PRAISE

"A worthy, page-turning debut that will keep readers guessing until the end. Readers of Liane Moriarty and psychological thrillers will not want to put this down."

—*Library Journal*

"Engrossing. Klehfoth's ability to draw in the reader shows that she's an author to watch."

—*Publishers Weekly*

"Fans of thrillers will have difficulty putting down this excellently plotted, gripping novel."

—*School Library Journal* (starred review)

"A compelling mystery. The story of a long-game revenge played out between generations."

—*Kirkus Review*

"This debut mystery gives readers a fun glimpse into the scandalous world of high-society boarding school and is reminiscent of Curtis Sittenfeld's *Prep* (2005)."

—*Booklist*

"This is going to be big."

—*Entertainment Weekly*

"Juicy, clever, and beguiling. An exceptional debut novel, deftly crafted and written with style. It is the perfect book to read at the beach. But be warned: you will get a sunburn, because you won't want to put it down."

—Cecily von Ziegesar, author of the *Gossip Girl* novels

THE

LOST

HEIRESS

OTHER BOOKS BY THE AUTHOR

All These Beautiful Strangers

THE

LOST

HEIRESS

a novel

ELIZABETH KLEHFOTH

LAKE UNION
PUBLISHING

Published by Lake Union Publishing, Seattle

www.apub.com

Amazon, the Amazon logo, and Lake Union Publishing are trademarks of Amazon.com, Inc., or its affiliates.

EU product safety contact:
Amazon Media EU S. à r.l.
38, avenue John F. Kennedy, L-1855 Luxembourg
amazonpublishing-gpsr@amazon.com

ISBN-13: 9781662529955 (paperback)
ISBN-13: 9781662529948 (digital)

Cover design by Erin Fitzsimmons
Cover image: © Husam Cakaloglu, © The7Dew / Getty

Printed in the United States of America

For Trevor, Milo, and Olivia

TOWERS FAMILY TREE

Towers Family Tree

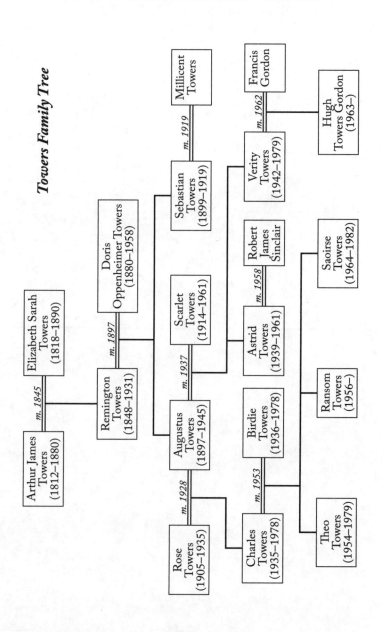

PROLOGUE

The workers found the body on Tuesday.

Well, not the body, but pieces of it. The left femur. The pelvic girdle. Part of a skull. The investigators erected their tent in the garden, graying bones assembled neatly on tarps as they crouched in the dirt with their trowels and brushes, like on some prehistoric dig.

Florence Talbot, the housekeeper, watched it all from the upstairs drawing room, a cup of chamomile tea cradled in her arthritic hands. The pain in her fingers was so bad this morning that she could barely grip the handle of the cup, which meant, of course, that it would soon rain. She glanced up at the pale-gray sky above her, and, as if to confirm her suspicions, a singular fat raindrop splattered against the windowpane.

The storms this year had been brutal and unrelenting, quite uncharacteristic for the Central Coast of California, where perpetual blue skies and sunshine were a far more familiar sight. Florence couldn't recall another year as bad as this one, except perhaps 1982. Then, as now, the rains had eroded the claylike soil under the Towers family home. And then, as now, Ransom Towers had hired a local construction company to refortify the east wing, which sat precariously on the cliffside, overlooking the Pacific. It was while digging down to the footings that the builders had found her, or what remained of her. For it was her, Saoirse Towers—Florence knew it deep in her bones, just as strongly as she felt the shifts in the weather. Before the DNA tests confirmed it—before the news choppers hovered over the house at all hours of the day and the reporters camped out at the gate of the front drive and all the headlines declared **Body of Young Heiress Found at Family Estate Nearly Forty Years After She Went Missing**—Florence knew.

Florence knew, like Florence knew everything that went on at Cliffhaven. She'd been there practically her whole life. Her soul, her mind, her heart were tethered to the weathered stones of this house, to this family. She loomed over it all, a stalwart captain of a lumbering ship, buoyed by an extensive network of eyes and ears in every nook and cranny of the estate, which granted her a sort of omnipotence that both impressed and terrified the staff. Even now, she'd enlisted Sally, the maid, to hover around the workers in the garden under the guise of fetching them tea or getting them fresh towels or being helpful in some way. Florence could see Sally's tall, lanky frame standing attentively next to one of the investigators in their navy windbreaker and then scurrying off toward the basement, probably to bring up a spare tarp before the storm hit.

The winds were picking up. Around the investigators' tent in the garden, the snapdragons, with their spires of pale-pink flowers, were bent at a forty-five-degree angle, as if in prayer. The winter daisies visibly shivered, their buttercup centers puckered, their delicate white petals trembling. Florence glanced back up at the sky, which was a more brutish shade of gray now. This storm would not be small. It would make its presence known. It reminded Florence in many ways of the night that Saoirse had disappeared.

Florence remembered it like it was only yesterday, for how could she not? It was Saoirse's eighteenth birthday party, one of the biggest social events of the season, and the party had taken all summer to plan. Florence had hired a caterer all the way from Los Angeles, flown crates of orchids in from Bogotá to fill the entry hall and ballroom. The champagne was Dom Pérignon, and it flowed from a fountain sculpted of ice that, prior to melting, stood nearly eight feet tall. Four engineering students from the local Cal Poly San Luis Obispo had been consulted in its construction, and they'd drilled through the foundation of the ballroom to place pipes that would drain away the water as the fountain melted, so as not to flood the hall. As the ice melted, it revealed a series of crystal letters spelling out s-a-o-i-r-s-e, a marvel within a marvel.

The cake was red velvet sponge with a thick cream cheese frosting, seven layers tall, with sparklers for candles that sent towers of flames soaring to the ceiling when lit. There was a dance floor in front of the stage, where Casey Hart and the Londoners had been flown in from Europe to play, and fireworks at midnight that got blotted out in the storm. Still, the party was a success; Florence took some small solace in that.

The guests—some of whom had come from as far away as Paris, New York, and Shanghai for the festivities—went to bed late and woke the next morning in various states of disarray, heads aching and stomachs sour from too much champagne. It was nearly two in the afternoon the following day before anyone realized that the birthday girl was missing. A maid was the one to raise the alarm. She'd gone to wake Saoirse and found her bed empty, the pillows still perfectly fluffed from the morning before, the coverlet neatly tucked in, crisp edges and corners the way that Florence always demanded. Indeed, the bed had never been slept in.

Quietly, discreetly, Florence had orchestrated a search party among the staff, but word that Saoirse was missing soon leaked to the guests, who filled their breakfast goblets with champagne and freshly squeezed orange juice from the buffet and stumbled down to the beach, calling Saoirse's name. They tripped and laughed and cursed the sand in their shoes. A few rolled up their pant legs or held up the hems of their dresses and darted into the frothy waves. Others, when word reached them, got up in haste, still dressed in the rumpled suits in which they had stumbled off to bed. They pushed back their shirtsleeves and thrust their socked feet into slippers, eager to join the search party. The women joined, still in their disheveled party dresses, pajamas, and robes. The group was a motley bunch of mussed hair and unshaven cheeks.

It started in good fun, for it was all a game to them, this "Find the birthday girl" brigade. The sun was shining, the salty air felt cool against their skin, and, back at the house, a full breakfast was waiting for them. Nothing bad had happened yet. They would find Saoirse, probably shacked up on the shoreline with a boy, his jacket tented over them as they slept. Or, perhaps, she had passed out in the stables after getting it into her head that she'd take a drunken midnight ride on her thoroughbred, Jack Abbott, and they would all have a good laugh about it. Like that time when Saoirse was twelve and she'd taken the family boat out by herself and crashed it into the crags off the shore of Catalina. The Coast Guard had found her hours later, sitting serenely atop the platform of a buoy, snacking on crackers and caviar, and remarking what a lovely day it was for a swim. Oh, Saoirse, their dear wild child. The things she got up to. It would be another story to tell after dinner when the wine was flowing freely, more fodder for the gossip rags and Page Six.

They combed the beach, but there was no sign of her anywhere. They checked the stables next, then the billiard room and the indoor theater, followed by an extensive search of the gardens and the tennis courts and a trek to the family's private airfield. As time crept on and the sun grew hotter, they started to sweat, shed their robes, unbuttoned their shirts, and complained about the heat. When a search of the observatory turned up empty, they retreated to the ballroom like refugees seeking asylum after a storm. Guests, now sober, congregated around tables like sailors clinging to lifeboats, the realization that something horrible had happened slowly washing over them, making them gasp for breath.

In the broad light of day, the grandeur of the ballroom had faded. The ornate walnut-paneled walls and gilded coffered ceilings felt claustrophobic and cage-like, the crystal chandelier that hung from the ceiling somehow grotesque. Flowers wilted in their centerpieces; the tablecloths, once stark white and crisp, were stained with rings of red wine and smeared with grease. Bloody pools collected around the edges of dirty plates that had been cluttered onto trays, the leftover flanks of dull-red steaks slumped in the middle. On every available surface—the windowsills, the dessert table, the ledge of the stage where the band had played—were clusters of glasses, half full of stale champagne, lipstick smears around the edges. And in the center of the room, where the champagne fountain had once proudly stood, were the letters s-a-o-i-r-s-e glinting in the waning daylight. The previous night, a proclamation. Now, a question that no one could answer.

As Florence had flitted among the guests, tending to their variable anxieties and neuroses, the police collected statements. Florence overheard more than a few harried whispers about the Towers family curse, which made the hairs on the back of her neck stand up straight. The untimely deaths that had claimed so much of Saoirse's family—the plane crash that had taken her parents; the skiing incident that had killed her brother, Theo; the horseback riding accident that had taken her late aunt; and, perhaps most infamously of all, the strange incident that had befallen her great-uncle Sebastian Towers, who'd drowned in the middle of Keany Square in Boston two days after his wedding, when a large storage tank exploded and unleashed a tidal wave of molasses. A string of unlikely tragedies had whittled the Towers family down to a few stalwart members. Could it be? Had the Towers family curse finally come for Saoirse too?

Now, the door of the drawing room creaked open, and Sally stumbled in, breaking Florence from her reverie. Florence turned to glance at the girl, who was still wearing her rain jacket and muddy boots from the garden. Tendrils of her red hair clung to the sides of her face, which looked unusually pale.

"Sally, your boots," Florence admonished her. She couldn't fathom what the girl was thinking, trekking through the house like that. She wasn't usually so careless. "You're dripping all over the mahogany floors."

Sally glanced down at her feet absently, but even staring directly at the toes of her boots, which were caked in slick red clay, and the wet, bloodlike smears they'd made on the polished hardwood, she didn't seem to register them.

"Oh, yes, I-I'm sorry," Sally stuttered. There was a panicked, hollow look in her eyes when she peered back up at Florence. "It's just, ma'am, well, they've found something. I thought you'd want to know."

Sally's words rattled Florence. "Found something?" she echoed. "What have they found?"

"A body," Sally said.

For a moment, Florence almost wanted to laugh. Was the girl daft? Had she hit her head?

"Yes, child," Florence said. "We're all well aware of that."

"No, ma'am." Sally cleared her throat. "I don't mean Miss Saoirse. I mean, they've found someone else. *Another* body."

"Another body?" Florence said.

It took a moment for the words to register. Florence took a step toward the window and peered down into the garden, but it wasn't any use. Despite it being midday, with the storm coming in, the sky was now as dark as evening, and with the heavy rain, the investigators' bright-blue tent was no more than an ominous dark figure crouched on the lawn, one that seemed to expand and contract, as if with breath, though Florence knew it was only a trick of the wind.

Sally watched her from where she hovered in the doorway. Florence Talbot—or Mrs. Talbot, as the staff all referred to her, even though she was not married—always seemed so ominous, so impenetrable, more of a force than a person. But as Sally looked at her now, she registered Mrs. Talbot's small stature for the first time. The woman couldn't be more than five feet four, and she looked her age, which was north of seventy, if Sally had to venture a guess. She looked old, frail.

Mrs. Talbot drew a shallow, rattling breath and dropped her teacup, which shattered unceremoniously on the floor.

"Mrs. Talbot, are you all right?" Sally asked, startled. She took a step toward her to come to her aid, but Mrs. Talbot raised a hand to stay her.

Sally couldn't help but wonder—Mrs. Talbot knew this house and the people in it, their intricate histories, their dark secrets. She'd made it her job, her life's work, to know them. But was it possible that after all these years, despite all her efforts, the house held its own secrets that even Mrs. Talbot did not know?

And if that was true, what else might it be hiding?

PART ONE

CHAPTER ONE

JUNE 1982—THREE MONTHS BEFORE SAOIRSE'S DISAPPEARANCE

The weather that year had been brutal, starting with one of the coldest winters on record. In January, a cold front blew down from Canada, sending snow and frost as far south as Texas and freezing the citrus groves in Florida. As late as April, blizzards shrouded the Northeast in two feet of snow. In California, storms surged along the coastline, sending heavy rains and mudslides. Waves eighteen feet high sucked homes off their foundations in Malibu, bit chunks off the Santa Monica Pier, and flooded the harbor in Santa Barbara. Farther north, the Towers family home had not escaped unscathed. Ana Rojas could see it as she drove along the cliffside in her old Saab—in the east wing, which she could make out from the road, the walls had been taken down to the studs, like an open wound.

Ana had never been this far north before. She'd grown up in San Bernardino, in the dry dust of the Inland Empire. Her whole life, she'd dreamed of the ocean—of those steel-gray columns of water and salt, and the roar of the waves crashing into the sand. When she was sixteen, her cousin Rosie had taken her to the beach in Santa Monica. They'd removed their sandals, and the sand had scalded the bare flesh of their feet as they walked. They lay on the towels they'd taken from the hotel and ate fresh slices of mango sprinkled with lime and salt and chili and stared out at the water—at the broad expanse of it, how it went on and on forever, like the desert. No, bigger than the desert. There was something comforting to Ana about the thought, because sometimes she felt like the desert and the things holding her there were so big that she might never escape them.

When Ana waded into the water, she went in alone. Neither Ana nor Rosie could swim, but that would not deter her. The water took Ana's breath away, how cold it was, like ice. She went only as far as she could touch, the sand shifting beneath her feet, until the water was up to her shoulders. She turned back toward the shoreline, searching for Rosie and their towels on the crowded beach, and so the wave surprised her. It encompassed her all at once without warning, the cold, dark wet of it. It swept her off her feet and then pitched her forward, without care, thrashing Ana's body this way and that, like a rag doll in a washing machine. In her shock, Ana went to draw breath, but she drew in water instead. The harsh salt burned the inside of her nose, her throat, her lungs. She kicked and clawed, and the wave spat her up near the shore. She landed hard on her hands and knees in the sand and sucked in dry air as the tide pulled out, leaving her soaked and bruised and bested.

She'd learned the hard way: Never turn your back on something bigger than you. Keep your eye on the horizon, on what's coming. Don't let it catch you off guard.

Ana turned off the road onto Cliffhaven's winding drive and stopped to give her name at the gate. As the gate swung open, she peered up at the giant house on the cliffside: tall and austere. The white stone facade caught the sun like it was lit up from within.

In some ways, Ana couldn't believe her luck. When she'd seen the ad in the paper calling for a young woman, age twenty to twenty-five, to serve as a caretaker for the summer, she'd imagined pushing an elderly woman around in a wheelchair, parceling out daily medications, inhaling the putrid smell of diapers, running a sponge over wrinkled, stooped shoulders in a hot bath. But the pay—eight dollars an hour, plus room and board—had been too good to pass up. The family had not given their name in the ad, only the name and address of a secretary to send her résumé to, and so Ana had shown up to the interview blind as to who her potential employers might be.

The interview had taken place over tea at the Peninsula in Beverly Hills. As soon as Ana walked in, she immediately felt underdressed in her JCPenney khaki skirt and plain button-down shirt—the clothes she wore to church on Sunday with her grandmother, the nicest things she owned. Even the tables were dressed nicer than she was, with fine white china that had scalloped edges and elderflowers around the trim, and thick cloth napkins neatly folded into the shape of a rose.

"Ana Rojas," she said at the hostess booth. "I'm here to meet Jacqueline Yates."

The hostess smiled kindly at her and escorted her across the parquet floors to a table near the fireplace. There was a pretty young woman sitting there, thin and blond. Sitting next to her was a man, his back to Ana. The young blond woman smiled when she saw Ana and whispered to the man, "Our three o'clock is here." The man turned, and when Ana saw his face, she forgot to breathe.

She recognized Ransom Towers immediately. He had coiffed dark hair, an angular jaw, an aquiline nose, and pensive gray eyes the color of the sky before a storm. The papers had nicknamed him "Handsome Ransom" when he made his first bid for public office. He was a congressman now, for was there anything else for a Towers man to be? The Towerses were one of the great American political dynasties, their names whispered alongside those of the Kennedys, the Roosevelts, honored and revered. Ana had read their names in her history books in school, just as she had read about their current counterparts in her glossy *Seventeen* magazine after school, sprawled out on her bed. The Towerses were beautiful and elegant, slinking into the backs of limousines in gorgeous silk gowns, smiling and waving at the cameras in their crisp tuxedos at fancy charity galas.

When Ana reached out to shake Ransom's hand, she couldn't help but recall the first time she'd ever seen him, in a picture in

People magazine. The paparazzi had snapped a photo of him on the rugby practice field at Stanford shortly after his parents' plane crash. Something about the sorrowful set of his eyes had made him look so young, like he was just a boy.

"Congressman Towers," he said, taking her hand. "And this is my personal secretary, Jacqueline Yates."

"Pleased to meet you, Ana," Jacqueline said. "Please, have a seat."

On the table between them stood blush-colored hydrangeas in a tall vase and a tiered tray piled high with cucumber-and-dill finger sandwiches, smoked salmon and capers, and currant scones. There were strawberries in a large glass bowl, topped with a dollop of fresh cream. Ana felt like she was in a daze, like she had fallen asleep and woken up in some kind of wonderland, where everything felt strange, the proportions all off.

"Let's get you something to drink, shall we?" Jacqueline said, signaling a waiter over. "I'm sure you're parched after your long drive."

Ana ordered a pot of spearmint tea, the only tea she could think of offhand, the kind her grandmother drank with her breakfast every morning, though her grandmother called it *hierba buena* and grew the leaves fresh in her garden.

"Now, Ana, before we get started, we have a bit of paperwork to take care of," Jacqueline said, her tone friendly and upbeat. She slid a stapled stack of paper across the table to Ana.

Ana scanned the top of it—a confidentiality and nondisclosure agreement.

"I know this may feel very formal and strange for a job interview," Jacqueline said, "but I'm sure you understand, with the Towerses being a very public family, there are certain private matters that may come up in our conversation that must remain private."

Ana nodded.

Jacqueline offered her a pen, and Ana took it, her hand shaking slightly.

"Please, take all the time you need to review it," Jacqueline said, sipping her tea. "It's very standard for an NDA, I assure you. Basically, it precludes you from discussing any matters that may come up in this interview with anyone outside the Towers family. That includes the media, of course, but also your own friends and family members. Any breach of this contract could result in legal action."

"Right," Ana said. "Okay."

She skimmed the pages quickly, feeling, not for the first time, as if she were in over her head. **The Candidate agrees that the Candidate will not directly or indirectly disclose the Client Family's Private Family Information to any person or entity who is not a member of the Client Family. Should the Candidate disclose or threaten to disclose Private Family Information, the Client Family will be entitled to seek injunctive relief and punitive damages.**

Ana felt self-conscious with Jacqueline and Ransom sitting right there across the table from her as she read, so she quickly signed and dated the last page and handed it back to Jacqueline.

"Wonderful," Jacqueline said with a reassuring smile as she tucked the signed agreement into her notebook. "Now, on to more pleasant matters. Tell us a little about yourself," Jacqueline prompted. "I saw on your résumé that you're studying nursing at California State University, San Bernardino?"

"Yes," Ana said. "I have one year left there."

"Splendid," Jacqueline said. "I hope you don't mind me saying so, but you look so young. Hardly eighteen. You must have started your degree quite early."

Ana cleared her throat. "Actually," she said. "I'm twenty-three. I got a bit of a late start. My mother was sick, and I had to put off school to look after her."

"My, I'm so sorry to hear that about your mother," Jacqueline said.

"Thank you," Ana said.

The waiter arrived then with Ana's tea and set it down in front of her, and Ana took that moment to steal a glance across the table at

Ransom Towers, but he wasn't looking at her. He was staring down at his watch, his brow furrowed, looking intensely displeased. Had she said something wrong already? Ana slid her sweaty palms against the thighs of her khaki skirt.

"And what are your hobbies?" Jacqueline asked.

"My hobbies?" Ana repeated, confused.

"Yes, what do you do for fun?"

"Oh, I, um, I read. And I love horseback riding."

"Horseback riding—that's perfect," Jacqueline said, jotting something down in her notebook.

"Yes, my uncle owns a cattle ranch," Ana said. "I grew up riding. Is that, um, relevant?"

Jacqueline laughed. "I'm sorry," she said. "You must think my questions rather odd. I suppose I should explain myself. The position you applied for was *caretaker*—and that's true, to an extent, but it's probably different than what you were expecting. You'll really be more of a . . . *companion* . . . for Ransom's younger sister, Saoirse. She's seventeen. As a companion, it would be helpful, I think, to have some common interests with her. And Saoirse, you see, loves horseback riding."

"Oh," Ana said. Saoirse Towers's face flashed in her mind. Over the past few years, she'd seen Saoirse's visage—heart-shaped face, steely gray eyes, and swollen lips—splashed across the covers of countless glossy gossip magazines, Saoirse smiling mischievously at the camera as she ducked into Lutèce, arm in arm with Eve Vanderbilt. Ana had read a story somewhere—she couldn't remember where now—that once the maître d' at a fancy restaurant had refused to seat Saoirse because she was wearing trousers, and without batting an eye, Saoirse had stripped out of her pants right then and there and marched to an open table in her heels and blazer, her long bare legs on display for all to see. The maître d', red faced and dismayed, had simply handed her a menu and recited the daily specials.

But Ana couldn't make any sense of it—that beautiful young girl she'd seen on the cover of magazines needed a caretaker? The thought seemed hard to square.

"And what . . . *care* . . . does she need exactly?" Ana prompted.

"Are you familiar with long QT syndrome?" Jacqueline asked.

Ana shook her head.

"It's a heart condition," Jacqueline said. "Saoirse's prone to fainting and seizures. She's had to withdraw from school and social activities over the last year due to her condition, and she's been confined to the house."

"I'm so sorry," Ana said. "I didn't know—I hadn't heard anything about that."

"Yes, well." Jacqueline tapped the nondisclosure agreement before her with the back of her pen and smiled. "Discretion is very important to us. We do our best to keep private matters private."

"Of course," Ana said.

"Anyway, with Saoirse's condition, she needs constant supervision," Jacqueline went on. "That's why your medical training is of particular interest to us. I assume you know CPR?"

"Yes," Ana said.

"Lovely," Jacqueline said, making another note in her book. "But I'm afraid Saoirse's isolation has made her quite miserable, and the caretakers that Mrs. Talbot has hired in the past haven't been quite the right fit."

"Mrs. Talbot?"

"The housekeeper," Jacqueline said. "Ransom and I thought if we could find someone with the right medical background who was closer in age to Saoirse and shared some of her interests, things might go more smoothly."

"I see," Ana said. "So I wouldn't be the first person to fill this position?"

"Not the first, no," Jacqueline said. "Milk?"

"I'm sorry?"

"For your tea," Jacqueline said. "You haven't touched it. And I've been such a boor over here, drilling you with questions. I haven't offered you cream or sugar or milk, and you've been too kind to interrupt me. Would you like some milk, dear?"

"Oh, yes, thank you," Ana said and reached for the small pitcher that Jacqueline handed her. She poured some into her cup, anxious not to spill and look totally inept in front of Jacqueline and her potential future employer.

"The accommodations for the position are quite good," Jacqueline went on, smiling broadly. "You'd be staying at the family home, Cliffhaven, near San Luis Obispo. There's a full staff there to take care of you. All meals would be provided. You'd be six days on, one day off. We're looking for someone to start immediately and go through the end of September."

"Yes," Ana said, setting the pitcher down. "I could do that."

"Miss Rojas," Ransom said, and his voice took Ana off guard, partly because it was the first time she had heard him speak since he had introduced himself, and partly because his tone was less than friendly. "Of all the summer jobs you could apply for, why did you want this one?"

Ana looked straight into his steely gaze, and for a moment, she thought about telling him the truth. "To be quite . . . blunt," Ana said. "I applied because of the pay. Eight dollars an hour for a caretaker is a very good rate. I'm putting myself through school while helping to take care of my family, and I really need the money."

Ransom seemed to consider this. "I appreciate your honesty, Miss Rojas," he said. "So I will be honest as well. My sister's condition may be delicate, but Saoirse is headstrong and difficult to manage. We've eliminated three caretakers in as many weeks, and I'm quite desperate to find someone who can last through the summer. And to be as . . . blunt . . . as you were with me, I'm not sure you have the constitution we're looking for."

"I'm sorry—the constitution you're looking for?" Ana repeated, confused.

"Yes, between Mrs. Talbot and my sister, you wouldn't last a day," Ransom said. "Now, I don't enjoy wasting anyone's time, particularly my own, and I know you have a long drive ahead of you, Miss Rojas, so I'll do you a favor and cut this short so you can beat the afternoon traffic."

Ransom turned and signaled the waiter for the check.

Ana sat there for a moment in cold disbelief as the reality of what had just happened washed over her.

It was over. Just like that.

The interview had seemed to be going so well—the position was in her grasp—and then, just as suddenly, it had been ripped away from her.

But that was the story of her life, wasn't it? The things she wanted—really wanted—were always out of her grasp. This was as close as she was ever going to come to them—right to the gatekeepers, close enough to peer in, close enough to see what she was missing out on, only to be told no, to be turned away. Anger seared inside of her; tears stung the backs of her eyes.

"Please don't cry, Miss Rojas," Ransom said. He handed her the cloth kerchief from his jacket pocket. "You're a nice girl. But that's the problem, you see? We're not looking for a nice girl."

A hot flash of resentment flickered in Ana's chest, that he could misread her tears as a sign of sadness, disappointment—no, weakness. She wasn't sad, and she most certainly wasn't weak. She was furious.

"Do you know what it's like, Mr. Towers," Ana said, leaning forward, eyes narrowing, "day in and day out, to care for someone who you love very much and watch them die, little by little, knowing that there's nothing you can do to stop it? To hold their hand and tell them everything is going to be all right, when you know it's a lie? If you had deigned to ask me, I would have told you I can manage difficult things. Rude, self-important assholes like yourself—those are certainly an annoyance, but not such the insurmountable hardship that you seem to think."

She stood, the legs of her chair scraping noisily against the parquet floors. She was aware she was drawing people's attention now; they were starting to stare. She could feel their judgmental gazes on the back of her neck. Let them look. She didn't care. What kind of people had tea at three o'clock on a Thursday anyway? Rich, rude, self-important assholes, that's who. To hell with them and their currant scones.

"And, might I suggest," Ana went on, "for the next *nice* girl you interview—if that is all the consideration you are going to give her: a few paltry questions about her interests and her hobbies and then a cold dismissal—a simple phone call will do? When you factor in the two hours of driving, both ways, the money for gas—and five dollars for a valet! That may not seem like much to you, but to me, it's something. It's not trivial, the hoops you make people jump through, all so you can tell them no." She balled up the kerchief he had handed her and dropped it on his plate. "So if you really want to do me a favor, Mr. Towers," Ana said, "you can fuck off."

Ana turned on her heel and marched across the parquet floor into the hotel lobby and out the front doors without a backward glance. She wasn't sure, but she could have sworn she caught a glimpse of Ransom's face before she turned—he had almost seemed to smile, the corners of his lips twitching up nearly imperceptibly, as she left the table. Or had she just imagined that? No, he was probably laughing at her, the asshole.

Ana was out of breath when she handed her card to the valet. She stood off to the side to wait and jumped when she felt a hand on her shoulder. She turned to see Jacqueline standing behind her.

"Miss Rojas," Jacqueline said.

"Yes?" Ana said, startled. She readjusted the strap of her purse on her shoulder. What could this woman possibly want from her? She was probably here to admonish her for talking to her employer in such a public and disrespectful manner, or to drag her back to the table, her tail between her legs, to issue some sort of apology. Well, to hell with that.

"I'm not sorry," Ana went on quickly, before Jacqueline could get a word in. "I meant what I said. I'm not going to apologize."

"Oh no, of course not," Jacqueline said, waving her hand like that was a ridiculous suggestion that hadn't even crossed her mind. "Can you start next Tuesday?"

"What?"

"Mr. Towers is offering you the position," Jacqueline said with a smile. "He wants to know if you can start on Tuesday."

"Oh," Ana said, taken aback. She could hardly process this swift change of events. "Why?"

Jacqueline laughed. "I suppose he liked your moxie."

Ana considered this for a moment. "Yes, Tuesday is fine," she said, still not fully believing it. "I can do Tuesday."

"Wonderful," Jacqueline said. "I'll send the starting paperwork to your address." She handed her a crisp bill. "For the valet."

Ana took it, still trying to recover from her confusion. "Thank you," she said.

"And, Ana?" Jacqueline said, her voice very serious.

"Yes?"

"Remember—don't be nice. *They* certainly won't be."

Ana pulled to the end of the drive, where it opened up into a motor court. She parked in front of the stone steps that led up to the grand front doors.

"You can do this," she said to herself, her hands braced on the steering wheel. She took a deep breath. "I can do this."

Ana pulled her duffel bag over her shoulder and tugged her suitcase out of the trunk. She looked up at the cold stone house, which did nothing to welcome her. If anything, the windows, with their wrought iron grills, looked like judgmental eyes glaring down at her. A chilly coastal breeze pushed up against the house, and Ana shivered.

She made her way laboriously up the front steps, hauling both bags herself. By the time she reached the top, she was out of breath. Her shoulder was sore where the strap of her bag dug into it. She went to ring the doorbell, but before she could, the door swung open.

A middle-aged woman stood there, dressed in a black dress and sturdy black oxfords, her hair pulled back into a sharp chignon at the base of her neck. Ana couldn't help but wonder if the woman had been there the whole time, watching her struggle up the steps.

"Oh, hello," Ana said. She put her suitcase down and shifted the bag on her shoulder to free up her hand, which she extended to the woman with a friendly smile. "I'm Ana Rojas, the new caretaker. You must be Mrs. Talbot?"

Mrs. Talbot only looked at her. She did not return Ana's smile or extend her hand. "The help's motor court is around the side of the house, by the kitchen," she said and then promptly shut the door in Ana's face.

Ana stood there a moment, shell shocked at the greeting. If she had not been warned about Mrs. Talbot's temperament, she might have thought she was playing a joke on her, some sort of initiation prank. Ana stood there for a full minute, waiting for the door to open again, to be admitted into the house, and when she wasn't, she turned and laboriously lugged her duffel and suitcase back down the stairs to her car.

She was still out of breath when she unloaded them again a few minutes later in the cobbled motor court along the side of the house.

"Leave your things and your keys with the car," Mrs. Talbot called from the kitchen doorway.

Ana looked over to see her standing in the doorframe, her arms folded sternly across her chest, as if Ana had crossed her once again.

"I'll have Manny bring them up to your room," Mrs. Talbot said.

"Oh, I don't mind," Ana said, her grip tightening on the handle of her duffel. "I don't have that much. I can get them."

"Shall I have Manny leave early, then, without pay, since you're determined to do his job for him?" Mrs. Talbot asked. "Will you cook and clean as well? Should I tell the maid and the chef to go home, too, since you're perfectly capable of cleaning a toilet and making toast? Shall I let go of the whole staff?"

"Oh, no, I wasn't—" Ana said.

"You're dawdling," Mrs. Talbot said. "I have much to do and very little time, and if you put me off my schedule, I shall be cross indeed, and none of the staff will thank you for that."

Ana hesitated a moment, not wanting to let go of her bag, to leave it there in the custody of a complete stranger. What kind of place was this, after all? Who were these people? Would they riffle through her things—out of instruction or idle curiosity—or, perhaps, even unpack them for her, all her underwear and socks, her nightgown, touched by strange hands? Ana shivered at the invasion. But what choice did she have? She couldn't risk upsetting Mrs. Talbot further; if she protested at all, it would seem like she was being unruly. So Ana reluctantly put her duffel bag and suitcase back into the trunk for the third time that day and left her key in the trunk lock.

"I would prefer to unpack the bags myself," Ana said as she joined Mrs. Talbot in the kitchen. "If that's all right."

Mrs. Talbot gave her a wild, disapproving look. "We're not here to wait on you hand and foot, if that's what you're expecting," she said.

Relief washed over Ana, and she realized she had been holding her breath. "Oh, no, of course not," Ana said.

She glanced around at the kitchen. It was the largest kitchen she had ever been in, and she had worked for a summer at the Desert Grille, a steak house in San Bernardino that sat a hundred. There was a long rectangular warming-and-prep table running down the middle, and along one side of the room stood a stainless steel three-compartment sink and drainboard, cabinets housing the dinnerware and glasses, chests of flatware, a commercial twelve-burner gas range with a griddle and two convertible ovens. There were four large refrigerators lined up in a row and, beyond that, a pantry. It was an industrial-size kitchen, meant for serving large parties, not just catering to a family home.

"We have a way of doing things here, as you'll quickly learn," Mrs. Talbot said. "I trust you won't be disruptive and that you won't question my authority again. I will not tolerate *insubordinate* characters."

"Yes," Ana said quickly. "I mean, no. I didn't mean to be difficult."

"Very well," Mrs. Talbot said and then went on. "Breakfast is served at eight o'clock sharp on weekdays, nine a.m. on weekends. Lunch is at noon, dinner at seven p.m. You'll eat with Saoirse in the dining room or on the terrace if the weather permits. Tea is served at three thirty p.m. in the blue room," Mrs. Talbot rattled on, barely pausing for breath.

Ana searched in her purse for a pen but found none. She felt like she should be writing this down.

"Do you have any dietary restrictions?" Mrs. Talbot asked.

Ana shook her head. "No, none."

"Very good," Mrs. Talbot said, as if that was the first thing Ana had said or done since she met her that she found agreeable. "This way."

Ana followed her through double doors into a dining room, which had a tall arched ceiling, two stories high. Light spilled in through the windows, which started halfway up the walls. There was a long oak table lined with upholstered chairs, and in the center of the table, every couple of feet or so, were vases overflowing with orange dahlias.

"The formal dining room," Mrs. Talbot said, "where you'll take your meals. The table seats sixty, so it's used for smaller, more intimate gatherings. For larger parties, we use the grand ballroom."

Ana would hardly call a dinner party of sixty a *small, intimate gathering*, but she wasn't about to voice that thought, so she simply nodded and followed Mrs. Talbot as she continued down the hall.

"The house was built in 1897 by Remington Towers as a wedding present for his young bride, Doris Oppenheimer, the oil heiress," Mrs. Talbot went on. "Well, I should say, Remington Towers *started* building the house in 1897. It wasn't completed until 1935. Doris Oppenheimer Towers had exacting tastes. This is her, here."

They paused outside a parlor, where there was a large oil painting of a couple in a baroque frame hanging over an ornate mahogany fireplace.

The young woman in the painting was seated in an upholstered chair. She wore a pale-blue tea-length dress with a square neckline that exposed her collarbones. Her dark wavy hair was secured in a low twist with a jade comb at the nape of her neck. She had wide-set eyes and cheeks that still held the plumpness of a child's.

"She looks so young," Ana said.

"She was seventeen when they wed," Mrs. Talbot said. "Remington was forty-nine. Such an age gap wasn't unusual, back in the day."

Ana looked at the man standing behind Doris in the painting. He had dark hair and dark eyes and a full beard that was beginning to gray around the edges. He was tall and rugged; he wore a Stetson hat and boots with his gray three-piece suit, like a cowboy who had not fully surrendered to being a gentleman. He was handsome, to be sure, and Ana could easily trace the family resemblance to his great-grandson, Ransom Towers. But still, she couldn't get over the predatory grip of his hand on the back of Doris's chair, nor the immense age gap between him and Doris, however "normal" it may have been for their time. Forty-nine years to Doris's seventeen. Remington was nearly three times her age when they were wed and seemed better suited to be her father than her husband. Ana peered into the young woman's eyes in the portrait. She couldn't help but wonder: How had Doris felt about the arrangement? Had she had any say?

"This was Doris's favorite room in the house," Mrs. Talbot said, gazing wistfully at the parlor in which the painting hung, with its tall coffered ceilings, the large velvet tufted sofas, and the pianoforte near the picture window.

"It's still arranged just to her liking," Mrs. Talbot said. "She used to sit and play Chopin at that piano in the afternoons."

Ana took a step forward, toward the room, and Mrs. Talbot grabbed her briskly by the forearm.

"You mustn't go in," Mrs. Talbot said sharply. "No one is allowed to step foot in this room, except the maid twice a week to clean."

"Oh, I see," Ana said. "Sorry."

It felt absurd and outlandish to her—a room this large and grandiose, kept for an occupant who was long since deceased? The whole thing was appalling, really—a house this size, all for one family, and so much of it unused, unoccupied space.

Ana turned to follow Mrs. Talbot, who had fallen silent, only to realize that Mrs. Talbot had not moved. She was looking at Ana appraisingly, as if waiting for her to offer some remark about the room. Ana racked her brain. What compliment had she paid to the dining room? She didn't want to repeat the same thing and seem insincere. Come to think of it, had she offered a compliment to the dining room, or had she simply nodded? She certainly hoped that Mrs. Talbot wouldn't be stopping at each room, as this house was huge and Ana could think of only half a dozen ways to say, "Wow, nice digs."

She cleared her throat. "It's lovely," she said.

Mrs. Talbot smiled at her, but the smile did not meet her eyes. "*Lovely*," Mrs. Talbot repeated, but on her tongue, it sounded belittling, as if Ana had referred to the room as *cute*.

"Yes, well, I suppose good taste is not a virtue everyone inherits," Mrs. Talbot said. "This way to the family's quarters, where you'll be staying."

She turned, and Ana followed her up the grand staircase to the second floor and then down another hall, unsure whether she should be grateful that Mrs. Talbot did not stop to show her any other rooms along the way or insulted that Mrs. Talbot clearly thought she didn't have the requisite taste to admire them properly.

"Miss Saoirse's room," Mrs. Talbot said, nodding toward a closed door as they passed it. They halted at the door just beyond it. Mrs. Talbot paused with her hand on the knob. "This will be your room for the duration of your stay," Mrs. Talbot said. She nodded at the room across the hall from Ana's. "That is Mr. Ransom's room. I trust I don't need to impress upon you the extreme discretion you'll need to practice living in such close proximity to the family."

"Is he home often?" Ana asked. "Ransom, I mean?"

Mrs. Talbot's left eyebrow shot up at the question, and Ana felt like she had once again overstepped some sort of invisible line.

"*Congressman Towers*," Mrs. Talbot said, enunciating his official title, as if Ana were not familiar enough to use his Christian name, "is not here when the House is in session, but he's home as often as he can be. And when he is home," Mrs. Talbot said sternly, "he is not to be disturbed."

Ana nodded. It took her a moment to realize that Mrs. Talbot was waiting for some sort of verbal affirmation that she wouldn't be a nuisance.

"Oh, um, got it," Ana said. "When I'm not needed, I'll make myself scarce."

That seemed to satisfy Mrs. Talbot, because she nodded and turned the knob.

Ana let out a low whistle when they entered the room. It was the biggest, most luxurious bedroom she had ever seen. There was a four-poster bed dressed with silk sheets and piled high with throw pillows, a tall rosewood dresser, a full-length mirror, a writing desk, and, in the corner, a sitting area next to a fireplace, complete with a sofa and reading chairs. There was a private bathroom with a soaking tub, a pedestal sink, and French doors that led out onto a veranda that overlooked the garden. And somehow, her suitcase and duffel bag were already there, sitting neatly at the foot of her bed.

"I take it the room is to your liking?" Mrs. Talbot asked.

It's a bit much for one person, Ana wanted to say, but she'd gotten the sense that Mrs. Talbot took great pride in the house and the family, as if they were extensions of herself, so she bit her tongue.

"The room's love—" Ana said and then caught herself. "The room's great."

"The maid will be in every morning at ten a.m. to clean and bring fresh towels," Mrs. Talbot said. "If you've forgotten anything, just let the maid know, and she'll get it for you. Would you like a moment to freshen up before you meet Miss Saoirse?"

"Yes, actually, if you don't mind," Ana said. "It was kind of a long drive."

"Very well," Mrs. Talbot said. "I'll meet you at the bottom of the stairs in fifteen minutes to make the proper introductions."

"I'll be ready," Ana said, giving her a compliant smile.

Ana waited until Mrs. Talbot had left and closed the door behind her before hurrying over to her duffel bag. She thrust it onto the bed and unzipped it. Half in a panic, she pulled out her toiletries bag that was sitting on top and tossed it carelessly onto the bedcover next to her. Her hands groped blindly through her pile of T-shirts and jeans until she found her nightgown at the bottom, balled up—or, rather, wrapped tightly around something small, compact, and heavy. She pulled it out and unwrapped it—nested inside the cloth gown was a matte black snub-nosed revolver.

Ana placed the gun carefully on the bed beside her and felt around in her duffel bag for her socks next, searching for the only pair of thick wool ones she had brought with her. When her fingers found purchase on the scratchy cloth, she pulled them out and released the fat, squat cartridges that she had tucked inside onto the bedcover—five in all, as many as the revolver would hold.

Ana surveyed the room. She needed a place to hide them, somewhere the maid wouldn't happen upon while cleaning. Across the room, next to the fireplace, she spotted a copper bucket piled with logs. It occurred to her that this was the perfect hiding place—no one would have any reason to disturb that bucket this time of year. It was in the dead heat of summer, after all. There would be no need for a fire.

Ana made quick work of removing the logs and placing the gun and the sock full of cartridges at the bottom. Then she stacked the logs back on top just as she had found them and checked her watch. Somehow, ten minutes had already gone by. She had better make her way to the staircase to meet Mrs. Talbot; she didn't want to be late. She had already made too many missteps today—she couldn't afford another one.

Ana could feel her heart beating in her chest, a loud thundering thud. She glanced at her reflection in the mirror above the fireplace and took a deep breath to steady herself.

"You can do this," she told herself, but the girl staring back at her didn't look like she believed her.

She had plaited her hair into a French braid this morning after her shower, when it was still wet. It had looked immaculate then, her dark hair in crisp, clean lines, everything lying flat. But since then, her hair had dried, and the braid looked messy now, a bunch of flyaways crowning the top of her head.

Her reflection disheartened her—standing there with her messy braid, in the striped shirt and overalls that were wrinkled now from the drive, and without a stitch of makeup, she looked so young. And plain. And out of place with the Versailles-like background of the room behind her. What was she doing here?

Frustrated, she tried to pat her hair flat, but the gesture didn't do any good—her flyaways defiantly stood up straight as soon as she took her hand away. Ah, well. There was nothing she could do about it now. There was nothing she could do about any of it, except to move forward. She turned and took a step toward the door.

It was time to meet her charge.

CHAPTER TWO

PRESENT

Detective Michael Church knew the Towerses' place from a distance. Everybody along the Central Coast did, and he had grown up just south in Morro Bay. It was hard to miss the thing when driving up the Pacific Coast Highway, the giant stone building, which looked more like a museum than a personal residence, standing by itself on the bluff. Staring up at the stone facade from the back seat of his mother's car as she drove him to T-ball practice, he'd imagined that the house was a castle, that King Arthur and his knights lived there, protecting the town from evil. Of course, he had stopped believing in all that a long time ago—in fairy tales, or God, or that any benevolent being was watching out for them. After the things he had seen, either there wasn't a God, or he wasn't benevolent.

As Detective Church pulled up to the front gate of the Towers family home, he cursed under his breath at the sight of the reporters and photographers camped out front. There was a patrol officer posted at the gate—Deputy McPherson—and Church stopped and lowered his driver's side window to speak with him.

"Jesus Christ," Church said.

Deputy McPherson shook his head. "Total shitstorm, I'm telling you, Church. Never seen anything like it. And now they've got eyes in the sky."

Church squinted upward. The sky was a weak pale-blue this morning, without a single wisp of cloud. "How many?" he asked.

"Counted three news choppers so far today," McPherson said. "I just hope they got my good side."

The deputy waved him through, and Church inched forward as the gates opened. The reporters slowly parted around the hood of his truck, their microphones pointed hungrily at his windshield, their barrage of questions muted by the glass.

Getting a sit-down with Ransom Towers—*Senator* Towers now—had proven trickier for Detective Church than he had imagined it would be. Twice now the senator's assistant had scheduled and then rescheduled for Senator Towers to come down to the station and talk. Just this morning, their interview had gotten moved again—but this time, Senator Towers couldn't make it down to the station at all. He had another obligation. Would Detective Church mind coming to Cliffhaven instead?

Church did mind, quite a bit. He preferred the sterility of the station's interrogation room—the bland linoleum flooring and laminate table, the plastic vinyl chairs. There was nothing to distract the interviewee there—no clock marking the passage of time, no barking dogs or ringing doorbells at inopportune moments. The interrogation room at the station was a quiet, unhurried, controlled environment. But Church had to take what he could get.

When Detective Church arrived at Cliffhaven, he was escorted to the senator's in-home office by his assistant, Robin, an androgynous twentysomething redhead who wore an earpiece that she was perpetually speaking into, so Church was never quite sure if she was talking to him or not. She gave two brisk knocks at the open door to the senator's office on the second floor and then walked inside, announcing, "Senator, your two o'clock appointment is here—Detective Church."

Senator Towers got up from behind his desk to greet him. The senator was in his mid-sixties now, his hair salted around the temples, but he still had a lean, athletic figure that made him seem younger than his age.

"Detective Church," the senator said, "it's nice to meet you." He gave Church a firm handshake and looked him square in the eyes. "I apologize for all of the rescheduling," Senator Towers went on. "It's been a hectic few weeks—election year, you know."

"I appreciate you making the time to meet with me in the midst of all the chaos," Church said. "I know you're a busy man."

"Senator," Robin said, "the *Town & Country* photographers are downstairs. I'm going to go make sure they have everything they need to set up. I'll be back in thirty to get you."

"Thanks, Robin," the senator said.

And with that, Robin ducked out, closing the door behind her.

"Please," Senator Towers said to Church, "sit."

Church was getting the sense that nothing the senator did was without intention—the constant rescheduling, then moving the interview at the last moment from the police station to the senator's own home office. Even how they were positioned in the room now—the senator sitting behind his desk while Church sat in a chair facing him. Everything was meant to undermine Church's authority, to establish the senator's dominance.

"You have a beautiful family," Church said, nodding toward a framed photograph on the senator's desk. In it, the senator stood on a beach in a tropical printed shirt, his bare feet in the sand, his tanned arm around a beautiful dark-haired woman, pulling her close. The waves foamed at their ankles, and in front of them were two preteen girls, both with braces on their teeth, smiling at the camera.

"Thank you," the senator said. "That's from our trip to the Dominican, many years ago. The girls are all grown up now. Evie works for a nonprofit in New York, securing funding for arts in underprivileged schools," he said. "Liv is still at Yale, studying political science."

"Following in her old man's footsteps?" Church asked.

The senator chuckled. "Don't try to tell her that. She's very determined to forge her own path."

"You must be very proud," Church said.

"Yes," the senator said. "I'm a very lucky man." The senator cleared his throat and leaned back in his chair, brow furrowed, his hands clasped across his middle. "So tell me, Detective, what's this I hear about a second body?" Senator Towers asked.

Church was taken off guard by the senator's question—not least of all because the sheriff's office had not released any information to the public yet about their discovery.

"Come again?" Church asked.

"The second body," Senator Towers said. "The one that was dug up in the garden the other day."

"Where did you . . . ?"

"My housekeeper informed me," the senator said.

"I see," Church said, his mouth drawing into a grim line. He'd have to have a word with the forensics team—they needed to be more discreet. "Unfortunately," Church continued, "as this is an ongoing investigation, there's very limited information that I can share with you at the moment."

The senator waited for him to go on, and when he didn't, he prodded, "So what *can* you share with me?"

"The sheriff will be making an official statement at the press conference tomorrow," Church said. "Anything that can be shared with the public will be relayed then."

"You're joking," Senator Towers said, leaning forward in his chair.

Church shook his head. "I'm quite serious."

"I don't understand," the senator said. "Detective Vance always kept us informed of any movement in the case."

Detective Richard Vance had been the original detective assigned to the case nearly forty years ago, when Saoirse Towers had first gone missing. He'd been retired for over a decade now. Church didn't know him personally—their times at the sheriff's office hadn't overlapped—but

Church had gotten a good sense of Vance through reading Saoirse Towers's case file. From the beginning, Vance had treated it as a missing person case, not a homicide, and he had never treated Senator Towers as a potential suspect. Instead, he had adopted an open-door policy with the senator—sharing any leads the department had gotten, their persons of interest, details that had not yet been made public. But as far as Church was concerned, the senator *was* a potential suspect, and he intended to treat him as such. Nine times out of ten, victims were killed by someone they knew, someone in their inner circle. And you didn't get more inner circle than your own brother.

"Yes, Detective Vance had his own way of doing things," Church said, not wanting to speak ill of his predecessor. "But, Senator, please try to understand—there are certain things I cannot tell you in order to protect the outcome of the case. Now, I'm coming at this with fresh eyes, and part of that is getting fresh statements, which is what I'm here to do. So if you would indulge me?"

The senator seemed taken aback by this. He shifted in his chair. This was clearly not how he had expected this conversation to go. He had thought he'd be the one asking the questions, but now, he found himself on the other end of things, not the receiver of information but the giver of it. He glared at the detective, and Church unwaveringly held his gaze.

"Yes, fine. Very well," the senator said after a moment.

"Senator Towers," Church said, "it was reported by several eyewitnesses that you left the party early the evening of your sister's disappearance. Where did you go?"

The senator was silent. He'd clearly never been treated as a potential suspect before, and he bucked at being treated like one now.

There were two things that made Church a great detective—he listened more than he talked, and he didn't trust anyone, ever. (His granny, of course, was exempt from this. As far as he was concerned, that woman walked on water.) Church's first talent meant that he could sit cool as a cucumber in an awkward, uncomfortable silence. He didn't rush to fill it; he could wait it out. And the longer the silence—the more uncomfortable—the better, even. It never ceased to amaze Church what the suspect would rush to fill it with. Not once but twice, a person he'd been interviewing had implicated themselves in a serious crime just to fill a lengthy pause in the conversation. Social awkwardness—it was a much more effective interrogation technique than torture, and it didn't break any federal laws.

"To my room," the senator said finally. "I went to my room to smoke a cigar and read a book and escape the noise. Parties aren't really my thing. I'd made an appearance, played my duty as host, met my obligations for the night. I watched the fireworks from my balcony and went to bed."

"So you were in your room the rest of the evening," Church said, "alone?"

"Yes," Senator Towers said.

Which meant, of course, that there was no one who could corroborate his alibi that he had been asleep in his room when Saoirse went missing.

"What about the next morning?" Church asked. "Take me through the next day."

The senator thought for a moment. "I suppose I did my usual routine," he said. "Woke up early, exercised, showered, ate breakfast, read the papers. Did some work here in my office."

Controlled, Church noted. *Methodical.*

"Then, later in the morning," the senator went on, "I went down to the ballroom to greet the guests as they came down for brunch. Around noon, a few of us decided to take the boat out. We didn't get back until late in the afternoon. By then, the whole house was in a frenzy."

Was it odd, Church wondered, that the senator had left the house with a few of his friends for such a length of time when there were so many guests at his home to attend to? Seeking a respite from a large group of people was perhaps within his character, but shirking his responsibilities as host didn't seem to be. Perhaps he didn't want to be present when people discovered that Saoirse was missing?

"When you returned, did you join in the search for your sister?" Church asked.

"No," the senator said. "I called the police. They arrived shortly after."

"And how would you describe your relationship with your sister, Senator?" Church asked. "Did she confide in you anything that might shed some light on her mindset that night?"

The senator was silent for a moment. "We were very different people," he said. "I was not in her confidence, no."

"So the two of you didn't really get along?" Church prompted. He already knew the answer to this, but he wanted to see if the senator would cop to it. From what Church had read in the case files, Saoirse was a loudly leaning liberal. She'd attended the Gay Pride Parade in San Francisco and a feminist pro-abortion rally in Los Angeles. She had once even claimed to be a Buddhist. And it wasn't just that Saoirse and her brother didn't see eye to eye when it came to politics; Saoirse liked to make a scene. She was photographed once at the Troubadour as a minor—a gin and tonic in one hand, a joint in the other—and another time stumbling out of the Whisky a Go Go at two in the morning, barefoot, strappy heels bunched in one hand, mascaraed racoon eyes blinking sleepily into the paparazzi's lenses. Saoirse provided unending fodder for the gossip rags and Page Six. Maybe the senator had seen her as a liability, an embarrassment, that he couldn't sustain.

"We didn't always see eye to eye on what was in Saoirse's best interest," Senator Towers said.

A very apt answer for a politician, Church noted.

"I understand you pulled her out of school the year before her disappearance. Is that correct?" Church asked.

Senator Towers shifted in his chair. "Saoirse's health had taken a turn," he said. "She suffered from long QT syndrome, a dangerous arrhythmia."

"And how did Saoirse respond to being removed from school?"

"Poorly," the senator said, "as most teenage girls might. But I had to weigh the risks, and ultimately, I felt that Cliffhaven was the safest place for her."

"And that decision caused a rift between the two of you?"

"There was some friction, yes," Senator Towers said. "But I had to behave like a parent, not a friend, not an older brother. I made a decision that I felt was in Saoirse's best interest, and if I had to go back, I'd make the same decision again."

Church was silent a beat. "And the money," Church went on. "Saoirse's inheritance. Whatever happened to that?"

The senator was quiet a moment. "Her trust reverted back to the family," he said. "To her next of kin."

"To be clear, that would make you the sole beneficiary, since your brother and parents are deceased?" Church asked.

"It would, yes," the senator said.

"And in order to do that, you had your sister legally declared dead?" Church said.

"I did, yes," Senator Towers said, "about five years after she disappeared. It was a legal formality at that point."

"And did you believe your sister to be dead?" Church asked.

The senator shifted in his chair. "To be honest," he said, "I didn't know what to believe. At first, I thought she might have run away. It wouldn't have been the first time, and Detective Vance said there was no evidence of foul play. I suppose I kind of hoped, for a long time, that that was the case—that she was out there, living her life somewhere. But as time dragged on and there was no sign of her—well, that seemed less and less likely."

"You said she'd run away before?" Church asked. "When was that?"

"When I first had her pulled out of school," Senator Towers said. "Instead of getting on a plane to come home, she took a train from Choate to the city. I found her a week later, camped out at the Plaza Hotel."

"Is there anyone you can think of who would want to hurt your sister, Senator Towers?" Church asked.

The senator leaned back in his chair and rubbed his chin. "Anybody who'd want to hurt her? No. But someone who might hurt her if the alcohol was flowing and he saw something he didn't like? Maybe."

"Who's that?" Church asked.

"Teddy Mountbatten," the senator said.

"Saoirse's ex-boyfriend?" Church said, and the senator nodded. "And what makes you say that?"

"Teddy was a jealous man," Senator Towers said. "And when he got jealous, he could be . . . violent. I saw it with my own eyes."

"The night of Saoirse's party?" Church asked.

"No, not then," the senator said. "But a tiger doesn't change his stripes."

"So he'd been violent in the past?" Church asked.

The senator nodded. "Teddy and Saoirse were on and off for years," he said. "They were both dramatic by nature. When they were together, they were either very affectionate or at each other's throats. The smallest comment or gesture could be incendiary. I was at a New Year's Eve party with them two years prior," the senator went on. "They were together then. I saw them from across the room, fighting. Saoirse shoved him. Teddy grabbed her by her upper arms, roughly, and shook her. He screamed in her face. I got up and walked toward them. Teddy saw me over Saoirse's shoulder, and he let her go. But the look in his eye—there was so much anger. Like he could have killed her. I don't know how far he would have taken things if he hadn't looked up and seen me standing there."

"Do you know what the nature of their fight was that night?" Church asked.

"Yes," the senator said. "Teddy had seen Saoirse flirting with another boy, and he'd confronted her."

"I see," Church said. He shifted in his chair. "And you believe, the night of Saoirse's birthday, a similar scenario played out—only this time, you weren't there to intervene?"

Senator Towers nodded. "It's the only thing that makes any sense to me," he said. "My sister wasn't always the easiest person to get along with, Detective, but I don't know anyone who actively wished her harm."

Church knew that the police had interviewed Teddy three times. Once, the morning after the party, along with all the other guests. Teddy had claimed the last time he had seen Saoirse was when he'd pulled her out of an argument with another guest, and then they'd gone their separate ways. He'd noticed she was in distress, and he'd rescued her; she hadn't told him what her disagreement with the other guest had been about, and he didn't pry. She'd seemed distracted and wandered off, and that was the last he'd seen of her.

Later, when several guests corroborated that they'd seen Saoirse and Teddy in the ballroom together after the argument, sharing more than one drink, the police interviewed Teddy again. This time, they'd gone out to New York to meet with him. Maybe he'd had a drink with Saoirse in the ballroom after the argument, he said this time. He'd drunk heavily that evening, and his memory was fuzzy. When asked if he'd escorted her down to the beach for the fireworks, he'd adamantly denied it. He'd been having an amorous encounter, as he called it, with one of the servers in a supply closet. When asked the name of the girl so that the police could corroborate it, he grew quiet.

The third time the police interviewed Teddy, he brought a lawyer. And not just any lawyer. He had retained Alan Dershowitz, who had represented Patty Hearst when she went on trial for helping her captors rob a bank. Word on the street was that Dershowitz had also recently been retained by Claus von Bülow, the British socialite who was accused of killing his wife. Teddy hadn't said a word that time, hadn't answered a single question. With no physical evidence or anything to charge him with, the police had let him go, and the trail had grown cold.

There was a knock at the door, and both the senator and Detective Church looked up to see Robin standing there.

"I'm sorry to interrupt, Senator," she said, "but they're ready for you downstairs."

"Yes, thank you, Robin. I'll be right down," the senator said. He stood and straightened the lapels of his jacket. "Detective, I hate to cut our time short," the senator said, though he didn't look like he hated it at all. In fact, he looked relieved. "I trust you've gotten everything you need?"

"Yes, this has been very helpful, thank you," Church said. "If it's not too much trouble, I'd like to get a tour of the house. You know—get a sense of the rooms where everything transpired and the layout of things."

"Yes," the senator said. "Mrs. Talbot, our housekeeper, can show you. I daresay she knows the house even better than I do." Senator Towers retrieved his phone from his pocket and typed out a text. "I'll have her meet you in the foyer," he said.

"I appreciate it," Church said, standing. "Thank you again for your time."

The senator nodded. He extended his hand to Church, and Church shook it, noting once again the strength in his grip.

Maybe it wasn't about the money, Church thought, or the differing political ideologies or the family reputation. Maybe it was simpler than that. Maybe it was about control. The senator was a man who liked to be in control of all aspects of his life, and Saoirse was wild and unpredictable and had bucked all his attempts to rein her in. She had been turning eighteen the night of her party, a powerful age. An age that legally declared her independence and adulthood, an age when her brother lost the authority to dictate every aspect of her life.

One thing was certain: If it was Senator Towers who had murdered Saoirse, it had not been some flight of fancy or a moment of rage. It would have been premeditated, perfectly planned, immaculately executed.

It made sense, in a way, for the senator to do it in an environment that he knew well, the home that he had grown up in. And to do it at a party that he had overseen. He'd know who would be there and what the itinerary would be—what would be happening and when. Had the chaos of the party provided the perfect distraction to mask his devious actions? Perhaps he had said good night to his guests early and retreated to his room under the guise of going to bed, as he claimed. But maybe he had slipped down to the beach after. It was his home—he knew how to navigate the back halls, the servants' stairs, well enough so as not to be seen. In guests' last reported sighting of Saoirse, she was drunk and stumbling down the stairs to the beach with an unidentified man. Perhaps that had been Ransom Towers? Someone Saoirse knew, someone she trusted.

Controlled. Methodical.

Perhaps, once again, Senator Towers and Saoirse had not seen eye to eye on what was best for her. Or, rather, on what was best for the senator.

CHAPTER THREE

JUNE 1982

When Ana rejoined Mrs. Talbot on the stairs, Mrs. Talbot gave her a quick once-over, from her flyaway braids to the same yellowing Chuck Taylors that she had worn on her drive, and then a disapproving look, as if Ana should have more to show for the generous fifteen minutes of freshening up that she had been so graciously granted. Still, Mrs. Talbot didn't say anything, and so neither did Ana. Ana followed her silently down the stairs to the hall, where they went left this time through another grand-looking room. The house felt like a giant maze, and Ana felt lost and disoriented. She tried to memorize the rooms and their orientation to one another, but again, Mrs. Talbot kept a brisk pace, which left no time to study anything. They made their way out onto a white stone terrace that overlooked the back garden.

A young woman sat there. She had a tray on a table in front of her, and she stared out absently at the garden, her chin propped in her hand, as if she were deep in thought. She wore a smart white jumper that skimmed her slender figure and showed off her deep tan, and her long dark hair fell loosely around her shoulders. She was quite possibly the most beautiful person Ana had ever seen, outside of the movies.

"Miss Saoirse," Mrs. Talbot called gently as they approached. Saoirse's head turned toward them then, and it was like a switch went on behind her eyes when she saw them. Gone was the dreamy expression, immediately replaced by animated excitement.

"You must be Ana," Saoirse said as she pushed back her chair.

Ana put out her hand, but Saoirse embraced her warmly, drawing Ana into her tall thin frame. She smelled of vanilla and elderflowers, delicate and fresh.

"It's so good to meet you," Saoirse said. "Ransom has told me all about you, and I feel as if we're friends already. Please, join me."

She motioned to the chair next to her, and Ana took it, feeling a little taken aback by such a friendly welcome.

"It's great to meet you too," Ana said, sinking into her chair.

"I'll leave you girls to get to know one another, then," Mrs. Talbot said. "Ring the maid when you're done, Saoirse, and she'll collect your tray."

"Thank you, Tabby," Saoirse said.

"Tabby?" Ana asked, when Mrs. Talbot was out of earshot.

"Oh, yes," Saoirse said, leaning toward her and whispering conspiratorially. "Absolutely *never* call her that. She will flay you alive. I'm only allowed because I started when I was two. Couldn't say my *ot*'s, and what kind of monster would scold a child with a speech impediment?"

"She's been with the family that long?" Ana asked.

"Oh, longer," Saoirse said. "I think they built her with the house." Saoirse winked, and Ana laughed.

Ana was relieved, really. Saoirse seemed neither sickly nor difficult. She was lovely, a breath of fresh air, especially after Ana's encounter with Mrs. Talbot.

Still, Ana couldn't help but wonder—this was the girl who had scared away three companions in as many weeks? She couldn't square it.

"I heard you like horseback riding," Saoirse said. "What do you say to a ride down to the beach?"

In the stables, they tacked up two of the most beautiful chestnut mares that Ana had ever seen, and then they were off, down a trail that followed the main road for a way before it veered off into the tall grass and made a gentle zigzagging descent down the hillside to the beach. At the bottom, they found themselves in a little cove surrounded by hills on either side and, in front of them, the frothy mouth of the sea.

It was hot, the sun still overhead, and when they dismounted, Saoirse untied her jumper and shrugged out of it. She had a stylish one-piece lime-green swimsuit on underneath.

"What do you say to a swim?" Saoirse asked as she tied her hair into a knot at the top of her head.

"Oh, I didn't realize we were going swimming," Ana said apologetically. "I'm not wearing my suit."

"It's a private beach," Saoirse said. "No one will see you here. And underwear is practically the same thing."

Ana shielded her eyes from the sun with her hand and looked out at the water. The waves arched and crashed loudly onto the sand.

"Looks a little rough out there," Ana said.

She didn't want to tell Saoirse that she didn't know how to swim, but she also didn't want to be a killjoy, not on the first day, not when they were getting along so well.

"You have to run in quickly when the tide pulls out," Saoirse said. "The bottom drops off a few yards out; that's why the waves break the way they do."

"Oh," Ana said, her heart sinking. "So it's too deep to touch?"

"It's perfectly safe," Saoirse assured her. "Trust me. I swim here nearly every day in the summer."

Ana bit her lip, feeling panic in her stomach. "I think I'll just sunbathe for a while," she said.

"All right," Saoirse said, clearly disappointed. "I'll sit with you."

They had brought a towel, a thermos of iced tea, and some cups. They spread the towel out on the sand and lay down facing the water.

"You'll get funny tan lines in those clothes," Saoirse said, glancing at her sideways.

Ana pursed her lips. She was hot and sweaty from their ride in the noonday sun, and she didn't want to deny Saoirse something else when she had already turned down her offer to go swimming. So Ana unbuttoned her blouse, undid the clasp of her shorts. She folded them neatly into a pile on the edge of the towel and lay back down in her underwear. She was secretly glad she had chosen to wear her new cream-colored underwire bra and a trusted pair of cotton briefs this morning: nothing fancy, but also not too dowdy or worn.

"Thirsty?" Saoirse asked, handing her the thermos.

"Yes, parched, thank you," Ana said.

She took a swig. It was cold and sweet, with a bitter aftertaste that Ana couldn't place. She wiped the corners of her mouth with her fingers.

"What kind of tea is this?" Ana asked.

"Persimmon with a hint of turmeric," Saoirse said. "My own secret recipe."

Turmeric. That must be what she'd tasted.

"I'm going to take a dip to cool off," Saoirse said. "You sure you don't want to join me?"

Ana shook her head.

"Suit yourself, then," Saoirse said.

Ana watched her saunter toward the water, all slender long legs and bronzed skin. When she was gone, Ana lay down on her back. She hadn't realized until just now how tired she was. She had risen before the sun this morning to pack her car and make the drive up north. And she hadn't really slept much the night before. She'd tossed and turned, her stomach roiling with anticipation and nervousness for the coming day.

She decided she would close her eyes, but just for a moment. The warmth of the sun covered her body like a comforting blanket, weighing down on it, pressing her into the sand. And the sound of the waves breaking on the shore was a lulling melody.

She heard Saoirse come back at some point and ask for the towel, and she'd scooted off it, still half asleep, and then she'd dozed some more.

When Ana woke, the sun had inched lower in the sky. The sand next to her was bare—Saoirse wasn't there. Ana sat up quickly and scanned the water, but aside from some gulls lolling on the surface farther out, it was empty.

"Saoirse?" Ana called.

It took her a moment to realize that her clothes and shoes were also gone. So, too, was the thermos and, to Ana's horror, both horses.

Jacqueline's words from her interview the previous week echoed in her head: *"Don't be nice. They certainly won't be."*

Saoirse's friendly welcome had been merely a ruse, Ana suddenly realized. She'd wanted to lower Ana's defenses, lure her into a vulnerable position so she could strike. Ana felt humiliated—how easily she had fallen for it.

Seething, Ana wrapped her arms around her middle. The wind was picking up, sending a chill that raised goose bumps on her bare skin. She had two choices: wait there in the hope that someone from the house would eventually notice she was missing and come find her, or walk back to the house, along the highway, in her underwear.

Ana stood up; she had never been the type to wait to be rescued.

The climb up the hillside was steep and long and treacherous, especially without shoes. The path was rocky, the jagged edges cutting into the flesh of Ana's bare feet. Her thighs and glutes ached, and she gasped for breath as she neared the top. She stumbled twice, dirt and rocks crusting themselves into the skin of her knees and the palms of her hands.

When she reached the road, she could see the house in the distance, about two miles away. The asphalt was hot but bearable to walk on, and she kept to the edge of it, facing oncoming cars. The road was not a busy one, and Ana couldn't decide if that was a good thing or a bad thing.

After a while, she could hear a car approaching from behind, and she glanced back. It was a blue convertible with its top down and a solitary driver—a man. She looked forward again and pulled herself up straighter, bracing herself for a humiliating encounter. Perhaps he would honk or whistle at her, and she would flip him the bird.

But the car didn't honk. In fact, as it got closer, Ana heard it slow to a crawl. The hairs on the back of her neck stood up, and she thought longingly of the gun hidden uselessly back at the house, near the fireplace in her room. Why hadn't she brought it with her? She'd heard of the I-5 Killer, who'd raped and killed women all along Interstate 5, all the way from Washington down to California. They'd caught him last spring, but still, there were bad people out there, and right now, she was an easy target.

When the car reached her, it stopped, and Ana felt real, hot panic pulse in her chest. She glanced to her left, but there was nothing but cliffside—a steep drop-off, maybe twenty-five feet to the water, and it was probably too craggy and shallow to jump. She looked forward toward the house on the hillside, but it was still so far away—too far for Ana to run if she had to. Besides, this man had a car, and Ana didn't even have shoes. She couldn't possibly outrun him. She was trapped. She wondered if she screamed, if anyone in the house would hear her, and if they did, if they would come to her aid.

Ana swallowed and reluctantly looked over at the car—a sleek robin's-egg blue convertible. The driver was a young man—late twenties, early thirties—and he was jeering at her.

Ana hugged her arms across her chest, trying to cover as much of her bare skin as possible. She couldn't let him know that she was afraid.

"Get a good look, you fucking pervert?" Ana shouted. "This isn't a free show, you know. Get lost."

She started to walk again, at a brisker stride this time. The car started to move, too, keeping pace with her. Ana could hear her heart thudding in her ears. *Fuck.* She needed a way out, but she couldn't think of one. She willed another car to drive by, but she could see a good way in either direction, and the road was empty.

"My apologies," the man said. "I promise, I wasn't laughing at you; it's more the situation. Let's just say you're not the first young woman I've picked up on this road dressed only in her underwear."

Ana stopped cold. She looked over at the man. What was he talking about? He made a habit of picking up young women in their underwear on the side of the road?

"You must be Saoirse's new caretaker," the man went on, by way of explanation. "She's done this sort of thing before. You didn't drink the tea, did you?"

The fear that had filled Ana only a moment ago was gone in an instant, replaced by white-hot anger.

"She put something in my tea?" she asked.

"Benadryl," the man said. "Hardly lethal, but it will knock you right out."

"Fuck," Ana muttered.

"Count yourself lucky. The last girl got a snake in her bed," the man said. "I'm Salvador Santos, by the way. Saoirse's tutor."

"Ana," she said. "Ana Rojas."

"Well, Ana-Ana Rojas," Salvador said, "here."

He reached into the back seat of the car and grabbed a jean jacket that was lying there. He tossed it to her.

Ana caught it reflexively.

"Thanks," she said. She slid one arm in and then the other and pulled it tightly closed over her chest. It was far too big for her, running past the tips of her fingers and halfway down her thighs, and she was glad for the cover, to no longer be nearly naked in front of this complete stranger, kind though he may be.

Salvador reached across the car and unlocked the passenger-side door. "Get in," he said. "I'll give you a ride to the house. I'm headed back there myself. I just borrowed the car to run some errands in town."

Ana crossed the street quickly and climbed into the front passenger seat.

"Thanks," she said again as she buckled her seat belt.

"Don't mention it," Salvador said. He winked at her. "Us help have to stick together."

He had a kind and attractive face. Almond-colored skin; dark, wavy hair; warm chocolate eyes, with swirls of gold around the edges. She couldn't fathom what Ransom had been thinking, hiring a tutor for his sister who looked like that.

"I can't believe I fell for her nice act," Ana said, pressing the back of her head into the headrest. "They warned me what she would be like—and still! I feel like such an idiot."

"Don't be so hard on yourself," Salvador said. "Saoirse puts everyone through the wringer."

"Yeah?" Ana said. "What'd she do to you? Whoopee cushion on your chair? Frog in your desk?"

"Something like that," Salvador said with a smile as he turned down the drive to the Towers home.

His English was very good, but there was something about the intonation of his voice, how he sometimes stressed the end of the word instead of the first syllable, and a slight, almost undetectable roll of his *r*'s, that betrayed that English was not his first language.

"And she just gets away with it?" Ana asked.

"Well, I'm sure if Ransom finds out, he'd do something to punish her," Salvador said. "Take away some privilege to vex her, give her a firm scolding whenever he does come back into town, though who knows when that will be."

"And Mrs. Talbot?" Ana asked.

"You won't get any help from Mrs. Talbot. She likes to do all of the hiring for the house, and she's none too pleased that Ransom took things into his own hands for this position. She'll be rooting for you to fail."

"Well, that's comforting," Ana said.

She was on her own, then. That was all right. She had been on her own for a long time.

As they approached the front of the house, Ana reached for the handle of the passenger-side door.

"Let me out here, if you don't mind," she said.

"Mrs. Talbot prefers that we use the—"

"I know," Ana said. "But I prefer to get out here."

"All right," Salvador said. He stopped the car.

"Do you mind if I return your jacket to you tomorrow?" she asked.

Salvador smiled at her, and she felt her stomach drop, but not in an unpleasant way.

"I guess I know where to find you if you don't," he said.

"Thanks," she said. "For everything."

He had done her a great favor, really. He had confirmed who her enemies were.

She got out of the car and marched up the grand stone steps to the front entrance, where, just that morning, Mrs. Talbot had shut the door in her face. But this time, she wouldn't knock. She wouldn't ask for permission and wait for it to be granted. She had done that routine most of her life, and it had gotten her exactly nowhere. She was tired of being told no.

"Ana," Salvador called to her, and Ana paused at the top of the stairs, her hand on the doorknob, and turned around.

"Yes?"

"What will you do?" he asked. "About Saoirse, I mean?"

"Why?" Ana said.

"It's just, you seem upset, and I know from experience that acting on impulse when you're angry rarely leads to a good outcome."

He acted like Ana's anger was something to be afraid of, but, on the contrary, Ana found anger to be a very useful emotion. It filled you with fire; it spurred you to action. Rage instilled in a person a sense of power. It was so much better than grief or fear, which drained you and left you feeling powerless, like a victim. Ana refused to be a victim. She had agency, and she would use it.

"Saoirse's brother, he can be a bit hard on her," Salvador went on, when Ana didn't say anything. "Especially after what happened with all the other caretakers—well, it probably wouldn't go so well for her if he were to find out."

"Don't worry, Salvador," Ana said. She wanted to tell him that she had known rage a long time. It was a familiar friend. She no longer allowed it to course through her veins unchecked like a drug, driving her to actions that were both reckless and counterproductive. Her rage was a tiger on a leash, sitting obediently at her heel, waiting for the command to strike. She was the master of it. "If Ransom finds out about Saoirse's tricks," Ana said, "it won't be from me."

She gave Salvador a friendly smile to reassure him.

"I'll see you around," she said.

Then she turned and opened the door and stepped over the threshold into the house.

CHAPTER FOUR

PRESENT

The young man waiting for her in the foyer couldn't possibly be the detective, Florence thought. He looked too young to be in charge of a case like this. He was practically a child.

"Detective Church?" she asked tentatively, and the man turned to face her.

"Mrs. Talbot," he said warmly, reaching out a hand.

Florence shook it. "Senator Towers informed me you'd like a tour of the house," she said.

"Yes, if it wouldn't be too much trouble," Church said.

"It's no trouble at all," Florence said. "We can begin with the ballroom, if you like? It's right down the hall here."

"Lead the way," Church said.

Florence turned, and Church followed her down the foyer and to the left.

"May I ask, Mrs. Talbot," Detective Church said as they walked, "how long have you been the housekeeper here?"

Florence had to think a moment. "Let's see," she said. "I believe Nixon was president."

"You've been with the family since the 1970s?" Church asked, sounding shocked.

Florence laughed. "Detective, I've been with the family since 1941. I was born here," Florence went on quickly. "Quite literally. My mother was a scullery maid; she was hired on during the war. Nobody knew she was pregnant with me until she went into labor while stacking peach preserves in the cellar. Gave the cook quite the scare."

"I can imagine," Church said. "Did your father work here as well?"

"No," Florence said wistfully. When she was a little girl, her mother used to show her a picture of a man in uniform that she wore in a locket around her neck. Blond hair, bearded face, a steady gaze. John Talbot was his name. Florence used to look at that photograph and try to puzzle out which parts of her belonged to him, but she never could settle on a likeness.

"He died in the war," Florence said, which is what she always said when someone asked about her father, though no one had asked about her father in a very long time. The truth was Florence didn't know if he died in the war, or if his name was John Talbot, or if he really was her father. The only thing she knew definitively was that he never came back.

"I'm sorry," Detective Church said.

Florence paused in front of a set of large wrought iron doors with glass inserts. She fiddled with the key ring she wore hooked to her belt until she found the right one.

"Here we are, then," she said, inserting the key into the lock and turning it. "The ballroom."

"Let me get that for you, Mrs. Talbot," Detective Church said, stepping forward to open and hold the door for her. "It looks heavy."

"Thank you," Florence said, a little taken aback. It had been ages since someone had held open a door for her. Once a routine gesture but nowadays a rare one, and it meant something to Florence.

The room was dark, and when Florence flicked on the lights, it took them a minute to come on—they sputtered and flickered across the space, as if they had been asleep for a long time and were slow to wake.

The room was long—at least a third of a football field in length, with a ceiling soaring over thirty feet high above them. It was empty, save for a stray round table scattered here and there, unadorned, and stacks of chairs. There was a chandelier in the center, at least twenty feet in circumference, lowered for cleaning so that it hovered just inches from the floor. A step stool and a bucket sat absently next to it. Across the room were floor-to-ceiling windows and two sets of large French doors leading out onto the terrace.

"I'll get the handyman to take a look at that," Florence said, glancing up at the one light directly above them that still refused to come on, leaving them standing partially in shadow. "It's been a while since the room has seen any use."

A while was a generous statement—the last time the room had been used was for a charity ball when the senator was still a congressman. There was so much dust in the air that it made Florence's eyes water, her nose itch.

"Do you mind if I take a few pictures?" Detective Church asked.

Florence shook her head. "By all means."

She watched the detective intently as he meandered around the room, stepping back into this corner or that to take a wide shot.

"If you don't mind me asking," Florence said, "how long have you been with the sheriff's office, Detective?"

Church clicked his camera and then glanced down to examine the shot on the digital screen. "Oh, about ten years now," he said.

"Ten years, my," Florence said.

"I started as a deputy straight out of the academy," Church went on. "Then moved up to detective in the Major Crimes Unit a few years later."

"And what year was that?" Florence asked.

Church smiled. "If there's something you want to ask me, Mrs. Talbot, you can."

"I hope I'm not being impertinent, Detective," Florence said. "But how old are you?"

"I'm thirty-eight," he said.

"Thirty-eight," Florence repeated. Not a child, then. Older, in fact, by nearly a decade than Detective Vance had been when he'd first taken on the case. Florence noticed, now that Church had stepped out of the shadows into the more brightly lit parts of the room, the specks of gray peeking out of his well-manicured beard.

"My apologies," Florence said. "I hope I didn't cause you any offense. That's the thing about growing old, I suppose. Everyone looks like a child to me now, even grown men."

"At my age, I'll take it as a compliment," Church said. "In truth, I'm probably closer to a hip replacement than I am to puberty."

Florence laughed, and the gesture caused her to sneeze, roughly. She felt around in her pocket for her handkerchief, but her pocket was uncharacteristically empty.

"My, I'm never without my hankie," she said.

"Here, take mine," Detective Church said, retrieving a handkerchief, neatly folded, from his inside jacket pocket.

"Thank you," Florence said, taking it. It was cotton and embroidered with his initials on the edge. "Are you sure you're only thirty-eight, Detective?" Florence asked. "I haven't had a man offer me a handkerchief for at least three decades."

Church laughed. "I'm a bit old fashioned in some ways, I suppose," he said. "I got my manners from my granny. She's the one who raised me, mostly."

"I see," Florence said. "You must be very fond of her."

"Granny's my favorite person in the whole world," Church said without hesitation. "I just spent this last Saturday with her at the nursing home, actually. Jell-O molds, canasta, and episodes of *Gunsmoke*. Don't threaten me with a good time."

He smiled, and Florence smiled back at him. He was a good seed, this one. Florence liked him immediately.

"If you wouldn't mind," Church said, "I'd love to get a sense of how the room was set up that night. I know it's been ages, but anything you can remember would be helpful."

"Not at all," Florence said, for she had spent months planning that party, and then for years, and then decades after, she had replayed the moments of that night, again and again, in her head. She took him through how the room was set up in great detail, as if they had only just taken down the tables and dismantled the dance floor. She showed him where the dinner tables had been—twenty-one tables in all, with some seating ten and others a dozen. There had been a bar on either side of the room and one outside on the terrace. The dance floor had been set up next to the stage where the band had played.

"And how many guests were there?" Church asked.

"Two hundred and thirty-four," Florence said, the number still sharp as a tack in her mind. Two hundred and thirty-four RSVP cards with the box next to "Accepts with Pleasure" checked. Two hundred and thirty-four place settings. Two hundred and thirty-four party favors in the form of gossamer bags stuffed with candied almonds—she had stayed up until nearly two in the morning the night before, tying the bags with ribbons.

"There are diagrams and seating charts," Florence went on. "I still have them, in case they would be of any use."

"Really?" Church said, as if he couldn't believe his luck. "Yes, that would be very helpful, thank you."

"I keep everything," Florence said. "I'm a creature of habit, I suppose."

"This must have been quite the event to plan," he said, looking around at the vast, empty room, as if he couldn't imagine all the work it took to fill it.

"Yes," Florence said with a deep, satisfied sigh. "Three months of planning."

"And what do you remember from that night, Mrs. Talbot?" Church asked. "I suppose you must have been very busy. Everywhere all at once."

"Yes," Florence said. "I was back and forth between the kitchen and the ballroom, mostly. The staff will say I was everywhere at all times. Omnipresent. The guests won't have seen me at all."

She smiled pleasantly to herself. Despite everything that had happened, everything that had gone wrong, at least that was a mark of a job well done.

"And what about Saoirse?" Church asked. "Did you see much of her that evening?"

"Sporadically," Florence said. "From a distance, mostly."

"You didn't speak with her?"

"I told her when it was time to cut the cake," Florence said. "She was having a drink with Mr. Mountbatten in the ballroom. She looked distressed, so I was glad to intervene."

"Teddy Mountbatten?" Church asked. "Her ex-boyfriend?"

Florence nodded. "That's the one."

"Did she tell you why she was upset?"

"Well, she was speaking with Mr. Mountbatten, so I figured he was the cause."

"Yes, I heard they had a volatile relationship," Detective Church said. "Did you know Mr. Mountbatten well?"

"Well enough to know that he was not what he seemed," Florence said.

"How do you mean?"

"Just that on the surface, Mr. Mountbatten may have been everything a man ought to be—attractive, charming, from a good family," Florence said. "But that only made him all the more dangerous. It hid his barbaric nature. Mr. Mountbatten was a wolf in sheep's clothing."

Detective Church paused a moment, as if he were struck by the severity of Florence's words. "Did you ever witness Mr. Mountbatten being violent toward Saoirse?" Church asked.

Florence smiled wryly. "Those kinds of men are good at hiding their ugliness from those whom they don't wish to see it."

"You speak as if you have some experience with the type," Church said.

Florence pursed her lips. "Something like that. Would you like to see the terrace?" she asked, already moving toward one of the French doors on the other side of the room. So Church followed her.

The terrace was long and wide, built of the same limestone as the house. Directly in front of them, in the distance, was a view of the ocean, and to the left, mountains. Curved staircases on either side of the terrace led down to the gardens and, to the left, an Olympic-size swimming pool.

Church emitted a low whistle. "That's quite a pool," he said.

"Augustus Towers built it for his second wife, Scarlet, as a wedding present," Florence said. "She was terrified of swimming in the ocean. All those things you can't see, you know, lurking beneath your feet. So he built her this pool and tiled the bottom with white stones from Sicily, to make it glow at night in the reflection of the moon."

"Augustus Towers," Church said. "That would be Saoirse's grandfather?"

Florence nodded.

"You must have known the whole family quite well," Detective Church said, "growing up here as you did."

"Yes," Florence said. "Charles, Saoirse's father, and her aunts, Verity and Astrid, we all came of age together. The four of us were thick as thieves when we were children."

Florence glanced down at the enormous pool below them. She remembered summers as a girl when she had practically lived in that pool. Charles would challenge her to breath-holding contests, and she would play Marco Polo with Verity and Astrid. Those summers were endless, bliss-filled days of picnics on the lawn, treasure hunts in the cove, and building forts out of old sheets in the playroom. They ran around barefoot and sunburned, their lips sticky and sweet from the lemonade the cook would make for them that they'd drink straight from the glass pitcher, too busy and bursting with energy to bother with cups. She and Verity would climb into their twin beds in the nursery at the end of the day, pleasurably exhausted, still dressed in their bathing suits, their hair wet and tangled.

Florence sighed and shook her head to clear it. She didn't usually allow herself to get swept up in nostalgia. There was too much that required her attention in the present to bother with that. "Would you like to see Saoirse's room?" Florence asked.

They took the short back hall from the ballroom to the kitchen next, and then the staircase up to the wing of the house where the family's quarters were.

Saoirse's bedroom was an odd mixture of ornate and adolescent, as if a bedroom at Versailles had been inhabited by a teen from the '80s. In the middle of the room was a large four-poster bed with a gossamer canopy, neatly made, a mountain of pillows resting against the headboard. There was a marble-top vanity and a floor-length, gilt-framed mirror to one side and a sitting area that looked out toward the balcony and the garden. But there were also posters of the Go-Go's plastered on the walls, and shelves of trophies and ribbons from Saoirse's dressage and show jumping competitions, and a memory board stuffed with photos of Saoirse with her friends and pinned with notes and old concert tickets, now yellowing and curling at the ends.

"It's just as she left it," Florence said. "The maids come in once a week to clean, but other than that, nothing has been touched or rearranged."

Detective Church walked around the perimeter of the room, snapping pictures, and Florence stood unobtrusively to the side. Her eyes skimmed the memory board next to Saoirse's bed, and a flash of bright pink caught her eye. She leaned forward to read the bubbly cursive on one of the notes pinned to the board. *Went to library to study. Meet me in Henley Hall after algebra final. Love, T.*

Florence's heart pinched in her chest. After all these years that had gone by, it was easy to forget that Saoirse had been just a teenager when she disappeared. An innocent child.

"Were you and Saoirse close?" Church asked, interrupting her reverie.

"Oh, yes," Florence said, a smile warming her face. "I daresay I knew her better than most. I was her nanny when she was just a baby. She was so tiny when she was born—barely six pounds. Had colic more times than I could count. I'd stay up all night with her in the nursery, holding her to my chest, rocking her. She used to cry—wail—when anybody but me or Charles would hold her."

"You must have felt very protective of her."

"I did," Florence said, "like she was my own."

"And how did you feel about Senator Towers removing her from school?" Church asked. "It sounded like Saoirse took that quite hard."

Florence was quiet for a moment. "Yes," she said. "But everything Ransom did was to protect her."

"So he acted in good faith," Church said, "but you didn't agree with his decision?"

"It wasn't my place to have an opinion," Florence said. "Ransom was her legal guardian, and he did what he thought was best. The poor boy was barely more than a child himself. It was tragic, really, losing both of his parents so young the way he did, and then his brother, Theo, too, not long after."

"The Towers family curse," Church said.

A chill went up Florence's spine, and she crossed herself.

"Are you superstitious, Mrs. Talbot?" Church asked. "I didn't take you for the type."

"Not superstitious," Florence said. "Catholic."

"Ah," Church said.

"You're not a religious man, Detective?" Florence asked.

Detective Church shook his head. "In my line of work, I've seen too many things to believe in God," he said matter-of-factly.

"I see," Florence said. "Yes, I imagine that is quite hard, day after day, to see the worst in humanity and believe we came from something better than us."

"That's the thing I never understood," Church said. "If we were made in God's image, then why do we do the things we do to one another?"

"Because we have a choice," Florence said. "And we don't always make the right one. But sometimes we do." Florence reached into the pocket of her dress and pulled out a small silver rosary ring. "When I was a girl," she said, "when I was lost and abandoned and in my darkest hour of need, someone showed me grace. They had no reason to do it, nothing to gain. But they did it anyway. My life today would be fundamentally different—unimaginable, really—if not for that act of kindness. That person gave this to me, and I've carried it around with me ever since. Not just to pray the rosary but to have something tangible to hold on to that reminds me of the good people are capable of, if only they choose it."

"That's a very noble way of looking at things, Mrs. Talbot," Church said.

"How we look at things is a choice too," she said. "People are rarely as simple as good or bad, right or wrong. In my experience, they're a bit of both, somewhere in between. Here." Florence handed him the rosary ring. "I daresay you need this more than I do."

"Oh, that's very kind of you," Detective Church said, "but I couldn't—"

"Take it, please," Florence said. "You don't have to use it for prayer. Just—you know, in the midst of all the chaos and the darkness that you see, let it remind you of the good."

Church reached out hesitantly and took it. He ran his thumb thoughtfully along the burnished silver beads on the edges of the ring and then slipped it into his pocket. "Thank you, Mrs. Talbot," he said.

"Please," she said. "Call me Florence."

CHAPTER FIVE

JUNE 1982

For breakfast that morning, the chef had prepared a Gruyère-and-porchetta omelet, and Saoirse dug into it zealously with her fork and knife. She was ravenous. The cheese lent a rich, creamy texture to the eggs. It was sweet and salty at the same time, with a divine nutty taste that Saoirse didn't think she could ever get enough of. The savory pork roast was so tender it practically melted in her mouth. She didn't know if she had ever tasted anything so divine.

"I heard what you did to that girl," Saoirse's mother, Birdie, said, and Saoirse lifted her head to see her mother sitting next to her, at the head of the table. She had a plate of fruit in front of her and a cup of coffee. The newspaper was splayed open on the table next to her so she could read.

"That was hardly Saoirse's fault," Tabby said.

Saoirse looked at Tabby, sitting across the table from her, dressed in black like she always was, a cup of tea in front of her.

"That girl isn't fit for her job," Tabby went on. "Falling asleep on the first day of work?" She made a *tsk* sound. "I don't know why I wasn't left to make the hiring arrangements. I would have found someone better suited."

"Mm," Birdie said, taking a sip of her coffee and turning her attention to her paper. "Still, it wasn't kind."

Saoirse stared down at her fork, at the bits of omelet speared on the ends of the prongs. Suddenly it looked revolting. She tasted iron and fat in her mouth, the tang of blood and meat. *What am I doing?* she wondered. She didn't eat meat. She didn't eat cheese or eggs or butter, hadn't for years. She dropped her fork, and it landed with a loud clang on her plate.

Saoirse looked up, expecting Tabby or her mother to scold her, but neither woman was looking at her. Tabby was stirring her tea, and Birdie was preoccupied with her paper. Saoirse studied her mother for a moment. There was something off about her nose—the slope of it— and the set of her eyes. It wasn't quite right.

She looked across the breakfast table to see if Tabby had noticed it too, but Tabby was drinking her tea as if nothing at all were amiss.

What the hell was going on?

Saoirse glanced down at the paper her mother was reading. On it was a picture of her father's face—handsome and smiling and dressed in a suit. Atop it, in large letters, the headline read: LOST: Mayor Charles Towers and wife Birdie presumed dead in plane crash off coast of Catalina.

A cold panic filled Saoirse's chest as she remembered. She didn't know how she could have ever forgotten it. Her mother was dead. She'd been dead for years. Birdie's plane had gone down in the Pacific one week before Saoirse's fourteenth birthday. It'd taken the rescue team twelve days to find the plane's wreckage off the coast of Catalina, 120 feet below the water's surface. The divers had found Birdie's body still strapped into the fuselage, next to Saoirse's father.

There'd been closed caskets at the funeral, with bright, smiling pictures in frames posed on top. Saoirse had stood before them, dry-eyed and numb, still too shell shocked to cry. She remembered wanting to pry open the top of her mother's casket, peer inside. She imagined her mother's beautiful face swollen now, her lips tinged blue, her face bloated. It would be horrible, but wasn't it always better to face the horrible truth than to live with whatever terrors your imagination cooked up? Saoirse thought if she could just see her, maybe she could stop thinking about what happened to a body at the bottom of the ocean, the way that skin absorbed water and peeled away from the tissue, the way fish and sea lice made a feast of one's flesh.

Saoirse looked at the woman sitting next to her now at the head of the table. Was she just imagining it, was it a trick of the light, or did the woman's lips have an oddly bluish tint to them? Her face looked fuller than it had a moment ago, her skin doughy. As the woman reached for the orange from her plate, Saoirse noticed how fat her fingers were, like stuffed sausages.

Saoirse's heart pounded in her chest. She wanted to get up from the table, to run screaming in the other direction, but she couldn't move. Her body felt impossibly heavy, as if it were held there by invisible weights.

"Who are you?" Saoirse asked, her voice sounding small and afraid.

The woman didn't even look up from her paper. She continued peeling her orange with her fingers, stripping away the peel. Her nails were broken at odd angles, as if she had tried to claw her way out of something.

Saoirse swallowed. Her throat was dry, and it hurt. "Who are you?" she said, louder this time.

The woman looked up. "I'm sorry, dear, did you say something?" she asked.

"Who. Are. You?" Saoirse said for the third time, her voice steely and loud, closer to a shout, an accusation, than a question.

"Who am I?" the woman repeated, laughing, as if Saoirse had told a joke. She looked over at Tabby, as if this was some sort of prank that Saoirse and Tabby had cooked up together and she was searching for the punch line. But Tabby just shook her head, clearly as lost as she was.

The woman looked back at Saoirse now, concerned this time. "Who am I?" the woman said. She reached out a hand and placed it on top of Saoirse's on the table. Her skin was cold and clammy, and when Saoirse tried to move her hand away, the woman only gripped it harder. Saoirse felt something tickle her wrist, and she glanced down to see a small black sea louse crawling along her forearm. Saoirse jumped, recoiling in disgust as a second louse dropped out of the cuff of her mother's dress and onto her arm. She desperately tried to wrest her arm away, but the woman held her there, pinning her arm to the table, her broken nails now cutting into Saoirse's skin. Saoirse opened her mouth to scream, but no sound came out, and when she looked up at the woman now, she saw that the flesh of her nose was gone, exposing a snub of gray bone. Foam dripped out of her open mouth, and her hair was a dark, wet, matted mess that hung down her back.

"Don't you recognize your own mother, child?" the woman said.

Saoirse woke with a start.

She was in the bath. She'd been in so long now that the water was lukewarm and her hands were starting to prune. Her heart still racing from her dream, she lifted her leg and turned the faucet knob on with her toes. It squeaked in protest, and Saoirse could hear the groan of the water coming through the pipes in the floor below her. After a moment, the water started to flow, filling the space by her feet with warmth.

She sat back in the bath again. Saoirse hadn't dreamed of her mother in a long time. She fingered the elaborate gold chain that rested on her clavicle and the heart-shaped locket with an inscription on the inside. It was a line from a poem by her mother's favorite poet—E. E. Cummings. In it, the speaker expressed an ardent love, one in which the object of the poem was the very center of their universe, their reason for being.

The necklace had been a gift from her mother—Saoirse remembered it with such longing that it made her bones ache. In the wake of her parents' plane crash, everyone had forgotten about her birthday. The search-and-rescue efforts were still going on—they hadn't found the plane yet, and so her brothers, Theo and Ransom, had gone to Catalina to be closer to the search. She'd spent her birthday alone at the house, eating ice cream out of a soup bowl on the sofa and watching reruns of *The Young and the Restless* in the living room. In the late afternoon, she'd wandered into her parents' bedroom and sat on the floor of her mother's closet. It was there she found the cache of gifts her parents had gotten her—all neatly wrapped with pale-pink paper and silver bows. She unwrapped them one by one—a beautiful hardbound book of poems by Rumi from her father, which made her feel sick with guilt for a million different reasons. She didn't want a stupid book; she loathed reading. But her father was always encouraging in her a love of learning, as if he thought if he could just find the right spark, it would ignite in her a dormant passion. She knew he did this because he loved her, but also because he saw a lack in her he wished to fill, and she didn't know how to square those two things—that he loved her enormously and that she disappointed him. Along with the book, her father had gotten her a pair of pointed-toe Manolo Blahnik pumps, embellished with a crystal buckle. They were beautiful shoes; she had seen a photograph in *Vogue* of Bianca Jagger wearing the exact pair, and she had begged and begged her father to get them for her. They were the most perfect pair of shoes that Saoirse had ever seen, and now she knew she would never wear them.

Saoirse unwrapped her mother's gift next—a long velvet box with the necklace in it—and she gasped. Unlike her father, her mother was not sentimental or affectionate. Saoirse wasn't even sure if her mother really liked her. She remembered with a particular cutting clarity one summer afternoon when she was ten and her mother had thrown a garden party for her book club. Saoirse had been roller-skating on the terrace, and she'd spent all morning mastering the backward skate. When she'd finally gotten it down, she had skated over to the landing and waved at her mother below to get her attention. Birdie was standing in a huddle of women in her white linen pantsuit and designer shades, daintily holding a martini. Saoirse called out to her, and just as her mother turned to look at her, Saoirse lost her footing and fell—all the way down the stone steps, landing in a tangled heap at the bottom in front of her mother and all her friends.

It was one of the other women who helped her up, calling her "poor dear," brushing off her dirtied pedal pushers, exclaiming over her skinned elbows, while Birdie, still holding her martini, shielded her eyes from the sun and looked past her, up the stairs, her lips pursed in displeasure.

"Where's Mrs. Talbot?" Birdie asked.

When Tabby appeared at the top of the stairs, two lemonades in hand, and saw what had happened, she'd run down the steps as quickly as her legs could carry her, sloshing ice and sticky sugared water over the edges. She'd pulled Saoirse into her arms and let out a gasp of relief when she saw there were just scrapes and bruises and no broken bones.

"You have to keep a closer eye on her," Birdie scolded. "She's always getting into things."

But perhaps somehow, Saoirse had misunderstood her. Every gesture of her mother's that she'd read as aloof or inattentive, every word she'd interpreted as blatant dislike, had really been something else. Here, this necklace—its inscription—was proof of what her mother really felt toward her but, for whatever reason, could never say out loud, could never show her. Saoirse slipped the necklace on, and even now, she rarely took it off, even in the bath.

Saoirse sat up reluctantly. She had better get out and get ready for the day. Breakfast would be over soon, and Tabby was always so strict about sticking to a schedule. Saoirse's stomach was still queasy after her dream. She didn't know if she could eat, but she would have some coffee at least, to get her through her morning lessons.

She gripped both sides of the tub and stood.

Saoirse heard them before she saw them—a woman's laugh and a man's voice, low and rumbling as he told some story. As she rounded the doorway to the dining room, she saw them—Salvador, with the girl from yesterday. Ava or Alice or Abigail—Saoirse couldn't remember which. She hadn't given her another thought, really, after she'd left her sleeping nearly naked on the beach. She'd thought surely that would be the last time she'd ever see her. But here she was, looking fresh and cheery and completely unruffled as she ate her breakfast, Salvador next to her. The girl's eyes sparkled with something as Saoirse entered the room. With what, Saoirse couldn't say, exactly—bravado? Smugness? Whatever it was, Saoirse didn't like it.

"Good morning, Saoirse," the girl said brightly, smiling up at her from the table. "We were about to send in the cavalry to wake you. You almost missed breakfast."

Saoirse didn't say anything.

"The cook made a lovely omelet this morning," the girl said. "Shall I ask him to make you one?"

Saoirse glanced down at the remnants of egg and bacon and potatoes on the girl's plate. She thought of her dream, and her stomach squirmed. She pressed her lips together tightly so she wouldn't throw up.

"I'll pass," Saoirse said. "Just coffee."

The girl went to the sideboard and retrieved an empty mug. "How do you take it?" the girl asked. "Cream? Sugar?"

"Black," Saoirse said dryly, "like my heart."

The girl smiled at her little joke. She filled the mug from a carafe and then walked back over to the table and handed it to Saoirse. "Salvador was just telling me about the natural history museum down in Morro Bay," the girl said. "Have you been?"

Salvador? Saoirse thought. Not Mr. Santos? Why were they so chummy?

"I didn't realize you two knew each other," Saoirse said.

"Oh, yes, Salvador and I are old friends," the girl said.

"We met yesterday," Salvador said, by way of explanation, "on the road."

"Ah," Saoirse said. "I see."

"The museum is right near the estuary," the girl went on, "with a great view of Morro Rock. Might be something to see, if you have any interest?"

"I don't generally find rocks very interesting," Saoirse said, sipping her coffee.

There was a moment of awkward silence, and then Salvador pushed his chair back from the table and stood. "I suppose I should head upstairs and prepare for today's lessons," he said. "Saoirse, I'll see you in a few minutes." He looked over at the girl sitting next to him and nodded. "Ana, it was lovely having breakfast with you."

Ana. Saoirse clocked her name as she nursed her coffee. She supposed she would have to remember it now, at least temporarily. She had stopped bothering to remember their names weeks ago. What was the point, when they all left with such haste? She had found it was best to get rid of them quickly. Saoirse had made the mistake with the first one of being too subtle: itching powder in the woman's cold cream on the first night. The woman had simply thought she had allergies and hadn't put two and two together that she'd been purposely sabotaged. Then the next day, Saoirse had dyed all her garments a vibrant shade of pink. Again, the woman thought the maids had simply made a laundry blunder. It was starting to vex Saoirse at that point, this woman's benevolent view of the world, that any misfortune she might encounter was purely coincidental. It wasn't until Saoirse had put dye in her toothpaste to stain her teeth green that the woman finally understood she wasn't welcome and packed her bags. With the others, Saoirse had made grander opening overtures and they, swifter exits.

All the others had been older, middle-aged, cherry-picked by Tabby for their years of service. Most of them had been hospice workers or had been employed at long-term care facilities. They'd spent their days cleaning bedpans and giving sponge baths and holding old, webbed hands as souls passed from this world to the next. They wore sturdy, practical shoes and dour expressions, their hair pulled back from their faces.

But this girl was different. Saoirse studied her adversary sitting across from her at the dining table. Ana sipped her own coffee and looked back at her, unbothered by her stare or the silence. She was younger than the others by a couple of decades but also . . . softer, somehow. Saoirse wondered at her brother's choice in bringing her here. She would have thought he would have sent a seasoned, stalwart mercenary to crack the whip. A worthy opponent.

But maybe Saoirse had underestimated the girl. She was, after all, still here.

Ana checked her watch. "Shall we go up?" she asked. "We don't want to be late."

"Yes," Saoirse said. She tilted her head back and drained what was left of her cup. "Let's get on with it."

She set her cup down hard on the table.

This girl, if Saoirse had anything to say about it, wouldn't last the week.

CHAPTER SIX

JUNE 1982

On Thursday, Ransom Towers sat down for lunch with his godfather, William Bass, at the Old Ebbitt Grill on Fifteenth Street. It was the sort of place to see and be seen in DC, which is why Bass preferred it. Ransom didn't care for that sort of thing, but he liked the building itself. The restaurant was old, and it had a story to it that was reflected in every aspect of each room. Large-game trophies hung on the walls, shot by Teddy Roosevelt himself. There was a mahogany bar that ran the length of the room, and oil paintings hung in gilded frames. There were murals painted on the ceiling and antique gas chandeliers and large exposed crossbeams. It felt warm and homey, lived in.

They were seated in the main dining room at a white-clothed table, a platter of iced New England oysters between them.

"I miss these when I'm away," Bass said, prying the tender meat from its shell with his oyster fork.

Ransom took a bite of his own oyster, the meat sweet and firm and briny, like tasting a bite of the ocean. It reminded him of home. It reminded him of Cliffhaven.

"Oh, there's Gordon Bailey," Bass said, nodding toward the other side of the room. He raised his voice, calling out, "Gordon!"

A portly middle-aged gentleman ambled toward them from a booth in the corner. He had ruddy cheeks and was well dressed in a nicely tailored suit.

Ransom gave a small, polite nod to the man and then averted his gaze back to his oysters, not wanting to be drawn into tiring pleasantries and small talk. These types of interactions were as choreographed as a dance; Ransom was familiar with the steps, but he did not wish to partake. One man would inquire about the well-being of the other. The other would make some joke about aching knees or a bad back. He would, in turn, ask about the other's family. They would schedule a tee time and part ways. There was a measured rhythm to it, like a waltz. *One, two, three, four. And one, two, three, four.*

"Terribly nice fellow," Bass said when the man had gone. "Owns a telecom company out of Boston. Not a bad person to know. Not a bad person to know at all."

Ransom gave a noncommittal grunt. He hated schmoozing, networking, the transactional nature of forced social interactions, even as he recognized their necessity. It made him uncomfortable, and he had no interest in it. He did it because he had to, not because he liked it. As a boy, he had always imagined for himself a quiet sort of life, outside the public eye. Or, at least, as much outside the public eye as someone with the last name Towers could get. He'd wanted to earn his architecture degree and settle somewhere off the beaten path in a house he built with his own hands. He dreamed of working for himself, designing homes and churches, community centers, and schools for small towns. Places people lived and breathed in, slept and dreamed in. Nothing like the glossy monstrosities that existed in the city or the sprawling stone house that he had grown up in. But all that had vanished with a single phone call.

Ransom still remembered where he was when he heard the news of his brother's passing.

He was at Columbia, in his first semester of his master's in architecture program. He'd been in the library, reading *The Death and Life of Great American Cities*, when he'd gotten a page from Bass. Ransom had called him back from a phone booth in the front hall.

"We've been trying to reach you," Bass said. "Theo's had an accident."

Theo had been skiing with his friends in Tahoe, celebrating his twenty-fifth birthday. He'd fallen on a particularly steep and slick run and hit his head. He'd drifted into a coma before they could get him to a hospital, and when the doctors tried to airlift him to San Francisco for emergency surgery, he died in transit. Epidural hematoma, they said.

Ransom had wandered back to his reading booth in a haze to gather his things. He'd closed his textbook and never reopened it. After that, it still amazed him how quickly the pieces of his life had rearranged themselves. With Theo gone, there was a legacy to be upheld, a duty to be done. Towers men were not private citizens; they were public servants. His father had taught him that. The Towerses were congressmen and senators, mayors and governors. Ransom's great-great-grandfather, Arthur James Towers, was a simple settler who had come west before California was even a state, looking for land and fortune. When he'd heard the Mexican government was going to expel them from their land, he led a group of thirty men to take control of a Mexican outpost in Sonoma and arrested General Mariano Vallejo, in what became known as the Bear Flag Revolt. He gave an impassioned speech declaring California to be an independent republic and raised a white flag with a grizzly bear and a red star.

During the following year, in the Gold Rush of '49, Arthur James Towers became independently wealthy, and when California was annexed by the United States in 1850, he ran for one of the two seats in the Senate and won. Every generation who came after him, every son and son's son, had followed suit. His son, Remington Towers, had served in the United States Congress and was a driving force in creating Yosemite National Park. Augustus Towers, Ransom's grandfather, had been governor of California, was a close friend of President Harry S. Truman, and had played an integral part in the creation of the United

Nations. And Ransom's own father, Charles, had served in the House of Representatives for twelve years. He was instrumental in the Civil Rights Act of 1964, and when he withdrew from Congress to be closer to his family, he became mayor of San Luis Obispo, a job he held until his untimely death.

There was a rarity and an honor in the legacy his father and forefathers had built; Ransom understood that. How many people knew the history of their family beyond living memory? How many people knew the names of their great-great-grandfathers? Their occupations? The marks they had left on the world? The Towers family history was interwoven with the history of their nation. As long as it persisted, they would too.

Was all that to end with him? When Theo was alive, he could carry that banner. But now, there was no one but Ransom. For him to slink off into anonymity, to serve only himself and his own desires, would be selfish. He was a part of a whole, a cog in a wheel, a piece of something much bigger than just himself. He was a Towers, first and foremost, "Ransom" a very distant second. His family name was like a shiny cape draped around his shoulders, one that he could never take off. It was the first thing people noticed about him and, his father had taught him, the most important part.

"How's the new caretaker working out?" Bass asked, pulling Ransom back to the present.

Ransom shifted his weight in his chair. "Good, I think," he said. "It's been . . . quiet."

He'd been back in DC for two weeks now, and he'd yet to hear a peep from Cliffhaven. No frantic phone calls that Miss Rojas had quit in the middle of the night. No telegrams about snakes in her bed, or superglue in her mascara wand, or Ex-Lax in her coffee. And no news was good news. Perhaps Saoirse had finally settled down, accepted her confinement, and put an end to her childish pranks and hazing rituals. More likely, Miss Rojas had endured them quietly and was proving that she could handle herself.

Ransom knew that none of Saoirse's antics were really aimed at her victims; it was *him* whom Saoirse was trying to punish. She resented him for keeping her there at Cliffhaven, like a child, like a prisoner, locked away from the world, under constant supervision. When he'd pulled her out of Choate, she'd railed against him. Instead of coming home, she'd taken a train to New York City and booked a suite at the Plaza Hotel, where she slept all day and threw loud parties all night, drinking excessively and running up exorbitant room service bills. He'd sent the police to collect her then, and there was nothing she could do. He was her legal guardian, and in the eyes of the law, Saoirse was a child. Somehow, he'd managed to keep that affair out of the papers.

At home, Saoirse had tried to buy a bus ticket to Tijuana, so he canceled her credit cards and froze her bank account. When she tried to drive herself, he revoked her license and took away her keys. Now, when he sent someone to look after her, she sent them packing. It was a chess game played from three thousand miles apart, a whole country between them.

"It has been quiet," Bass repeated, a thick crease between his brows. "Yes, I've noticed that too."

"Saoirse's still not speaking to you either, then?" Ransom asked.

Bass shook his head. "No," he said. "It's unsettling, this quiet, like the quiet before a storm."

"You think we need to do something to get back in Saoirse's good graces," Ransom said, as if reading his mind.

Bass nodded. "Yes. Before it's too late."

Ransom didn't have to ask him what he meant; they both knew. When Saoirse turned eighteen, she came into her trust, and there was little they could do to contain her then. Ransom could picture it: the morning Saoirse turned eighteen, her bags would be packed. With her newfound adulthood and inheritance in tow, she'd be out the door as soon as the clock struck midnight—to LA, to New York, to London, to God knew where. And he'd have no recourse to stop her.

"What do you suggest?" Ransom asked.

"Her spirits are low. We should give her something to look forward to," Bass said. "A chance to see that we're her friends, not foes. That we're not as obstinate as she seems to think. A party, for her birthday."

Ransom bristled at the idea, but he tried to keep an open mind. "How many people?" he asked.

"No more than two to three hundred," Bass said. "The guest list should be substantial but exclusive."

Ransom's eyebrows shot up. "Absolutely not," he said. "That's out of the question." He shuddered to think about all the ways his sister could expose herself in front of that many people.

"Think of it this way," Bass said. "Better to have it under your own roof, where you have some control of things, some oversight. If we do not give it to her, she will just go elsewhere to find it. You know what happened in New York."

Ransom sighed. "Yes," he said. "I know what happened in New York."

He couldn't afford another fiasco like that. He might not be able to keep it out of the papers this time.

"I can take care of the details, make the arrangements," Bass said. "I just need your blessing."

As his godfather and his father's best friend, Bass had been a constant fixture in Ransom's life, a presence at every birthday party, every Thanksgiving, every family Christmas celebration. It was as if, in lieu of having a family of his own, Bass had become a part of theirs. Now, with Ransom's parents gone, Bass was the closest thing he had left to a father. After the plane crash, Bass had been the one to break the news to him and his brother and sister. Bass had arranged the funeral, sat next to them in the front pew during the service, stood vigil at the reading of the will. He had always had their best interest at heart. He wouldn't steer them wrong.

Ransom sighed. He didn't like it, but perhaps Bass was right.

"Very well," Ransom said. "Make the arrangements."

PART TWO

CHAPTER SEVEN

1948

I don't know how she could have found out about it," Mrs. Abbott said as she rolled out the dough for the morning bread on the center prep table. She had flour in her hair and dusting her temples, and her apron was tacky from where she had wiped her hands after making the mix.

"She must have overheard one of the maids talking," the housekeeper, Mrs. Wilson, said.

Florence watched them from her place a few feet farther down the prep table, where she stood polishing the silverware. One of the kitchen maids had found a milk crate for her to stand on so that she was at the appropriate height and didn't have to stand on her tiptoes to reach the forks and spoons.

"Now she wants to see the girl," Mrs. Wilson said, rubbing the back of her neck, as if it ached. "She asked me to bring her upstairs."

Florence had become accustomed over the last several weeks to people speaking about her as if she wasn't in the room, or as if she were deaf and mute and couldn't understand what they were saying. But Florence was six, and she could understand them very well.

"I never would have hired that woman in the first place if I'd known that she was pregnant," Mrs. Wilson said. "But once the baby was here, I couldn't very well just turn them out into the street, now could I?"

"Of course not," Mrs. Abbott said, slicing the dough vigorously with her bench scraper. "That woman put you in a very unfair position."

"And now she's gone and left me with her mess," Mrs. Wilson said, and Florence understood very plainly that the mess Mrs. Wilson was referring to was her.

Florence had always felt Mrs. Wilson's dislike of her, noticed the way the corners of her mouth pinched together tightly anytime Florence came within her sight line. Florence tried to stay out of her way, to make herself as small and unnoticeable as possible. Until six weeks ago, she had lived with her mother in a small cottage on the edge of the estate. She followed her mother like a shadow—a small, quiet shadow—as she worked. When she was very small, Florence slept in a laundry basket swaddled in old towels in the kitchen while her mother washed dishes. Now that Florence was older, she'd sit on the stone floor near the sink, playing with the doll that her mother had made for her out of straw and a dress she had sewn out of a cast-off dinner napkin.

Thinking of her mother now made Florence's insides squeeze together painfully; it made her whole body ache. She missed her mother desperately, missed sleeping next to her each night in their cottage's one bed—how, when it was cold, Florence would press her toes into the warm flesh of her mother's calves to warm them. She missed her mother plaiting her hair into twin braids after her bath, humming strands of Bing Crosby's "I'll Be Seeing You." Since her mother had died, Florence had been forced to sleep on the floor in one of the maids' rooms; no one made sure she bathed, and when she did bathe, no one plaited her hair, no one sang. Everywhere she went, people looked at her with a mixture of pity and irritation and asked what should be done with her. She'd heard talk of a convent up north, and it made Florence sick to her stomach to think of being sent away. To lose, in the space of less than two months, not only her mother but also the only home she had ever known. To have her whole world taken away.

"This is how she repays my kindness," Mrs. Wilson said.

Mrs. Abbott shook her head. "No good deed goes unpunished."

"Well, I suppose there's nothing to be done about it now except to take the girl upstairs," Mrs. Wilson said. She turned to Florence. "Come along now; get down off there."

Florence obediently set down the spoon she was polishing and climbed off the milk crate.

Mrs. Wilson surveyed her from head to toe with that familiar pinched-lip look, as if she could find nothing about Florence that she approved of.

"Stand up straight," Mrs. Wilson said. "Shoulders back."

Florence did as she was told, and Mrs. Wilson took her firmly by the hand, not in the way her mother had—there was nothing comforting or reassuring about the gesture—but rather to tether Florence to her, as if she might wander off and get into mischief if she didn't. They stepped out of the kitchen and into the dining room. Florence had never been in this part of the house before. She had been in the kitchen and the cellar and the servants' quarters, but never in the part of the house that the family lived in. She marveled at the tall ceiling, the big windows, the fine upholstered chairs.

"We don't have time to dawdle," Mrs. Wilson said curtly and pulled her sternly along. Florence did her best to keep up with Mrs. Wilson's brisk pace as they wound their way through the labyrinthine halls to Doris Oppenheimer Towers's private parlor. It was a beautiful room. Florence's mouth gaped open when she saw it. There was forest green wallpaper with gold embossed flowers, a mahogany fireplace, and velvet sofas. On one of the sofas sat a woman who Florence could only assume was Doris Oppenheimer Towers herself, based on the way Mrs. Wilson reverently angled her body toward her from the doorway and gave a little bow of her head. Doris was dressed elegantly in a taffeta tea-length dress that nipped in at the waist, and she held a book in her hands, which she set down in her lap as soon as Mrs. Wilson and Florence entered. Next to her was a younger woman—pretty, but in an understated way, with dark hair and dark eyes and a fine silk dress that was modest and elegant in its simplicity. She wore a gold crucifix around her neck, and Florence guessed that this must be Scarlet Towers. She'd heard talk in the kitchen that Scarlet was very religious. She never ate meat on Fridays during Lent, which meant the cook had to prepare endless fish dishes, something he complained about because of the smell. There was another woman sitting in an armchair off to the side. Florence recognized her. Her name was Maggie, and she was Scarlet's lady's maid. Florence saw her sometimes in the servants' quarters, and she was always kind to her. Maggie smiled at Florence now, as if to reassure her and give her courage.

"This is the girl, ma'am," Mrs. Wilson said to Doris, dropping Florence's hand and pushing her forward for inspection. "Florence Talbot. Her mother passed six weeks ago. Tuberculosis."

Doris examined her sharply.

Florence clasped her hands nervously in front of her and tried to stand up straight, as Mrs. Wilson had instructed her. Her hair was unwashed and hung lankly down her back, unplaited, uncombed. Her dress was a hand-me-down and two sizes too big, dwarfing her, making her look even tinier in her petite frame. It was worn, the edges fraying and rumpled because she'd slept in it the past two nights. There was grit beneath her fingernails and a smudge on her forehead from where she'd scratched an itch. In short, she looked every inch the destitute orphan that she was.

"Mrs. Wilson," Doris said, the disapproval heavy in her voice. "She looks awfully thin."

"She gets three square meals a day, ma'am," Mrs. Wilson said, which was not a complete lie, Florence supposed. There was always food set out in the servants' hall, and they all sat down to dinner together while the family was eating, though after her mother had passed, no one made sure she ate, and no one missed her if she wasn't at the table. And so, since Florence's stomach was too full digesting her grief to eat, she had subsisted on very little—a bowl of porridge in the afternoon, a roll taken from the bread basket in the evening.

"I see," Doris said. She turned back to Florence. "What's your favorite thing to eat, child? If you could have anything at all?"

"Cake," Florence said, without hesitation. The cook had made one for her last birthday, small and round, with pink buttercream frosting and her name spelled out in white chocolate drops across the top.

Doris smiled, as if there were something in Florence's answer that she approved of or, at least, that she found amusing.

"Maggie," Doris said, "would you run down to the kitchen and bring up a bowl of that potato stew and some rolls? And see what can be done about a cake."

"Yes, ma'am," Maggie said. She set her needlework down and disappeared down the hall.

Florence looked around the room. She wasn't used to being fussed over in this way, as if she was of any consequence. She was used to being looked past, looked through, but rarely looked *at*. When people asked her things, they were more accusations than questions. *Where have you been? What are you doing? Why would you do that?* It felt strange and unfamiliar, the warmth of someone's care. It made Florence's heart pinch; it made her miss her mother.

Her eyes caught on two large oil portraits above the fireplace. In the portrait on the left sat a much younger Doris Oppenheimer Towers in a pale-blue dress, a man standing behind her, who Florence could only suppose had once been her husband, though she couldn't guess at his name—he had been dead a long time. In the portrait on the right was the most recent iteration of the Towers family. Scarlet Towers was seated in the middle, her husband, Augustus, standing behind her. Florence had only a vague memory of him. There had been a big to-do in the servants' quarters a couple of years back when he had died suddenly of a ruptured ulcer in his spleen. Charles, Augustus's son from his first marriage, stood behind them in the portrait, and Scarlet and Augustus's daughters stood to either side. The smallest girl had a bunny-slope nose and an impish grin. The other girl was striking in her beauty. She had a heart-shaped face and large, round violet eyes.

"How old are you, dear?" Scarlet Towers asked.

Florence tore her gaze away from the portrait. "Six," Florence said, but her voice was so small and meek that it came out almost a whisper.

"Six," Scarlet repeated brightly. "That's a wonderful age. I have a little girl, you know, who's six exactly. Her name is Verity."

Florence nodded.

"Come sit next to me, child," Doris said. "I'd like to take a closer look at you."

Florence glanced back at Mrs. Wilson, and Mrs. Wilson nodded.

"Go on, now," she whispered curtly.

Florence ambled forward, her chin tucked down, too frightened to look Doris Oppenheimer Towers in the eyes. She glanced back at Mrs. Wilson as she sat down between Doris and Scarlet, and she thought she saw her cringe as her dirty dress made contact with the immaculate velvet sofa.

They all sat there in weighted silence for a moment. Florence was too terrified to breathe, let alone speak. She kept her head down, her eyes catching on Doris's hands and, in particular, a ring she wore on her index finger. Florence had never seen anything quite like it before. It was a beautiful silver ring, with little beads and a cross.

"Do you like it?" Doris asked, catching her stare.

Florence immediately looked away, embarrassed at being caught.

"It's quite all right," Doris said, slipping the ring off her finger. She held it out in the flat of her palm for Florence to see. "Go on, then," Doris said. "Try it on."

Florence hesitantly obeyed, taking the ring and slipping it onto her index finger at first, just as Doris had worn it, but it was far too large. So she put it on her thumb next, where it was a snugger fit. She marveled at wearing such a thing on her finger. She had never worn jewelry before.

"You can keep it if you like it so much," Doris said.

And Florence finally had the courage to look up at her, to study her expression, to see if she was serious.

"It's a rosary ring," Scarlet interjected from Florence's other side. "The beads represent the Hail Marys, and the cross is the Our Father."

"Never mind all that," Doris said. "I wear it because it's pretty. And I think it's just fine to wear something because it's beautiful, because it brings you joy."

Florence could feel Scarlet stiffen next to her, but she didn't say anything in return. Instead, she tilted her needlework toward Florence so she could see it.

"Do you know how to cross-stitch, dear?" Scarlet asked her, and Florence shook her head. "Well, every girl should know how to cross-stitch," Scarlet went on, showing her how to hold the needle, how to push it in through the fabric and pull the thread taut. Florence pursed her lips as she concentrated and made a stitch on her own, and then another.

"Very good, dear," Scarlet commended her.

Doris turned back toward Mrs. Wilson. "The child has no other family?" Doris asked.

"No, ma'am, none," Mrs. Wilson said. "The sisters of Saint Mary's Convent in Sacramento have agreed to take her in. It's a very good home, I assure you. She'll be brought up in the way of the Lord. Communion every Sunday."

"I see," Doris said.

Florence could feel Doris's gaze on her, observing her, and she tried very hard to keep her hand steady with the needle.

"You're a quick study, Florence," Doris said approvingly. She was quiet a moment. "Child," Doris finally said, "how would you like to come stay in the nursery with Verity? You could take your lessons together. I daresay, Verity could use the influence of a companion with a sharp mind or, at the very least, the company."

Florence looked up at her with wide eyes. She could hardly believe her luck. But before she could say anything, Mrs. Wilson interjected.

"But, ma'am," Mrs. Wilson started. "I'm sorry, ma'am, I mean no impertinence; it's just—I'm not sure Florence is the proper company for Miss Verity to keep. She has not been brought up in the proper way. Nothing against her mother, ma'am, as I will not speak ill of the dead, but the child has not been taught manners and has never been to a day of school. She does not know how to read."

"All the more reason, then," Scarlet said, speaking up from her place next to Florence and placing her hand on Florence's shoulder. "The Lord instructs us, 'Rescue the poor; and deliver the needy out of the hand of the sinner.' The Lord tells us, 'The stranger and the fatherless and the widow, that are within thy gates, shall come and shall eat and be filled: that the Lord thy God may bless thee in all the works of thy hands that thou shalt do.'"

"Yes, ma'am," Mrs. Wilson said. "That is all very well, but there are things you do not know."

"Yes?" Doris prompted her.

"I do not wish to speak indelicately," Mrs. Wilson said, "but I am not entirely sure the child's mother was married. I wouldn't wish that stain upon your household, ma'am."

Florence stared down at the fabric of the couch, heat rushing into her cheeks. Next to her, she felt Scarlet grow silent and withdraw her hand from her shoulder. Florence felt ashamed of herself, of her very being. She ran her fingers along the velvet sofa under her as the words repeated in her head. *A stain. A stain. A stain.*

"Remarkable," Doris said. "A woman who was able to evade matrimony. I'm very sorry now I didn't get to meet her. I'd have liked to ask her how she managed such a thing."

"Doris," Scarlet said, in a scandalized whisper.

"Oh, come off it, Scarlet," Doris said. "Either this woman took her pleasures where she could find them—a thing men do often enough— or she was taken advantage of and is deserving of our sympathy. Either way, that's hardly the child's fault." Doris turned once again to Florence. "So I ask you again, Florence. Would you like to stay here?"

Florence did not look at Mrs. Wilson or Scarlet. She stared straight up at Doris Oppenheimer Towers and nodded vigorously. "Yes," she said, her voice small and gravelly from lack of use.

"Very good. It's settled, then," Doris said. "Mrs. Wilson, you can have Florence's things brought up to the nursery."

"As you wish, ma'am," Mrs. Wilson said, resigned.

Maggie returned then with a tray of steaming stew and a platter of rolls with a fresh dab of butter.

"The cake's in the oven," Maggie said as she set the food down in front of Florence.

"Eat a bit, Florence, and then you can have some cake," Doris said.

But Florence hardly needed prompting. The smell of thyme and rosemary, pepper and cream and potatoes and leeks, made her mouth water, and she barreled spoonful after spoonful into her mouth, suddenly ravenous.

That night, after Florence had packed up her things from the cottage, which all fit neatly into a cloth sack, Mrs. Wilson took her once again by the hand and led her upstairs to the nursery. Florence could see in the glow of the night-light that it was a big beautiful room, with a giant bay window and two feather beds, one on each side of it. In one bed, Florence saw a dark mop of hair spilled across the pillowcase and a lump under the covers. That was Verity, she figured. Florence glanced up at Mrs. Wilson, and Mrs. Wilson pressed a finger to her lips.

"Don't wake her," Mrs. Wilson whispered sternly. "You can meet her in the morning."

She pointed toward the empty bed, and Florence set her sack down at the foot of it and climbed in. Florence looked up at Mrs. Wilson, and Mrs. Wilson stared down at her. Florence knew better than to ask her to tuck her in.

"Good night, then," Mrs. Wilson said gruffly.

When Mrs. Wilson had gone, Florence sat up in her bed and looked around the room, taking it all in. The walls were painted to look like the sky—baby blue with soft, billowy clouds. There were more toys than

Florence had ever seen before—a miniature kitchenette and table and chairs, dolls, stuffed animals, blocks, a train. There was a dollhouse, three stories tall, painted pale pink, with white shutters and an attic at the top. Every room was carpeted, and there was decorative paper on the walls, and furniture—real furniture carved out of wood—and a whole family of dolls that lived there, one for each of them: Doris Oppenheimer Towers, Augustus and Scarlet Towers, and the children: Charles, Astrid, and Verity.

Florence lay back down on her back and stared up at the ceiling in the soft glow of the night-light. She whispered the three words that she had never thought to question until a few weeks ago, when she learned it could all be taken away from her.

"I am home," she said. "I am home."

"Mother says we get to keep her," said a voice excitedly.

"She's not a pet," said another voice.

Florence slowly drifted into consciousness. She could feel the sunlight, heavy and bright against her eyelids, and she blinked her eyes open.

There were two girls in the room with her, one kneeling next to her bed, though the girl wasn't looking at her anymore. She was half turned toward the other girl, who was sitting on the bed across from them, absently swinging her legs.

Florence knew the girl kneeling next to her was Verity, even though she couldn't see her face. She recognized the girl's dark mop of hair from the pillowcase the night before. And the girl across the room from them, who was a couple of years older, was Astrid—the one with beautiful raven waves flowing down her shoulders, and violet eyes, and a perfectly symmetrical face. Florence had seen her in the Towers family portrait hanging above the fireplace in Doris's parlor.

"I *know* that," Verity said. "I'm just saying. And she gets to stay here in my room with me. In your old bed."

"Good," Astrid said. "Maybe now that you don't have to sleep alone again, you'll stop wetting the bed every night."

"Not *every* night," Verity said sheepishly. "It was just the one time."

"Twice, at least," Astrid said.

"Well, it's scary, being in here all alone at night," Verity said. "I hear strange noises. The house is haunted—I told you that."

"You're *such* a baby," Astrid said, rolling her eyes.

"Am not," Verity said.

"Look," Astrid said. "She's awake."

Verity's face swung back toward Florence, her eyes alight with excitement. "Hello!" Verity sang. She gave a little wave. "I'm Verity. You're Florence, I know. Mother told us all about you. I'm sorry that your mom is dead."

"Verity!" Astrid reprimanded her. "You're not supposed to talk about her mom, remember?"

"Oh, yeah," Verity said. "Sorry. Would you like to see my toys?"

"You can show her your toys later," Astrid said, sliding off the bed. "We're supposed to meet Charles at the pool, remember? For Marco Polo?"

"Right," Verity said. She looked back at Florence. "You should come too."

Florence's mind was still a little foggy from her sleep. She blinked, trying to clear it. She glanced back at the foot of her bed and saw the cloth sack that held all her belongings lying there on the floor.

"I don't have a swimsuit," Florence said.

"You can borrow one of mine," Verity said, already heading across the room to her dresser. "We're about the same size." Verity dug through the top left drawer and tossed her a purple one-piece. "The bathroom is over there, if you want to change," Verity said, giving a little nod of her head.

Florence clutched the purple bathing suit in her hands and looked over at Astrid, unsure, as if she were waiting for permission.

"Yeah, all right," Astrid said, clearly irritated. "But hurry up. We're already late."

As Florence headed toward the bathroom, she overheard Verity whisper to her sister, "Astrid, you're supposed to introduce yourself, remember?"

"She already knows who I am," Astrid said, not even trying to keep her voice down.

"How?" Verity asked.

"Because," Astrid said. "They all know who we are."

"Who knows who we are?"

"The help," Astrid said.

"That's my room," Astrid said a few minutes later as they passed a large bedroom painted pink with a big canopy bed in the middle. "You can't go in unless I'm in there, and even then, I need to invite you first."

Verity gave Florence a commiserating look. "She tells me the same thing," Verity said.

Only a few moments later they were outside, crossing the terrace and then descending the steps to the tiled patio and the giant pool. Florence had seen the pool a million times from a distance, but it was something completely different to be standing this close to it now with the intention of actually going in. It felt ginormous—a wide, unsettling sea of blue.

A boy stood up from his lounge chair, a striped towel thrown over his shoulder. He was almost a teenager, tall and sinewy.

"Hello," he said, sticking out his hand with a friendly smile. "I'm Charles."

Florence reached out and took his hand. It was dry and warm and steady. "Florence," she said.

"Florence," he repeated. "It's nice to officially meet you. Will you be joining us?" He inclined his head, indicating the pool.

"I, um, I don't know how to swim," Florence said sheepishly.

"How do you not know how to swim?" Astrid asked, as if Florence were stupid.

"It's fine," Charles said, giving Florence an encouraging smile. "We'll stay in the shallow end, where you can touch."

Behind him, Astrid sighed heavily, as if this were a huge inconvenience.

"And later, I can teach you, if you want," Charles said, his voice lower so only she could hear.

Florence beamed and nodded.

The days passed quickly, one day blurring into the next, until it all felt completely natural to Florence—crawling into the twin feather bed in her and Verity's room at night, swimming lessons with Charles in the early morning before the girls woke up, games of Marco Polo in the afternoon. Packing a pail of tuna sandwiches and cold Coca-Colas and trudging down to the beach to eat their picnic in the sand. In the evenings, they'd lie side by side on the sofa in the playroom, their feet propped up on the ottoman, an afghan thrown over their legs, as they listened to episodes of *Murder at Midnight* on the radio. Verity would bury her face in Florence's shoulder during the really scary parts, and Astrid would tease her for being afraid.

Verity, Astrid, Charles, and Florence. Florence, Charles, Astrid, and Verity. They were the four musketeers, one inseparable entity as they shuffled into church on Sunday mornings and sat side by side in their pew. One lockstep unit as they came down to breakfast in the morning or went upstairs to brush their teeth before bed.

So it came as a cold shock to Florence when Christmastime came and Verity, Astrid, and Charles went to visit their grandparents on the East Coast, and Florence was left behind. She sat at the long dining table all by herself on Christmas Day, the honey ham glistening on the platter before her, looking intimidating with its girth, and making her feel all the more small and alone.

"Why the long face?" Mrs. Wilson asked as she set a basket of rolls down next to Florence's plate. "You've been touched by an angel's wing, child. They've opened the door to you; they've let you in. But you must remember this—they haven't made you one of them."

The words swirled in Florence's head; they made her dizzy. She tried to push them away, tried to keep them from seeping into her, but she realized that no matter how much she didn't want Mrs. Wilson to be right, she was: Florence may sleep in their beds and eat their food, she may laugh at their jokes and guard their secrets, but she was not, and never would be, a Towers.

No matter how much time passed, it would never stop feeling strange to Florence, being both on the inside and outside of something at the same time.

CHAPTER EIGHT

On Sunday, her one day off, Ana got up early. She fumbled in the dark to turn off her alarm clock before anyone else could hear it and, in her haste, knocked over an alabaster bowl holding potpourri and sent a picture frame tumbling to the floor.

"Shit," she mumbled in the dark.

Ana sat up and turned on the lamp on her nightstand. She silenced her alarm and then sat there for a moment, holding her breath, listening.

For such a large home, Ana felt she scarcely had any more privacy than she'd had growing up in her parents' house, with eight people sharing two bedrooms and a single bathroom. Here, there were always people milling around: maids cleaning up after her, a chef preparing her meals—poached eggs doused in hollandaise sauce and freshly squeezed orange juice for breakfast every morning. Even her room wasn't a private space. The maids came in at least twice a day: once in the morning to get her laundry and make the bed, and then again in the evening for turndown service. It made her feel lazy, like an overgrown child, to have other people doing things for her that she was perfectly capable of doing herself. She was used to a certain level of utility, self-sufficiency, independence. To have that taken from her felt stifling. If someone had told her only a month ago that this would be her life now, she wouldn't have believed them. She had never had a hunger for grand things. That had always been her cousin Rosie.

Rosie, who after high school had moved to Los Angeles to study hospitality at Santa Monica City College. She worked night shifts as a clerk at the front desk of the Duchess Hotel in Beverly Hills. The Duchess was a historic landmark. Shirley Temple had learned her famous stairstep dance on the grand staircase of the Duchess's lobby. Clark Gable had jumped into the hotel pool, still dressed in his tuxedo, at an Oscars after-party after winning Best Actor for *It Happened One Night*. In the '60s, the Rat Pack were spotted so regularly at the Sunset Lounge, the Duchess's restaurant, that they reportedly had their own designated booth. All that glitz and glam did nothing for Ana, but Rosie was drawn to it like a moth to a flame. She used to tell Ana stories about the brief but electrifying encounters she had with the celebrities who stayed there. Once, she had checked in Brooke Shields, and Miss Shields told her she had nice hair. Another time, she had delivered an extra set of towels to Keith Richards's suite, and he had answered the door stark naked, with two women in his bed. Clint Eastwood had stayed there while filming *Every Which Way but Loose*, and Rosie was responsible for giving him his wake-up call every morning at 4:00 a.m.

"Just think, Ana," Rosie had told her once teasingly, over one of their frequent phone calls, "you're talking to the voice that starts Clint Eastwood's day."

Rosie was an only child, something Ana had always envied about her. Ana was one of six, sandwiched between two older sisters and three younger brothers. She'd shared the attic with her sisters, where the walls sloped on both sides, so you could only stand up straight when you were standing in the middle, and there was a dusty single-pane window that never let in enough light. Ana existed on hand-me-downs from her sisters until she was old enough to work and put aside some of her own money. Everything she owned was inherited, worn, starting to pill under the arms from too many washes. Nothing ever fit her just right; nothing was exactly to her taste.

But her cousin Rosie had her own room. A proper room with four straight walls and two windows that let in unending light. Rosie's mother, Ana's aunt Magdalene, took Rosie shopping for a new set of clothes before each school year started, and Rosie had her own closet with things that she had picked out herself, that no one had ever worn before her.

Rosie was two years older than Ana but closer to her in age than either of her sisters, so Ana spent as much time as she could at Rosie's house growing up. Rosie's father owned a cattle ranch, and they would spend their time helping with chores, watering and brushing the horses. On the weekends, they would play house in Rosie's bedroom, build forts with old linens, and whip egg whites with Aunt Magdalene in the kitchen for the tres leches cake they'd eat after dinner. When they were older, Rosie was the one who taught Ana how to curl her lashes and pluck her brows. When Rosie moved away to college, Ana felt a hollow ache beneath her ribs, like a piece of her was missing.

Ana still felt that familiar ache when she thought of Rosie, but it was different now. It'd grown sharper edges. She stared at the receiver on her bedside table. She wished it was that simple, that she could pick up the phone and call her cousin, tell her of the strange life she was living now. No one would understand it better, no one would appreciate it more, than Rosie. But, of course, that was impossible. She hadn't talked to Rosie in years.

When Ana was sure that no one in the house had heard her, she threw back her bedcover and pulled on a pair of jeans and a T-shirt, being careful to step over the shards of the alabaster bowl that littered the floor. She would clean it up later. For now, she had a plan she had to get to; she had to move quickly.

Ana couldn't help but feel that she'd accomplished very little in her first two weeks here. It was too dangerous to go snooping around during the day. If she was going to make any progress, she could do it only when everyone else was asleep.

It didn't help matters that Saoirse had required her constant vigilance. Ana had to stay one step ahead of her at all times. On Ana's second day, she'd gone into town and bought a second set of toiletries, which she kept in the bottom of a large vase near the fireplace in her room. She didn't touch the toothpaste or the shampoo or the lotion she'd left out on her bathroom vanity—she'd heard stories of the itching powder in the night cream and the green dye in the toothpaste that had befallen her predecessors. She was sure that the maids helped Saoirse with her missions of sabotage, so Ana set out to befriend them. She learned their names, sought them out in the kitchen or laundry to chat, and, while she helped them fold linens or dry dishes, asked them about their family, their friends, their interests, and shared her own stories. Familiarity, friendliness, a sense of compassion would—in time, perhaps—save her. It was the only means she had at her disposal, for any bribe she could scrape together, Saoirse could match tenfold.

Still, every night before she got into bed, Ana stripped the sheets and remade it to ensure there were no reptilian surprises awaiting her. On her third night, she found a tarantula under her pillow.

Her younger brother Alejandro had a pet tarantula named Harold. They called him Harry for short. Despite their scary appearance, Ana knew tarantulas were docile creatures who rarely bit people, and if they did, the bite was next to harmless. Alejandro kept Harry in a glass aquarium, but he was always getting out, and Ana had, on more than one occasion, found Harry in the pantry or the garage and coaxed him back into his cage. So Ana handled this intruder with ease, shuffling it into a spare hatbox that she found above her dresser. The next morning, she set it free in the garden, where it was sure to find an abundance of grasshoppers to feast upon.

Ana said nothing of the encounter to anyone, just as she had never mentioned Saoirse abandoning her on the beach. Let them wonder what had become of the spider; let them puzzle out why their itching powder had no effect, why her teeth weren't stained green. No matter what they threw at her, she would remain calm, collected, and self-possessed. She would not be bested.

With Mrs. Talbot, Ana contrived to be subordinate, to never give her reason to be displeased with her. She had not won either Mrs. Talbot or Saoirse over yet, but she had managed to at least keep her head above water, which was no small feat.

Ana had made one real friend, at least: Salvador Santos, Saoirse's tutor—the man who had rescued her on the road that first day. Since then, Salvador always sat next to her at breakfast and regaled her with the latest house gossip or his own stories. He had been born in Rio Grande do Sul, Brazil, Ana learned. His grandmother had raised him. They didn't have a lot of means, but Salvador was smart and precocious and won his way into a prestigious boys' school and then a scholarship to Stanford, where he'd met Ransom. Salvador and Ransom weren't friends, exactly, but they were friendly. Salvador served as a de facto tutor for Ransom's fraternity, which Ana came to learn meant he wrote their term papers for them and secured answers to exams in exchange for cash. Salvador majored in languages and philosophy, and he spoke Portuguese, English, Italian, Spanish, and French fluently. His grandmother had passed away while he was at college, so when he graduated, he had no reason to return. Instead, he had traveled all over South America, offering translation services and tutoring to get by. And then, a year ago, he had gotten a call from his old acquaintance Ransom Towers, asking for a favor. So he had returned to California to oversee Saoirse's education. Salvador was, without a doubt, Ana's closest friend in the house.

Now, Ana opened her bedroom door and peered down the hall, first one way and then the other, squinting into the dark. It was empty.

She padded across the hallway quietly. She knew which door it was, even though she'd never been inside. In the dark, she had to feel around for the handle. It twisted in her palm, and she sent up a silent prayer of gratitude that it wasn't locked. She slipped in and shut it silently behind her.

Once inside, Ana flipped on the light.

In many ways, Ransom's bedroom was a mirror image of hers, though slightly larger and with a floor-to-ceiling bookcase in the far corner and a built-in desk. There was a fireplace and sitting area near the door, just like in her room, but his had a liquor cabinet against the wall.

Ana locked the door behind her. That would buy her at least a few minutes if someone were to try to come in, though in that case, her only recourse would be to go out on the balcony and scale the side of the house. Ana's stomach dropped at just the thought of it. Ransom's balcony overlooked the cliffside, meaning any misstep would result in a staggering drop four hundred feet down into the cold ocean and jagged rocks. Hopefully, it wouldn't come to that.

Ana turned on the dim desk lamp and switched off the bright overhead light in the hope that, should anyone pass by in the hall, they wouldn't see a light on under the door.

Now it was time to get to work.

It struck Ana as odd—unsettling, even—how neat and sterile and, well, *bare* the room was. This was the room that Ransom had grown up in, spent his whole childhood in, and yet there was nothing to suggest that a child had once occupied it—no school memorabilia hung on the walls; there were no trophies lining bookshelves or ribbons to denote past achievements. There were no photographs of Ransom with ruddy cheeks displayed in frames, his sweaty hair pushed back, his arms slung around the shoulders of his teammates on a rugby pitch—no pictures of him on a beach vacation with his family. There were no personal photographs at all. Instead, there were black-and-white landscapes—the sun peeking through clouds in Yosemite, snow-covered pines in a forest, a fallen tree in a still lake.

Even Ransom's bookcase lacked warmth or personality. There were no well-worn *Chronicles of Narnia* or *Hardy Boys* book sets, no Stephen King paperbacks or James Bond novels or guilty pleasure reads. Instead, there were only the classics, books by Pynchon and Gabriel García Márquez, books on architecture and large tomes of nonfiction like Gibbon's *The History of the Decline and Fall of the Roman Empire*. Shiny, leather-bound first editions. It was the kind of bookcase one might curate for a public space to give the appearance of being educated and well read, but surely not the kind of bookcase that reflected one's individual tastes and passions.

Who had a bedroom like this—so cold, so devoid of individuality or sentiment?

Ana pulled open Ransom's bedside drawer, thinking that surely there would be something there that marked Ransom as human—just flesh and blood like the rest of us. A stash of *Playboy*s, perhaps, a bottle of lube, a box of condoms—but she found only a Bible and a pair of spare reading glasses. She shoved the drawer closed.

"Fucking sociopath," Ana muttered.

She turned her attention to Ransom's desk next. It sat along the far wall, in front of the window. In the center was a thick taupe box with a screen, an Apple II. Ana recognized it from the commercials she'd seen on TV. She'd never known anyone who had their own personal computer before. The library at her school had a single Xerox Alto, but it was a large boxy station, and only the engineering students used it. She tried the main long drawer in the middle of Ransom's desk first, but there was nothing of significance in it, just a bunch of pens and paper clips, a bottle of Wite-Out, and a blank legal pad.

Next, she opened the top-right desk drawer, which was organized into a mini filing cabinet. This one took Ana a while to go through. There were contracts for the construction on the east wing, background checks and employment paperwork for the household staff, tax returns going back several years, and a will. Nothing of interest to her. She shut it with a growing sense of irritation and tugged on the handle for the bottom-right desk drawer, but this one wouldn't budge. She pulled on it again. It was locked.

Bingo.

Ana got a paper clip from the center drawer and went to work. It took her only about a minute, and she was in.

The drawer was mainly empty, aside from a thick black leather notebook and, on top of it, a silver frame.

Ana pulled the frame out first. The glass was dusty, so she held it with the sleeves of her sweatshirt pulled over her fingertips so she wouldn't leave prints. In the frame was a picture of a girl with dark auburn hair. She had on a heather-gray sweatshirt, a crimson *S* in the middle emblazoned with a tree. The girl was only half turned toward the camera, as if she had been walking in the other direction and the person taking the picture had called her name, so she'd turned around. Her hand was halfway to her face, and her mouth was open, as if she'd been caught mid-conversation. Behind her was a thicket of redwoods, soft afternoon sunlight dappling through the trees.

The photograph was so casual and spontaneous, so unrehearsed—a genuine moment caught and preserved behind glass—that it made Ana want to keep looking. It played out in her mind like a home video, or a memory—this girl walking through the forest on a crisp fall afternoon, her jeans tucked into her Wellington boots. In the shade of the tall trees looming overhead, the air had a wet chill to it, but when you stepped into a puddle of sun, it was pleasantly warm. The girl was talking about her art history class, some Swedish artist she had just learned about, and Ransom, trailing along behind her, had paused, raised his camera, called her name.

Just then, there was a rattling sound, and Ana looked up, pulled from her reverie. She glanced across the room, trying to figure out where the noise was coming from, and then she saw it: the black orb of the doorknob seemed to shudder, turning incrementally in one direction and then the other. Then the whole door moaned as someone tried to tug it open. Someone was trying to get in.

"Fuck," Ana said. She immediately lowered herself to the floor, hiding behind the desk. *Who would be up at this hour?* she wondered. *And who would need access to Ransom's room?* She'd been meticulous; she'd studied the maid's schedule. She came in only on Friday afternoons to clean it—Ana was sure of it.

She heard a mechanical click, and the knob turned again.

Double fuck, she thought.

Whoever it was, they had a key.

Ana ducked back down and held her breath as she heard the door swing open and then the echo of several purposeful strides against the wood floor as someone entered and closed the door behind them. She chanced a peek over the desk. From where she was, she could see only the figure's back. From the breadth of their shoulders and their height, she guessed that he was male. He carried a bag, which he set down on the upholstered bench at the foot of the bed.

What is this guy doing? Robbing the joint?

Ana got onto her knees and crawled to the other side of the desk to get a better look. The man took off his jacket and sat on the edge of the bed. The lamp she had turned on on the other side of the room was still illuminated, so she could make out his face when he turned.

Ransom.

Ana recoiled behind the desk. *What the hell is he doing home?*

He wasn't supposed to be here. Ana had heard nothing from Mrs. Talbot or Saoirse or the maids about Ransom being expected back at Cliffhaven this weekend.

She took a deep breath and peeked around the corner of the desk again. Ransom had unbuttoned the collar of his shirt and was shrugging out of it. Underneath, he had on a white undershirt that hugged his chest tightly. She could see the way his biceps bulged at the sleeves.

Ana swallowed hard. She drew back behind the desk and shook her head. She had to focus. There had to be a way out of this.

Maybe she could wait until he fell asleep, and then she could tiptoe across the room to the door. But she would have to pass by his bed if she did that, and the lamp was still on on that side of the room, so if he woke up or opened his eyes and looked over, he would surely see her. Whereas, where she was now, on the far side of the room, was at least shrouded in shadow.

She glanced toward the French doors that led out onto the balcony, only a few feet to her left. Her stomach dropped at the thought of having to traverse the stone railing in the dark and maneuver onto the thin ledge along the side of the house, absolutely nothing standing between her and a four-hundred-foot free fall into the water and rocks below.

But what choice did she have? She couldn't risk getting caught now. She'd come this far.

Ana heard footsteps—Ransom was up off the bed now—and a moment later another light flickered on somewhere in the room. Ana's heart started to race. Of course Ransom was the type of person who would dive into work at 5:00 a.m. on a Sunday after taking a cross-country red-eye.

Fucking sociopath, Ana thought for the second time that morning.

She steeled herself for the moment he would discover her there, crouched behind his desk. She took a deep breath and closed her eyes— here was the end of it, after everything she had put into this, after the years of waiting, the planning, the sacrifices she had made.

Ana heard a spray of water against tile, the gurgle of a drain.

She peered around the corner of the desk again. It was the bathroom light that had been turned on. Ransom was in the shower.

Ana exhaled sharply.

Thank God.

Still, she wasn't out of the woods just yet; she had to move fast. She glanced down at the frame she still held in her hands. When she went to put it back in the half-open drawer, she saw the black notebook lying at the bottom.

Ana paused. What secrets might lurk in a notebook locked away in one's bottom desk drawer? Her fingers itched to take it, but was it too risky? The frame that had rested on top was dusty. Maybe Ransom never went in this drawer. Maybe it was a drawer full of memories too painful to look at but too precious to discard.

Before Ana could think better of it, she reached in and grabbed the notebook, slid it under her sweatshirt.

Maybe it was time for some secrets to see the light of day.

CHAPTER NINE

JUNE 1982

Ransom had told no one that he was coming. He woke early—before the sun rose—dressed, and left the house without eating breakfast.

There was a cool, dense fog this early in the morning that obscured his view as he drove, but he'd taken this route so many times that he knew the view by memory. He drove south down the 101, which hugged the coastline near Pismo Beach and then veered inland, through the lush green valley of Santa Maria. He passed through the farmland, with its crops of squash and beans; through the city; and to the other side. When he saw the old white mission, he turned off the road and took the unpaved path that wound through the sycamore trees. Through the clearing, there was a singular white planked house with a black shingled roof and a chimney choking smoke into the sky.

He got out and reached for the briefcase on the front passenger seat and carried it with him to the front door.

Ransom knocked once and had to wait several minutes for someone to answer the door. When it did open, it inched open hesitantly, like a question, and an old woman wearing a habit poked her head out.

"Good morning, Sister Mary," Ransom said.

"Ransom?" Sister Mary said, opening the door wider. "We weren't expecting you. What a pleasant surprise. Come in, come in. I was just making breakfast."

He followed her into the house, which was not large. He could hear the hiss of bacon frying in a pan on the stove in the kitchen just to their right and smell something sweet—cinnamon—baking in the oven.

"Sit, make yourself comfortable," Sister Mary said, gesturing toward the couch. "Can I get you anything?"

"Oh, no, thank you. I'm fine," Ransom said as he sat. He put the briefcase he carried on the coffee table. "How is she?" he asked.

"Oh, very well," Sister Mary said. "It's been a good week."

"Good," Ransom said, nodding. "That's good."

They stayed in silence for a moment, and then Sister Mary cleared her throat.

"Well," Sister Mary said, "I'll go get her for you."

And she shuffled back down the hall and up the stairs.

Ransom leaned forward, fidgeting with his hands. He stared at his briefcase and told himself not to be nervous.

Above him, he heard the exchange of muted voices, an excited yelp, the quick patter of footsteps down the stairs and then the hall. A woman entered hurriedly, still dressed in her pajamas, robe, and slippers. Her hair was still mussed from sleep. She stopped abruptly when she saw him, smiled, and clasped her hands behind her back, like an equally shy and eager toddler. It was never not jarring, the juxtaposition of her childlike gestures articulated by a grown woman's body. She was tall, like their father, but she had their mother's face—soft and heart-shaped, with steely gray eyes.

"Hello there, Vivi," Ransom said, standing.

Her smile deepened, and she stared down at the floor, still too shy to look him in the eye.

"I brought you something," Ransom said. "Would you like to see it?"

She nodded eagerly, and he motioned to the seat next to him on the sofa. She crossed the room, pigeon-toed, and sat, cross-legged, next to him.

He opened his briefcase and took out first the glossy page of a *Seventeen* magazine. He had come across it while waiting at the dentist's office and surreptitiously torn it out and folded it into his pocket when no one was looking. It was a picture of him from the most recent Met Gala. He was dressed in a navy Versace suit, staring haughtily into the camera. The caption read, **Hunk! American royalty Ransom Towers looks dashing in Versace.**

"Hunk?" Vivi said. "What's that?"

"Just—uh—you can cut that part out," Ransom said, feeling sheepish.

He hated pictures of himself. He felt ridiculous taking the magazine page in the first place and carrying it around with him in his pocket. But Vivi had a scrapbook she kept of her siblings, the edges of the pictures delicately cut into patterns—scalloped or zigzags—and labeled with a child's scrawl. The last time he had brought her some news clippings with his picture, she had asked for something in color.

"You look very nice," Vivi said, staring admiringly at his picture, as if she were very proud.

"And this is for you too," Ransom said, taking out a small cardboard box.

He opened it. Inside were a dozen pale-pink blooms, flattened and dried.

On her daily walks, Vivi collected flowers, and at home, she'd dry them and press them into the pages of her book. She'd shown him her collection on his last visit. When he had told her about the cherry blossoms that bloomed in DC in the spring, she had looked at him with wide-eyed wonder and remarked how much she'd like to see them.

So, in March, he'd stopped to gather a handful of blooms as he walked along the Tidal Basin. At home, he'd dried the petals and pressed them into fresh parchment paper between two large volumes of Proust's *In Search of Lost Time.*

"You'll take me to see them bloom?" Vivi asked. "Maybe next year?"

"Yes," Ransom lied. "Maybe next year."

This was all still so new to him. He had lived the majority of his life without ever knowing he had an older sister. Ransom had only learned of her existence when his parents died and Bass relayed the great family secret to both him and Theo.

Her name was Vivienne Smith, Bass told them. She'd been Theo's twin. But she'd come out wrong, the umbilical cord wrapped around her neck. She'd gone without oxygen for two whole minutes. The doctors said she might not survive and, if she did, that she might never be quite right. And that was true. As a child, she was always small for her age, and she developed slowly. She didn't walk until she was three, and she spoke her first words at five. Now age twenty-eight, she had the IQ of an eight-year-old, and she struggled to read past the first-grade level. She lived in Santa Maria in a house their parents had built for her, on the property of the Sisters of the Sacred Heart, attended by a full-time nurse and the nuns who lived there.

As Ransom had gotten to know Vivi, he'd realized she lived a full and happy life. She was active; she enjoyed swimming and hiking and tennis. She was curious about the world around her—catching bugs in mason jars, collecting local flora and fauna and pinning them onto boards. Mostly, she was congenial and friendly. She laughed hard and often. But she also had a quick temper and sometimes threw violent tantrums. They came on like a summer storm, with little warning. One small thing would turn her mood, and then there was screaming and crying, kicking and throwing. When she had learned her parents died, she'd given a nurse a black eye. It wasn't Vivi's fault, Sister Miriam said. Vivi didn't understand her own strength. She had emotions too complex and painful for her to process or control.

It was hard for Ransom to square what his parents had done to Vivi, what they had done to their whole family, by separating her and shrouding her existence in secrecy. Ransom knew his parents had grown up in a different time, under the awning of social Darwinism and eugenics, when any kind of physical or mental disability was considered shameful, something to be feared or pitied. The disabled were shuffled into institutions, subjected to lobotomies and forced sterilizations and electric shock therapy. Their own president, Franklin Delano Roosevelt, who had been crippled by polio, hid the symptoms of his illness, never allowing the press to photograph him in his wheelchair. Instead, he was always filmed standing at the podium or in his car without any assistive device, terrified that his country would think him weak if they knew he was disabled. Perhaps Ransom's parents had only wanted to protect Vivi from the ire and condemnation of public scrutiny by hiding her away; or, perhaps, they had only wanted to protect themselves.

The tragic irony was that now, public opinion had shifted. Disability rights were a hot-button issue. The civil rights movement had happened—a movement his father had participated in wholeheartedly; state hospitals were deinstitutionalized, activists were lobbying for equal rights. While his parents' actions toward Vivi would have seemed, in their day, justifiable, even kind, today they would be seen as cruel, barbaric. To claim Vivi as his sister now and reveal her existence to the world would be to subject his parents and his family to insurmountable censure. The Vivi affair would be a stain on the family that would never come out. He had no choice but to become complicit in the whole thing, to keep her existence a secret, even from Saoirse. He visited Vivi as often as he could, but it was never often enough to assuage the guilt he felt.

"Who's hungry?" Sister Mary asked, parting Ransom from his thoughts as she entered the room carrying two plates laden with bacon and cinnamon rolls.

"Me!" Vivi sang out, raising her hand eagerly into the air. "I am!"

"Here we go, then," Sister Mary said, setting the plates down on the coffee table. "Bon appétit."

Vivi pulled her plate into her lap and grabbed a spear of blackened bacon, which she eagerly bit into.

"There's crawdads in the creek already," Vivi said as she chewed.

"They're early this year," Ransom said, and Vivi nodded.

"Wanna go catch some after we eat?" Vivi asked.

She had a small aquarium tank in her room, which she used to house the crawdads she caught in the creek each summer. She'd name them and feed them cabbage leaves and shrimp and let them go when the fall came.

"Sure," Ransom said. "That sounds nice."

By the time Ransom returned to his car, it was midday and the fog had burned off, replaced by the hot, dry sun. He stood for a moment facing west, toward the broad expanse of the Pacific Ocean, which he could not see from where he stood, but he could smell it—the salt and the brine still thick in the air, carried by the wind. He closed his eyes and took a deep, steadying breath.

Sometimes, his father had told him, you had to do things in service of the family name. You had to make sacrifices that people without a name would never have to make. You had to hide parts of yourself, fold them up, and push them down and smile, even if their pointy edges bit into your rib cage with every breath you took.

Ransom thought for a moment of his brother, Theo, who had at least shared in the weight of this secret for the brief window between their parents' death and his own. Sometimes, Ransom couldn't help but wonder if all the tragedy that had befallen his family was some kind of divine retribution for the sins they had committed. He felt like Atlas, condemned by the gods to stand at the edge of the earth and hold up the sky. Maybe death had been Theo's punishment, and this was his—to forever carry the weight of his family's sins, silent and alone.

CHAPTER TEN

JULY 1982

On the northwest side of the house, past the garden, was a staircase down to the beach. The structure hugged the steep cliffside, one flight dropping down to a landing and then another flight going back in the same direction, so that it stood in what had once been a tall, neat column, five stories high. The staircase had been built with the house after Doris Oppenheimer Towers, on one of her annual visits out west, had proclaimed that it was a travesty to live in a house so close to the beach without direct access to it. What good was owning a hundred acres of land along the coastline if all you could do was look at it, and, to get to the nearest beach accessible by foot, you had to go two miles down a public highway? She wanted to walk out her door and put her toes in the sand. So Remington Towers had commissioned a staircase to be built off the garden, leading down the cliffside to the beach. Rumor had it that after the staircase was built, Doris Oppenheimer Towers had used it exactly once. She'd descended the stairs, taken off her shoes, dipped her toes in the sand, pursed her lips as if to proclaim it good enough, if not entirely satisfactory, and then climbed the stairs again.

The beach that the staircase led to hardly warranted the name. It was a stretch of sand no more than a hundred feet long and fifty feet deep. When the tides came in, they swallowed half of it, leaving only a narrow sliver of sand. The cliffs rose steeply like walls on all three sides around the beach, making it feel even smaller than it was. Barely anyone from the household used that beach. It was a long descent down those five flights of stairs and an even more arduous climb back up. The beach was small, hard, and cold—and inhospitably windy. The family much preferred the beach two miles down the road, with its soft sand and sunshine, where there was room to spread out.

Because no one used the beach, the staircase leading to it had gradually fallen into disrepair. The sun dried out the timber. Salt water settled into the cracks, pushing the fibers of the wood apart. The result was that now, instead of standing in a tall neat column, the staircase slumped noticeably to the right, as if it had grown tired of standing up straight. It creaked and swayed when you walked on it. Birdie Towers, proclaiming it to be both an eyesore and a hazard, had campaigned to have it taken down. But Charles and Florence Talbot, who both had strong attachments to Doris Oppenheimer Towers, quietly but resolutely dissented, and so the staircase stayed where it was.

Saoirse was the only one who used the staircase, secretly and often. That little scoop of sand was the one place she could be sure to be alone, where no one else would bother her. That was where she found herself that morning, the wind pressing into the cliffside in galloping gusts, the waves violently pounding the shore. The morning fog had not yet cleared. Saoirse sat on the bottom step of the staircase, her feet in the cold, wet sand. She shrugged deeper into her cardigan, her hair whipping behind her.

It was the Fourth of July; her brother was home. Her godfather, William Bass, had arrived the night before.

Normally, Saoirse was thrilled to see Bass. They'd always enjoyed a special relationship, unlike any of the relationships she had had with the other adults in her life. Her mother had either ignored or criticized her; her father had doted on her, but he was good in a way she never could be, and she knew she constantly disappointed him with her temper and her wayward antics. But Bass was different. With him, it was never about rules or discipline, expectations or behaving oneself. It was always about having a good time. When, at six, Saoirse had baldly told a visiting congressman's wife that her hair looked like a dead rat, her mother had nearly spat out her wine and then harshly glared at her and sent her to bed without supper. Her father had apologized to the woman profusely and then brought Saoirse a bit of bread and soup in her room, gently chastising her for the way she had made the woman feel. But Bass had only laughed when he'd heard her remark and given her a Toblerone. Saoirse's one regret was that she'd made the remark right before a family-planned trip to the Maldives, and after, there had been talk about whether she would be allowed to go. She'd overheard her mother, father, and Bass discussing it one night in her father's study as she pressed her ear against the door.

"I personally find it refreshing when a young lady speaks her mind," Bass said. "And she was telling the truth—the woman's hair did look like a dead rat. Honestly, I think Saoirse was doing the woman a favor by telling her. I don't see why she should be punished for it."

"She's a child, Will," Birdie said. "I don't care if Angela's hair looked like the pope; she was mortified. Now just see if I'm ever invited back for canasta."

There was a pause, and Saoirse could picture her mother taking a drag on her cigarette. "That girl is impetuous," Birdie said, "and I will not stand for it."

"I don't believe Saoirse had any malicious intentions," Charles said. "But she must be taught that her words have consequences and that we have an obligation to the feelings of others."

"You don't want Saoirse to grow up to equivocate, to pussyfoot around things," Bass said. "You want her to know her mind and speak it. Don't punish the girl for doing exactly that."

In the end, Saoirse had been allowed to go on the family vacation, but not without a very long lecture by her father that she had genuinely tried to pay attention to—but she'd ended up counting the panels in the ceiling above his head instead.

That was not the first or only time that Bass had rescued her. When Saoirse was ten and had broken the heel of one of her mother's favorite pairs of vintage pumps while playing dress-up, Bass had sourced another pair and helped her replace them in her mother's closet before Birdie was any the wiser. When Saoirse was twelve and had gotten into a fight at school with another girl, it was to Bass whom Saoirse took her pink slip, Bass who accompanied her to her parent-teacher conference, Bass who defended Saoirse's conduct, all while her parents were kept blissfully unaware. Saoirse had always felt she could confide in Bass her secrets, her true opinions, without fear of judgment or reprimand. He understood her in a way few other people did. Partly, perhaps, because they were so similar. They both loved to have a good time, to entertain, to be the center of attention. They were impulsive and had quick tempers that could be slow to cool.

Bass was the first person she'd tried to plead her case to when Ransom pulled her out of school and dragged her back to Cliffhaven. She'd fully expected him to be on her side. She remembered phoning him from her father's old study because Ransom had had the phone removed from her room. She'd sat huddled in the alcove under the desk, lest a maid passing by in the hall see her and try to take the phone away or disconnect the call. She'd pressed the receiver to her ear so hard it hurt, desperate, and almost dropped it when she heard Bass's voice on the other end, she was so relieved to have finally reached a lifeline, someone who could do something to help her. She'd told him the whole sordid story, the words tumbling out of her like one long tangled rope of hurt, barely pausing for breath between relaying one betrayal after another. When she finished, she gulped down air and waited for Bass's response. She'd expected him to be shocked, confused, outraged. To ask questions and shout expletives.

Instead, his voice came over the phone steady and measured. "I understand that this is hard, Saoirse," he said. "And I hate to see you so upset."

The cold realization washed over her then—he'd already known what had been done to her, and he hadn't done anything to stop it.

Maybe, even, he had helped Ransom orchestrate the whole thing. Saoirse felt dizzy then and very, very small.

Bass was talking again, only this time, she wasn't listening. She was a castaway on a remote island, half starved and out of provisions, shooting her last flare to capture the attention of a passing plane. Only, the pilot had seen her and just smiled and waved and passed on by.

"Just trust me that this is for the best," Bass had said.

He'd been trying to placate her ever since. Frequent visits. Lavish gifts. Saoirse had met each one with icy indifference. A part of her hated the rift that had opened between them—to lose someone she'd loved, a confidant. But a bigger part of her roiled with anger at his betrayal.

Why did men always get to do exactly what they wanted and expect to be forgiven? Why was she never allowed the same courtesy?

And why could she never hurt Ransom and Bass the way that they had hurt her? To make them feel powerless and small? To take away their freedom, their autonomy, the way they had taken hers?

But, of course, that was impossible. What power did she have to take anything from them?

Saoirse sat up straighter. Maybe she couldn't do exactly to them what they had done to her, but she could certainly hit them where it hurt.

She stood and started to make her way hurriedly up the stairs, back toward the house. She knew exactly what she had to do.

Lunch was served on the beach that afternoon. At noon, the six of them—Saoirse, Ana, Tabby, Salvador, Ransom, and William Bass—set off on horseback from the stables down to the private beach off the highway. There, the servants had erected a tent, and underneath, there was a table dressed with white linen and china and more food than could be eaten by all six guests if they were to feast on it for a week. There were skillets of clams cooked in garlic and butter, oysters on ice, and mussels in tomato broth, with crab cakes and lobster. For sides, there was grilled zucchini and mushrooms, mashed cauliflower, buttered asparagus, a leafy green salad, and sourdough rolls. Between the food sat carafes of ice water and bottles of wine.

Saoirse sat on one side of the table, between Florence Talbot and Ransom, and on the other side, Bass sat on the end, next to Salvador and Ana. Salvador pulled out Ana's chair for her, and Saoirse watched him whisper something in her ear. Ana laughed, and Saoirse immediately felt a twinge of irritation. This Ana was proving more challenging to get rid of than she had thought. She shook her head to clear it. That was a problem for another day.

The waiter poured them each a glass of wine, and Bass stood to make a toast.

"On this day, two hundred and six years ago, our proud nation was born," Bass said. "Let us not forget that it was a group of farmers, mostly, who wrested their freedom from what was, at the time, the most powerful empire in the world. And that is an important lesson for all of us: that no matter who you are, where you come from, who stands above you in the food chain, you can make of your life what you want; you can rewrite the hierarchy, if only you have the grit and the will to do so."

Saoirse bit her lip to keep from laughing. It was equally irritating and endearing that Bass would find a way to make any speech, any occasion, in some way, about himself.

"To friends, new and old," Bass said, and they all clinked their glasses.

Saoirse picked up a shell and extracted the meat with a tiny fork, dipped it in the broth, and then discarded the shell into a separate bowl.

"Saoirse, my dear, I'm surprised to see you partaking in your lunch with such vigor," Bass said. "I would have thought you'd be outraged. Or are you taking a vacation from your diet?"

She set down her fork, a tinge of annoyance racing up her spine. "I don't think you can take a vacation from a deeply held belief, Uncle, or you must not hold it very deeply," Saoirse said. "You can betray your values in a moment of weakness, but you cannot part yourself from them completely."

"You have a philosopher's soul, my dear," Bass said.

"My sister is a victim of PETA," Ransom explained to Ana and Salvador, who looked confused.

Saoirse bristled. "Not a victim, an advocate," she corrected. She turned toward Ana and Salvador. "I don't eat anything that can feel pain or experience fear. Shelled mollusks don't have brains or central nervous systems, so they don't experience either." Saoirse turned back toward her brother. "And honestly," she went on, "after you read PETA's investigation into the suffering of those poor monkeys at those research facilities in Maryland—and see the pictures, my God," Saoirse said. "I don't know how anyone wouldn't support their cause. Even you, Ransom. And how you continue to eat meat after I've shown you the pictures of what happens in those factories to those poor pigs, I'll never understand."

"Campaigning for the ethical treatment of animals and not eating meat are two entirely different matters," Ransom said.

"I hardly see how," Saoirse said. "How is raising a sentient, feeling being for the purpose of slaughter ethical? You've been conditioned by society into a very barbaric practice."

"Come now, Saoirse, you'd really go so far as to say eating a steak or enjoying a hamburger is barbaric?" Bass asked. "Isn't that a bit dramatic?"

Saoirse fumed. She knew she was losing her temper, but she couldn't do anything to stop it. "If we came down to this beach and there was a dog stewed in that pan instead of crab, we'd all be revolted," she said. "No one would think it dramatic for a display of outrage then. And yet how is a dog any different from the pork that you eat regularly? Pigs are more intelligent than dogs. More intelligent than three-year-old humans, even. They feel joy and fear and loneliness. And yet you raise them in factories, where they never know what it is to do anything natural to them—they never run across a pasture or feel the fresh wind in their face. They're taken from their mothers when they're only a few weeks old, crowded into a dirty pen, and fed a steady diet of drugs to make them grow fatter, until they're crippled under their own weight and then inhumanely exterminated. So, yes, I do think *barbaric* is the right word, and no, I do not think I'm being dramatic."

She was out of breath when she finished. It was maddening to her, the way her brother and Bass went after her deeply held beliefs, as if she belonged to a brainwashed cult.

"Need I remind you that grilled pork chops with balsamic caramelized pears used to be your favorite meal?" Bass said. "You'd have the cook make it for your birthday."

Saoirse felt the heat rush into her cheeks. "Yes, well, I'm not pretending to be above reproach," she said. "But when our understanding changes, so, too, should our actions."

"Apt words," Salvador said brightly, clearly trying to steer the conversation into safer waters. "We should all strive to expand the boundaries of our own understanding. I find reading extremely helpful in this regard. Speaking of which, has anyone read *The Heart of a Woman*? I've been meaning to pick up a copy. I thought *I Know Why the Caged Bird Sings* was illuminating. Transcendent."

"I admire your fortitude, however misguided it may be," Bass said to Saoirse, ignoring Salvador's attempt to lead the conversation elsewhere. "I shall just bite my tongue and wait for this fad to pass, as they always do. I never understand them. Have you heard of these cleanses the young people are doing now? Or these diet pills?"

"Don't provoke her, Uncle," Ransom said under his breath, "or we'll never be able to get through this meal in peace."

"I assure you, this is not some 'fad,' as you put it," Saoirse said, sitting up straighter and raising her voice. This was the time. Here was her chance. It had arrived quicker than she had planned for or hoped. "And I fully intend to put my money where my mouth is," she went on, "once I'm legally able to do so."

"Don't tell me you're actually going to give money to that PETA organization?" Bass said with a laugh. "Those liberal radicals are a foolish investment, Saoirse. They're poorly run, and mark my words, they'll be defunct in the next year unless they can pull the wool over the eyes of enough bleeding-heart donors like yourself. I hope you won't put too much into them."

Saoirse took a deep breath. "No, Uncle," Saoirse said, her voice calm. "What I meant was, I plan to divest my holdings in Bass Corp."

Bass had been in the middle of taking a drink from his wineglass when Saoirse said this, and he stopped cold. He coughed, a deep, guttural cough that sounded as if he might be choking.

Ransom leaned forward, his face strained and looking very, very serious. "Saoirse, what are you talking about?" Ransom asked.

Saoirse swallowed. She couldn't lose her grit now. "I'm getting out of Bass Corp. when I turn eighteen," Saoirse said, trying to keep her voice level. "I cannot hold a majority share—or any share, for that matter—in a company that subjects animals to the cruelty of factory farms and slaughter. No matter how lucrative it may be."

Saoirse looked over at Bass, who was still stuck in the middle of his coughing fit. His face was beet red, there was sweat pooling at his temples, and his hair—had it always been this gray? He looked old and tired, and there was an anger in his eyes that she had never seen directed at her before.

In her mind, this scene had played out differently. She had imagined looking Bass in the eye and saying coldly, without an ounce of feeling, *I understand that this is hard. And I hate to see you so upset. Just trust me that this is for the best.* She'd imagined how satisfying it would feel, how pleasing that moment of revenge would be, when she could take something away from him while reciting back the same words he had said to her when she had come to him in her most desperate hour of need. But as she looked across the table at him now, the reality felt very different from how she had imagined it.

"At first, I thought you were just naive and foolish," Bass said, finally regaining his voice. "But now I see your delusions have driven you to self-destruction. Surely you're astute enough to separate business from this . . . this . . . ridiculous cause you've taken up?"

"I assure you, I cannot," Saoirse said, her voice quiet. It felt like her throat was closing up. She couldn't breathe. What had she done? She could see it plainly in his eyes—he hated her. *Hated* her. And she realized in that moment, too late, that she didn't hate him, not really. She was angry, but she didn't want to lose him completely, and she couldn't stomach his ire.

Bass turned to Ransom. "Aren't you going to reason with her?" Bass asked.

"This is really not the time or place to discuss business," Ransom said. "Can't we all just enjoy the—"

"Man was made to eat meat!" Bass said, slamming his fist down hard onto the table. Saoirse yelped, as if he had struck her.

"Would you shame a lion for eating a wildebeest?" Bass asked. "It is in its nature for the lion to hunt and for the wildebeest to be eaten. It's the circle of life, and death is a part of it, however unpleasant that may seem to your delicate sensibilities." He stood and threw his crumpled-up napkin onto his plate. "And to think, you're going to throw your whole financial legacy away for a pig!" He stormed off down the beach toward the water.

Saoirse stared after him, her heart galloping in her chest. She felt like she had just run a mile. Her face was red; she felt flushed.

"Really, Saoirse, did you have to provoke him?" Ransom asked. "You know he has a heart condition, and it's not good for him to get riled up like this."

"Me?" Saoirse asked weakly. "He—he started this."

"He has your best interest in mind," Ransom said, "and you know he can't help himself but get carried away, especially if he thinks you'd come to harm."

Ransom looked sternly across the table at her, and there was something in his eyes that Saoirse was all too familiar with: disappointment. She'd seen it in her mother's eyes every time she looked at her; she'd seen it in her father's eyes, even Tabby's on occasion. Maybe she had been the one in the wrong. Again. How did she always manage to make such a mess of things?

"I'll go talk to him," Saoirse said, pushing back her chair and discarding her napkin on the table.

She would make it right. She had to.

Tabby put a hand on her arm to stay her. "Really, a grown man of his age should have better control of his temper," she said. "If he was a toddler, we'd spank him and send him to bed without supper. I don't know why you would indulge him by running after him and coddling his pride. In my opinion, our company is much improved by his absence."

"I have to, Tabby," Saoirse said. "I'll be right back."

Saoirse saw Bass's figure down the shoreline. He had stopped and was facing out toward the water, his hands in his pockets—whether because he was waiting for her to come and apologize and bring him back or because he had simply run out of beach, Saoirse didn't know. She took off her shoes and held them in one hand as she made her way toward him.

William Bass was a tall man, like her father. He still had a full head of hair, despite his forty-seven years of age, though now it was salted with gray. He'd grown slightly portly in the middle, as most men his age did, but he wore it well. It struck Saoirse suddenly, took her breath away—the realization that from a distance, with a glance, Bass might be her father. In their youth, Bass and Charles were markedly different: both tall, but Bass had been lean, whereas Charles had been stocky; Bass all bronzed skin and brassy hair, while Charles had the trademark dark mane of the Towerses. But now, age had likened them. Bass had thickened; his hair had grayed. If Charles had still been alive, it might have been her father standing there.

"Are you going to punish me forever?" Bass asked, when she had caught up with him.

Saoirse came to stand beside him and looked out at the water too. "I'm not punishing you," she said.

Bass cocked an eyebrow at her, and Saoirse relented.

"Well, okay, yes, maybe I was punishing you a little bit," she said. "But I really do feel that way, that I can't be involved in something that goes against my beliefs. I would be a hypocrite if I did."

Bass nodded. "How long have you been thinking about this?" he asked.

"A while," Saoirse said. "And it did occur again to me this morning, this time with the aim of pissing you off." She smiled a little; she couldn't help it. She went on. "But as soon as I said it, I realized I don't want to hurt you. But I do need to do this. I feel in my heart that it's the right thing to do."

Bass didn't say anything.

"You've always encouraged me to speak my mind, to follow the beat of my own drum," Saoirse said. "Won't you still encourage me to do that, even though my mind, for once, is not aligned with yours?"

"It's not so simple, Saoirse," Bass said. "It's hard for me to encourage this behavior when I see the harm that it will do to you, and all for a cause I don't understand. You're giving up a financial legacy that your father and I built for you. Does that mean nothing?"

"Of course it means something," Saoirse said.

"And have you given any thought to what you will do with the money, once it's divested?" Bass asked. "You can't just let it sit there.

When I think of the way that money will depreciate, wasting away in a bank account, my God. You have to have a plan for it."

"I will," Saoirse said, though in truth, she hadn't thought that far ahead.

"I'm not sure what terrifies me more—the money sitting there, wasting away in a bank account, or where you might choose to put it. It's fine to have a cause you believe in, but to invest your entire financial future in it is an entirely different matter. Just causes do not always equate to wise investments. Saoirse, you could lose everything. And then what?"

She didn't answer.

"Promise me, at least, that you won't do anything rash," Bass said. "That you'll really think things through and exercise caution. Let Ransom and I put together a plan for you to take a look at. Something reasonable."

Saoirse pursed her lips. It sounded sensible, everything Bass was saying. But after what Bass and Ransom had done to her, she didn't know how to trust them again.

But what could she say? No, she wouldn't consider their carefully crafted proposals, meant to protect her assets and secure her financial future? They did, after all, know far more about financial planning and investments than she did.

It was useless to argue about this, just as it had been useless to argue about them keeping her here. *We are doing it for your own good, for your own protection,* they would say. And maybe that was true.

"I'll think about it," Saoirse said finally.

This seemed to soften Bass a little. "Let's not fight," Bass said. "Let's talk of happier things. I have a surprise for you. We were going to wait to tell you, but I suppose now is as good a time as any."

"Tell me what?" Saoirse asked.

"We're throwing a party, for your birthday," Bass said. "And not just any party—something really grand. Two, three hundred guests. A live band or orchestra. Dinner, dancing, fireworks. We'll make it the party of the year, the event to be at."

For a moment, Saoirse's heart leaped. *People.* She'd missed being around people. The conversation, the laughter. A hug, a handshake, being touched. Dancing. She'd missed live music and getting dressed up.

"Ransom agreed to this?" Saoirse asked, skeptical.

"He did," Bass said.

"He's not worried about all the ways I might expose myself?" Saoirse asked.

Bass was quiet for a moment, thoughtful. "We both know that the past year has been hard on you," Bass said. "I won't rehash the past. You know our reasoning, even if you don't agree with it. We'll always fight to protect you, Saoirse, even if the person we're fighting is you." He cleared his throat. "But this is a new chapter we're embarking on. Let's leave the past in the past and start anew. Shall we?" He held out his arm to escort her back to the table.

Saoirse looked at him. Was it a bribe she was accepting, or an olive branch?

Why couldn't things ever be simple? A godfather watched over his godchild. A brother looked out for his little sister. Saoirse didn't doubt that either of these things was true. But were they more true than a CEO wanting to avoid a large divestiture in his company by one of its biggest shareholders? Or a congressman wanting to protect his image? Which was it? Could it be both? Which was it more of?

Was she being naive in trusting them, or coldhearted and stubborn by refusing a genuine peace offering?

Saoirse sighed. She put on a smile and took Bass's arm.

She would go along with it, on the surface, but she would have her guard up.

"Lead the way," she said.

She could be more than one thing at once too.

CHAPTER ELEVEN

JULY 1982

The night sky had deepened into a blue-black bruise; the ocean, though just a stone's throw away and hundreds of feet beneath them, was no longer visible, but they could hear the rhythmic assault and retreat of the waves on the shore. Anytime now, and the fireworks would start.

Ransom sat with Florence at one end of the table on the terrace, his chair pointed toward the open sky.

"I was hoping the rift would last longer," Florence said.

Saoirse and Bass sat at the other end of the table, sipping their champagne, heads together, talking, friends once again. They had made up as quickly and animatedly as they had fallen out. They were exactly alike in that way—they ran hot and cold, loved a heated argument if there was a captive audience, and drew great pleasure from being deeply displeased. All it had taken was Bass telling Saoirse about the party they were to have for her birthday, and all was forgotten and forgiven in the glee with which they took up debating the guest list—whom to invite and whom to snub.

"They're too similar to quarrel for long," Ransom said. "And too similar *not* to quarrel."

Florence scoffed.

"You don't think so?" Ransom asked.

"I wouldn't insult anyone with a likeness to Bass, even if it were true," Florence said.

She did not care for William Bass and hadn't from the day she met him. Florence still recalled, with vivid clarity, their first encounter. She was twelve. It was summertime, and Charles was coming home from his first year at Yale. He was bringing a friend—his roommate, a boy by the name of William Bass. Florence was over the moon to see Charles; the day he was due home, she was one big ball of nervous energy, almost sick to her stomach with excitement. She'd put her swimsuit on and walked down to the outdoor pool with a towel thrown over her shoulder, determined to work out some of her nervous excitement with a swim.

The day was overcast and the water cold, but Florence quickly warmed herself by doing laps—freestyle in one direction, and backstroke in the other. She was so concentrated on her strokes that she lost track of time. As she neared the edge of one side of the pool, on her back in the water, she suddenly noticed there was a man standing over her at the edge of the pool.

"Hello, little fish," the man said.

Florence stopped. She turned over and held on to the side of the pool with one hand while removing her goggles with the other. She pinched the water out of her nose and looked up at him. He was tall—all bronzed skin and blond hair and blue eyes, like some sort of Greek god.

"Hello," she said, a little breathless.

He crouched down so he was closer to her eye level. "I was watching you out there," he said. "You have quite the sophisticated backstroke for someone your age. Do you compete?"

Florence shook her head. "I just do it for fun," she said.

"For fun," the man said, as if that were a refreshing novelty he hadn't heard before. "Well, I'm sure all the other girls your age who do swim competitively are grateful. You'd whip them all. No contest."

He smiled and winked at her, and Florence beamed. She felt warm, as if she were standing in a swathe of sunlight, even though the day was chilly.

"I'm William Bass," he said, holding out his hand. "Charles's roommate. You must be Verity."

"No, actually," she said, drawing her hand out of the water to shake his. "I'm Florence."

"Oh," he said, and she saw the flicker of interest in his eyes go out, as if someone had flipped a switch. "Right." He limply shook her hand and grimaced a little at the wetness of it. Florence drew her hand back, embarrassed.

"I'm sorry," Florence said, because she hated to be the cause of anyone's discomfort.

William Bass didn't say anything; he just stood up and turned away from her, and Florence felt the brisk shadow of his indifference. He put his hands in his pockets and glanced back down at her. "Which way to the stables?" he asked. "I'd like to see the horses."

Florence pointed, and he nodded and took off in the direction she had indicated without so much as a thank-you or a "Nice to meet you" or a goodbye. Florence blinked, a little shocked and rattled by the encounter.

Charles called him by just his last name—Bass—Florence learned, and so everyone else did too. She watched as Bass charmed the family, one by one. He had a unique talent for identifying the one thing that a person cared most about and leaning into it. At family dinners, he led them all in such a devoted and elegant prayer that Scarlet practically swooned in her chair at the head of the table. He complimented Verity on her sense of style and vehemently fanned the flames of Astrid's vanity. Every Towers at Cliffhaven seemed to be under Bass's spell—all except for Doris Oppenheimer Towers, who was the only one besides Florence who saw right through him.

"I've never met someone who thinks so highly of himself, and I've met the pope," Doris said one afternoon to Florence as they played cards together in the living room. "I mean, the boy grew up on a poultry farm in Wisconsin. He's attending Yale on scholarship. I don't know what he's done to warrant his intense sense of superiority." Doris laid down a card on the table and picked up another. "Charles could do better," she said.

Florence had to agree—everywhere Bass went, he was too loud and too sure of himself. He made special requests of the chef (half a grapefruit to be served to him after every meal; no pork dishes for dinner). He rang the butler to help him dress for dinner, like some French king at Versailles. The whole summer, Florence couldn't wait for him to leave, but when he finally did go, Charles did too—back to New Haven for school.

"Mrs. Talbot?"

A voice broke into Florence's reverie, and she turned to see Grace, one of the kitchen maids, standing next to her on the terrace.

"I'm sorry to bother you, ma'am," the girl said, "but there's been a mix-up in the kitchen. I think you better come down, straightaway."

Florence sighed. The fireworks were about to start, and now she would surely miss them. But what was she to do about it? She lived her job; she never left it.

"Duty calls," she said to Ransom and got up to follow the maid.

Ransom nodded at Florence. He always enjoyed her company, but tonight he was grateful for the solitude; it had been a long and trying day.

He watched Salvador standing a little way off, leaning against the railing, talking with Ana. She leaned her head back and laughed heartily. It was dark, but Ransom thought he saw Salvador lean toward her, his shoulder touching hers. Ransom had seen them whispering and laughing together at lunch. Perhaps they had grown a romantic attachment. He wouldn't be surprised. Salvador was a ladies' man. In college, he always had a different girlfriend hanging around him, though he would never call them that, because they weren't permanent attachments. Ransom had never understood the appeal in that type of laissez-faire relationship. He himself had been involved with just one girl, the only girl he had ever been, and probably ever would be, in love with: Gabi Martin. Such a common, nondescript name. She had red hair and green eyes and freckles across the bridge of her nose and on her shoulders. She had a lean, athletic frame and strong legs. She played on the Stanford girls' soccer team and majored in English. She wanted to be a high school English teacher so she could read and talk about books the rest of her life.

They had met at a football game the fall semester of their freshman year. His friend Freddie Astor, whom he had known for four years at Andover, was dressed as a tree, and the girls in the row directly behind them complained that his branches were too tall to see over. Freddie, who had always had a short fuse, turned around, but—finding the central complainant to be short, cute, and blond—he became charming rather than combative. After several minutes of flirtatious teasing, it was decided by both parties that the only remedy for the situation was for Freddie to switch seats with the short blonde's friend, and that is how Gabi came to be seated next to Ransom for the second half of the game. He offered to share his Cracker Jacks, which she accepted.

Gabi talked a lot, but Ransom liked that about her. There were no awkward silences that he had to stretch himself to fill. After the game, the newly assembled group walked to a diner for burgers and fries and then to the blonde's dorm room, where they drank cheap beer and listened to records and passed around a joint. In the early predawn light, Ransom walked Gabi back to her dorm room across campus, and as he said good night to her on the limestone steps, he couldn't help but find her inexplicably alluring, even though the cardinal red war paint she had streaked across her cheeks was now smudged and her hair was mussed from the hours they had spent in the beanbag chairs on the floor of the blonde's room. She wasn't shy or vain, self-deprecating or overly confident. She was just Gabi.

He went home with her one weekend a month after Christmas break. Her parents lived in San Francisco, in Haight-Ashbury, in an old Victorian that had been sectioned off into a duplex. They had the second floor, accessible through a single rickety staircase. He and Gabi kept their shoes on and piled their heavy coats and hats into the closet off the front hall. Gabi's mother greeted them, her painter's smock still on, bifocals on the bridge of her nose. She enveloped her daughter into a warm, full-bodied hug and gave Ransom the same, even though they had never met before. She ushered them down the hallway to the living room, talking a mile a minute (that must have been where Gabi got it from) about the project she was working on and asking about their trip (Was the bus on time? Had Gabi seen anyone she knew from the neighborhood on the walk from the bus stop?) and then about school (How had Gabi done on that paper on Chaucer she turned in last week?). Family photographs hung on the walls of the narrow hallway, and the floorboards were worn and squeaky. There were chips on the baseboards where Gabi had kicked her soccer ball around inside and smudges of fingerprints on the walls where her brothers had steadied their weight during impromptu hallway wrestling matches. There was a single bathroom off the hallway that they all shared and a damp towel on the handrail by the sink. The living room boasted two bay windows that let in enormous amounts of light, and her mother's easel was set up there with a canvas, still wet with paint. There was a buttery leather couch—the seats worn in the middle, covered in hand-knit throws—and a television. Every inch of the room was taken up, every surface occupied with books and knitting needles and skeins of yarn; there were half-drunk mugs of cold tea on the coffee table and a puzzle of Versailles that was three-quarters done. The Christmas tree was still up in one corner of the room, even though it was three weeks past Christmas. The room smelled of evergreens, and there were pine needles collecting in heaps on the carpet that no one had bothered to sweep up. To Ransom, it was perfect. The house felt small and full and lived in. It felt like a home.

Later, when Gabi's father and brothers were there, they ate crowded together in the small kitchen. Gabi's father brought Chinese takeout, and they spooned the rice and noodles and garlic chicken onto plates and reached over each other for the sweet-and-sour packets, lost in a cacophony of three separate conversations all going on at once. Gabi's father was a dentist, and she had two younger brothers still in high school—twins, redheaded like her. After dinner, they played the most spirited game of Yahtzee Ransom had ever participated in, with allegations of cheating dogging whoever might be ahead that round and rolls where one die landed off the table hotly contested. When the game was over, they curled up on the couch, which could just barely fit them all, and watched reruns of *Happy Days* that Gabi's mother had taped, until Mr. Martin fell asleep, his head cocked back on the couch, and Mrs. Martin chastised him for snoring too loudly for them to hear the show, and then she herded them all off to bed.

Ransom slept in Gabi's brothers' room on a makeshift bed of blankets and pillows on the floor. He lay awake for a long time in the dark, feeling strangely content and satiated, listening to the humming of the radiator and the whooshing of cars going by on the street below.

At school, Gabi slept over in his dorm room, the two of them wedged together in his single bed. She wore an oversize T-shirt, her hair still wet from the shower. She'd read aloud passages from Wordsworth or Austen or Byron—anything she found beautiful or profound—lying on her back in his bed, her bare feet propped up on his cinder block wall.

"Listen to this," she'd say. And he would.

On Saturdays, they used the kitchen in the common room to make pancakes and ate them quickly, drowned in syrup. There was Frisbee golf to be played on the quad, and open mic poetry readings in the student center, and volunteer day trips for beach cleanups. Their days were alternately lazy and too full, filled with studying and drinking, sports practice and sleeping in.

The fall semester of his junior year, Ransom took Gabi as his date to a charity gala his parents threw every year for the Los Angeles Philharmonic. They drove down the coast together in his convertible, Gabi's feet on the dash. She fiddled with the radio dial every time a station grew fuzzy and pleaded with him several times to stop at Cliffhaven on the way. She wanted to see where he had grown up.

"There isn't time," Ransom told her.

When she pouted, he put her hand to his mouth and kissed it.

"On the way back, we'll stop," he said. "I promise."

At the hotel in the city, they changed into their evening wear: Ransom a tux, and Gabi a long green sheath dress and heels. The limousine took them downtown to the Dorothy Chandler Pavilion, where there was a line of cars waiting to let out the crème de la crème of LA society. When it was their turn, Ransom got out first, emerging into the blinding flashes of photographers' cameras with a practiced smile and a steady gaze. He turned to give Gabi a hand and saw her dazed expression, the way she squinted into the bright lights, as if they were an unwelcome intrusion. Her heel caught in the hem of her dress as she exited, and there was a horrid ripping sound as part of her train tore. She winced and looked back to survey the damage as a flurry of cameras leaned in to capture the moment.

Click. Click. Click. Click. Click.

They sounded like some sort of herd of hungry animals about to consume them.

Ransom slipped his arm around Gabi's waist and leaned in toward her ear. "Just smile," he whispered. "No one will notice about the dress."

He held on to her hand tightly as he led her down the carpeted entrance. Near the doors, they had to stop and pose for pictures. Ransom stood with his shoulders back and a ready smile, while Gabi stood awkwardly next to him, seemingly unsure of how to position her hands or where exactly she should be looking when there were cameras in every direction. Someone asked for her name.

"Gabriella Martin," Ransom said, even though he only ever called her Gabi.

"Who are you wearing, dear?" a woman asked.

Gabi glanced down vacantly at her dress, as if she had forgotten she had it on. "Oh, um, Sears, I think," she'd said.

Inside, Ransom wished fervently that he could whisk her away to the quiet and safety of their seats in the theater, but it was still too early for that. He grabbed two champagne flutes from a passing tray and handed her one, hoping it would help calm her nerves. She clung to the glass with a viselike grip, as if it were a life raft and she were adrift in a turbulent sea, on the verge of drowning.

Ransom introduced her to some friends of his parents and tried to engage her in the conversation, but Gabi was quiet—so unlike herself— more of an observer of the conversation than a participant in it. Ransom was relieved when the lights in the foyer finally flashed and they could take their seats. In the theater, he placed his hand palm up on the armrest between them, but Gabi never reached for it.

They walked past a newsstand on their way to breakfast the next morning, and there, on the cover of one of the tabloids, Ransom saw a picture of them from the night before. In it, he looked steadily into the camera, smiling, while Gabi looked haplessly in the wrong direction. The Prince and the Pippi, the headline quipped. Ransom tried to turn his body slightly to shield Gabi from seeing it too, but when he glanced over at her and saw the hurt in her eyes, he realized he was already too late.

On their way back to school, Ransom kept his promise. Just south of San Luis Obispo, he turned down the drive to Cliffhaven. He looked over at Gabi as she took it all in and tried to see it through her eyes—the tall stone house in the distance, perched on the cliffside. They had lunch on the terrace, overlooking the ocean. But the day was cold and windy, and Gabi shivered in her sweater. A strong gust knocked over her half-empty water glass, wetting the tablecloth and the front of Gabi's jeans. Afterward, Ransom gave her a tour of the grounds, and in the garden, under the hydrangeas that hung as big as church bells and swayed in the wind, Gabi started to cry.

Ransom put his arms around her, held her close, but he could feel her slipping away all the same. He could see their future, which was no future at all. How she would start to spend more and more nights at her apartment than his; how she would claim a headache and turn over on her side and switch the light off—no more passages read aloud of Proust or Austen, nothing beautiful or profound. How studying took more time than it used to and nights out with friends became more common. Breaking one by one the threads that had bound them together. The slow, drifting dance they'd pretend to do, to make it more bearable, when really, it had happened in a moment, the chasm that had opened between them that could never be crossed.

After his parents' plane crash the spring semester of his senior year, Ransom answered a knock at his apartment door to find Gabi standing there. They'd been broken up for eight months at that point and hadn't seen each other or spoken for almost as long. He held the door open, and she came in, holding her arms to her chest like she was carrying something heavy.

They drank scotch on his couch and listened to the new Elvis Costello album on his record player, trying to fill the large swathes of silence that pressed up against them. And then they were kissing, because that was easier than trying to find the right words. He held her in the dark, warm body to warm body, and felt all the things they could not say pass between them.

They didn't talk again after that. He had seen her at graduation, standing with her friends across the quad, her auburn hair set off against her white cap and gown. She'd leaned into another girl for a photo, laughed at a joke he couldn't hear.

She was married now. He'd found out through a friend of a friend. She was settled in Oakland with a doctor; they had a little boy. She taught English at a private all-girls' school. Ransom could imagine their life easily—a blue-shuttered two-story on a quiet cul-de-sac, azaleas growing unchecked in the front yard. Stacks of Shakespeare essays to grade on the kitchen table, takeout eaten from the carton in the living room, bath time and *Goodnight Moon* and night-lights. And Gabi, dressed in a large T-shirt, her hair still wet from the shower, lying on her stomach as she read aloud to her husband her favorite passages of Hardy. Beautiful and profound.

"Mind if I join you?"

Ransom looked up to see Ana standing next to him, gesturing at the chair that Mrs. Talbot had vacated.

Ransom only nodded. He glanced behind her at the now-empty terrace.

"Where has Salvador gone off to?" he asked as Ana settled herself into the chair.

"To help Mrs. Talbot in the kitchen," Ana said. "There was some mix-up with the new kitchen hand, and she needed someone who speaks Spanish."

"Ah," Ransom said. "Do you not speak Spanish, Miss Rojas?"

"No," Ana said. "My older sisters do, but my parents were adamant we not speak it in the house, because they wanted us to learn English. I can pick out bits and pieces when they talk to each other, but I never learned it properly. My younger brothers, they don't understand it at all."

"That's too bad," Ransom said. "Bilingualism is an amazing asset."

Ana pursed her lips. "Yes, well, I think my parents were more concerned with us fitting in, you know? My father, he picked oranges for a living. He was a field-worker. He was forty-two before he could carry on a very rudimentary conversation in English, and he never learned to read in it. To him, English always felt like a foreign language, something he was on the outside of, trying to find his way in. He never wanted English to be a second language to us."

Ransom wished he could rewind the past few seconds, unsay what he had said. Languages had always been to him a matter of cultural capital, denoting intelligence, class. A shiny bead on your achievement bracelet. He had never experienced language as a barrier before—something keeping others out—but of course it was. What a privileged asshole Ana must think he was.

"I didn't mean—" he started.

"No, of course not," Ana said quickly and forced a smile. "So tell me the truth," she said, changing the subject. "So far, I've survived three weeks with Mrs. Talbot and your sister. Are you surprised to see me still standing?"

Her green eyes flashed at him, and it struck him, for the first time, how pretty she was. The first time he had seen her, he had registered only how unexpectedly young she looked, with her hair pulled back into a ponytail, and no makeup, and that khaki skirt. But sitting next to her now in the dark, with the candles on the table illuminating her face, he saw how pleasing her green eyes were, and with some color in her cheeks from being in the sun all day and her dark hair loose around her shoulders, she looked older.

He cleared his throat. "This was one time I was glad to be proven wrong," he said.

Ana laughed. She crinkled her nose, and something about the gesture struck a chord in him, like a sense of déjà vu. He couldn't help but feel that strange sense of familiarity he had felt that first time he'd met her. Like it wasn't the first time, like they'd crossed paths before.

"Miss Rojas—"

"Ana, please."

"Ana," Ransom said. "You're absolutely sure we haven't met before?"

Her eyes flashed again at him, and there was something new there—fear? Uneasiness? He couldn't quite get a read on it.

She looked away. "I get that a lot, actually," she said, tucking her hair behind her ear and making her voice light. "I guess I just have a familiar face."

He opened his mouth to press the issue further—to ask about her travels, if she had ever spent time in Los Angeles, if she had family in other parts that she visited—for surely their paths had crossed before, but just then, there was a loud, piercing shriek across the sky, followed by a thundering boom. Ransom turned to see the sky ablaze and glittering.

"Ah, it's starting," Ana said. "I'm going to go grab Salvador; he'll be bummed if he misses this," she said, already halfway out of her chair.

Ransom only nodded at her, but he couldn't shake the feeling that she was grateful for the sudden interruption, that she couldn't get away from him and his question fast enough.

CHAPTER TWELVE

PRESENT

S ergeant Wallis had an intimidating presence, even sitting down. He was a tall husk of a man, broad shouldered and big boned. He had a voice to match, low and deep and rumbling.

"You see this?" he asked, setting the morning paper down on his desk. It was the front page of the *San Luis Obispo Herald*. Detective Church didn't have to look to know what it said. He'd read it this morning, and not just in the *Herald* but in the *Washington Post* and *USA Today* and the *National Enquirer*, the headlines getting more and more brazen and salacious as the credibility of the paper declined: Cold Case Heats Up: Second Body Discovered in Saoirse Towers Case and Towers Case Becomes a Double Homicide: How Many More Skeletons Is the Senator Hiding? And Church's least favorite: S.L.O.(W) County Sheriff's Office Misses Not Just One Body, But Two.

"I saw," Church said.

The press conference the other day and the announcement that a second, unidentified body had been found on the Towers property had ignited even more public interest in the case and, consequently, more ire in the direction of the San Luis Obispo County Sheriff's Office. In Church's opinion, the whole department looked like a bunch of Barney Fifes. Not only had they misclassified Saoirse Towers as a missing person for over four decades, but her body had been found at the very location from which she had gone missing. And now there wasn't just one body that had been missed, but two.

Sergeant Wallis leaned back in his chair.

"Listen, I'm bringing Detective Leland in on this one," he said.

For a moment, Church thought he had misheard him. "Leland?" Church said.

Sergeant Wallis nodded.

Church was used to—and very much preferred—working alone. There were seven officers in the Major Crimes Unit, but the Cold Case Unit, where Church worked, was only him. There was nothing Church enjoyed more than the solitude of his own desk and an afternoon spent sifting through an old, dusty case file.

"With all due respect, Sarge, Leland's never worked a case this old," Church said. "He won't know what he's doing. He'll just get in the way."

"Saoirse Towers is still your case," Sergeant Wallis assured him. "But I've got two bodies now. I need two detectives. Detective Leland will be focused on ID'ing this Jane or John Doe. He'll stay out of your hair."

Church was silent a moment. "Tell me this isn't because of the Riley case," he said.

Sergeant Wallis shifted in his chair. "Listen, this is a big case," Wallis said, and it wasn't lost on Church how Wallis had sidestepped his question. "There are a lot of eyes on this. I want you to have a second set of hands. You don't have to like it, but you do have to accept it."

There was a knock on Sergeant Wallis's office door, and the department secretary, Judy, ducked her head in.

"I have the DA on line two for you," she said. "Looks like they're moving up the court date for Dean Williams."

Judy smiled at Detective Church when she saw him, mouthed a friendly hello, and Church gave her a nod.

"Put him through," Wallis said.

"Will do," Judy said, ducking back out.

Wallis fixed Church with a hard stare. "Do we understand each other?" he asked.

"Yes, sir," Church said. "Understood."

As Wallis reached for the handset on his desk, Church stood and headed for the door. He was halfway through it when Wallis called his name.

Church paused, turned back around. "Sir?"

"Take Leland with you to Santa Barbara," Wallis said. "Whatever BFS has to say, Leland should be there too."

The Bureau of Forensic Services was a state-run crime laboratory located in Goleta, about an hour and a half south of San Luis Obispo and just east of UC Santa Barbara. Church had been there many times. The lab assisted local law enforcement agencies with forensic testing and analysis. Their accreditations and state-of-the-art facilities far surpassed the small crime laboratory at the San Luis Obispo County Sheriff's Office, which was better equipped to run blood samples in DUI cases than to conduct a forensic analysis of bones.

As Church and Leland waited in the lab, Leland eyed the two cups of coffee that Church held.

"One of those for me?" Leland asked.

"No," Church said but offered no further explanation.

They had driven down separately. They could have driven down together, but Church had purposely scheduled an interview directly after with Teddy Mountbatten, Saoirse's ex-boyfriend, who resided in Los Angeles now, so as to make carpooling impossible. Church didn't like the idea of being trapped side by side in a car with Detective Leland for a whole hour and a half, both ways. In truth, he didn't know Leland that well. Leland was one of the newer detectives in the Major Crimes Unit, and Church never went out of his way to get to know anyone, preferring instead to keep to himself. Leland was young, still— late twenties. As far as Church had been able to form an impression, Leland reminded him of a golden retriever—friendly, eager to please, and not the sharpest tool in the shed. Church suspected Leland had been promoted to detective only because he was the sheriff's nephew, and he had probably been assigned to this case for the very same reason.

"This is so much better than the morgue," Leland said, looking around at the bones assembled neatly on stainless steel tables.

"How so?" Church asked.

"Dude, the smell," Leland said, as if it should be obvious.

It'd been years since Church had had to attend an autopsy, but no matter how much time had passed, he could still conjure up the stench of rotting flesh—like rotten eggs and cabbage and days-old meat that had been left out to spoil in the sun.

"What do you think this thing does?" Leland asked, picking up a caliper from a tray on the table and turning it this way and that to examine it.

"Don't touch anything," Church said sharply.

Just then the door opened, and Dr. Nisha Laghiri entered. She was in her mid-thirties, her dark hair pulled back at the nape of her neck in a low ponytail, secured with a black elastic band. She wore a plain long-sleeve black shirt underneath her lab coat, cargo pants, and steel-toed work boots. Nisha was always practical, and Church liked that about her. They'd worked together for over five years now on cases where all that remained of the victim was skeletal, which, in Church's line of work, was often. Nisha approached life with the levelheaded certainty of a person who believed everything was an equation with an exact answer, if only you had the patience and reason to solve it.

"Good morning," Nisha said with a smile. "Hello, Michael. Nice to see you again."

Nisha was the only one besides his grandmother who ever called him that, and he had never corrected her. To everyone else, he was Mike or Detective Church. The formality of his full first name never seemed to fit him, but for some reason, he didn't mind when she used it.

"Thought you might need reinforcements," Church said, proffering the second cup of hot coffee, black. Nisha preferred her coffee like everything else: plain, without fuss or embellishments.

"Thank you," Nisha said, taking it. "And who's your friend?"

"This is Detective Leland," Church said. "He's looking into the identity of the second body."

"Ah, tracking down our John Doe," Nisha said.

"The victim's male?" Leland asked.

Nisha nodded.

"And you can tell that from just, well, this?" he asked, gesturing dubiously at the bones assembled on the table nearest him.

Nisha smiled. "You can tell a lot about a person from their bones," Nisha said. "Not just sex, but height, relative age, weight. Here, I'll show you." She took a sip of her coffee and then set it down, out of the way, and pulled on a pair of rubber gloves. "May I?" she asked, pointing to the caliper Leland still held in his hand.

"Oh, yeah, of course," he said sheepishly, handing it to her.

Nisha adjusted the caliper's clamp over the left femur shaft. "The femur shaft width, when taken in relation to the victim's height and sex, can give us a relative approximation of their weight," she said. "Looks like two point thirty-four centimeters in diameter," she said, reading from the caliper. "Which, knowing the victim is male and roughly six feet tall, means he would have weighed around one hundred and ninety-six pounds."

Nisha was the one who'd taught Church that bones were particular, that they told a story. By measuring the length of the femur, the largest bone in the body, they could approximate a person's height. By examining the width of the hips and the anatomical differences in the frontal brow, eye orbits, and lower jaw, you could assign sex. The epiphyses—the caps at the ends of the bones—could tell you whether a body had made it into adulthood.

"What about cause of death?" Leland asked.

"There was no evidence of perimortem trauma in our John Doe, unfortunately," Nisha said.

"Perimortem?" Leland asked.

"It means no injuries that were caused at the time of death," Church said. "At least, none that are visible on the skeletal remains."

"But we'll run a full tox report," Nisha said. "It could identify trace amounts of drugs or poisons in the victim's system."

Leland's eyebrows shot up. "Even this long after death?" he asked.

"It won't be as definitive as what you'd get from blood or soft tissue," Nisha said, "but yes, drugs and toxins can be absorbed into the bone tissue and detected long after death."

Leland whistled appreciatively. "That's impressive."

"We've also made impressions of the teeth for possible dental identification," Nisha went on, "and we should be able to construct a DNA profile to run through CODIS and MPDP. Oh, and this is interesting." Nisha moved around the back side of the table and reached over it, indicating one of the victim's lower arm bones.

"What am I looking at here?" Leland asked.

"It's the radius," she said. "There's evidence of antemortem trauma."

"Antemortem?" Leland said.

"It means the injury occurred prior to death," Church said.

"The shaft of the distal end of the radius is crooked," Nisha said. "It was broken and then joined back together. See how the edges are rounded and smooth? There's evidence of healing—that's how we know it didn't occur at the time of death or after."

"Can you tell how long prior to death the injury occurred?" Church asked.

"Based on the amount of healing, I'd say several years, at least," Nisha said.

"Right," Leland said, and from the blank look on his face, Church could tell he wasn't connecting the dots, that he failed to see the significance of what an injury sustained by the victim years before death could have for him.

"A broken bone is like a scar or birthmark," Church said. "We can use it to identify the victim or rule people out. Anybody who's never had a broken arm, not our guy."

"Can't we just wait for the DNA analysis?" Leland asked.

"That will take weeks, maybe months, to come back," Church said. "And even when it does, there's no guarantee we'll get a match. In the meantime, I'd check the local missing persons records in a one-hundred-mile radius for anyone matching the description. And the staff list as well. The family hired out the caterers, entertainment. That type of workforce can be transient. There were a lot of people in and out of the house that night. It's possible someone went missing and nobody noticed; they slipped through the cracks."

Leland nodded. "Right. Good idea. I'll make sure they're all accounted for."

"Now, our other victim, Miss Towers, is a more straightforward case," Nisha said, rotating to the other table. Church and Leland followed her.

"Miss Towers died of blunt force trauma to the back of the head," Nisha went on. She picked up the skull gingerly and turned it over so they could see. "There's a depressed skull fracture on the parietal bones, here. It would have been instantly fatal."

"Do you know what sort of instrument would have caused it?" Church asked.

"It's consistent with a hard, heavy object with a small contact area," Nisha said. "Possibly a rock, a pipe, the barrel or handle of a gun, something of that nature. But it's also possible she wasn't struck with anything at all."

"How do you mean?"

Nisha pursed her lips. "There's significant overlap in fracture patterns between a fatal blow and a fatal fall. It's difficult, maybe impossible, to definitively distinguish between the two."

"I see," Church said.

"Maybe she tripped and fell," Leland said. "Maybe it was an accident."

"Then why hide the body?" Church said. "And what about the second victim?"

"I'm just brainstorming with you here," Leland said. "Throwing things at the wall and seeing what sticks. You know what they say—there are no dumb ideas."

"There are definitely dumb ideas," Church said. "How about you stick to your victim and I'll stick to mine?"

Leland scratched the back of his head. "Sure, Church. Whatever you say." Leland turned toward Nisha. "Which way to the men's room?" he asked.

"Out the door and to your left," Nisha said.

"Thanks."

When he was gone, Nisha gave Church a hard look.

"What?" Church asked.

"You should go easier on him," Nisha said.

"He's an idiot," Church said.

"He's young, and he's learning," Nisha said. "I remember a time when you didn't know your perimortem from antemortem trauma either."

"Yes, well, you have more patience than I do," Church said.

"Fruit flies have more patience than you do," Nisha said with a smile.

Church laughed. "Yes, I suppose that's true."

"So what do you make of it all?" Nisha asked, looking down at the bones spread out on the table.

"I'm not sure yet," Church said. "It still feels like a riddle of sorts. How does a young woman vanish at her own birthday party without anybody seeing anything?"

Nisha nodded. "And then throw a John Doe into the mix."

"Right," Church said.

He stared down at the weathered bones on the table. He used to find a certain solace in physical evidence. Unlike witnesses, physical evidence didn't lie. It didn't obfuscate, manipulate, or deceive. It could, however, be misinterpreted. Church had learned that the hard way. Facts, physical evidence—you had to be careful in how you strung them together, how you constructed meaning out of them. He'd learned to be distrustful when they took you too easily to exactly where you wanted to go. Facts and evidence, they could become a mirage of sorts—especially when you were in the middle of a hard case where every lead had seemingly dried up.

Church knew better than anyone—when you were thirsty like that, and desperate, facts and evidence could lead you further away from the truth, rather than closer to it, and, ultimately, to your own destruction.

CHAPTER THIRTEEN

1951–1958

When Astrid turned twelve, she went off to boarding school on the East Coast, and Verity followed her two years later, leaving Florence back at Cliffhaven to attend public school in the nearby town. Without Charles, Verity, and Astrid, the house felt, for the first time since her mother died, too big and lonely. Florence tried her best to make friends at the local school she attended, but she was shy and awkward. She ate her lunches alone in the school library, arrived right before the first bell in the morning, and left promptly after the last bell rang so she wouldn't have to hang about the halls by herself. She felt her aloneness like a presence, heavy and shameful, an embarrassing stench that followed her that everyone could smell as soon as she entered the room.

One afternoon when Florence was feeling particularly despondent, she allowed herself to cry. She made sure she was alone first, without any witnesses, and climbed into the window seat in the parlor. She pulled her knees to her chest and let the tears come, like she was opening a spigot slowly. She buried her face in her knees and felt her salty tears dampen the thin cotton of her dress.

"Florence."

She looked up at the sound of her name. She was no longer alone— Doris Oppenheimer Towers was standing there, her purse over her shoulder, clearly on her way out somewhere. She glanced at Florence curiously.

Florence opened her mouth to say something—to apologize, perhaps, for the inconvenience of her public display of emotion—but no words came out.

Doris sat next to her on the window seat, setting her purse in her lap.

"Well, what's the matter?" Doris asked matter-of-factly.

"Nothing," Florence said. "I'm sorry. I just—I had something in my eye."

"If you're going to lie, you have to do it better than that," Doris said. She glanced down at her watch. "I have a hair appointment to get to, so out with it. Why the tears?"

Florence shifted in her seat and took a deep breath. "I suppose it's because . . . well, at school, I don't—I don't have any friends," Florence said sheepishly.

Doris blinked at her. "Well, of course you don't, darling—you have elevated tastes," Doris said, as if it should be obvious.

Florence had never thought of it that way, as if there were something lacking in her classmates, rather than something lacking in herself.

"I recognized a kindred spirit in you the first time we met," Doris said. "We're a rare breed, Florence, you and I, and not everybody understands us. And we certainly don't want to bother ourselves with them if they don't. Listen to me: we don't take guff from anyone. We do things our own way, which is how they should be done."

Florence didn't see anything in herself that resembled Doris, but she was delighted that Doris did.

Doris handed Florence her kerchief. "Now, dry your eyes, dear," Doris said. "If you're going to cry over someone or something, make sure they're really worth it. Tears dry out the skin terribly." Doris stood up. "Grab your purse, Florence. Nothing soothes the spirit quite like having your hair set."

On weekends, Doris took Florence to the nail salon to get their nails done, to the fortune teller to have their palms read, to the antique store to get an eighteenth-century tufted ottoman that no one was ever allowed to rest their feet on. Doris instructed Florence in the ways of the world. *Never trust a man who doesn't marry. Always wear gloves when leaving the house. Be generous with your maid and stern with your children.*

Doris Oppenheimer Towers was the most glamorous person Florence had ever met. Doris adored fashion and was an advocate for Dior's "new look": the boned girdles, the dresses with full skirts that nipped in at the waist. "A woman should look like a woman," Doris said, eschewing the shapeless shift dresses that had dominated the previous decades. Twice a year, she went to Paris to order her wardrobe for the new season. Dior, Balenciaga, Givenchy. She wore bold colors—poppy red, canary yellow, bright persimmon—in delicious fabrics: lace and taffeta, twill and tulle. She always wore gloves and a silk scarf in her hair.

Scarlet insisted that everyone in the house, including the staff, attend church on Sunday, but Doris never did. When Florence asked her about this, Doris said, "If God has a problem with my absence in the pew on Sunday morning, he knows where to find me." And when Florence asked her why Scarlet never said a thing about it, Doris laughed and said, "Darling, make no mistake—this is my house, not hers."

For it was Doris's house, Florence learned. It had been built for her by her late husband, Remington Towers, as a wedding gift back when they were married in 1897. Doris loved to regale Florence with the family history on weekday afternoons while Florence sat at the writing desk in Doris's room and did her homework. Remington Towers was a cowboy in every sense of the word, Doris told her, flush with money his family had made in the Gold Rush of '49. He had come east to find a bride, and he had fallen head over heels for Doris from the very first time he laid eyes on her across the way at the opera house on Dudley Street in Boston. He'd brazenly shown up at her parents' house the next afternoon to call on her without an introduction.

For her part, Doris did not much care for Remington. He was forty-nine years old to her seventeen; he was unshaven and wore leather cowboy boots and a Stetson hat instead of the black pointed shoes and top hat that were the fashion among gentlemen. But he had money. Lots of money. And Doris—the daughter of the respected Oppenheimer family, who had helped settle the city of Boston, and heiress to a now-dilapidated oil fortune—did not. So she married him.

As his wedding gift to his young bride, Remington purchased one hundred acres of land on the Pacific Coast and started building a house for her. Cliffhaven, he christened it. Every year, Doris would make the long trek out west to see the house, and every year, Doris would proclaim it wasn't finished yet, and she'd return east, to her family home in Boston. There, she birthed their sons, Augustus and Sebastian, and raised them, as out west, Cliffhaven grew steadily bigger and grander as the years wore on.

It wasn't until Augustus had graduated from school and his father had grown ill that Augustus moved west to care for him. Doris didn't immediately follow. But when Augustus's wife died in childbirth, Doris stepped in to mother her grandchild. She doted on Charles and couldn't bring herself to part with him. It was Charles's arrival that finally satiated Doris's appetite for building, the final piece that allowed her to proclaim—finally—that the house was indeed complete.

When Doris died at the age of seventy-eight, it was not something quick and dignified, as it should have been, but a cancer that drained her slowly.

Florence took leave from school to care for her, sitting stalwartly by her bed when Doris could no longer leave it. Florence read to her from her favorite gossip magazines, and she did the things that Doris was no longer able to do herself: pinning up her hair—which Doris still insisted must be done—putting on her lipstick in the morning, applying her Pond's Cold Cream at night.

When, one morning, Florence found Doris in particularly bad shape, she begged her to let her call the doctor.

"Don't you dare," Doris said. "I'm in such a state. I'd rather die than have a stranger see me like this—my hair uncurled, my nose unpowdered."

And so Florence was the only one in the room with her when Doris took her last rasping breath. Florence held on tightly to Doris's cold hand, and she sat there long after she knew that Doris was gone, alone in the room with the weight of her grief. She felt the loss more keenly than she had that of her own mother.

Afterward, there was the funeral, which the whole family attended, the girls back from school and Charles home from DC. Florence sat in the front pew with the Towers family and, at the lectern, read a poem she had written. At the reading of the will, Florence learned that Doris had left her her favorite pendant necklace—a canary yellow diamond, surrounded by pearls. Astrid gasped aloud when she heard this.

"Why would Granny leave the necklace to *her*?" Astrid hissed under her breath. "She knew it was my favorite."

In the privacy of her own room, Florence slipped the necklace on over her head and clasped it with both hands to her chest. She lay down on her bed and wept.

The house should have been in mourning. Florence wanted nothing more than to be left alone to wallow. To dress in all black, to sleep until noon, to have the space and quiet to feel her own wretchedness. But it was summer, and Astrid had just finished school and returned to Cliffhaven with all the destructive energy of a hurricane.

Astrid was nineteen now, wild as ever, and in single-minded pursuit of a husband. She refused to wear black, or hang her head and look dour, or sit out at parties, at such a crucial time as this. Instead, she paraded around in colorful couture dresses with full skirts and impossibly small waists. She had brought home with her a pair of cigarette pants and a knee-length pencil skirt that hugged her thighs so tightly that Florence wondered how she could walk in it. When Scarlet saw these, she ordered the maids to confiscate them and then burned them in her fireplace.

They were too sinful to donate—why encourage a vice in someone else that one would not tolerate in their own house?

This, Astrid saw fit to mourn. She came to the breakfast table the next morning with red, swollen eyes and protested her mistreatment.

"I will not have a daughter of mine dressing like a hussy," Scarlet said sternly, which put an end to it.

Astrid threw herself into her social calendar with abandon. She attended a string of parties in San Francisco, Los Angeles, Palm Springs—doing Lord knows what when she was away from her mother's prying eyes. At Cliffhaven, Astrid hosted an unending rotation of girls she'd met at school. They'd sit by the pool in their bikinis, lathered in baby oil, sipping tall glasses of Long Island iced tea and gossiping. Florence could hear them at night as she lay awake in bed—their rock albums played too loudly, their shrieks of laughter drifting through the wall. Florence would turn on her side and bury her head under her pillow so she could sleep, sending up a silent prayer that Astrid would find a husband soon so he would take her off their hands.

Perhaps God heard her prayers, because it did not take long for Astrid to snare a husband. She met him at a yacht party off the coast of Catalina. Two weeks later, they were engaged.

His name was Robert James Sinclair—RJ, to his friends. He was a wealthy banker from London, devastatingly handsome, with striking bright-blue eyes and brown hair, like a young Paul Newman. Somehow, Florence suspected the real reason Astrid had chosen RJ had nothing to do with his money or looks and everything to do with her wanting to get as far away from her mother as she could—to put a whole ocean between them.

Of course, Scarlet disliked RJ. He was too charming, too rich, too good looking to be trustworthy, but she knew the sort of pious man she would have preferred for her daughter was someone Astrid would never consent to. It was a whirlwind to pull the wedding off before RJ had to return home overseas, so that his young bride could accompany him, and Florence could hardly believe her good luck that barely a month after she'd sent up her silent prayer, she'd finally be rid of Astrid forever.

Then, the other shoe dropped.

One afternoon about a week before the wedding, Scarlet called Florence into her sitting room for tea. Scarlet looked harried, like she hadn't had a good night's sleep in days.

"Florence, I have a great favor to ask you," Scarlet said, cradling her cup and saucer. "I wondered if you wouldn't want to accompany Astrid on her honeymoon and then settle with her in London for a while? You're a very sensible girl, with a solid head on your shoulders, and I know Astrid could desperately use your influence."

Florence couldn't help it—she laughed. What influence could Scarlet possibly think Florence had over Astrid? It was preposterous. Nothing could be further from the truth.

"I'm sorry," Florence said, feeling ashamed for having laughed. She put a hand to her lips. "It's just that—well, Astrid—she doesn't listen to me, ma'am. I don't think my being there will have any effect on her."

"But just your presence, your example, might ground her," Scarlet said, grasping.

Florence opened her mouth to protest further, but before she could, Scarlet went on hurriedly.

"And if it wouldn't be too much to ask . . . perhaps you could write to me?" Scarlet said, looking down at the cup in her lap, slowly stirring her tea with her little spoon. "Keep me informed of Astrid's well-being, the things she gets up to. It is very hard on a mother, you know, to be so far away from her daughter."

Florence let out a breath. She knew now what Scarlet was really asking her. She didn't have any delusions about Florence's influence on Astrid. She just wanted Florence to spy on her. Anywhere Astrid went in the States, Scarlet knew people, Scarlet had eyes and ears. But across the pond, Scarlet had no one. It would be a big black vat of darkness, of not knowing.

Florence fiddled with the cup in her own lap. There was nothing she wanted less than to leave the only home she had ever known, a home she loved, to accompany a person she didn't care for halfway across the world.

"I know it is a great favor," Scarlet said, "and I wouldn't ask it unless I truly found it necessary." She looked at Florence with wide, desperate eyes. "Please, dear."

It was not lost on Florence that this was the very room into which she'd been brought all those years ago as a young girl, newly orphaned. This was the same couch, even, where she had sat between Doris and Scarlet as Scarlet had shown her how to cross-stitch and then Doris had offered her a place at Cliffhaven, a chance to stay. They had shown her mercy in her darkest hour of need. They had rescued her, made Cliffhaven her home. How could Florence deny one of the women who had saved her, who had taken her in and raised her as practically her own?

Besides, there were other factors to consider. As a child, Florence's place at Cliffhaven had always felt secure. She was an orphan, in need of looking after. But now, Florence was nearing eighteen, and when she came of age, what was to become of her? Things felt more tenuous, her place at Cliffhaven uncertain. Surely, she'd be expected to marry or to go off and make something of herself in the world—but what? Florence had no prospects, no special talents, no burning desires or ambitions. All she really wanted was to stay at Cliffhaven, but that was impossible. She could not expect to stay at Cliffhaven forever.

Florence raised her cup to her lips and took a sip. Then she rested it in her lap and looked up at Scarlet with a smile she did not feel.

There was no choice in the matter, really. There was only one answer she could give.

"Yes, ma'am," Florence said. "Yes, of course."

CHAPTER FOURTEEN

JULY 1982

Cousin Hugh had come for a visit.

As usual, there was no notice given. Hugh had simply shown up one afternoon in the middle of the day, in a sleek red convertible with the top down, his Chanel luggage piled precariously into the back seat. He might stay a month or be gone the next day; with Hugh, one never did know.

Saoirse was delighted to see him. Hugh was her only cousin, but even if she'd had two dozen, she was sure he'd still be her favorite. They set up court by the pool, basking on lounge chairs, lathered in baby oil, foil reflectors poised delicately below their chins, twin Long Island iced teas sweating on the table between them.

"So why didn't you tell me your new nanny is a dish?" Hugh asked, taking a sip of his drink.

Saoirse rolled her eyes. "Who, Ana?"

"Uh-oh, I know that tone," Hugh said. "Is she a total bitch? She looked more Wendy Darling than Cruella de Vil."

"It's not that," Saoirse said. "I just can't seem to get rid of her."

"Oh," Hugh said. "So *you're* the bitch."

Saoirse laughed. She'd been called worse.

Hugh set his drink down and picked up his foil again. "Aren't you going to ask me why I'm here?" he said.

"You mean it's not to see *moi*?"

"Well, there's always that," Hugh said, reaching over and giving her an affectionate tap on the tip of her nose. "But this time, the impetus was far less cheerful. Parker and I broke up."

The smile slipped off Saoirse's face. "Darling, I'm so sorry," she said. "What happened?"

Hugh fell in love often and indiscriminately—male or female, young or old, rich or poor. But he rarely stayed in love for long. Saoirse had trouble keeping up with his dalliances.

"I don't know," Hugh said. "I'm sure he explained it to me, but the trouble was, I wasn't really listening, and he always said me not listening was a pet peeve of his, so I didn't have the heart to ask him to repeat himself. So I came here to mope and drink copious amounts of alcohol."

"I have something better," Saoirse said.

"Better than a martini?" Hugh asked doubtfully.

"A distraction," Saoirse said, a self-satisfied grin on her face.

Hugh sat up. "Go on."

"I'm throwing a party for my birthday," Saoirse said. "And not just *a* party; I want it to be *the* party. Something people remember. Something people talk about. The bigger, the better. And I could use your help. You're a genius at this sort of thing."

"Ransom knows about this?" Hugh asked, skeptical.

"Of course he knows," Saoirse said. "He's the one footing the bill."

"Well, I'll be a monkey's uncle," Hugh said.

"I know," Saoirse said. "I think he feels guilty. And he should."

"There should be burlesque dancers, for starters, and a champagne fountain," Hugh said, sitting back in his chair. "I know a guy; I can put you in touch. Obviously, a caviar and raw bar is a must, and—oh—synchronized swimmers in the pool. How do we feel about exotic animals?"

"Yeah, I'm not big on the whole 'subjugation of animals for people's amusement' thing," Saoirse said.

"Fair enough," Hugh said. "Guest list?"

"Two to three hundred," Saoirse said.

"And, dare I ask, is His Dickship invited?"

Saoirse made a face. They had special names for her ex, Teddy Mountbatten. It was a game they played between just the two of them—who could come up with the most creative, derisive nickname. His Dickship. Lord Fuck-Face. Sir Ass-Wipe. They rarely used the same name twice. It amused them, and it helped to blunt Saoirse's pain. Even thinking about Teddy was like pressing on a bruise, tender and sharp.

"Honestly, I haven't decided," Saoirse said. "On the one hand, I don't want him to think I care enough about him to *not* invite him. On the other, if I do invite him, then I have to see him."

"Yes, but think of it this way," Hugh said. "How many of us get to design, down to the smallest detail, the first moment we see an ex after a breakup? There you'll be, at your party, dressed to the nines, surrounded by all your friends, everyone there to celebrate *you*. You'll have to see him sometime. What better opportunity than this?"

Saoirse sighed. She set her sun foil down and closed her eyes. "I don't want to think about it," she said.

But it was all she could think about now: Teddy Mountbatten. As if she had summoned the specter of her hurt to haunt her again, had released it from that box in her chest where she had tried to keep it locked away.

Saoirse had first met Teddy Mountbatten at a yachting club in Newport the summer she turned fourteen. She would always remember the first time she saw him. He was beautiful: blond haired and blue eyed, with honeyed skin, stuck somewhere between a boy and a man. He was sixteen then, tall and slender, with dimples that dipped into both cheeks when he smiled, something that made Saoirse's stomach drop when she first saw it. He was standing on the pier, one foot on the bottom rung of the railing as he looked out over the water, talking to a group of kids around his age. Saoirse noted the way they were all slightly turned toward him. He was wearing leather Top-Siders and a soft pink Lacoste shirt, his golden hair blowing in the wind.

Her friend Tessa Montgomery, whom she'd be staying with all summer, introduced her.

"This is my cousin Teddy," Tessa said. "Teddy, this is Saoirse. She'll be rooming with me at Choate in the fall."

"A Choate girl, huh?" Teddy said.

"Teddy's at Andover," Tessa explained.

"My brothers went there," Saoirse said. "Well, Theo didn't make it past his freshman year. He got kicked out for detonating a cherry bomb in the faculty bathroom."

Teddy's eyes flashed at her, full of interest. "Theo Towers is your brother?" he asked.

She could see the gears turning in his mind, and she wanted to kick herself. If Theo Towers was her brother, then Teddy knew she was one of *those* Towerses. Why couldn't she ever just be Saoirse, first and foremost? Her family name trailed her like a shadow she could never step out of.

"Yes," Saoirse said, "but my family is the least interesting thing about me."

"Oh, I don't doubt that," Teddy said.

Saoirse quickly learned that back at Andover, Teddy Mountbatten had a girlfriend. She was seventeen and looked like Christie Brinkley, big chested and thin waisted, with wavy blond hair. Teddy kept a picture of her in his wallet. But that didn't intimidate Saoirse. She liked a challenge.

On the beach, the girls spread out their towels in the sand and lay down to tan, their *Cosmo* magazines splayed out in front of them. When the boys started to divide themselves into teams for a game of touch football, Saoirse sprang up to join them. Teddy paired off to guard her.

"Don't worry—I'll go easy on you," he said.

Saoirse rolled her eyes. Nothing put a fire in her belly more than a heavy dose of misogyny and being underestimated.

When the play broke, she feinted left and then went right, darting out of Teddy's grasp. She sprinted down the beach, her arms open, calling for the ball. The quarterback tossed it to her, and she ran it all the way past the makeshift goalpost they had set up in the sand.

When Teddy caught up to her, he was winded. "You're faster than you look," he said.

Saoirse shoved the ball into his chest, hard. "Don't worry," she said. "I'll try and go easy on you."

At the midpoint of the game, they took a break, and Saoirse retrieved her water bottle from her towel in the sand. Teddy sat down next to her.

"Thought we could talk strategy before the next half starts," he said.

"You're not on my team," Saoirse said.

Teddy lowered his voice, leaned close to her so only she could hear. "I'm a double agent," he said. "Don't tell anyone."

"Ah, that makes a lot of sense, actually," Saoirse said. "I thought you were just really bad at this. Now I see it's all an act." She took a swig from her bottle and let the liquid burn down her throat, warm her stomach.

"Yeah," Teddy said, scratching his chin. "But, I was thinking, it might be a bit too obvious at this point. So maybe in the second half, you let me get a run in, just to throw people off our trail."

"Mm," Saoirse said.

Teddy glanced at her water bottle. "Can I have some of that?" he asked, and Saoirse reflexively handed it to him, forgetting for a moment that it was filled with vodka, not water.

Teddy took a sip before she could warn him. His eyes got big for a second, and then he wiped his mouth with the back of his hand and screwed the cap back on.

"All right, then," he said as he handed the bottle back to her. He had a look in his eye like he was reappraising her.

"Stop fraternizing with the enemy, Mountbatten," one of his teammates called.

Teddy stood up. "I'm just buttering her up so she'll go easy on us, is all," he said. He winked at her so only she could see. "Don't worry—I've got her right where I want her."

When Saoirse's team won, Teddy bought her an ice cream, and they walked along the pier together, feeding pieces of her sugary cone to the seagulls and talking.

"Has anyone ever told you you have the most amazing eyes?" Teddy asked. "Like, they're really quite large. Like saucers. They're stunning."

Saoirse laughed. "You make me sound like the wolf in 'Little Red Riding Hood,'" Saoirse said. "Why, Granny, what large eyes you have."

"No, not like a wolf," Teddy said. "Cuter than a wolf. Like a meerkat. A mongoose."

"Oh my God," Saoirse said, but she couldn't help but laugh. "You sure know how to make a girl feel good about herself, calling her a mongoose."

Teddy shrugged. "It's a compliment. It's all in how you say it. My little meerkat. My little mongoose."

Saoirse laughed and threw a piece of her cone at him. "Please stop talking now," she said.

There was rarely a day that summer that they didn't spend together, always in a group, but somehow, they always sought each other out. At an outdoor concert, Teddy lifted Saoirse onto his shoulders so she could see the stage, and the bare skin of her thighs burned where he held on to her. She could barely focus on the song the band was singing, even though it was one of her favorites. Another time, in the air-conditioned room of the town's dark theater, Teddy sat next to her, his arm laid out next to hers on the armrest, just barely touching.

Part of her wished she could go back in time and warn that skinny, knobby-kneed fourteen-year-old version of herself. She'd take her by the shoulders and shake her. *Get out while you still can*, she'd say. *This isn't the sweet young puppy love you think it is. You don't know what's coming.*

The thing was, no one knew the real truth about her and Teddy, the full extent of it. She'd never even confided it to Hugh. It was a secret both too shameful and painful to look at. So she kept it wedged beneath her rib cage, next to other dangerous things.

CHAPTER FIFTEEN

A t noon, Detective Church sat down for lunch with Teddy Mountbatten at the Beverly Wilshire. The meeting place had been Teddy's idea; it was not Church's scene at all. They were seated on the outdoor patio, and at the table next to them, a middle-aged woman had a Pomeranian in a baby stroller. She rocked and cooed at it as she picked at her salad, her designer shades perched high on her forehead. Church had had to look twice to make sure he'd really seen what he had thought he'd seen.

"If I were a client, I'd tell myself not to talk to you," Teddy said, taking a sip from his iced tea. He was sharply dressed in a designer suit and leather loafers, still handsome despite his age.

"And why's that?" Church asked.

Teddy smiled good-naturedly. "It's always people wanting to help that gets them into trouble," he said. "'Silence is the true friend that never betrays,' I always tell them. But people can't help themselves. The guilty ones are overconfident and think they can't be caught, and the innocent ones think they have nothing to hide and share guilelessly. I'm not sure which is worse, honestly. They both do as much harm to themselves."

Teddy Mountbatten was a criminal defense lawyer now, and not just any criminal defense lawyer—a very famous one. Teddy was known for taking on headline-making cases. His first claim to fame had been serving on the defense team for Dr. Mark Morrison, a neurosurgeon who had been accused of murdering his pregnant wife. It had seemed, at first, to be an open-and-shut case: Dr. Morrison was the only one home at the time of his wife's murder, and he was covered in her blood. Later, it was discovered he'd been having an affair with a young lab technician from the town over. But Teddy was an expert at introducing seeds of reasonable doubt and nurturing those seeds until they took root and grew, cracking the perfect facade of the prosecution's case. He knew how to tease out an admission, how to poke holes in a testimony, how to make a person seem untrustworthy, unreliable, inaccurate. How to implicate and insinuate with subtle inflections or the nuanced way he worded a question.

Teddy had brought in a blood-spatter expert to argue that the perpetrator must have been left-handed, while Dr. Morrison was right-handed. He sidled up to the jury booth when giving his arguments; he knew how to make each juror feel like he was speaking directly to them. And they warmed to him; they couldn't help themselves. Teddy was handsome and charming and good at getting people on his side. When the jury returned a verdict of "not guilty," the public was shocked, and the world took note of Teddy Mountbatten. "Teddy the Tenacious," they called him. In his long tenure as a criminal defense lawyer, Teddy had never lost a case that had gone to trial.

"I assure you I'm not here to get you into any trouble, Mr. Mountbatten," Detective Church said. "I'm just trying to establish a baseline of events from the people that were there that night. What they saw, what they remember."

Teddy leaned forward, elbows on the table. "Detective Church, let's be honest with one another—no bullshit," Teddy said. "You have a job to do, and that is to find the person responsible for all this. And sure, I bet you'd like to find the right person. But we live in an imperfect world. Witnesses lie or obfuscate or misremember. Physical evidence is incomplete or contradictory or nonexistent. You do the best you can with what you have, but in order to do your job, you must find the *seemingly* most right person—a *viable* person—nothing more. And I am a seemingly viable person, I think we can both agree. So let's cut the pretense, shall we, and get straight to what you came here to ask me."

Detective Church shifted in his chair. He hated talking to lawyers. They had such a skewed sense of the justice system. To them, it had nothing to do with justice or truth at all; it was about winning, no matter what side they were on.

"Okay, Mr. Mountbatten," Church said. "I'll get right to it, then. You and Saoirse used to date?"

"On and off, yes," Teddy said.

"And why was that—the on-and-off nature of it?" Church asked.

"I suppose because we were young," Teddy said. "We were long distance sometimes, and that was hard. I'd forget to call one evening because lacrosse practice ran late, or she'd think I was flirting with another girl—things like that. We'd get into an argument on the phone, and one of us would hang up, and we wouldn't speak for weeks."

"So you fought often?"

"Not any more than I would say is usual for a young couple."

"And was it just arguments, these fights? Or did they ever turn physical?"

Teddy thought for a moment and smiled wryly. "Saoirse threw a plate at my head once," he said, "but I ducked."

"But you were never physical with her?" Church asked.

"Never," Teddy said.

Church was silent for a moment. "Mr. Mountbatten," Church said, "the family reported that Saoirse came home once from a trip she took with you to Catalina with a black eye. They claimed you were the one who gave it to her."

Teddy had a very unusual reaction to this. He smiled, and then he started to laugh. "Of course they did," Teddy said, rubbing his chin. "Not exactly clever—rather uninspired, actually—but sometimes that's better. People like tropes, familiar stories, recognizable characters. It's an easier sell."

"I apologize," Church said. "I'm not following."

"Isn't it obvious what they're doing?" Teddy asked. "They're trying to cast me in this role of the violent ex-boyfriend. Maybe I liked to knock her around a bit. Maybe the night of the party, I saw Saoirse with another guy, I got a little jealous, and I took things a little too far. It's an easily digestible narrative. A jury would understand it, eat it up."

"Are you saying the family is propagating a fake narrative to implicate you?" Church asked.

"I'm saying they're trying to cast doubt on my character, to undermine me, to give me a plausible motive," Teddy said. "I should know. It's what I do for a living."

"And why would the family want to point a finger in your direction?" Church asked.

"Because this is what *they do*," Teddy said. "They're good at making people see what they want them to see and keeping hidden things hidden."

"How do you mean?"

Teddy paused for a moment, as if he were unsure if he should say. "They're very good at stories, Detective. I'm sure you know that they had Saoirse removed from school her junior year?"

"Yes," Church said. "Saoirse had a health condition, and her brother was worried about her safety."

"Yes, and isn't that a pretty story?" Teddy asked. "Poor, frail Saoirse, and her big brother looking out for her, protecting her."

"You're saying it isn't true?"

"Saoirse didn't have an arrhythmia," Teddy said. "They made that up so they could take Saoirse out of school without anyone batting an eye, without anyone becoming wise to the truth."

"And what was that?" Church asked. "What was this truth you think they were so intent on hiding?"

"Saoirse wasn't sick," Teddy said. "She was pregnant."

At first, Church was sure he had misheard him. "Pregnant?" he echoed.

"Yes," Teddy said. "Saoirse told me so herself. She used to call me sometimes, without them knowing. She was furious with her brother for hiding her away and keeping her under lock and key the way he did. Always with a caretaker—someone to keep an eye on her every move. And before you ask," Teddy said, returning his attention to his Cobb salad, "it wasn't mine—it happened when we were broken up."

Church was still trying to process this sudden turn of events. "Did you ever see her pregnant?" he asked.

Teddy shook his head. "The next time I saw her was at her birthday party," he said. "And she obviously wasn't pregnant then."

Church shifted in his chair, his mind racing. "If the baby wasn't yours, do you know who it belonged to?" he asked. "Who Saoirse was involved with?"

Teddy shrugged. "She wouldn't say."

"But the child," Church said. "There would be hospital records, a birth certificate—"

"Not for a home birth," Teddy said. "Not if they used a private doctor and paid him to keep his mouth shut."

"But what happened to the baby?"

"I don't know," Teddy said. "Saoirse told me they planned to make her give it up. She didn't know where or to whom. She was sick over the whole thing, that all this was happening to her and she didn't have a choice."

Church considered this. On the one hand, the story sounded preposterous. A secret pregnancy, a secret child, that no one had breathed a word about for the past forty years? But Church doubted Teddy would make something like that up. It was too much of an over-the-top story for someone as sly as Teddy Mountbatten to bandy about, even if his intent was to throw suspicion back in the direction it had just come from, at the Towers family themselves.

"Is there anyone who can corroborate this?" Church asked.

Teddy shrugged. "The staff—anyone who was working there at the time would have known."

Florence Talbot's face flashed in Church's mind. She was working with the family when Saoirse disappeared. But she seemed very protective of the Towers family, willing to keep their secrets. If Church was going to find someone who had been working there and would willingly corroborate Saoirse's pregnancy, he might have to look elsewhere.

"Why didn't you come forward with any of this before?" Church asked.

"Saoirse told me all of this in confidence," Teddy said. "When she first disappeared, I thought she'd merely run off. Maybe she'd found out where they'd sent the baby and she'd gone to find it. Then, as more time went by and I never heard from her, my mind took a darker turn. I thought maybe she hadn't run off. Maybe they'd found a way to silence her forever. And who would want to cross someone like that?"

"You were afraid of her family?" Church asked.

Teddy set his fork down and finished chewing. He gave a wry smile. "Well, they aren't just any family, are they?" Teddy said.

"No," Church said. "No, I suppose they're not."

After they'd finished their lunch and Church had paid the bill, he leaned across the table toward Teddy.

"Can I ask you just one more thing?" he said. It had been nagging at him since they'd started their conversation. "Why talk to me at all?" Church asked. "'Silence is the true friend that never betrays' and all that?"

Teddy smiled. "I suppose either I am guilelessly innocent or I have some hubris myself that my good sense cannot cure me of."

CHAPTER SIXTEEN

JULY 1982

When Ana descended the steps to the front drive at 8:00 a.m. sharp that Saturday, she saw Ransom there, leaning against the same blue convertible that Salvador had rescued her in that first day.

"At least one of you is on time," Ransom said when he saw her.

Well, hello to you too, Ana thought.

Ransom had insisted on taking Saoirse to Los Angeles himself to find her a dress for her party. Ana had initially thought this was a kind, brotherly gesture, until Saoirse had assured her that there wasn't anything benevolent about it—Ransom just wanted to make sure that she didn't pick out something that could be interpreted as inappropriate or salacious by Page Six.

"Is this all you're bringing?" he asked, reaching for her bag.

"I thought we were only going for one night?" Ana said.

"We are," Ransom said. "I've just rarely seen a woman pack so economically."

As if to prove his point, his assistant, Jacqueline Yates, appeared on the steps behind them with a bulging suitcase.

"Is this really necessary, to start so early?" Jacqueline asked, yawning. "Or did we all do something truly revolting in our past lives that requires such punishment?"

"We need to make the most of the day," Ransom said, stepping forward to take her bag next. "Besides, I've been up since six a.m."

"Dear God, why?" Jacqueline said.

"I always get up at six a.m.," Ransom said.

"I know, but that doesn't make it okay," Jacqueline said. She spotted Ana then and waved limply. "Ana, hello," Jacqueline said. "It may not sound like it, but I'm very happy to see you. I'm just incapable of showing enthusiasm for anything before nine a.m. Do you prefer the front or back?" Jacqueline asked, motioning to the car.

"Back," Ana said quickly. Something about spending the whole drive sequestered in the front seat next to Ransom sent a wave of panic through her.

"Great, I'll ride up front, then," Jacqueline said. "I'd ask Saoirse what her preference is, but you know what they say: early bird gets shotgun, late riser rides bitch."

"Speaking of Saoirse, did you see her on your way down?" Ransom asked, checking his watch. "Is she close to being ready, or should I send someone up after her?"

"Ransom, for the love of God, please, just sit down and be still," Jacqueline said, pinching the bridge of her nose, as if she had a headache. "Your avid punctuality is giving me a migraine."

They all got in. Ransom put his elbow on the driver's side door and leaned his head against his hand, restless. Ana could see his leg bouncing anxiously up and down through the gap in the seats.

"I've been rooting for you, you know," Jacqueline said to Ana, half turning to face her. "I love Saoirse to death, but she's a handful. And that Mrs. Talbot!"

"Yes, she's . . . ," Ana said, trailing off, searching for the right word. *Awful, the worst, so mean.* She wasn't sure whether it was okay to criticize Mrs. Talbot in front of Ransom. From what she could tell, Ransom and Mrs. Talbot had a particular regard for one another.

"She's terrifying—I know!" Jacqueline said, finishing her sentence for her. "I want to be her when I grow up. I mentioned to her one time—just once—that I'm allergic to peanuts, and to this day, she remembers. At a charity auction Ransom hosted here, this awful man, Mr. Brookes, had a Snickers bar in his pocket, and Mrs. Talbot told him if he wanted to eat it, he'd have to do it outside. You should have seen his face! That woman doesn't take shit from anyone."

"I wish she hadn't done that," Ransom said, sounding displeased. "Mr. Brookes donates a lot of money to our campaign."

"That's the only redeeming thing about him," Jacqueline said. "He cheats on his wife and abuses his staff."

"How do you know that?"

"I talk to people, and they tell me things," Jacqueline said.

"For the love of God," Ransom said, looking in his rearview mirror.

Ana turned to see the butler setting two large suitcases down near the rear of the car.

"She must be joking," Ransom said under his breath. He opened his door and got out. "Robert, hang on a moment, please."

"Oh, good, we caught the early show," Jacqueline said, giving Ana a wink. Jacqueline flipped her visor down so she could see it all play out in the mirror without having to turn around in her seat.

"What's the matter?" Saoirse asked, emerging from the house with yet another bag.

"We're only going for one night!" Ransom said.

By the time they actually got on the road, they were an hour behind schedule, and they had to skip lunch to make their appointment at the Giorgio Beverly Hills on Rodeo Drive. A woman greeted them personally at the front of the store, dressed sharply in a chic black dress, a kerchief tied around her neck, and offered them champagne. It was nothing like the beige-carpeted stores Ana normally shopped at, with their dim fluorescent lighting and racks packed tightly with dozens of copies of the same uninspired garment. Here, the mahogany floors gleamed in the brightly lit room, and the racks were sparsely populated with singular garments—floor-length evening gowns;

tailored, high-waisted pants; and sleek jumpsuits. Designer handbags were arranged just so on the shelves, like pieces of art in a gallery.

"I have your room ready," the woman said. "Come, right this way."

"Elizabeth Taylor shops here, you know," Jacqueline whispered to Ana as they were escorted to the back of the store. "And Princess Grace of Monaco."

In the dressing rooms, there were pedestals with three-paneled mirrors and a buttery leather sofa to lounge on.

"Miss Towers, I pulled a few things already that I thought might be to your taste," the woman said.

Saoirse handed her glass of champagne to Ana so she could survey the selections that hung on the rack next to her dressing room.

"My taste, or my brother's?" Saoirse asked skeptically. "You pre-vetted these, didn't you?" she asked Ransom, but Ransom didn't respond. Saoirse flipped dismissively through the first three dresses and paused on the fourth, pursing her lips. "This one isn't awful, I guess," she said, running her hands down the silk fabric.

Ana took a seat on the sofa next to Ransom, setting both glasses of champagne on the sleek oak coffee table in front of them. Ransom was thumbing through a discarded magazine, already bored and impatient to leave.

"So are you looking forward to the party?" Ana asked, trying to make conversation.

"I'm looking forward to it being over," Ransom said, not glancing up from his magazine.

Bah, humbug, Ana thought.

"Surely there must be something about birthday parties that you enjoy?" she said.

Ransom gave a noncommittal grunt. "Personally, I find birthday parties a little self-indulgent and unnecessary," he said.

Jesus, Ana thought.

"I don't think that's fair at all," Ana said. "Birthdays are some of my favorite memories as a kid. I mean, I never had my very own birthday party. Growing up, we always had these parties in the summer to celebrate all of us in the family who had a summer birthday. My uncle threw them at his ranch. There'd be a mariachi band, and my aunt would hang a piñata from the old oak in the backyard, and all of my uncles would take a swing at it, blindfolded, after they'd been drinking Tecates all day. Me and my cousins would stand back under the old string lights and watch them and just laugh so hard we cried."

For dessert, her grandmother would make her famous rice pudding and sopaipillas, dusted with sugar. Ana's mouth watered now at just the thought of them.

"You didn't mind sharing it?" Ransom asked. "Your birthday party, I mean?"

Ana shrugged. "I guess I never really thought about it like that."

There was so little in her life that she hadn't shared, she supposed it was just second nature.

Ransom looked at her for a moment. He opened his mouth to say something, but just then, Saoirse came out of her dressing room in her first selection: a strapless Calvin Klein dress, dark as night, with boning in the bodice and a taffeta skirt.

"I feel like Princess Barbie," Saoirse said, her mouth in a dour line. She stood on the pedestal, turning this way and that in front of the mirror, surveying her appearance at every angle.

"No, you're a vision," Jacqueline said, emerging from her own room clutching the large skirt of a red floral-lace Valentino with a flowy tulle overlay. It had a high neck and was belted at the waist. She looked stunning.

"It's too dark and constrictive," Saoirse said, still looking at her own reflection. She tugged at the top of the dress, pulling it up.

"Beauty is pain," Jacqueline said as she stepped onto the mirrored pedestal next to Saoirse. "I can't breathe at all in this one, but I never want to take it off. Ransom, what do you think of my dress?"

"It's loud and over the top," Ransom said.

"Perfect," Jacqueline said. "I'm getting it."

While Jacqueline changed back into her clothes, Saoirse tried on another dress: a sleeveless silver silk concoction by Halston. The dress had a plunging neckline, a fitted waist, and a flowing skirt. Saoirse looked like a Greek goddess in it with her tall, slim figure and dark hair.

"Now, this is more like it," Saoirse said, glowing.

"You're like a glimmer of moonshine," Jacqueline told her. "Like a streak of starlight."

"I don't recall seeing that one before," Ransom said, the disapproval heavy in his voice as he glanced over the top of his magazine.

"I may have added one or two things to the selection at the last minute," Jacqueline said nonchalantly. "She's turning eighteen, not eighty. Let her live a little."

"It's very low cut," Ransom said.

"Hardly," Saoirse said. "I saw Bianca Jagger wearing something twice as low at her birthday party, and everybody couldn't stop talking about how stunning she looked."

"Bianca Jagger?" Ransom said. "That's hardly the argument to win me over."

Saoirse sighed. "Fine. We could put in a few stitches here and there and some strategically placed fashion tape. At that point, I could practically wear it to church."

"For God's sake, it's a Halston, Ransom," Jacqueline said. "Jackie O. wears Halston. It's not exactly scandalous."

Ransom was quiet for a moment. "Miss Rojas, what do you think?" he asked.

Ana was a little caught off guard that he was asking her opinion about anything, let alone a decision that he had flown all the way across the country to make himself in person.

"Honestly? I think it's very pretty," Ana said. She lowered her voice so only he could hear. "And in the interest of making our dinner reservation, it may be the best compromise you're going to get today."

Ransom thought a moment and then sighed heavily. "Fine," he said, barely placated. "I can see I'm outnumbered."

As the shop attendant started taking Saoirse's measurements for alterations, Ransom turned back to Ana.

"You're not going to try anything on?" he asked.

Ana couldn't imagine what one of these dresses would cost—probably her entire paycheck for the summer. Maybe more. What a waste to spend so much money on something you'd wear once and then hang in the back of your closet.

"I'm more of a JCPenney girl," Ana said.

"I see," Ransom said. He turned to one of the shop attendants. "Alexandra, see if you can't find something for Miss Rojas here. And put it on my tab."

"Oh no, you don't have to—" Ana started, but Ransom ignored her.

"The blue-green Yves Saint Laurent dress in the window would suit her," Ransom said.

"The strapless crepe gown?" Alexandra asked.

"Yes, that's the one."

"Excellent choice, sir," Alexandra said. "I'll be right back."

In the dressing room, Ana stood still as Alexandra slipped the dress on over her head and then did the zipper and clasps at the back. She felt ridiculous having someone dress her, but the closures on the dress were too cumbersome and out of reach to manage by herself.

The dress was a deep ink blue, almost teal. It was simple, in a way: strapless, cut straight across the bodice, falling in a column to the floor. One side of the skirt was draped and pinned to the bottom of the bodice, which ended at the natural waist, and the other had a thigh-high slit that made the dress easy to walk in. Ana hated to admit it, but she had never felt anything so luxurious and smooth against her skin before, and when the clasps were done, it fit her body just so.

Once she was dressed, Alexandra ushered her out into the common area of the dressing room. Ana begrudgingly stepped up onto the pedestal, facing the three-paneled mirror, and took in her reflection.

She was still herself, but it was as though the dress heightened and underlined her best features. The color brought out the radiant blue-green of her eyes, the dark olive of her skin. The cut skimmed her slim figure and showed off the sharp blades of her collarbones, the soft slope of her shoulders.

"What do we think?" Alexandra asked, although Ana couldn't help but feel the question was directed more at Ransom than herself. She glanced up at his reflection in the mirror. He was holding the magazine absently in his hands, as if he had forgotten it existed. His gaze swept her body, but she couldn't read his expression. His mouth was drawn in a tight line, and for a moment, he didn't speak.

"It's impeccably cut," he said, his voice a little hoarse. He cleared his throat. "Exquisite craftsmanship."

"We'll need to take it in at the waist, just a bit," Alexandra said, surveying her. "And have it hemmed. But this dress was made for you. You're a knockout in it."

Ana caught sight of the price tag—the dress was over a thousand dollars. She felt sick to her stomach.

"I really don't think I can accept this," Ana said. "It's too much."

"I insist," Ransom said.

She opened her mouth to object, but Ransom cut her off.

"In the interest of making our dinner reservation, Miss Rojas," he said, leaning forward conspiratorially, "take the compromise."

Ana locked eyes with him for a moment in the mirror. There was something heavy in her throat; she couldn't swallow. Then, Ransom looked away.

Afterward, they went to their hotel—the Duchess in Beverly Hills. It was just as Ana had always imagined it would be from the way Rosie had described it: pearl white, five stories tall, with arches in the entryway and palm trees dotting the drive. The valet came running to take Ransom's car as soon as they pulled up, and as they walked through the marble lobby, Ana couldn't help but glance at the hostess desk, even though she knew that Rosie wouldn't be there.

Through the lobby and to the left was the Sunset Lounge, with its white-clothed tables and forest green velvet booths. The busboy filled their water glasses from a pitcher as soon as they sat down, and another boy brought a basket of bread rolls warm from the oven.

"Do you always stay here?" Ana asked as she opened her menu. "At the Duchess?"

"It was Mother's favorite," Saoirse said. "We stayed here anytime we were in the city. So it sort of feels like a home away from home now, I guess."

When the waiter returned, Ransom ordered bluefin tuna tartare for the table to start. Ana chose lobster risotto in parmesan and mascarpone cheese for her meal, because Rosie had told her that was the best thing on the menu. Rosie used to sneak bites of it from the half-eaten room service trays in the kitchen.

Ana heard her name, and she glanced up to see the whole table looking at her.

"Sorry?" she said.

"Where were you just now?" Jacqueline asked. "You looked a million miles away."

"Just tired, I guess," Ana said.

"We were asking if you'd want to go see *Sweeney Todd*," Jacqueline said. "It's playing at the Pantages tonight."

"The one where a mad barber slits men's throats with his razor blade?" Ana asked.

Jacqueline nodded enthusiastically. "And bakes their remains into meat pies," she said. "It's supposed to be terribly fun."

"Sorry," Ana said. "I think I'll sit this one out."

"Spoilsport," Jacqueline said. "Ransom, what about you?"

"I have some reading to catch up on," Ransom said. "But you ladies go and have a good time."

"Just us, then," Jacqueline said to Saoirse, raising her water glass. "To a proper girls' night out."

They emphatically clinked glasses.

"So, Ana, tell us," Jacqueline said, taking a sip of her water. "Do you have a special fella in your life?"

"Or girlfriend," Saoirse interjected.

"Mm, yes, of course," Jacqueline said. "All types welcome. We're not puritans here."

"Oh, um, no," Ana said. "I'm not really looking for anything like that at the moment."

"What about Mr. Santos?" Saoirse asked.

"Oh, yes," Jacqueline said. "He's a very nice-looking man."

"I guess," Ana said, wanting desperately for this line of questioning to end. She shifted uncomfortably in her seat. "Objectively speaking."

"The two of you are always sitting next to each other at the breakfast table, whispering together," Saoirse said. "You're not sweet on him?"

Ana could feel Ransom's eyes on her, but she couldn't bring herself to look at him.

"I don't think we *whisper*," Ana said, perturbed. "We converse at a normal volume."

"Well, I can never hear what you're saying to each other."

"Well, maybe that's because we're not talking to you," Ana quipped. She recoiled a bit at her own words. She hadn't meant to lose her cool.

Jacqueline laughed. "Zing, darling!" she said.

Saoirse rolled her eyes. "Jesus," she said. "It was just an observation."

Luckily, the tuna tartare arrived then, and the table was distracted by the distribution of appetizer plates and placing more drink orders.

After dinner, they went upstairs to their shared suite on the top floor. Ana had never stayed in a suite with multiple rooms before. This one was like a large, expensive apartment. There was a formal living room and a separate dining room with a long table and twelve high-backed chairs. They had a balcony with a view all the way to the ocean and three bedrooms all with their own bathrooms.

As Saoirse and Jacqueline got ready to go out, Ana took a hot bath and then put on her pajamas. She lay down, but sleep evaded her, so after an hour or so, she got up and padded out to the living room to watch some TV. She was surprised to see Ransom there. She figured he would have retired to his own room by now, but he was sitting on the sofa, writing in a notebook. He closed it quickly and set it aside when he saw her.

"Sorry," Ana said. "I didn't realize you were out here."

"No, it's fine," Ransom said. "Come in."

Ana hesitated. "I was going to watch something, but I don't want to bother you."

"Help yourself," Ransom said, picking the remote off the coffee table and handing it to her. "It won't bother me."

Ana took the remote and settled on the other side of the sofa, an arm's length from where Ransom sat. She turned on the television and flipped to MTV. The music video for "Our Lips Are Sealed," by the Go-Go's, was playing. Ransom turned off the overhead lamp he'd been using, and the room was sheathed in darkness, dimly lit by the glow of the television.

"What were you writing?" Ana asked, glancing over at him.

"Just taking some notes about my day," Ransom said.

"You keep a *diary*?" Ana asked, her voice teasing.

"Not a diary," Ransom said, "a journal. I'm not a thirteen-year-old girl."

"Clearly."

"What?" Ransom said defensively. "A lot of respectable people keep journals: Leonardo da Vinci, for one. Frida Kahlo. Mark Twain."

"Judy Blume heroines."

Ransom cracked a rare smile. "What do you have against journaling?"

"Nothing," Ana said. "I'm just having a hard time squaring it with your character is all."

"How so?"

"I mean, you always seem so serious and, like, dour," Ana said. "Not someone who reflects on how their day went or how they're feeling."

"Dour?" Ransom repeated.

Ana shrugged. "*Sociopathic* is maybe the word I'd use. No offense. It's just how you come off."

Ransom laughed. "If I tell my publicist you said that, she'll want to include you in my next focus group."

"You focus group your personality?" Ana asked in disbelief.

"Not my personality, the public perception of my character," Ransom said. "It's not unusual in my line of work."

"I guess," Ana said. "But what's wrong with just being yourself? Or do you not trust people to like you for that?"

"It's not that simple," Ransom said. "My job depends on how people see me. I don't get to leave that at the office at the end of the day or take a vacation from it. And no, I don't trust the media to portray a nuanced or generous illustration of who I am or for the public to grasp it from a ten-second sound bite on the nightly news or a headline splashed across the tabloids."

"But don't you think that's a little like lying?" Ana asked. "To . . . I don't know, *consciously construct* how you come across to other people? It sounds a little manipulative."

Ransom shrugged. "I don't think so. Everyone has two selves, a public self and a private self, whether they're cognizant of it or not."

"I don't," Ana said.

"Okay," Ransom said, "then tell me the last time you masturbated."

Ana scoffed, heat rushing into her cheeks.

"See?" Ransom said. "Everyone has things they prefer to keep to themselves."

They were quiet for a moment. A commercial for nacho-cheese Doritos came on the screen. Ana's eyes flitted to the closed journal on the coffee table in front of them. What she wouldn't give to skim those pages. She'd thought when she took the black notebook from Ransom's locked desk drawer that she had been pilfering a diary, but it had, quite disappointingly, turned out to be a sketchbook, full of drawings and diagrams of buildings from some architecture class. A huge bust.

"Those big family birthday parties you were telling me about earlier today," Ransom said after a while. "Does your family still have them?"

Ana looked over at him. She was surprised he remembered that. She didn't think he had really been paying attention. "My uncle doesn't throw them anymore," she said. "My cousin—his only child—she passed away, in a terrible accident."

"I'm sorry to hear that," Ransom said.

"Yeah," Ana said. She looked down at her hands, picked at a loose thread on the armrest of the sofa. "You know that saying that you can never go home again?" she asked. "I never understood it until my cousin died. Home isn't a physical place. It's a point in time when you felt loved and protected and safe. It's a person who made you feel that way. And when that's gone, it changes everything, you know?"

"I do," he said, his voice quiet.

Ana believed him, that he really did know the feeling. It was rare for Ana to get to talk to someone around her own age who had experienced grief and loss and understood it as acutely as she did. There was a certain comfort in sharing that burden, in not having to explain it or sit there while someone felt sorry for you and groped for the right words that wouldn't come because they didn't exist. There were no right words. There was no right thing to do that could take away the sting, erase the pain. Oftentimes, she ended up having to comfort and reassure the person who was there to comfort her.

"My brother, Theo, and I, when we were younger, we used to have this game we'd play," Ransom said. "Our great-aunt Peggy, she'd get everyone the same thing for Christmas every year—a tin of these handmade marzipan candies from this monastery in Switzerland. The candies were all made to look like her little pug, Sir Winston, whom she was obsessed with but nobody else could stand, because he'd either drool all over you or bite you or—sometimes, if you were particularly unlucky—both. It was an awful and bizarre gift—what kid likes marzipan? And shaped like a dog that nobody liked? So Theo and I, to get rid of them, we'd hide them in each other's things, you know, just to mess with each other. The more random and well hidden, the better. Sometimes you wouldn't find them for months, and then you'd go to put on your ski jacket and find one tucked into your pocket, half melted, or you'd go to pull your driver out of your golf bag and find one there. We called it getting Pugged. When Theo passed, I put one in his suit jacket pocket to be buried with. It was the sort of thing he'd have had a laugh at. One last Pug.

"Several weeks ago, I pulled out my old chess set, the one my father had gotten me ages ago. And when I opened the box, I saw it there—a marzipan pug, sitting there with all the other pieces. And I just . . . I—" Ransom trailed off, was quiet a moment. "He must have hidden it ages ago, of course," Ransom went on. "But it was just so like Theo, to still be playing. To make one more move when you thought the game was over."

Ana smiled gently. "He sounds like quite the character," she said. "You must miss him terribly."

Ransom shifted on the sofa. "He was a lot of things."

"You know, you're not exactly how I imagined you'd be," Ana said after a while.

"And how's that?"

"Well, based on your politics, I always kind of assumed you were . . . I don't know, a little cold. Morally bankrupt, maybe. But, it turns out, you do have feelings."

Ransom cocked an eyebrow at her.

"Just some of the policies you support," Ana went on quickly. "Cutting funding for welfare programs, like food stamps, for one."

"Sometimes you have to do the wrong thing for the right reason," Ransom said.

"What's that supposed to mean?"

"Just that no one in government has the luxury to vote solely in line with their own conscience," Ransom said. "By supporting that federal budget cut, I got the votes I needed to push through legislation for my disability rights bill. Sometimes you have to scratch someone else's back so they'll scratch yours."

"That sounds like a spin to me," Ana said.

"I'm not spinning anything," Ransom said. "Things are more complicated than just *right* and *wrong*. Democracy is a giant wheel, and I'm just a small cog in it. I can't make it turn by myself. There have to be enough of us, all going in the same direction. And sometimes that means you have to make sacrifices, compromises."

"I think if you're truly confident that you're doing the right thing, you should do it without compromise," Ana said.

"Someone who believes they're always right and single-mindedly pushes forward their own agenda without compromise—that's an autocrat, a dictator," Ransom said. "That's not a democracy."

"Maybe," Ana said. "But how do you know when you've compromised too much?"

His eyes flashed at her. "That, Miss Rojas, is the million-dollar question."

They sat there for a moment, looking at one another in the dark, the glow of the television softly illuminating their faces. Somehow, while they'd been talking, they had shifted closer together on the sofa. Ana's knee was just inches from Ransom's thigh.

"You can call me Ana, you know," she said. "Miss Rojas feels so formal."

He held her gaze. There was an intensity in his stare that sent a shiver down Ana's spine.

"Ana," he said.

An electricity pulsed between them when he said her name. Ana sat very still. Ransom leaned forward, and before Ana knew what she was doing, she closed her eyes and waited to feel his lips against hers.

After a few moments when nothing had happened, she opened her eyes again. Ransom was no longer sitting next to her. He had gotten up, was already standing on the other side of the couch.

"I should get to bed," he said, his hands in his pockets. "We have an early morning tomorrow. Good night, Miss Rojas."

Ana felt an ache of disappointment between her ribs, and then a jolt of shame.

What the hell was she doing? Did she just have a stroke and forget that this was Ransom Towers she was talking to? The man who, prior to this conversation, she had always seen as a cold, pompous—hell, *sociopathic*—asshole?

Oh God. Had he seen her close her eyes in anticipation of a kiss? She swallowed, hard. She was glad the room was dark and that at least he couldn't see the blush rising from her collarbone to her cheeks. Her face felt like it was on fire.

"Yeah, right," she said. "Good night."

She sat there for a while in the dark after he had gone, waiting for her heart rate to return to normal.

CHAPTER SEVENTEEN

PRESENT

D etective Church leaned back in his chair and rubbed his temples. His head was starting to throb from all the reading he'd done, the strain of studying small text and puzzling out handwriting in the old case files, which had never been digitized. Instead, there were several large binders full of typed and handwritten reports, microfiche, and photographs that had degraded with time. The pages had yellowed, the ink had faded, and everything smelled musty, like an old library book. Church had been through the whole thing now, catalogued timelines and persons of interest. The details swam around in his head, untethered.

A cold case was like a giant puzzle that had been partially assembled, the edges and corners filled in, the middle a patchwork of center pieces and the maddening empty spaces between them. Normally, Church enjoyed the slow, laborious process of examining each piece and figuring out how they fit together; he loved the challenge of looking for the needle in the haystack that someone else had missed.

But the Towers case was frustrating. Often, crimes were solved by one of two things: witness testimony or physical evidence. What was perhaps most remarkable about Saoirse Towers's case was the scarcity of either, when one would think the circumstances under which she disappeared would have lent themselves to an excess of both. How was it, Detective Church wondered, that in a house full of guests gathered for the express purpose of celebrating Saoirse's birthday, nobody had noticed that the guest of honor was missing? Surely somebody would have seen or heard *something*? Anything.

But when the police interviewed the guests the evening after Saoirse disappeared, the timeline they were able to cobble together of Saoirse's activities the night prior was piecemeal and fuzzy. One guest claimed to have seen her floating on a swan raft in the outdoor pool, sipping champagne, at the same time that another saw her eating cake in the ballroom. One guest might have seen her crying in the bathroom. She had given her handkerchief to a tall dark-haired girl in a silver party dress weeping over the sink, but it could have been someone else—she didn't get a good look. On only three points were the guests decidedly unanimous: the night was dark, the drinks were flowing, and the storm was loud. The party and the weather worked in unison to create the perfect cocktail of chaos and distraction. Part of Detective Church couldn't help but wonder if that was purely coincidental or by design.

When the police searched the house and grounds the next day, they were dismayed to find that the whole scene had been compromised. The household had known about Saoirse's disappearance for hours before they alerted the authorities. By the time the police arrived, any evidence that the storm had not washed away had been destroyed by the guests in their search. The halls were smeared with muddy footprints going in every which direction, the gardens trampled, every surface in Saoirse's room touched by dozens of hands.

Detective Church shook his head to clear his frustration. So no evidence to go off of, then, and a suspect list that included everyone in the house that night—312 names, to be exact, when the staff and entertainers were factored in along with the guests.

The last sighting of Saoirse had been around midnight, when several guests claimed they had seen Saoirse barefoot and inebriated, clutching her shoes in one hand and laughing as she headed down to the beach for the fireworks. A man was with her, but it was dark, and they couldn't see who.

Was it Teddy Mountbatten? Church wondered. *Ransom Towers? Or someone else?*

Church had tried to substantiate Teddy's claim that Saoirse had been pregnant when she was taken out of school. He'd asked Nisha whether there was any way to determine, based on Saoirse's remains, whether she had ever been pregnant or given birth. Nisha told him that sometimes there were parturition scars on the pelvic bones from childbirth but that they were not always present and certainly wouldn't be present if Saoirse had had a C-section or miscarried. As it was, Saoirse had no such scars. So Church tried to find another witness to substantiate Teddy's claim. The family doctor was deceased, but Church had been able to track down a gardener who had worked at Cliffhaven during the time in question. The man was in his eighties now, living in Sacramento with his daughter. Church had sat with him for over an hour, but he had no recollection of Saoirse being with child and claimed to have spent very little time in the house.

Church sighed. There was only one thing left for him to do. He would have to go back to Cliffhaven and talk to Florence Talbot.

It was Florence herself who answered the door when he showed up at Cliffhaven unannounced.

"Detective Church," she said brightly. "I was wondering when I might see you again."

"I'm sorry for not phoning ahead," Church said. "I hope I'm not intruding."

"Not at all," Florence said and waved him in. "Come into the drawing room; I have something for you."

Florence ushered him into the next room and onto the sofa, while she orchestrated an order of tea to be brought out and a box to be brought up from the storage closet. She inquired about his grandmother and made sure he had exactly the number of lumps of sugar and milk that he wanted. Not long after, a maid entered, carrying an old, dusty box.

"Ah, here it is," Florence said, setting down her own cup on the coffee table and waving the maid over. "You can set it down here, Jenny. Thank you. Would you go check on Rebecca and make sure she takes her break now?"

Jenny nodded and left the room.

"What's this?" Church asked, looking at the box.

"Just some old party-planning things," Florence said. "Odds and ends."

When he still looked confused, Florence went on. "Seating charts, from the night of Saoirse's party. RSVP cards. Some old photographs from that night, like we talked about."

"Oh, yes," Church said. He had forgotten all about that. "Yes, thank you."

"Of course," Florence said. She looked at him for a moment, a crease of concern forming between her brows. "You look tired, Detective," Florence said. "Bone weary."

Church rubbed his jaw. He thought about denying it, but he *was* tired, and he knew he looked it. "Lots of long nights lately," Church said.

"Yes," Florence said, nodding. "Maybe you should do something to take your mind off of it? Just for a little bit. I read somewhere that the subconscious mind is better than the conscious mind at solving problems, that even when you're not actively thinking about something, the subconscious is at work, making connections."

"I believe that's true, yes," Church said. "My best breakthroughs in a case usually come when I'm playing hearts with my grandmother."

Florence laughed.

Church looked at her thoughtfully for a moment and then said, "Florence, can I ask you something?"

Florence set down her cup of tea and nodded. "Yes, of course," she said.

"Was Saoirse ever pregnant?"

She blinked at him, and Church clocked the real confusion on her face as she processed his words.

"What?" she said.

"The year before she died, when Ransom pulled her out of school and brought her home," Church went on. "Did he do that because she was pregnant and he wanted to hide it? Was Saoirse's illness a cover?"

"Wherever did you hear such a thing, Detective?" Florence asked.

"I'm afraid I can't disclose my source," Church said.

"Was it Mr. Bass who told you this?"

"Who?"

"William Bass," Florence said.

The name tickled Church's brain. *Bass.* He had come across that name more than once in the case files.

"Saoirse's godfather?" Church asked.

"Yes," Florence said.

"Why would you think it was him?" Church asked, sidestepping Florence's question.

"Because it's just the sort of thing he would say," Florence said. "If he found himself in a tight spot, his back against the wall, he would say anything, even if it was hurtful, even if it was untrue."

Church was thrown off by her remark. "I thought Bass was quite close with the Towers family," he said. "Why would he want to strike at them with such a damning allegation, if it were false?"

"It wouldn't be the first time he's betrayed the family," Florence said.

"How do you mean?" Church asked.

"I mean," Florence said, "that Charles gave Bass his start in life. Bass could never have founded his company without Charles's investment or sustained it when it fell on hard times without Charles's continued support. Charles made Bass godfather of his children, executor of their trust. And what did Bass ever do for Charles? He lent him a plane that took him straight to his watery grave."

Church furrowed his brow. "The plane that Charles and Birdie went down in, it belonged to Bass Corp.?" Church asked. He had never read that in any of the case files.

Florence nodded. "Charles and Bass had had a fight the week before the crash, practically a falling-out," she said. "The plane, the lending of his vacation home on the island, was Bass's goodwill gesture to patch things up. Bass was supposed to join them, but at the last minute, he backed out. He insisted they still go on without him. You tell me what that looks like."

Church scratched his chin. "Did they find any evidence of foul play in the wreckage?" he asked.

Florence shook her head. "The official ruling was that the crash was a result of equipment failure. But I have my doubts."

Church's mind was reeling. If this was true, if Bass was responsible for Birdie's and Charles's deaths, then that established a pattern of behavior. He was looking not just at a killer but at a serial killer.

"Do you know what Bass and Charles's falling-out was about?"

"What else? Bass Corp.," Florence said. "Charles wasn't happy with the way Bass was running things. He didn't feel comfortable investing more money unless there was a significant change in direction."

"Charles told you this?"

"Birdie did," Florence said. "She and Mr. Bass were close. She was concerned about a rift in Charles and Bass's friendship, what it would do to the family. I told her we were all better off without Bass, but she didn't listen. When Bass extended an olive branch—the private plane, the weekend getaway—they took it."

"And suddenly, without them in the picture, Bass became guardian of the children, executor of the family estate," Church said, putting it all together, "in control of the finances he needed for his company, and in control of his own destiny again."

"Exactly," Florence said.

"And," Church went on, "the only thing standing between Bass and Charles's money at that point was Charles's children."

"Yes," Florence said, the disdain clear in her voice. "Ransom looked up to Bass, trusted him implicitly. Saoirse, on the other hand, was much more difficult to manage."

"You think Bass got rid of Saoirse to get at her money?" Church asked. "But I thought Ransom, not Bass, stood to inherit her trust if something happened to her?"

"He did," Florence said, "but don't you see? That's exactly what Bass would have wanted. Saoirse didn't want anything to do with Bass Corp. She made it very clear that when she turned eighteen and gained control of her trust, she was getting out, which would have sent Bass Corp. into a tailspin. But Ransom and Bass were close; Bass could have counted on Ransom to keep his shares invested, which is exactly what he did when he inherited her estate."

"I see," Church said.

It certainly established a motive. And Bass had plenty of means and opportunity as well.

"What does your gut tell you, Florence?" Church asked. "Do you think he did it?"

Florence didn't hesitate. She looked him square in the eyes and said, "I think there's no morally decrepit act that man wouldn't make, if it benefited him."

CHAPTER EIGHTEEN

JULY 1982

The next morning, both Jacqueline and Saoirse slept through breakfast, so it was just Ana and Ransom at the table. Their suite had a dining room adjacent to the living room, and room service had brought up platters of eggs Benedict with a side of roasted potatoes for each of them and a bowl of steel-cut oats with currants and coconut for Saoirse, which currently sat covered and untouched. Ana sat next to Ransom, who was seated at the head of the table, a cup of coffee in one hand and the morning paper in the other. Ana was glad for the paper—it was a nice distraction, something for Ransom to pay attention to that wasn't her. She didn't know how to look at him after last night, how to talk to him when she had made such a fool of herself. Her mind replayed the scene in vivid detail—how she had closed her eyes and leaned in—how obvious she had made it that she had thought he was about to kiss her. And in response, he had gotten up and moved away from her. It was mortifying. She didn't know how she was supposed to endure a whole four-hour car ride with him back to Cliffhaven without spontaneously combusting from embarrassment.

"Are you all right?" Ransom asked as he set the paper down. "You seem a little off this morning."

"I'm fine," Ana said, keeping her eyes trained on her breakfast tray and spearing a cube of potato.

Ransom glanced at his watch. "We should get on the road soon," he said. "I suppose I shall have to go wake them."

"Did they get in late?" Ana asked.

"You didn't hear them? It was like the storming of the Bastille at two in the morning."

"Two in the morning?" Ana said. "The play was that long?"

"No," Ransom said. "They seemed to have enjoyed themselves after the play was over. And if either of them regurgitates any of last night's enjoyment in my car today, I will be cross indeed. I've just had the upholstery cleaned."

Ana didn't say anything and took another bite of her eggs Benedict. She could feel Ransom surveying her, and her face felt suddenly warm.

"Have I done something to offend you?" Ransom asked after a moment.

"No," Ana said. Still, she couldn't bring herself to look at him. She busied herself with her napkin instead. "Why would you ask that?"

"Because you've barely made eye contact with me all morning," Ransom said.

Ana sighed and forced herself to look at him. "You're imagining things."

"Ana, kindly, don't insult my intelligence," Ransom said. "Just tell me what I've done to upset you."

"It's nothing," Ana said. "It's just—I feel a little weird around you after last night and the . . . the kiss."

"What kiss?" Ransom asked, looking confused.

"Well, it wasn't an actual kiss," Ana corrected herself. "It was more of an almost kiss." She felt even more insane and silly saying this all out loud. "Last night, in the other room, on the couch. See?" She nodded toward the aforementioned couch, which sat in perfect view of their table, just through a set of open French doors. The couch existed, and therefore the kiss—or the almost kiss—had too. "We were talking," Ana went on, "and I thought you were going to—you know—but then you didn't."

Ana stared down at her plate. She desperately wished for a shovel so she could dig a hole through the floor and escape from his gaze. She could feel his eyes focused so intently on her, and her cheeks flamed. Why did she open her mouth? Why had she started talking at all?

"But I did want to kiss you," Ransom said matter-of-factly. "That's why I got up and walked away."

Ana looked up at him. "See, that's not usually what someone does when they *want* to kiss someone."

"I wanted to, but I didn't think I *should*," Ransom said. "I'm your employer. And I'm older than you."

"Not so much older," Ana said quickly.

"Yes, well, still your employer," Ransom said. "I don't think it's a good idea for us to get romantically involved."

"Oh, yes, I'm in complete agreement there," Ana said heartily.

"You are?"

"Absolutely," Ana said. "I'm not *in love* with you, Ransom. It was a momentary attraction thing. And I'm very happy for it never to happen again."

"Good," Ransom said. He was quiet for a moment. "At the same time," Ransom went on, "I don't think we need to avoid each other completely. I like spending time with you. I enjoy your company."

"You do?" Ana asked.

"Is that so hard to believe?"

"Kind of," Ana said. "You so rarely look like you enjoy anything."

Ransom laughed.

"So where does that leave us, then?" Ana asked.

"Well, I don't see why we can't be friends," Ransom said.

"Friends," Ana said, as if it were a foreign word she was trying on for the first time. "Yes, all right. Friends."

Ransom reached out his hand.

"What are you doing?" Ana asked.

"Shaking on it," Ransom said.

"Is a verbal agreement not enough?"

"Don't be so contrary, Ana," Ransom said. "People have been using handshakes to solidify deals and alliances for centuries. Medieval knights would shake hands to show they weren't carrying any weapons."

"Fine," Ana said, rolling her eyes but extending her hand all the same. "I'm just saying, I have a lot of friends, and we've never shaken on it. Things have turned out fine so far."

Ransom took her hand in his. His hand was so much bigger than hers. It was warm and steady, and the way he held on to her made her stomach do a not-unpleasant twist.

Ana swallowed. "Is there anything else we need to do?" she asked. "Exchange blood oaths, perhaps? Do some sort of chant?"

Ransom smiled but let her hand go. She immediately missed the weight of his hand on hers, his warmth.

"No, that will suffice," Ransom said.

"Good," Ana said.

She drew her hand back into her lap under the table. As she absently traced the lines of her palm with her left thumb, she sent up a silent prayer that the promise they'd both made wouldn't be so hard to keep.

CHAPTER NINETEEN

PRESENT

William Bass was eighty-seven now and living in Buena Villa, an old, graying hacienda just outside of Santa Barbara that had been converted into a nursing home. By the looks of it from the outside—the shingles curling on the roof and covered with moss, the shutters in need of painting—Bass's fortune was all but gone.

Detective Church had done his homework: Bass's bad business decisions that had caused turbulence in the '70s continued to plague his company into the early '90s. Eventually, a costly trademark infringement lawsuit, followed by a massive recall on turkey dinners due to plastic being found in the mashed potatoes, were the death knells. Bass held on as long as he could, liquidating all his assets to keep his business afloat, but in the end, he had no choice but to dismantle the company and sell it off, piece by piece, at pennies on the dollar, until there was nothing left. Which meant, Church thought, if Bass had killed Saoirse to keep her from divesting her shares in his company, her death had only prolonged the inevitable by several years. Such a maddeningly pointless loss.

Bass's nurse, Wanda, met Church at the front desk when he signed in. She was middle-aged, African American, with close-cropped coarse hair. She had on white tennis shoes and purple scrubs with pink hearts. She smiled at Church warmly.

"This way, honey," Wanda said. "I'll take you to him."

The carpeted halls were narrow and dimly lit; they smelled faintly of Pine-Sol and incontinence. Most of the doors they passed were closed, but through one open doorway Church caught a glimpse of an elderly woman sitting up in bed, eating her lunch from a tray.

"I'm so glad you're here," Wanda said. "Mr. Bass doesn't get many visitors. He's a bachelor, you know. No family." She paused outside of a closed door at the end of the hall. "It's this one here," Wanda said. "Now, I will warn you that Mr. Bass can be a bit . . . prickly. I wouldn't take it personally. It's just the loneliness talking. I find the best approach in these sorts of cases is to just smile and kill them with kindness."

She knocked twice and then opened the door with the fortitude of a soldier going to war, and Church followed behind her. Inside was a single-size bed and an en suite handicap bathroom. The bed was made; a quilt was folded neatly at the end. Bass sat in front of it in a wheelchair, facing a small television. He was portly now and balding but clean shaven. He wore a velvet robe and silk pajamas—once nice but now mottled with age and wear.

"I'm back, honey," Wanda said. She went over and gave Bass's arm a comforting squeeze. "I brought that guest we talked about."

"Out of the way, will you?" Bass said, shooing her out of his view. His eyes were trained on the TV behind her. "Olivier is giving his speech."

"Why don't we pause this, just for now, sugar?" Wanda said. She picked up the remote and clicked, and the screen froze. "Laurence Olivier will take right back up where he left off when you're done. Now, this is Detective Church. I told you he was coming today, remember?"

Bass's eyes flickered reluctantly from the television to Church. "Have you seen this program?" Bass inquired.

Church glanced at the screen but couldn't place the image on it.

"It's *Brideshead Revisited*," Wanda said, "Mr. Bass's favorite. He watches it nearly every day."

"It's magnificent," Bass said. "Laurence Olivier plays Lord Marchmain. He's really very good. I saw him once, you know, in *The Merchant of Venice* on Broadway. Spectacular. Are you a theater man, Detective?"

"No," Church said. "I'm sorry to say I never really cared for it."

"Hmm," Bass responded, as if Church's lack of enthusiasm for the theater revealed something inauspicious about his character.

"I'll leave you boys to it, then," Wanda said. She leaned down and pressed what looked like a remote buzzer into Bass's hand. "Just press the call button if you need anything, honey. I'll be just down the hall."

Wanda gave Detective Church an encouraging smile as she walked past him and out the door. For a moment, Bass and Church just looked at one another. Then, Church cleared his throat.

"Well, as Wanda said, my name is Detective Church," he said. "I'm here to talk to you about Saoirse Towers and what happened the night she disappeared."

He pulled up the only other chair in the room that he could find, which was next to the TV, and moved it in front of Bass, directly facing him.

"I'm talking to everyone who was there that night," Church went on as he sat down. "What they saw, what they heard, what they can remember."

"Everyone should go to the theater," Bass said animatedly. "Even philistines."

Church blinked at him, caught off guard by the sudden about-turn in the conversation. He wasn't sure what to say in response, so he just said, "Yes, well, I'll have to give it another go." He shifted in his chair and tried again. "Mr. Bass, on the night that Saoirse Towers disappeared, several eyewitnesses claimed you had an altercation with Saoirse in the ballroom," Church said.

"An altercation?" Bass huffed. "My, that's dramatic. No, no. It was more of a—a conversation."

"A conversation?" Church repeated.

195

"Yes," Bass said. "You know, one person says something, and then the other person responds, and so on and so forth."

"Witnesses reported raised voices," Church said.

"My voice carries," Bass said. "And the acoustics in that room—well, sound travels well."

"According to onlookers, you grabbed Saoirse roughly by the arm," Church went on. "Then she pushed you away and told you not to touch her."

"Well, I don't recall any of that," Bass said, shaking his head.

"All right," Church said. "Do you happen to recall, in this . . . *conversation* that you and Saoirse were having, what it was about?"

Bass was silent for a moment. "Laurence Olivier came from nothing, you know," he said. "His father was a clergyman. But Olivier, they made him a lord."

"I'm sorry?"

"Laurence Olivier," Bass said, louder, as if Church were stupid. "He was born Laurence Olivier, but he died *Sir* Laurence Olivier. Isn't that something?"

"I suppose," Church said. He wondered at Bass's lucidity. Maybe, in his old age, he had grown senile. "Now," Church went on, trying to keep Bass focused on the conversation at hand, "perhaps this will jog your memory. That night, the conversation with Saoirse Towers, was it about Saoirse's plans to divest her shares in Bass Corp.?"

Bass blinked at him and then laughed a deep, rumbling laugh that turned into a violent hacking cough. His shoulders shook violently, and Church wondered for a moment if he should get the nurse, but Bass held out a hand to stay him.

"Rumors!" Bass said, when he finally caught his breath. He swatted at the air like the word was a pesky fly. "People like to talk, don't they? But that's all it is—a bunch of hot air. Saoirse always had the acumen to separate business from her personal beliefs. Period. She was never going anywhere."

Church couldn't help but feel there was something threatening in that proclamation: *She was never going anywhere.* And in the end, she hadn't, had she? She'd stayed right there at Cliffhaven, and her money had stayed invested in Bass Corp.

"What about the necklace?" Church asked.

Bass cleared his throat. "What necklace?"

"The one she always wore," Church said. "It was given to her by her mother when she was just a girl. It had a locket with an inscription on it and a very distinctive chain—twenty-four karat gold, with little gold stars woven into it."

"I'm afraid I don't recall that," Bass said.

"Here," Church said, reaching into his pocket. He pulled out a plastic baggie that he had signed out of the evidence room that morning. He leaned forward and placed the bag with the necklace in Bass's lap, and Bass flinched, either from surprise at the gesture or from seeing the necklace again after all these years—Church wasn't sure which.

"Care to explain how this necklace found its way into your room the day after the party?" Church asked.

In the case file, Church had read how Bass had seemed agitated and flustered when the police had first questioned him, and he couldn't account for Saoirse's necklace being there among his things. Later, when they brought him into the station for further questioning, Bass claimed he'd found the gold chain on the floor of the ballroom the night of the party. He'd recognized it as Saoirse's, picked it up, and put it in his pocket to give back to her the next time he saw her, but then he'd forgotten that he'd had it. Church was curious if Bass would give a different answer now.

"I don't know," Bass said. "A faulty clasp? Perhaps you should consult a jeweler instead of harassing me, Detective, with your inane questions."

"A faulty clasp?" Church said. "You're going to have to do better than that, Mr. Bass."

Bass balked at the bald statement. "How dare you speak to me in such a manner," Bass said.

But Church kept going. He thought that if he applied pressure, he might get somewhere with Bass. He had read, in the case files, about Bass's volatile temper. "Saoirse was hell bent on divesting her shares in Bass Corp.," Church said. "You went to her that night, tried to talk her out of it. A last-ditch effort. But Saoirse was stubborn; she wouldn't listen. You grabbed her, and she screamed at you to let her go. There were witnesses, then, in the ballroom. But later, when you sought her out, there weren't witnesses then, were there? You made sure of that."

A vein pulsed on Bass's neck. "Well, I've never been so egregiously treated in my entire life," he said.

"It was the only thing you could do to save your company, to save yourself, wasn't it?" Church went on. "You had to take Saoirse out of the equation forever."

Bass looked around Detective Church toward the doorway. "Wanda?" Bass called, and when she didn't immediately appear, he clicked the call button in his lap repeatedly. "Wanda, I need you!"

Wanda appeared in the doorway a few moments later, partly out of breath. "Yes, sugar?" she huffed.

"I want to watch my program," Bass said, gesturing toward the TV.

"Are you two done talking already?" Wanda asked as she shuffled into the room.

"Yes," Bass answered firmly. "The detective was just leaving."

"All right," Wanda said as she retrieved the remote from the tray on his side table and pointed it toward the television. "Let me get you all set up here . . ."

She bit her lip in concentration as she fiddled with the buttons, and when Laurence Olivier's face unfroze and his voice filtered into the room, she said brightly, "There you go, sugar," and set the remote back down.

"And show the detective out," Bass said, not even looking in Church's direction. "He seems confused, and I wouldn't want him to get any more lost than he already is."

"That's all right, Wanda. I can find my own way out," Church said, standing. "But, Mr. Bass, I will need the necklace back."

"What?" Bass said absently and then glanced down at his lap. "Oh, yes, this. You can have it." He picked it up with his trembling, liver-spotted hand and dropped it unceremoniously on the floor next to his wheelchair.

"Very dignified of you," Church said. He leaned down to retrieve it and then headed toward the door.

"Oh, and, Detective?" Bass called.

Church didn't want to, but he paused, turned around. "Yes?"

"If you wish to talk with me again, I want my lawyer present," Bass said.

"That's probably a good idea," Church said. "Maybe he can help you come up with a better story." Church held up the plastic baggie with the necklace in it. "From the looks of it, this thing was torn from Saoirse's neck. It wasn't a matter of a faulty clasp. The chain was broken."

CHAPTER TWENTY

AUGUST 1982

Would you ever sleep with someone that you worked with?" Saoirse asked one morning at breakfast.

She had learned this trick at school—to come out bluntly with the question you really wanted to know. The more shocking, the more salacious, the better. It unseated your opponent immediately, knocked them off their feet, and then you had them right where you wanted them: unguarded, unprepared, submissive on the ground before they even knew what hit them.

It seemed to have the desired effect: Ana almost choked on her mouthful of eggs. She coughed, finished chewing, and took a sip of her orange juice.

"What?" she asked, a little hoarse.

"Would you ever sleep with someone that you worked with?" Saoirse repeated.

"I—" Ana said, clearly ruffled, which only piqued Saoirse's suspicions more. "Where's this coming from?"

"It's coming from me, the inquisitive creature sitting before you," Saoirse said.

"I don't think this is an appropriate line of questioning," Ana said.

"You and Salvador seem really close is all," Saoirse said, watching her closely. "You always have your little tête-à-têtes at the breakfast table. I saw you drive off together the other day. Where did you go?"

Saoirse had been observing them for a while now—the way they always seemed to pair off together when they were in the same room, put their heads together, talk. The way Ana would throw her head back and laugh, and Salvador would smile in a self-satisfied way. They sat next to one another at the breakfast table, side by side, every morning, chattering in low voices so she could never hear what they were saying to each other when she came in. Salvador would always finish breakfast first and then head upstairs to prepare for Saoirse's lessons. He had done the same today, pushing back his chair once his plate was cleared and giving her a friendly, *"Miss Towers, I expect I'll see you shortly. On time today would be a pleasant surprise, yes?"* He had touched Ana's shoulder in parting as he'd gotten up, which did not go unnoticed by Saoirse.

"Salvador and I are friends," Ana said.

"So were John Lennon and Yoko Ono," Saoirse said. "They were also fucking."

Ana glared at her, but Saoirse couldn't tell whether Ana was simply annoyed at her questioning or if she had hit a nerve.

"You don't seem like an obvious pair," Saoirse went on. "Salvador is—well—handsome. Charming. Accomplished. And you're more . . . how should I put this? Subtle in your attractions. It's hard to see what the two of you might have in common, though I suppose sometimes opposites attract, or so they say."

Ana remained quiet, unresponsive.

Saoirse sighed, angry now. Why wasn't she taking the bait? "Look," Saoirse said, "I think I have a right to know whether two people who are under my family's employment are amorously involved."

"Yes, you seem to think you have a right to a great many things," Ana said.

"What's that supposed to mean?"

"Giving employment to a person does not give you authority over a person's entire being," Ana said. "You don't own them. You can't dictate the details of their personal lives. People have a right to privacy."

Saoirse did not like how this was going. "You never answered my question," Saoirse said, frustrated.

"You're right; I didn't," Ana said before taking another bite of her eggs and chewing in a self-satisfied manner. She set her fork down and wiped her mouth with her napkin. "Now, let's follow Mr. Santos's advice and get you to your lessons on time today, shall we?" she asked brightly, pushing back her chair.

Salvador pursed his lips and made a contemplative sound, which is how Saoirse knew she had gotten the answer wrong.

"*Apprendre* is an irregular verb, remember?" Salvador said gently, standing over her, pointing to the place on her paper where she had incorrectly conjugated it. "You can't just drop the infinitive ending to find the stem and add the past participle ending. It follows its own rules. *Appris* is what you're looking for."

"Ah, right," Saoirse said.

She turned her pencil eraser end to paper and removed her mistake.

It wasn't like her to make such a careless error, but after her conversation with Ana at breakfast, she was having trouble concentrating. Why wouldn't Ana just answer her question? Did that mean she had something to hide? Or was Ana just trying to irritate her? Get under her skin by refusing to give her what she wanted?

Salvador returned to the other side of the table, where he was preparing the next part of their lesson. He had Ovid's *Metamorphoses* open in front of him, several pieces of text underlined, notes scribbled in the margins. Saoirse watched him as he bent over his book, deep in concentration. She hadn't really meant what she'd said at the breakfast table. Ana was pretty, though in a quiet, unassuming way, which was perhaps more dangerous than being overtly beautiful. People could be intimidated, awestruck, by beauty. It kept them at arm's length. But Ana's kind of beauty lured you in. It wasn't something otherworldly or unattainable. You could get close to it.

Of course, sometimes sex wasn't about attraction, or love. Saoirse's first time certainly hadn't been. Sex could be about so many different things, and that's what made it so complicated, so tricky to navigate.

At Choate, Saoirse had thought about Teddy. They had written to one another, long letters about the things that filled their days. Teddy never wrote about his girlfriend, and Saoirse didn't know if that meant that they were still together or if they had broken up. She couldn't bring herself to ask, to put the words down on paper.

One day in the fall, there was a party in the woods off campus with some of the students from the neighboring schools of Westover and Hotchkiss. It was October, and there was already frost on the ground. Saoirse and Tessa went together and shared a bottle of brandy, slipping it back and forth between them in their gloved hands until their bellies were warm and their bodies loose. Two Hotchkiss boys edged over to them and commended them on their choice of liquor. They asked if they could have a sip, and Tessa handed them the bottle.

One of the Hotchkiss boys told Saoirse his name. It started with an *M*, she thought—Miles or Martin, something bland and generic. He was cute, in his winter hat and thick wool coat, but unmemorable, which made him perfect. This boy had a name she could forget and a face she probably wouldn't remember in the morning. He didn't go to her school or share mutual acquaintances, so the possibility of running into him again was slim. They talked for a bit about benign things—the classes they were taking, the shows they watched. He kissed her, and his tongue tasted like candied oranges and dark chocolate—like Tessa's bottle of brandy. Saoirse took his hand and led him deeper into the woods, away from the crowd of people.

They found a picnic table in a small clearing not far away. Miles/ Martin smoothed Saoirse's hair out behind her as she lay down, and she thought how kind boys could be when they really wanted to be.

He kissed her, and his lips were cold. Saoirse wanted to tell him they could skip the prelude and go straight to the main event, but she didn't want to hurt his feelings. Boys could be very sensitive, she'd found, when it came to their sexual prowess. She'd once told a boy that it felt like he was trying to tune a radio when he was fondling her breasts, and he immediately became moody and withdrawn. The male ego was so delicate. It was best to just gently lead this boy in the direction she wanted to go, so she unbuttoned the top of his pants, unzipped his fly. That seemed to accelerate things.

He lifted up her skirt, pulled down her tights, but other than that, they kept their clothes on because it was cold and there were people nearby. They could still hear the voices and music from the party through the trees.

To Saoirse, sex seemed like a very intimate thing to do with someone she really liked. Especially the first time, when she knew it would be painful, and she'd probably be bad at it, and she might make some noises or expressions that she wouldn't want anyone who really knew her to see or hear. Besides, she was sure that Teddy had more experience than her. She needed to even the playing field, get her own experience, before wading into those waters with Teddy.

Saoirse felt the weight of the boy's body on top of hers, and then he pressed into her. There was a pinprick of pain between her legs. She expected it, so she pressed her lips together hard so she wouldn't gasp out loud. Then there was the fog of his hot, wet breath against her neck, and she stared up at the dark open sky above her.

The pain melded into something else as he thrust into her, not quite pleasure but something not unpleasant. He paused, and Saoirse felt his body shudder against hers. She knew that it was over.

She waited to see if she felt any different than she had before. Tessa said after her first time, she felt more like a woman after, more grown up, somehow. But all Saoirse felt was a dull ache between her legs.

When they rejoined Tessa at the party, Tessa nudged Saoirse hard with her elbow.

"So?" she whispered expectantly. "How was it?"

Saoirse shrugged. "It was fine, I guess," she said.

Tessa looked disappointed. "It's not a handshake," Tessa said. "You're supposed to feel something."

Saoirse shrugged and reached for the bottle of brandy. As she pressed the nearly empty bottle to her lips, she tried to push away Tessa's words, keep them from seeping into her skin, her bones, her soul.

It wasn't the first time that the thought had occurred to Saoirse or been voiced by someone else that something might be wrong with her, that something inside her might be inexplicably off. To Saoirse, it seemed so reasonable, it made so much sense, that her first time would be about the physical experience of it without any messy feelings or attachments thrown in. Practice, so she could know exactly what to expect when she did it for real. But maybe her ability to look at something so intimate with so much detachment pointed to some inherent defect within her. Maybe a part of her that was supposed to be there was missing.

It made Saoirse panicky whenever she thought of it, like a cold fist was squeezing her esophagus and she couldn't breathe. Maybe people could see it when they got close to her—that something about her was off, that she didn't feel what she was supposed to feel. Maybe that's what her mother had sensed in her, what had kept her at arm's length all her life: she'd recognized a void and couldn't bring herself to get too close.

CHAPTER TWENTY-ONE

AUGUST 1982

The first Sunday of every month when the weather was nice and both men were in town, Ransom Towers and William Bass had a standing engagement to play tennis at the Columbia Country Club. Today, when they took their places on the court, Bass went first, giving a gentle serve to warm up. Ransom returned the ball with a light volley.

"Don't think I don't know what you're doing, my boy," Bass said, hitting the ball short across the net. "Though, I was a bit shocked when I heard. Truth be told, I didn't think you had it in you."

Ransom missed the return volley and ambled across the court to collect the ball. "What's that?" he asked, tossing the ball back to Bass over the net.

"Don't be sly," Bass said. "I know. I know about the girl. The . . . oh, what's her name? Saoirse's companion?"

"Ana?" Ransom asked, confused.

"Yes, Ana," Bass said. "Saoirse told me the two of you hung back together at the hotel the other week in LA. Now, I'd be a hypocrite if I didn't admit that I've had my head turned by a pretty girl a time or two when I shouldn't have. But take it from me: getting involved with a member of your household staff, someone under your own employment—things can get messy. Not to mention, if it were ever to get out, it's not a good look. Especially in an election year. And especially with a girl like that."

Ransom's first impulse was to flatly deny the allegation—it wasn't, after all, true—but something about Bass's words struck a nerve. Ana's face flashed in his mind, and for some reason he could not name, he felt immediately protective of her.

"'A girl like that'?" Ransom repeated.

"Now don't get defensive," Bass said. "I've met Ana—she's lovely. And very pretty. But you must think of her, er, background and how things look. Besides, what do you really know about her? Where's she from?"

"San Bernardino," Ransom said flatly.

"You know what I mean," Bass said. He served the ball, harder this time. "Is she legal? Are her parents?"

"You cannot be serious," Ransom said, not moving from where he stood or attempting to hit the ball as it whizzed past him.

Bass looked irritated. "I could say the same thing," he said. "Come now, are we going to play or sit here bickering like a couple of housewives?"

Ransom reluctantly retrieved the ball and tossed it back to him over the net.

"What I'm saying is be careful, that's all," Bass said. "Have you at least looked into this girl? Into her family?"

Bass served the ball, and Ransom knocked it back across the court with equal gusto, hitting it toward the opposite end of the court so that Bass had to scurry to reach it. Bass was winded and grunted as he knocked the ball out of bounds.

"Ana's shared a great deal about her family with me, actually," Ransom said. "I know her father picked oranges. Her mother was a homemaker. She grew up with five brothers and sisters."

"That is not what I meant, and you know it," Bass said, growing increasingly angry, as if Ransom were teasing him.

"I'm sure I don't know what you meant," Ransom said.

"Come now, Ransom, be reasonable," Bass said. "Think about what you're doing. This is wanton recklessness, and you cannot afford it."

"Uncle," Ransom said. His blood was thrumming in his temples, but it had nothing to do with exercise. "I'm fully capable of making up my own mind when it comes to who I date, and if I want your counsel on the matter, I will ask for it. Until then, I expect you to keep your opinions on the matter where they belong: to yourself."

Bass was seething and red in the face. Still, he held up his hands and bit his tongue. "Have it your way, then," Bass said, as if he were washing his hands of the matter. "But remember this: even wise men can be fools in love."

CHAPTER TWENTY-TWO

JUNE 1958

The morning after Astrid and RJ's wedding, they flew to Rome. Florence had never been on an airplane before, and she gripped the armrests on either side of her chair as they waited for the coach passengers to board. It did not seem logical to her that something as big and substantial as this plane, and all these people, and their luggage (Astrid alone had packed three suitcases), would all soon be airborne. Surely that defied the laws of physics.

"Can I get you something to drink before takeoff?" the stewardess asked.

Florence pressed her lips together and shook her head. She thought if she opened her mouth, she might throw up.

"She'll have a glass of champagne," Astrid said from across the aisle. "And so will I. And my husband." Astrid placed her hand proprietarily on RJ's arm. "We're newlyweds, you know," Astrid cooed. "We just got married last night at the Beverly Hills Hotel. There were over four hundred guests. I'd wanted to invite more, but it was rather last minute."

"The mayor was there," RJ said. "Tell her, darling. And Bing Crosby sang a duet."

"Yes, with Marilyn Monroe," Astrid said. "Everyone said the dress she was wearing was pale pink, but I thought it was very pale—almost white, which was very inconsiderate, and you cannot convince me otherwise that she didn't know exactly what she was doing. Everyone knows it's gauche to wear white to a wedding."

"No one can hold a candle to you, darling, even Marilyn," RJ assured her.

The stewardess expressed her congratulations to the couple and then scurried back up front to prepare their drinks. Florence couldn't help but feel as though she was relieved to have an excuse to get away from them.

"Here," Astrid said when the stewardess was gone. She leaned across the aisle and pressed a pill into Florence's sweaty palm. "Take this with your champagne."

"What is it?" Florence asked.

"Miltown," Astrid said, "a mild tranquilizer."

"Are you supposed to take this with alcohol?" Florence asked, unsure.

"Yes," Astrid said. "It makes it work even better. You'll be dead asleep by takeoff."

Florence closed her fingers around the pill, and Astrid smiled. When the stewardess returned with their drinks, Astrid raised her glass in mock salute.

"Bottoms up," Astrid said. "I'll see you all in Rome."

When Florence woke up hours later, the cabin was dark. The window shades were pulled shut, and the woman next to her was sleeping, her head lolled back at an unattractive angle.

Florence looked across the aisle. RJ was asleep, reclined in his seat, but Astrid was up, another glass of champagne on the tray in front of her and a fashion magazine spread open.

"Where are we?" Florence asked.

"Somewhere over the Atlantic," Astrid said.

Florence imagined the dark swathes of cold water thousands of feet beneath them and suddenly felt lightheaded.

"Hey, can I ask you something?" Astrid said, lowering her voice slightly and leaning toward Florence conspiratorially.

"Um, sure," Florence said, grateful for the distraction. Though if Astrid asked her one more time what color she thought Marilyn's dress really was, she just might throw herself out the nearest emergency exit.

"Have you ever been in love?" Astrid asked instead.

Florence was taken aback. Astrid had never asked her anything about herself before.

"No," Florence said. "I haven't."

"You say that with so much confidence," Astrid said, "like you're really sure."

"I am sure," Florence said.

"But if you've never been in love, how do you know when you really are?" Astrid asked. "People say 'love at first sight,' like it can happen in an instant, with a single glance, without knowing a thing about the person aside from what they look like. And then people say 'falling in love,' like it's a process that happens over time. And people say 'falling out of love,' like it's something transient that can pass, like a flu or a summer cold. And Mother said she loved Daddy, but I never saw them so much as hold hands, and that does not seem like love to me. Sometimes it seems like love is like God—you get a different answer depending on who you ask, and everyone fervently believes in their version of it."

Florence thought for a moment. "I've always believed that romantic love has two parts," Florence said. "There's physical attraction. That can happen at first sight, obviously. But the second part, a real affection, can only be developed over time, after you've come to really know someone. I think that anyone who says they fell in love at first sight merely had their initial attraction substantiated later on by a deepening regard for the person as they got to know them."

Astrid considered this. "But how do you know when you really love someone?" Astrid asked. "How do you know when you're in love?"

"I think it's something you just know," Florence said. "Like when you're lonely or homesick, that hollow ache in your bones. No one has to tell you what it is. You just know."

Astrid thought about this for a moment and then took out the pill bottle from her purse. "Would you like another to get you through the rest of the flight?" she asked, rattling the bottle.

"No," Florence said. "Thank you. I'll just sit for a little bit and read."

When the sun came up, they landed in London, where they boarded a smaller plane for Rome. And when they arrived in Rome, a car took them three hours south to Amalfi, along the coast, to a place called Minori.

Minori was a small town wedged between the mountains and the sea. It was a labyrinth of narrow streets and alleys, overlooked by terraces of lemon groves. Bougainvillea cascaded everywhere from the rafters and rooftops.

They had two rooms at the Villa Romana Hotel, a mere five hundred feet from the sea. It was a beautiful hotel the color of cream, three stories tall, with a private pool, a courtyard dining room, and a solarium.

Astrid and RJ stayed out all night drinking and dancing at the local clubs. In the predawn light, they'd stumble home, laughing and drunk, and fall asleep, still clothed, on their bed, where they'd sleep until the afternoon. And so Florence was left mostly to herself, which was how she preferred it. She spent her mornings walking the promenade along the sea, looking out at the people scattered on the black sand beach with their umbrellas and chairs. She ate her lunch on the shaded beach patios—fresh mozzarella, handmade pasta, limoncello—and spent her afternoons visiting the local sights. She visited the ruins of an ancient Roman villa and then a baroque church with a pale-yellow facade called the Basilica di Santa Trofimena, which was built for the martyr Saint Trofimena. The nuns there told her the story. Trofimena was a young girl from Sicily. At age twelve, she was determined to dedicate her life to Christ, but her father, who did not share her beliefs in Christianity, wanted her to marry. When she disobeyed him, he killed her, put her ashes in an urn, and cast it out to sea. The urn washed up in Minori, her story inscribed on its lid. The villagers put the urn on a cart and carried her into town, but at a certain point, the ox pulling the cart refused to go any farther. So the villagers erected a church there in her name. Soon after, the Arabs tried to attack the village and convert it to Islam. The people of Minori prayed to Saint Trofimena for protection, and she sent a storm to sink the invaders' ships.

Florence was not Catholic. She did not believe in saints or martyrs. But something about Trofimena's story reminded her of Doris. Like Trofimena, Doris had known her own mind at a young age, and while she had not been able to escape matrimony as Trofimena had, she had found her own way to live the life she'd wanted, largely outside the confines of her marriage. At the altar, Florence lit a candle in remembrance of Doris, and even though Doris was not a religious woman, Florence felt she was there with her in that moment and that she understood the gesture.

At dinner on the last night, Astrid begged Florence to come out with them.

"I'm not really one for dancing," Florence said. "Or drinking, for that matter."

"Are you a prig or something?" RJ asked, lighting a cigar. "What do you have against a good time?"

Heat bloomed in Florence's cheeks. Astrid leaned over and put her hand on top of Florence's on the table.

"I know you've been very sad since Granny died," Astrid said. "I can see how much you loved her. But I know Granny, and I know she wouldn't want this for you, all this moping around. If she were here, she'd say, 'My girl, you're seventeen, not seventy. Go out and have a good time.' So do it for Granny. Do it for yourself. Come out with us. It's our last night here. Don't waste it."

For the second time that week, Astrid had surprised her. So often, Florence thought Astrid to be vain and flighty, and maybe she was. But she also had her moments of insight, her moments of compassion, however rare and far between they were.

"All right," Florence said, and Astrid smiled.

"Splendid," Astrid said, cutting into her steak with renewed vigor. "Come to our room after dinner, and we can get ready together."

Astrid insisted Florence borrow one of her dresses, a strapless cocktail gown that nipped in at the waist. Florence had never worn a strapless gown before, and she felt naked with her shoulders exposed. Astrid had to keep reminding her not to cross her arms in front of her chest, not to hunch forward.

"You're prettier than you think, you know," Astrid said as she applied blush to the apples of Florence's cheeks. "Besides, half of being attractive is believing you're attractive. People notice how you carry yourself before they notice the symmetry in your face or how slim your waist is. I saw it all the time at school—girls who, when you really stopped to look at them, were no more than average, getting all the attention from the boys, as if they were a nine instead of a six, and girls who really were quite pretty never getting noticed, because they wore the wrong clothes or hunched their shoulders. Believe you're worth looking at, and others will believe it too."

It surprised Florence, how much she enjoyed herself. The music at the club was loud. She could feel the thrum of the bass in the heels of her shoes as they stood in line at the bar, the vibration climbing her calves, settling into the base of her stomach. They did a round of shots first, and then Astrid handed her something red and sweet to drink that she didn't catch the name of. Florence let Astrid take her by the hand and lead her into the throng of the dance floor, so many bodies pressed together, the air hot and sticky and stale. Florence let some man she'd never met put his arms around her, and she closed her eyes and moved with the music. With alcohol coursing through her veins, she felt brave and alive.

When they left the club near dawn, Florence had to grip onto Astrid's arm so as not to stumble in her heels. RJ walked slightly ahead of them, fishing a lighter and a cigarette out of his pocket. The toe of his shoe caught on a loose pavestone, and he fell forward onto his hands and knees in the street, the lighter skittering away from him. Astrid and Florence laughed involuntarily, bleary eyed and drunk.

"Whoops-a-daisy," Astrid said, which only made Florence laugh harder.

"It's not fucking funny," RJ said as he retrieved his lighter and stood up. "I smashed my goddamn lighter."

"Okay, darling, I'm sorry," Astrid said half heartedly. "I didn't realize there were casualties, or I wouldn't have laughed."

Florence pressed her lips together to stop from giggling, but that only resulted in a very loud snort that set Astrid off again.

"Stop," Astrid chided, laughing still herself. "We're terrible people. We're monsters."

Florence went to Astrid and RJ's room with them because Astrid insisted they have another drink before bed. RJ fumbled with the keys and flicked on the light.

"Oh, darling, your pants," Astrid said, raising her hand to her lips.

Florence glanced over and saw the left knee of RJ's trousers was ripped.

"It must have happened when you fell," Astrid said, trying not to laugh. "Another casualty."

"We lost a lot of good ones tonight," Florence said, hiccupping.

It happened in an instant, the shift in the room. One moment, Florence and Astrid were laughing, and the next, RJ grabbed Astrid roughly by the throat and pushed her against the wall.

"Here's something funny," RJ said. "I could crush your throat like a kumquat."

He squeezed, his knuckles white, and Astrid sucked at the air, unable to draw breath.

Then he let go and walked across the room to pour himself a drink. Astrid coughed and sputtered, clutching at her neck, tears in her eyes. Her skin was red and splotchy where his hands had been. She sat down on the bed.

"You want one?" RJ asked Florence, motioning to the decanter of brandy in his hand, but Florence just stood there, unable to move, unable to talk.

"What's the matter?" RJ asked her, handing her a glass. "Come now, where's your sense of humor? Can't you take a joke?"

Florence barely slept. She tossed and turned all night, waking at the slightest sound. Twice she got up and went to the door, swearing she heard a quiet knocking. She was sure she'd find Astrid standing there in the dark, her jacket on, her suitcase by her side. *Let's go,* she'd say, glancing nervously behind her. *Before he wakes up. Before he knows we're gone.* But each time, the hall was empty. There was no one there.

In the morning, she met Astrid in the lobby. Astrid had on pedal pushers and a silk scarf tied around her neck.

"RJ's gone to get the car," Astrid said.

Florence reached out and touched Astrid's arm. "Are you all right?" she whispered.

Astrid smiled at her. "Oh, yes! Though I think I may have drunk too much last night. I have a bugger of a headache. How'd you sleep?"

Florence just looked at her, searching her eyes for a sign of distress, a secret SOS, and finding none. She couldn't understand it. For a moment, she doubted her own sanity. RJ had put his hands around Astrid's neck and pressed her up against the wall, hadn't he? That wasn't some crazed, alcohol-fueled dream? No, she'd seen the primal anger in his eyes and the fear on Astrid's face when she couldn't breathe. That was real, a wake-time nightmare—she knew it in her bones.

"Fine," Florence said, her voice a bit hoarse. "I slept fine."

CHAPTER
TWENTY-THREE

AUGUST 1982

Ransom Towers was distracted. In the House committee meeting on transportation and infrastructure, his mind wandered from the drafting of the Infrastructure Revitalization Act back to that last heated conversation he'd had with Bass on the tennis court. Where did Bass get off, prying into the private details of his personal life? Instructing him on what was appropriate or wise? Of course Ransom knew what the right thing to do was, and of course he had done it all on his own, without having to be expressly told. It was irritating—insulting, even—that Bass obviously did not trust his judgment enough to see through to the truth of the matter: that nothing untoward had happened between him and Ana in that hotel room in LA, however much Ransom had wanted it to.

Ransom thought of Ana then, how she had sat next to him on the couch in that dimly lit room. The way she had looked at him—so deeply, so intently—when he spoke, as if she were trying to figure him out as earnestly as he was trying to discern her. She had seemed so unaffected, so honest and sincere, so plainly herself that it intrigued him, drew him to her.

He was so intently focused on the image of her face in his mind's eye, so distracted, that he missed the cochair of the committee calling on him. He looked up, dazed, in the middle of the meeting, when another congressman reached over and tapped him on the shoulder.

All week it continued like that. In his staff briefing, he stumbled over his words and made Jacqueline repeat three times the schedule for the day. He had trouble keeping his thoughts in line or his attention where it should be. When he lay down to sleep at night and closed his eyes, it was Ana's face he saw—her bright-green eyes and those soft, slightly pursed lips.

So much of his life was about duty. He so rarely got to do what he actually wanted. It had almost become foreign to him to follow impulse, to chase desire, because he had denied himself those things for so long. He'd lost count of all the things he had given up, stopped cataloguing them in his mind, but he felt every day the two greatest losses: without putting up a fight or hesitating in the slightest, he'd abandoned both the career he'd dreamed of since he was a boy and the girl he had loved. The two defining coordinates of a person's life—what they did and who they spent it with. Maybe he had finally reached some sort of internal threshold of how much he could deny himself before he imploded.

And so late Saturday afternoon, after leaving a fundraising luncheon at the Mayflower Hotel, he hadn't gone back to his town house on the Hill but had gone to the airport, where he chartered a private jet to fly him home. He'd arrived at Cliffhaven around midnight, the whole house dark and sleeping, and crept off to his room as silently as he could.

"What, do you live here now?" Saoirse asked the next morning when she ran into him in the hall. He made an excuse about some work that had to be done for the party, and she rolled her eyes and continued on her way.

He found Ana in the dining room, eating breakfast. She was wearing overalls and Converse, one leg pulled under her on the chair, and she had her head thrown back, laughing, when he entered the room. Ransom quickly gleaned the source of her amusement—next to her was Salvador Santos, drinking a cup of coffee, smiling, and looking very pleased with himself, like the cat that got the cream. Saoirse's words from their dinner conversation at the Sunset Lounge the other week floated reluctantly back to Ransom, and something sharp and unpleasant tightened in his chest. *"The two of you are always sitting next to each other at the breakfast table, whispering together. You're not sweet on him?"*

"Ransom," Salvador called out as soon as he saw him. He scooted back his chair and rose to greet him. "It's nice to see you."

"Santos," Ransom said and crossed the room to shake his hand. His smile didn't quite reach his eyes. "How are you?"

"I can hardly complain," Salvador said, glancing back at Ana. "Good food, good company." He smiled at Ransom. "Come, join us. We were just finishing breakfast and talking about our plans for the day."

"Yes, Salvador is being boring," Ana said, taking a bite of her French toast.

"I'm afraid I've disappointed Ana," Salvador said. "I have errands to run in town."

"On our one day off!" Ana said, exasperated. "Meanwhile, I plan to be as lazy and unproductive as humanly possible."

"And how does one accomplish that?" Ransom asked.

"Guilty pleasure reads, lots of napping, and eating copious amounts of food with zero nutritional value," Ana said. "But I plan to start by hanging by the pool. It's beautiful out."

Ransom glanced toward the nearest window, where sunlight was streaming in. "It is nice out," he agreed. "Mind if I join you?"

"The more the merrier," Ana said. "Besides, it *is* technically your pool."

It was a hot day in the dead of summer, the sun blazing in the sky, so bright you had to squint to see, and so Ransom kept his Ray-Bans on as he floated on a tube in the shallow end and waited for Ana. The water felt pleasant in the heat—lukewarm. He tried to remember the last time he'd been in this pool. It'd been years. Theo had been alive, that he could recall. Yes, Theo had had friends staying over from college, and they'd played a game of chicken in the shallow end, not far from where he was now. Ransom recalled gripping the knees of a girl he didn't know as she sat on his shoulders and tried to wrest another girl from her place on Theo's shoulders.

"Howdy."

Ransom looked up to see Ana by one of the sun loungers, a T-shirt on over her swimsuit. Her hair was up in a ponytail, and she had a book in her hand.

"What're you reading?" Ransom asked.

"Probably something you wouldn't approve of," Ana said. She held up the cover. "*The Velvet Promise*. It's a romance novel."

"Are you not getting in?" he asked.

Ana hesitated a moment, as if she wasn't sure. "It's roasting out," she said finally. "I'll take a quick dip."

She pulled her T-shirt off over her head. She had a plain black one-piece on underneath. She was toned and lean and had more of an athletic build—straight with muted curves.

Ransom got out of the tube and held it out for her near the stairs as Ana waded into the shallow end.

"All yours," he said.

"What a gentleman," Ana said.

He helped her into it and then hung on to one end as she floated. Together, they drifted slowly across the pool.

"Is that what you normally read?" Ransom asked, nodding toward the book on her sun lounger. "Romance novels?"

"I read all sorts of things," Ana said.

"So what's your favorite book?" Ransom asked.

"Judy Blume's *Are You There, God? It's Me, Margaret*," Ana said without hesitation.

"A children's book?" Ransom asked.

"It's not just a children's book," Ana said. "It's the first book I remember reading that I completely lost myself in. My cousin lent it to me. She was a few years older than me, and she was obsessed with it, and I wanted to be just like her, so I read it too. And I just—I'd never had an experience like that before. Reading that book, it was like someone was in my head. They had written down my thoughts. My fears. My inhibitions. Everything I was insecure about or wondered about. I felt . . . understood in a way I hadn't before. Like, maybe I wasn't as weird or strange as I thought I might be. Maybe there were other people out there who were going through something similar. What about you?" Ana asked.

"*The Fountainhead*," Ransom said.

Ana made a buzzer sound, like he had answered incorrectly.

"What?" Ransom asked.

"*The Fountainhead* is not your favorite book," Ana said.

"Yes, it is."

"No, it's not," Ana said. "This is not a college application or a formal interview where you have to impress me with how smart and well read you are. I want your real, human answer. If you were stranded on a desert island and there was only one book you could have with you that you would have to read over and over again for the rest of your life, what would it be?"

Ransom thought for a moment. "Still *The Fountainhead*," he said.

"Unbelievable."

"I didn't give you a hard time about your favorite book," Ransom said.

"Yes, you did. You called it a children's book."

"To be fair, it *is* a children's book," Ransom said. "But you chose that book because of how it made you feel, and I respect that. I chose *The Fountainhead* because of how it makes me think. If I could only read one book for the rest of my life, it would be one full of ideas and moral complexity."

"Fine," Ana said, after thinking a moment. "I concede that *The Fountainhead* is a legitimate choice for your favorite book, and I'm sorry for mocking you."

"Thank you," Ransom said.

"You've really motored us a long way from where we started," Ana said, glancing around them. "Are we in the deep end now?"

"Yes," Ransom said.

"In all seriousness," Ana said, "please don't tip me over. I can't actually swim."

"What?"

"I can't swim," Ana repeated.

"Then what are you doing in the pool?" Ransom asked.

"I normally stay in the shallow end, where I can touch," Ana said. "Or, you know, hence the raft."

"That doesn't seem safe," Ransom said.

Ana shrugged. "If you don't leave your comfort zone every once in a while, you never really live."

"Yes, well, if leaving your comfort zone means potentially drowning, I'd stay put, or at least wear a life preserver."

Ana laughed.

"Jesus Christ," Ransom said, steering them back toward the shallow end. He felt immediately relieved as soon as his feet touched the bottom of the pool again. He steered the raft over to the side of the pool.

Ana tried to lift herself out of the raft, but she had sunk so far into it that for a moment, she struggled.

"I'm stuck," Ana laughed.

Ransom reached in and scooped her up. She was light and small in his arms. He lifted her onto the edge of the pool, where she sat, dangling her legs into the water.

"You're so miniature," Ransom said. "I could put you in my pocket and carry you around."

Ana laughed. "Stop," she said. "I'm a perfectly normal-sized person." She looked at him, and he held her gaze.

He reached up and tucked her wet hair behind her ear. She didn't flinch; she didn't look away. She looked steadily back at him. He trailed his finger down her neck, traced the curve of her bare shoulder. It was not remotely the most physically intimate thing he had ever done with a girl, but for some reason, it felt that way.

"Ana," he said, his voice thick in his throat. "I don't think I want to just be your friend."

She looked up at him, and something in her eyes made him believe she felt the same way.

"But we shook on it," Ana said. "Remember?"

For once, he didn't care who saw, or what they thought, or the things they might say. He just did the thing that he had so often denied himself—he did exactly what he wanted.

He leaned forward and kissed her.

CHAPTER TWENTY-FOUR

PRESENT

There was an incessant buzzing on Church's nightstand.

At first, he was so deep in his REM sleep he didn't hear it, so when he finally stirred to consciousness and grappled in the dark for his phone on his bedside table, it had already stopped. When the buzzing started up again, not two seconds later, Church rubbed his eyes and answered it without looking at the screen.

"Hello?"

"Detective Church," the voice said. It was male, stilted and icy, and Church's mind struggled to place it, still half caught in the stupor of sleep. "I trust you've read this morning's paper?"

Church glanced over groggily at the alarm clock on his nightstand. Who on God's green earth would be calling him this early? It was only 6:15 a.m., and he had had a late night. He'd been in the office until nearly 11:00 p.m., reviewing case files.

"You talked so much about the integrity of this case, Detective," the voice went on. "The last time we spoke, you went on and on about how you couldn't share any details with us so as to protect the sanctity of the investigation, did you not? So imagine my surprise when I opened my paper this morning to see all the things you could not tell us printed there in black and white for all to read."

"Senator Towers?" Church said, his mind finally catching up with him. He coughed to clear his throat. "I'm sorry—I'm not sure what you're talking about."

"The paper," the senator said, the irritation evident in his voice. "The *San Luis Obispo Herald*. They printed it this morning."

Church sat hurriedly up in bed. He put his phone on speaker so he could see his screen and thumbed opened a browser. He quickly googled *San Luis Obispo Herald Saoirse Towers*.

The headline struck him like a cold slap to the face: New Lead in Saoirse Towers Case: Was the Second Unidentified Body Staff?

He kept reading:

> Police have reason to believe the unidentified remains discovered on the Towers family property last month may be those of a staff member hired to work the party at which Saoirse, and this unidentified victim, were presumably killed. A probable cause affidavit filed on Wednesday reveals the victim was male, between twenty-five and thirty-five years old, and approximately 6 feet tall. The affidavit was filed with a search warrant requesting access to the Towers family tax returns from 1982, in an effort to track down the staff members who were hired to work the event.
> This would not be the first time a staff member attending to the Towers family has ended up dead. Readers may recall, in 1978, that a young woman working at a hotel where Theo and Ransom Towers were staying drowned while sailing on their yacht.

Church stopped reading.

"Shit," Church muttered under his breath. "Senator, I can promise you I didn't know anything about this," Church said.

"This came from your department, did it not?" Ransom asked.

"Yes, it did, but—"

"I've been cooperative, haven't I?" Ransom cut in. "Any questions you asked, I answered. I opened the door to my home. I instructed my staff to be open with you as well. When you told me you couldn't tell me anything about the investigation or the body found in my own backyard, I let it go. I acquiesced. And this is what I get in return? Details I wasn't allowed to know, splashed across the front page of the paper? Private truths about my family, out there for the whole world to read about? It's a transgression of my privacy, of my family's privacy, and our trust."

Church was silent for a moment. "You're right," he said. "You're absolutely right. This shouldn't have happened, and I can give you my word nothing like this will ever happen again."

"Your word means very little to me now," Ransom said. "Detective, you will find me less than cooperative going forward. I'm afraid both my understanding and my patience have run out."

And with that, the senator unceremoniously hung up.

There was a bar called Pour House on State Street in Santa Barbara, not far from BFS, where Church and Nisha met up occasionally for drinks to talk about the cases they were working on together. They'd throw darts, knock around a few balls on the pool table, sip their pints at the bar. And case talk would inevitably lead to talking about other things. Conversation with Nisha felt as easy as breathing—never forced.

Tonight, they didn't make it to the dartboard or the pool table; they just sat at the end of the bar with their pint glasses of beer and talked.

"I don't understand," Nisha said, taking a sip of her beer. "How did that reporter get all that information about the second body anyway?"

"From the search warrant that Leland filed for the Towerses' tax returns," Church said. "You have to file a probable cause affidavit, basically explaining to the judge why we need access to the documents we're requesting."

"And the public has access to those?" Nisha asked.

"No," Church said. "I mean, not if you petition to have them sealed, which any detective worth his salt would have, in this case."

"Ah," Nisha said.

"It was a rookie mistake," Church seethed. "And it's fucked me. The senator won't even return my calls now."

What really got under Church's skin was that Leland should never have been assigned to the case in the first place. He didn't have the experience. Church had told Wallis that from the get-go. If Wallis had only listened to him then, they wouldn't be in this mess now.

"I'm sorry," Nisha said. "That's awful. But—" She paused.

Church looked over at her. He cocked an eyebrow. "But?"

"Okay, just hear me out on this," Nisha said, raising her hands defensively. "I know Leland is super green, but I do think he's trying. He really wants to do well, and yeah, this time he fucked up, but it was an honest mistake, and he owned up to it. And, from what you're telling me, the sheriff and Sergeant Wallis really went at him hard for this. So, maybe, you could cut him some slack."

Church exhaled. He recalled with particularly cutting clarity the other day in Sergeant Wallis's office, as he had sat next to Leland while both the sheriff and the sarge basically chewed Leland a new asshole, and Leland just sat there, the tips of his ears red, looking chastened and embarrassed. He reminded Church in that moment so much of a wounded golden retriever, and while Church hadn't been able to bring himself to add to the barrage, he also had not come to his defense.

"I just think," Nisha went on, "let he among us who's never made an error when they're tired and overworked throw the first stone. That's it. That's all. I'll step down from my soapbox now."

"Thank you," Church said. He didn't want to talk about it anymore, didn't want to even think about it. "So what's new with you? I trust you've had a better week than me?"

"Well," Nisha said excitedly, "we're trying 3D forensic facial reconstruction on our John Doe."

"3D facial reconstruction?" Church asked.

"Yeah," Nisha said. "You basically digitize the skull with a CT scanner, and then you map the face onto it, with the help of tissue markers. It's painstaking. It takes *forever*. But it's a good idea, and it's worth a shot."

"That sounds promising," Church said.

"Leland suggested it, actually," Nisha said. "It was something he read about. He's been really focused ever since—well, you know. Head down. Serious."

"I don't really want to talk about Leland anymore," Church said. He took a drink of his beer. "You know what I've been wondering, though?" Church asked after a moment, changing the subject.

"What's that?" Nisha said.

"What made you want to spend all your time with dead people?"

Nisha laughed. "I'll tell you, but you'll probably think I'm morbid."

"I already think you're morbid."

"Well, then, good. The pressure's off, I guess," she said. "I actually went to school to be a dentist originally."

Church snorted, almost spitting out his beer.

"I know," Nisha said, "it's hard to picture. Anyway, first year of dental school, you have to take anatomy with the med students. You basically spend the semester dissecting a human body. It was my first time seeing one. It's quite a shock to the system, you know? The smell of formaldehyde and methanol from the embalming fluid, the feel of your scalpel cutting through skin, which doesn't feel or look like skin at all, really. It's tough and leathery, and the tissue and muscles are gray underneath."

She told him about the dissection of the body, how they kept the face and hands covered with a towel while they were working. Her lab partners didn't like to think about the body on the table as a man who had once lived. They didn't want to think of him as someone's father or brother or son, though of course he had been at least one of those things. They tried hard not to know him.

But, to Nisha, that was impossible. The human body was so particular. From the plaque in the arteries in the abdomen, she knew the man often ate red meat, and from the scars on the walls of his liver, she knew he enjoyed drinking. On his left leg, she discovered a healed femur shaft fracture. Nisha thought about that for months. What could this man have done to break the longest, strongest bone in his body? All over the body, it was like that. She found indications of stories, subtle signs of who the man had been.

"My classmates wanted to think of this man as just a body, but that didn't interest me at all," Nisha said. "I couldn't separate the body from the man, from the stories that made him. That was it for me. I changed my major the next semester. What about you?" Nisha asked. "What made you want to become a detective?"

Church took a sip of his beer. He so rarely answered this particular question honestly with anyone, but something about Nisha made him want to tell her the truth.

"When I was twelve," Church said, "me and my little brother, Bobby, and the neighborhood kids would play capture the flag in the park after school on Tuesdays. There was this one day in September, right after school started, and it was just like this perfect game. I stole the flag right out from under Joey McIntyre's nose and ran it all the way back to home base before he could tag me. Anyway, we decided to play another round. My brother, Bobby, had to go home early. We took turns helping my mom set the table for dinner, and that night was his turn. I was supposed to go home with him, but I didn't want to leave. It was still light out, and we lived three blocks from the park, and Bobby had his bike. He whined about it—he was sore that I got to stay and play and he had to go home early. I told him I'd watch him to make sure he got home all right. There was a clear sight line from the park to our house. I watched him walk his bike across the park to the street, and then the game started and I turned away. That was the last time I ever saw him."

What killed Church was that if he'd just been looking, like he promised Bobby he would, he would have seen him.

"Mr. Miller, one of our neighbors, was out watering his lawn, and he saw Bobby straddling his bike on the side of the road, talking to a man in a red Cadillac," Church said. "He looked away to turn off the hose, and when he looked back, both the Cadillac and Bobby were gone. They never found the man in the red Cadillac, or Bobby. He was ten."

Church didn't tell many people this story, because he knew they would try to fill the silence that followed. They would grapple for the right words to make it better, a balm to soothe the pain. They would have told him how sorry they were, how terrible it was, how they couldn't even imagine. How brave he was to do what he did every day, how Bobby would be proud.

Words that scraped at the surface of the tragedy that had shaped his life. How hollow and insufficient they would feel. And how much more alone he would feel in their wake. Because the words were true—it was terrible, and they couldn't imagine. But the words were also false. He wasn't brave. And Bobby wasn't proudly looking down on him from somewhere up there. Bobby was dead, buried somewhere, he was sure, in an unmarked grave in the cold, hard ground.

But Nisha didn't say anything. She understood the insufficiency of words. Instead, she sat there in silence with him, holding the weight of it all, and for a moment, he didn't feel so alone.

"Sometimes, I wish for the unforgivable," Church said quietly. He had never said this part out loud to anyone before. "I wish that Bobby was dead. That someone would find his body buried somewhere."

Missing was the worst sort of purgatory. For three years after Bobby went missing, his mother had insisted that someone always be at the house. They couldn't go on vacation or out to dinner or to a Sunday matinee, because someone had to be home for Bobby. His mother's worst fear was that Bobby would call and no one would answer, or that he'd come home to a locked and empty house. What would he think, she'd wonder—how would he feel? To be lost and come home to find his family gone, out to a nice meal or enjoying a ball game? It was unfathomable to her that they could do anything but wait.

Sometimes, hope seemed to Church a poison that was killing his mother slowly. If she could just let go, if she could just find peace, if she could just move on. But she couldn't or wouldn't—he wasn't sure which. His mother woke every morning and knelt next to her bed to pray. Hope—she consumed it like a drug. There were cases of the few who were found, the few who came back. Steven Stayner, a boy who had been taken when he was just seven years old, had reappeared seven years later, hitchhiking forty miles to a police station while his captor was at work. There was Jaycee Dugard, who disappeared off the street near her family's home in South Lake Tahoe when she was eleven while on her way to her school bus stop. She was found eighteen years later. And Elizabeth Smart, taken from her own home at the age of fourteen and found walking in broad daylight on a public street alongside her captors nine months later. Church's mother watched the news broadcasts, sitting up in her La-Z-Boy, a blanket draped over her lap, the TV screen casting a dull glow in their living room. She cut the news articles out of the paper, folded them up, and kept them in the Bible next to her bed.

Church did not like to imagine his brother afraid or alone or in pain. He wished for a quick and merciful death, that Bobby had died shortly after he was taken, before he realized the sinister intentions of his captor. Something quick and painless. But most of all, Church wished for certainty, for answers to the questions that plagued his mind when he lay down to sleep at night. He wished for an end to missing, for an end to waiting, for an end to hope.

Church had gone to therapy exactly once after Bobby disappeared. He hadn't had a choice. His grandmother had made him, determined that he wouldn't become the zombielike shell of a person his mother had, so crippled by grief that she was unable to live her life or care for the son she had left. The therapist was a middle-aged woman who sat across from him on a scratchy twill couch. He'd told her about his mother, how she kept Bobby's room exactly the same, how she stayed up late with the porch light on in case Bobby came back.

"Grief is like being stranded on a mountain," the therapist had said. "We all have to find our own way down."

He thought the words she didn't say—that some people never found their way down at all.

Now, Nisha raised her tumbler of beer.

"To Bobby," she said.

Church raised his glass too.

"To Bobby," he echoed.

CHAPTER TWENTY-FIVE

SEPTEMBER 1958

Dear Scarlet,

I'm sorry that it's taken longer than I intended to write to you, but let me start by allaying any worries you might have—all is well here. We have been busy to distraction these past several weeks, and that is the only reason for my delay in writing to you. So let me hastily fill you in, as I'm sure you're eager to hear all our goings-on.

The honeymoon was a dream. We stayed in a small seaside town called Minori, in a hotel a stone's throw from the beach. There was much to see and do there, including visiting the ruins of an ancient Roman villa and a very old church. The food was better than you could imagine. All the pasta was handmade, and the sauce came from the best San Marzano tomatoes grown in the countryside. I'm sure I could eat nothing but that for days on end and never grow tired of it. We all enjoyed ourselves very much and were sorry to leave.

Since returning from Italy, we've settled in London. Mr. Sinclair's townhome is large and grand and you cannot beat the location. Astrid says the furnishings and decor reek of bachelorhood, so she is determined to do up everything in a style that suits her, and Mr. Sinclair has given her free rein to do so. The remodel has kept Astrid very busy, but she has not neglected her duties as a wife. She has hosted many dinner parties for Mr. Sinclair and his friends and associates, and we have gone out to two operas and a ballet since we arrived. Astrid has been very well received here; everyone remarks on her beauty, style, and her good manners.

I realized that before I left I did not have a chance to put your mind at ease about the cut of Astrid's wedding dress. I know you thought it was too low, but I did see at least half a dozen women at the reception whose gowns were at least a half inch lower than Astrid's, and so I do not think anyone thought that her gown strained the bounds of propriety.

I hope you are well and I would love to hear what you have been up to since we've been gone. How is Verity doing at school? Did Charles's conference go well? How is Birdie? I miss you all so much.

Yours faithfully,

Florence

Florence reread the letter for the hundredth time. She could not find it within herself to outright lie to Scarlet, but she felt comfortable omitting certain truths. For instance, she'd written: *There was much to see and do there, including visiting the ruins of an ancient Roman villa and a very old church.* That was a factual statement. She didn't mention that Astrid and RJ had neglected doing either of these things and instead had spent their entire honeymoon drinking and dancing and staying out all night. Writing that would only give Scarlet a conniption, so it was best to leave it out.

Florence also left out the part about what had happened in the hotel room on their last night in Italy. She didn't know how to write about that. Neither Astrid nor RJ had ever mentioned it since. They acted like it hadn't happened or, if it had happened, that it didn't matter. And maybe it didn't. Florence had never been married before; how was she to know what a marriage was supposed to look like from the inside? The Bible said, "Wives, submit yourselves unto your own husbands, as unto the Lord." Astrid and Florence had laughed at RJ when they shouldn't have. Maybe it was right for him to be angry. In the Bible, even God was wrathful when people behaved wrongly. Maybe, if Florence told Scarlet what happened, Scarlet would be angry at Astrid for misbehaving. Or maybe she would be angry at RJ, but what then? Florence was sure Scarlet would never countenance a divorce. And was it really Florence's place to stir up strife in Astrid and RJ's marriage because of her misgivings of something she had witnessed? She was just a witness, after all, not an active party. It seemed devious to intercede.

Besides, all seemed well, or well enough. The townhome that Mr. Sinclair owned in Trafalgar Square really was beautiful—three stories tall, with coffered ceilings and a private garden. And he had given Astrid free rein to do with it what she pleased, with seemingly no budgetary restrictions. Astrid had hired two designers, one for the upstairs rooms and one for the downstairs, and an architect to enlarge the dining room. She threw herself into redecorating with a feverish passion, with fabric swatches, wallpaper samples, and catalogs unfurled on the coffee table in the living room, on her nightstand, in the downstairs hall. Twice before the construction started on the dining room, she had hosted a dinner for RJ and his associates from the bank and their wives. Everyone seemed to adore her—a pretty young American, lively and vivacious.

At a party one evening, Astrid and Florence were introduced to the Countess of Sandington, the first member of nobility they had ever met. She was very beautiful, with blond hair, striking blue eyes, and a long white neck.

"Cressida, please," the countess said, when they were introduced. "I inherited the title with my marriage, and anytime someone calls me Countess, I still look around the room to see who they're referring to."

"Yes, I know what you mean," Astrid said. "I'm still not used to being called Mrs. Sinclair. Every time someone uses it, I look around the room for RJ's mother."

The countess laughed. "I'm so glad to finally meet you," she said. "RJ and I are very dear friends."

"Well then," Astrid said, "you should come to dinner sometime. Any friend of RJ's is a friend of mine."

Later, Astrid and Florence found themselves in the midst of their usual group—the wives of RJ's bank associates, Gemma Thompson and Eloise Winthrop.

"Doesn't it bother you?" Gemma asked, her gaze sliding across the room and landing on RJ and the countess standing very close together, talking.

"What?" Astrid asked, following her gaze. "My husband talking to the countess? Oh, I've met Cressida. She's lovely."

"It would drive me crazy," Eloise said. "The way they're always seeking each other out."

"They're good friends," Astrid said. "I'm of the mind that members of the opposite sex can be friendly without there being anything untoward going on."

"You're more generous than I would be," Gemma said.

"I mean, she's very pretty," Astrid admitted, "but I hardly think I'm an ugly duckling in comparison."

"Yes, but I was referring to the fact that they were previously *engaged*," Gemma said. "I won't let George talk to his ex-girlfriends, let alone an ex-fiancée."

Florence was very glad she didn't have a drink in her hand, because she would have dropped it. She looked over at Astrid. Astrid had her lips pinched together slightly, but only for a moment before she smoothed them into a complacent smile.

"Did RJ ever tell you why Cressida ended things between them?" Eloise asked.

Perhaps she laughed at him, Florence thought but kept her mouth shut.

Astrid shrugged. "They weren't as compatible as they thought at first," she said. "It was amicable and mutual. Nothing salacious, I'm sorry to report. I love a good juicy piece of gossip as much as the next person, but there's nothing of that sort here."

She smiled and steered the conversation elsewhere, and it wasn't until much later, when it was time to leave, that she made her way across the room to RJ.

"Shall we go?" Astrid asked, keeping her voice light.

"Why? Aren't you having a good time?" RJ said.

"We have tickets to the ballet," Astrid reminded him.

"Who gives a fuck about the bloody ballet?"

"I do," Astrid said. "I've been looking forward to it all week."

"All right," RJ said with a sigh. He checked his watch. "I'll get you a cab. You go on ahead, and I'll meet you there."

"Curtain's in half an hour," Astrid said.

"I know, darling. I've plenty of time."

He hailed Astrid and Florence a cab.

At the theater, Astrid and Florence took their seats in the upper gallery. When the houselights dimmed, Astrid glanced back expectantly toward the doors.

"He probably got caught in traffic," she whispered to Florence.

Svetlana Beriosova was dancing the lead that night—Giselle, a young peasant girl who fell in love with a nobleman who had disguised himself as another. At the end of the first act, she realized that her beloved had misled her: he was not who he claimed to be; he was already betrothed to another. Svetlana descended into madness as she danced an adagio, whipping her pale, willowy limbs into a creamy pirouette, dipping low into an elastic plié. Florence followed the smooth lines of her body, saw the way her braid had come undone, the dark halo of curls that fell to her shoulders. The straps of her dress were loose, and even from a distance she could see the pink buds of her breasts showing through the gossamer tunic. Giselle's beloved watched her from the sidelines as she fluttered across center stage. Everyone watched her—her mother; her admirer, Hilarion, who had tried to warn her; and the villagers. They all watched, unable to console her, to stop her descent. She was despair; she was heartbreak—everyone understood that; she didn't have to say one word. When she collapsed onstage and the curtain fell, Florence looked over at Astrid and saw her surreptitiously wipe a tear from her eye. No one else saw; the theater was dark, and the seat Astrid had saved next to her was still empty.

CHAPTER
TWENTY-SIX

AUGUST 1982

Ransom was at Cliffhaven again that weekend. He seemed to be there all the time these days, which Saoirse found irritating. It was the party planning. He couldn't leave well enough alone. He had to know everything, down to the smallest detail. And he was always rearranging things, making adjustments behind her back. For instance, she'd put the raw bar outside on the patio, and he'd moved it inside.

"Who doesn't like fresh air and caviar?" she asked him.

But he'd argued it would be too warm out and that it would last longer, be fresher, in the house's AC.

Saoirse had wanted hot-pink dinner napkins, but Ransom called the color crass and replaced them with a pale blush color; he'd nixed the sword-swallowers and fire-breathers.

"This is not a circus," he'd said.

Now he had called her into his study, stood across from her as she took a seat in front of his desk. Uncle Bass was there too. He took the seat next to her, leaned toward her amicably.

"Here you go, my girl," Bass said, handing her a portfolio. "Ransom and I have been working on this for a while, and we think this is something that everybody can be happy with."

She flipped it open on her lap, skimmed the pages. To her surprise, it was not about the party. It was the plan they had discussed that day on the beach—how she might divest her shares in Bass Corp. and invest it elsewhere. Only, it was also decidedly *not* what they had discussed.

"Two and a half percent a year over five years," Saoirse said. "Until I reach a holding of twenty percent, which I would retain."

"We can give you a seat on the board as well," Bass said, sounding very satisfied with himself. "Think about what you might accomplish with that influence? Together, we could steer the company in the right direction, to a more ethical treatment of the animals—increasing stall sizes, incorporating grazing periods—things of that nature."

"A more ethical slaughterhouse?" Saoirse said. "If you still plan to off Wilbur, I doubt it makes much difference to him whether he has an extra few feet in his stall to stretch his legs."

"We could introduce a vegetarian meal option," Bass went on, keeping his voice upbeat, optimistic. "Some sort of pasta-and-veggie dish, perhaps."

"This isn't what we talked about," Saoirse said.

"Saoirse, be reasonable," Bass said. "This plan reduces your share of Bass Corp. by nearly forty percent, freeing up a large amount of assets to do with what you want—support your PETA, perhaps. You don't want to divest any more than that. You'd no longer be a significant shareholder in the company."

"I don't *want* to be a significant shareholder," Saoirse said. "I don't want any part of it. I thought I made that very clear."

Bass sighed, struggling to remain in control of his temper. He looked at Ransom, but Ransom said nothing.

"I know you feel that way now, but in time, you may come to regret that decision," Bass said, turning his attention back to Saoirse. "We're trying to protect you from making a life-altering mistake."

"I would gladly welcome a mistake—a regret—if it were my own," Saoirse said. "What I cannot live with is going contrary to what I believe is right, to live in opposition to my own beliefs."

"This is not just about you!" Bass snapped.

Saoirse sat back in her chair, startled.

"I'm sorry," Bass said. He sighed heavily again and looked pointedly at Ransom. "Do you want to jump in here?" Bass asked, irritated.

Saoirse looked at her brother. She couldn't figure out what was going on between the two of them. Usually, Bass and Ransom were in lockstep. But today, she could feel the silent tension simmering between them.

Ransom took a deep breath and said evenly, "If you divest all of your shares at once, Saoirse, it could be catastrophic for Bass Corp. It could cause the price of shares to free-fall. I don't know that the company would survive it."

"This is not just my legacy," Bass said. "Your father helped me start this company, to build it into what it is today. You talk about being true to your beliefs, and I understand that—admire it, even. But what of family and loyalty? Do you not believe in those too?"

Saoirse couldn't breathe. It felt like someone had wrapped their hand around her throat and was slowly constricting it. In her mind's eye, she saw her father's face—how he had looked the last time she had seen him. She was thirteen, sprawled out on the couch in the living room, watching something on TV. He had come in to say goodbye—he and her mother were going to Catalina for the weekend. She'd been so preoccupied with her show that she hadn't even initially looked up. He'd leaned over the couch, kissed her forehead. It was only then that Saoirse glanced up at him. She could see a spot on his neck, just below his chin, where he had nicked himself while shaving that morning and stuck a piece of tissue to stop the bleeding. He must have forgotten about it. She reached up and brushed off the tissue.

"You're a mess," she said.

"What would I do without you?" he asked.

"Walk around with tissue on your face, probably."

"I love you," he said. "Be good."

Be good. The last thing her father had ever said to her. Such seemingly simple instructions, and yet they weren't.

What did *be good* mean in this context? What was the "good" thing to be done? Was it to follow her conscience? Or to protect those she loved? Both of those things in themselves seemed good, but what if they were at odds with one another? What then?

Ransom cleared his throat. "There comes a time for all of us, Saoirse, when we have to lay aside our own desires and self-interests and think of what's best for the family," he said. "We all have to make sacrifices."

Sacrifices. What sacrifice had Ransom made in this? What sacrifice had Bass made?

"Stop," Saoirse said. "Just stop. Both of you."

Saoirse couldn't help but feel that she was being manipulated. It boiled her blood, the hypocrisy of it, for both of them to sit there and preach about how wrong it was for her to act in her own self-interest, when they had clearly only thought about themselves when putting this plan together. Their strategy had not been to give her what she had asked for while looking out for her financial well-being. No. It had been to give her as little as possible—just enough to make it look like they were placating her—while still protecting their own interests.

"Don't sit here and try and use my own father to—to emotionally coerce me into doing something that only serves you," Saoirse said. "I said I would listen to your plan, and I have. But I cannot in good conscience follow it. And I think if Daddy were here, he would—he would be on my side in this."

"Saoirse—" Bass said.

"No," Saoirse said, cutting him off. She'd done her fair share of listening, and now it was time for both of them to listen to her. "I'm going to divest my shares in Bass Corp. when I turn eighteen. All of them. And as quickly as possible," Saoirse said. She stood and deposited the portfolio where it belonged—into the trash can next to Ransom's desk—as both men watched.

The sad truth, Saoirse thought, was that if either of them had shown any consideration for her and her feelings in this plan, then maybe she would have done the same for them. But they hadn't.

And maybe that was the problem—they didn't know what it felt like for someone else to make a decision on their behalf that greatly impacted them, one that they themselves had no say in. One that they couldn't do anything about.

But it was certainly time that they learned.

CHAPTER
TWENTY-SEVEN

AUGUST 1982

Well," Ransom said after Saoirse had stormed out, "that could have gone better."

He was used to seeing his sister upset by now. The past two years had been especially hard, full of loss and disappointment, isolation and restraint—and she had obviously taken this financial plan that he and Bass had carefully drawn up for her as yet another blow, even though it hadn't been meant that way in the slightest. It irked Ransom, burrowed under his skin, that even though everything he'd ever done was to protect her, Saoirse seemed determined to interpret it as some kind of punishment.

What Saoirse didn't seem to realize or appreciate was that all this had been equally hard on him—these were decisions he didn't want to have to make. He took no joy in taking things away from her, in removing her from school and sequestering her at Cliffhaven, in participating in this vicious war between them, this tense, cross-country chess game that they had been engaged in for two years now. He hadn't asked for any of this. If he had his way, he'd be Saoirse's brother, plain and simple— nothing more, completely uncomplicated—perhaps someone she felt she could turn to and confide in, instead of her jailkeeper whom she railed against.

"I need a drink," Bass said. He got up and crossed Ransom's study to the liquor cabinet, busied himself with pouring a glass of brandy, neat.

"I think we pushed her too hard," Ransom said. "We should give her some time to cool off, and then I'll talk to her, try to get her to come around."

Bass took a long sip of his brandy as Ransom surveyed him from across the room. His relationship with Bass had always been easy, uncomplicated. They'd always been on the same side of things, seen things the same way, implicitly trusted one another. But ever since their heated argument on the tennis court a few weeks prior, things hadn't been the same between them. There was a silent tension simmering beneath the surface, thin and taut, that they danced around, pretending it didn't exist. Ransom wasn't sure how to address it without giving ground that he wasn't willing to give. Bass had questioned his judgment, scolded him like a child. He couldn't let Bass think that he could control him, tell him what to do. He was a grown man, after all.

"Maybe we're going about this the wrong way," Bass said after a while. "Maybe there's a simpler answer staring us right in the face."

"Like what?" Ransom asked.

"We could, perhaps, simply not release her assets when she turns eighteen," Bass said.

"How?"

"I don't know, but there must be something—some sort of legal precedent we can lean into here," Bass said. "After all, she's a teenager, and this is a large sum of money at stake. She's clearly not emotionally equipped to handle that responsibility."

Ransom thought about this. The trust had converted into an irrevocable trust upon his parents' death, and they hadn't placed any contingencies on Saoirse's inheritance other than age.

"The trust doesn't give you that sort of discretion," Ransom said. "Saoirse could file to have you removed as trustee. She could sue."

"It would buy us some time at least," Bass said. "Time for her to come around."

"I don't think she'll ever come around if you do that," Ransom said.

"Well, what if we had her declared incompetent?" Bass asked. "We could set up a conservatorship."

"On what grounds?"

"I don't know!" Bass said, slamming his glass down on the table. The amber liquid sloshed over the sides, onto the wood. "Christ," Bass said. He put his head in his hands. "What was Charles thinking?"

There was only so much they could do. Ransom was slowly, reluctantly, coming to that realization. They were running out of options. They were running out of time.

"I'm at my wit's end, trying to keep this family from throwing it all away," Bass said. "Why won't anyone listen to me? Why won't anyone listen to reason?"

In that moment, Bass looked every bit his age standing there, leaning over the liquor cabinet for support. Crumpled. Wilted. Old.

Ransom crossed the room to him, put his hand on his shoulder. "We'll figure something out," Ransom said. "She'll come around."

He said it even though he didn't fully believe it, that Saoirse would change her mind, listen to reason. He was beginning to think she would never come around. And what option did that leave them then?

"I had one of my guys look into Ana," Bass said.

It took Ransom a moment to process Bass's words. "What?" he said.

"I had a bad feeling about her, Ransom, and I couldn't let it go."

Ransom dropped his hand from Bass's shoulder. "I thought I made my sentiments on that matter perfectly clear," Ransom said.

Bass turned around to face him. He looked like he'd regained some of his strength, some of his composure. "You did," Bass said. "But I knew I'd have no peace of mind until I'd at least done my due diligence."

"So you deliberately went against my wishes?"

"Just hear me out—"

"No," Ransom said. "No, I will not."

"Are you as foolish and obstinate as your sister?" Bass asked, exasperated. "What hold has this girl got on you that you will not listen to reason? The Ransom I knew cared about the facts. And this is what I have to tell you, Ransom. This is what I'm bringing you: the facts."

If being in politics had taught Ransom anything, it was that there was no such thing as cold, hard, objective facts. It was all in how you presented them. You could spin anything in your favor or against someone else. And Bass had made his dislike of Ana plain enough; Ransom knew the way he would spin things, whatever he had. How he could make things look. This wasn't about Ana, not really. It was about control. Bass wanted things a certain way, and he would keep pushing until he got it.

"I don't want to hear," Ransom said. He turned away from Bass, but Bass grabbed him by his arm, hard.

"She's been lying to you, Ransom," Bass said sternly. "About everything."

Ransom tried to shut out the sound of Bass's voice. He didn't want to listen; he didn't want to know. "Remove your hand," Ransom said, "or I will remove it for you."

Bass removed his hand, but he kept talking. "Ransom," Bass said, "at least hear this: her name isn't Ana Rojas."

PART THREE

CHAPTER TWENTY-EIGHT

MARCH 1960

Florence's letters to Scarlet became fewer and farther between. There was more going on that she had to omit than there was that she could relay. Just the other day, Astrid had told her how RJ had stumbled home again at two in the morning. She heard him take off his shoes at the edge of the bed—two loud clunks as they hit the floor. And then he had crawled in next to her still fully dressed and put his arms around her. She could feel his want sticking into the small of her back, smell the whiskey on his breath. She told him if he was going to do it, to hurry up and get it over with so she could go back to sleep.

"And then, of course, he just got charming," Astrid said, taking a long drag on her cigarette.

RJ told Astrid she was impossible to please, and Astrid told him with the way he was built, he couldn't please any woman. Florence didn't have the gall to ask if that were true.

"It's terrible, the things we say to each other," Astrid said. "The things we don't mean. The things we do."

Scarlet was eager for news of grandchildren; she hinted at it in nearly every letter. Florence suspected this was because Scarlet thought that motherhood might tame Astrid in a way that marriage had not, that it might finally settle her.

My friend Mrs. Bennet was here the other day, Scarlet wrote. *You remember her—she has a daughter around Astrid's age. She and her husband just welcomed a baby boy. I wonder when Astrid might be so blessed as to enjoy a similar happiness? There is nothing like a child to humble a person, to give them proper perspective.*

And in another letter: *When you come home for Christmas this year, I wonder if I might need to air out the nursery and have the maid assemble the crib? I know it is still several months away, but these things do take time and I want to be sure I have the proper notice.*

Florence didn't know how to answer her. Privately, she wished that a baby would not enter into the mix. With RJ's drinking, the other women, and the bruises that Astrid hid under long sleeves and silk scarves in the summertime and thick turtleneck sweaters in the fall, they had enough to worry about without involving an innocent child.

Besides, there were other secrets Florence was keeping on Astrid's behalf. Astrid barely ate, and she exercised to exhaustion. She had taken up ballet.

When the remodeling was finished and there was not one wall left unpapered, nor a single ottoman left to be reupholstered, Astrid turned to dance. There was a studio in a fourth-floor walk-up in Notting Hill, where Madame Petrov taught classes in her thick Russian accent. "This is what it means to dance," Madame Petrov said as Astrid leaned over the barre, bruises blooming in her inner thighs where the muscles had torn. "You must break yourself down into your smallest parts and then put yourself back together."

RJ came to see her practice, just once, in that fourth-floor walk-up studio. He stood in the corner, lighting a cigarette, puffing smoke into the room—a room already stale with sweat and the smell of glue from busted toe shoes. Florence heard the other girls whisper among themselves. They began to eye RJ from their places at the barre or on the floor. He was handsome, this husband of Astrid's. They knew he was the one who kept her in delicate organdy skirts. A blush-colored one for early morning. A pale-blue one for after lunch because she liked the way it looked in the afternoon light that filtered in through the skylight overhead. RJ kept Astrid in black tights without runs, in fresh canvas shoes. And they had all seen her tutu—the fine layers of tulle, the steel spiral boning, the hooks, the eyes, the bars, the silk ribbon. Astrid, who had never danced in a real ballet. Astrid, who, at twenty, was just beginning to dance at an age when many were peaking in their careers.

"Please don't," Astrid told RJ, waving away the cigarette smoke. "It makes the girls sick."

"Come out with me tonight," RJ said, taking another drag. "You never come out anymore."

"I have to practice," she said.

"I wish you wouldn't take this all so seriously," he said, but Astrid was already drifting back toward center floor.

Florence went with Astrid to the studio to keep her company. She sat on the floor near the mirror, watching, a notebook open in her lap so she could write down everything Madame Petrov said and give Astrid her notes later.

One afternoon, after they'd had their lunch and Astrid had changed into her blue organdy skirt, they sat on the warm floorboards of the studio together. Another girl, Mary, was sitting on her knees in a group of girls just to their left. She had something in her hands—something they couldn't see—and the girls were giggling and conversing in whispers.

"She's married to a prince, you know," one of the girls said, and for one dreadful second, Florence thought they were talking about Astrid.

"Yes, but it's a tragic story," another one said. "I heard their son died in an accident when he was just a boy—fell through the ice in the winter. Her husband has gotten into gambling. They've lost all of their money. That's why she teaches."

"Anyone worth knowing is a tragic story," Astrid said loudly, inserting herself into the conversation. "It makes them interesting, gives them angles."

Of course, Madame Petrov had never told any of the girls these things about herself. She was always telling them stories, but none of them were about her.

"Ballet is a long tradition," Madame Petrov was always saying. "If you look at it as just a set of techniques you must memorize and master, you will never learn them. You will always be on the outside of them. But if you learn their history, if you learn about the people who first danced them and why, you will not only learn the move but become a part of it."

The other week, Madame Petrov had told them about the ballet rivals, Sallé and Camargo.

"Men used to be the stars of ballet, not women," Madame Petrov had said. "Yes, it is true. Women used to wear high heels while they were dancing—can you imagine?—and these full hoopskirts that reached all the way to the floor. They couldn't do any of the flashy techniques the men did—and even if they had been able to do them in those heels, those heavy skirts would have hidden them. But Sallé and Camargo—they cut off their heels, they let down their hair, they shortened their skirts. While performing the role of Galatea in *Pygmalion*, Sallé wore nothing more than a flimsy muslin tunic. Can you imagine? And Camargo was the first to perform the entrechat quatre and the cabriole, which before only men had done. Now when you do a cabriole, think of Camargo, and I bet you dance it differently."

Mary leaned toward Astrid, holding the photograph in her hand. "Did you see?" she asked.

Astrid took it. It was a photograph of a young dancer, posed en pointe. Her back was to the photographer in the shot, but she'd half twisted her body around to face the camera. It was staged in the forest, and the dancer was pale and wearing a long white tulle skirt.

"It's Madame Petrov. From her time in the Imperial Ballet in Russia," Mary said. "When she danced the role of Myrtha in *Giselle*. I found it in the library."

The photograph was yellowing, and the edges were rough. Mary must have ripped it from an old newspaper.

"It's lovely," Astrid said.

In the photograph, Madame Petrov was younger than Astrid was now. Her hair was dark and full and piled on top of her head. And in her eyes, Florence thought she saw what Madame Petrov meant every time she told Astrid to lift herself.

"Do you think Madame Petrov will be pleased?" Mary asked. "I was going to give it to her after class. Perhaps she could frame it and keep it on her dressing table?"

Mary was always bringing Madame Petrov presents—flowers and fresh fruit—even though Mary lived by herself in a one-room studio and had only two practice skirts (one taupe, one faded gray), which she washed herself in her sink and hung out the window each night to dry. Madame Petrov had hired her to play the piano during afternoon lessons and let her use the studio for free in her spare time. *"Poor Mary,"* Astrid was always saying. *"Poor, poor Mary."*

"She'll love it," Astrid said, handing her back the photograph. But when Mary turned away, Astrid whispered to Florence, "If it were me, I would hate Mary for reminding me that once I was young and beautiful."

"Levez-vous! Levez-vous!" Madame Petrov said. Florence looked up to see Madame Petrov entering the studio, dressed head to toe in heavy black chiffon, as she always was, as if she were in mourning. Her salted hair was gathered into a chignon on the top of her head, and her skin caught in rivulets at the creases of her eyes, her mouth. She was stockier here than in her photo, her waist thick, her shoulders stooped.

"Il faut casser le noyau pour en avoir l'amande," she said, and everyone rose from the floor to take their places at the barre.

In Astrid's first lesson with Madame Petrov, Astrid had told her about Svetlana Beriosova, about *Giselle*.

"I must learn to do that," Astrid said.

"You are too old," Madame Petrov said. "Why did you come to me so late?"

That whole first week, Madame Petrov made Astrid stand facing the barre, holding it with both hands, learning how to do nothing more than move her head properly. She taught her how to turn out her hips, how to align her body. The way she was supposed to lift herself.

"Ballet is about forward movement, even when you are standing still," Madame Petrov said. "More of your weight should always be on the balls of your feet, not your heels. And lift your chest."

Astrid moved through each position with port de bras and épaulement. There was so much to think about besides her feet—her entire body needed her attention all at once.

"It's not just the position that matters but how you get there," Madame Petrov said. "Do it again. And again."

Astrid watched the girls in the center of the room, the ones practicing pirouettes and pas de bourrées, their toes skimming across the floorboards. She was tired of gripping the barre, of doing pliés and tendus.

"These are too easy," she complained to Madame Petrov. "I've been bending my knees since I was a child. Look. I'm ready for the floor."

"If it's easy, then you are not doing it right," Madame Petrov had said. "Here we are building your foundation. The plié is the origin of every jump, every turn. If there is an imperfection in the foundation now, later the building will crumble."

Now, Astrid joined the girls when they transitioned to the floor. Mary played the piano, and Astrid moved along with the others, practicing her entrechats, her glissades. When the others rose to their toes in their pointe shoes, she stayed on the floor on her canvas soles. Finally, when they moved exclusively into pointe work, she headed toward the dressing room.

"You will tell me when I'm ready?" she said to Madame Petrov, who was standing next to the piano. She asked this every day.

"I will tell you about Marie Taglioni," Madame Petrov said. "Marie Taglioni—an ugly girl, by all accounts: hunchbacked, with long arms. Everyone told her to do something else, but she wouldn't. She loved ballet. Her father trained her, choreographed a ballet for her, *La Sylphide*, the first full-length ballet on pointe. She performed it—she rose onto the tips of her toes, and she flew across the stage. Before, dancers had needed wires and pulleys backstage to do that, but she did it all by herself. She flew.

"Taglioni was a star," Madame Petrov went on. "Her flaws became a thing of beauty. When she danced, her arms were always bent at the elbows or folded across her chest—designed that way by her father, of course, to hide their unattractive length. But they became classic Romantic poses. After her last performance, a group of young dancers cooked her pointe shoes and ate them. All this after they said she could never make it as a dancer—they loved her so much they ate her shoes."

At dinner that night, Astrid told RJ about her upcoming recital.

"A recital?" RJ asked. "You're going to perform in public?"

"Well, yes," Astrid said. "That is sort of the point."

"I thought this was just a hobby," RJ said. "Something to occupy your time."

"I hope it can be more than that," Astrid said. "I know I've gotten a bit of a late start—"

"A late start? You're a grown woman," RJ said. "You cannot be serious."

"Yes, I assure you, I'm quite serious."

"I don't want you going there anymore," RJ said, returning his attention to his steak.

"Where? The studio?"

"Yes," RJ said, taking a bite. "Look how thin you've gotten. You don't fill out your clothes anymore the way you used to. Where have your hips gone, your breasts? You've turned into a wisp of a woman."

"I rather think a slender silhouette is becoming more fashionable these days," Astrid said in her own defense. "Look at the sheath dresses in the storefronts at Harrods. They're not at all flattering if you have any sort of curves."

"I do not care for sheath dresses, nor the type of woman that they flatter," RJ said. "And what of your social obligations? You never come out anymore or call on any of your friends. It's as if I'm married to an eccentric recluse. Cressida just remarked to me the other day that you hadn't called on her in over a fortnight."

"I rather think Cressida prefers your company to mine," Astrid said, and RJ didn't even have the decency to color or look ashamed at the barely concealed accusation. "Besides, all those women—they're a bunch of bores. I admit, if I'm half drunk, they're almost tolerable, but nothing like the girls at the studio. Or Madame Petrov. Now, there's someone worth knowing. We should have her over for dinner one night. The stories she has, the life she's lived. Oh, I can only imagine."

"We are not having that woman over to this house," RJ said. "I've been more than patient. I thought this . . . thing . . . you do was a passing fancy, something you'd grow bored of. But every day you fall more and more into it, grow more and more delusional. I now see that I've indulged this far too long."

"Come now, RJ—" Astrid said.

"I did not marry a ballerina!" RJ said, slamming his fist down on the table. Both Astrid and Florence jumped in their seats. Florence dropped her fork on the floor, and the butler rushed to the kitchen to fetch her a clean one. Astrid took a sip of her drink and stared down at the table, but Florence could see the way the color had drained from her face, the way her hand shook as she set down her glass.

The next morning, they did not go to the studio. Astrid greeted her husband at the breakfast table with a kiss on the cheek, dressed in a blue Chanel scoop-neck tea-length swing dress that brought out her eyes. The dress was belted at the waist, accentuating the hourglass figure that RJ had claimed was diminishing the night before.

"You look chipper this morning," RJ said over the top of his newspaper.

"I thought I'd do some shopping," Astrid said. "Givenchy's fall line just came out. And then I was thinking of calling on Gemma. It's been too long since I've seen her."

"That sounds like a marvelous day," RJ said.

"It does," Astrid agreed, taking a sip of her coffee.

RJ helped Astrid and Florence into a cab as he headed off to work. They took a left off the street, and as soon as the house disappeared behind them, Astrid redirected the driver to Notting Hill.

"Harrods isn't in Notting Hill," Florence said.

"No, it isn't," Astrid said with a smile.

At the dance shop, Astrid asked for her first pair of pointe shoes. She sat in an upholstered chair by the window as the salesgirl measured her feet and examined her arches. She brought out an armful of boxes from the back.

"Stop looking so dour," Astrid told Florence. "You're dampening the mood."

Florence bit her lip. "I'm sorry. It's just . . . last night, RJ seemed really serious."

"I'm sure he was," Astrid said. "But so am I."

"What if he finds out?"

Astrid shrugged. "He's not going to find out. I'll eat some cake, put on a couple pounds. This bra and crinoline are doing a lot of the heavy lifting right now, which is fine, but I won't always be wearing them when I'm with him."

"But what about your feet?" Florence asked. She glanced down at Astrid's bare feet—the toes that were bruised and bandaged, the rough calluses on her heels. "Won't they give you away?"

"I'll soak them," Astrid said. "And powder them if I have to. If there's one thing RJ's not going to be looking at when I'm naked, it's my feet."

The shop attendant slipped a pink satin slipper onto Astrid's foot. "How does that feel?" she asked.

Astrid flexed and relaxed her ankle. "It's so delicate, so intimate," Astrid said. "Almost like wearing lingerie on your feet." Astrid turned to Florence. "What do you think?" she asked.

For a moment, Florence didn't answer. It was one thing for Astrid to defy Scarlet. Scarlet would burn her cigarette pants in the fireplace and chastise her at the breakfast table. But RJ was a different story. Florence thought back to that night in Italy when they had merely had a laugh at his expense. She shuddered to think what he might do if he found out that Astrid had openly defied him.

"They're lovely," Florence said.

They left the store with two pairs and some ribbons and elastics that Florence would sew into the shoes herself.

CHAPTER
TWENTY-NINE

Ransom found that he could not stay away from Cliffhaven. Even when he was on the other side of the country—in a committee meeting, conversing with his staff, or eating dinner alone at night at his townhome in Dupont Circle—his mind would wander back to that stone house on the cliffside and the people in it. Ana, in particular, was at the forefront of his mind. She was not who she claimed to be; that much was certain.

There was an Ana Rojas, age twenty-three, from San Bernardino, California, who studied nursing at CSUSB, but the girl under Ransom's employment was decidedly not her. That Ana Rojas was still living in Colton and was spending her summer working part time at a local Dairy Queen. When Bass's guy had gone to the home address that "Ana" had listed on her application, he'd found a girl claiming to be Ana Rojas living there. She was short, barely five feet tall, with traces of auburn in her dark hair and a constellation of freckles across the bridge of her nose—definitely not the Ana Rojas who was in residence at Cliffhaven. Furthermore, the real Ana Rojas had no idea who the girl was who'd been impersonating her all summer. When Bass's private investigator had shown her a picture, she stared at it blankly, claiming she'd never seen the girl before in her life.

Bass had wanted to confront the imposter immediately and have her promptly removed from the house, but Ransom had stayed his hand. He preferred to go into any encounter, especially a confrontation, sure footed, armed with the facts. And at that point in time, the only thing they knew about the girl for sure was that she wasn't Ana Rojas. So he'd hired his own investigator to look into their false "Ana," but weeks had ticked by now, and he had learned, frustratingly, nothing about who this woman actually was and what she was doing there. Every potential lead that the investigator had tried to track down had resulted in a dead end. Ransom was left only with his own speculations and wild conjectures, which his mind spun, unprompted, at all hours of the day and night.

The most likely scenario, which Ransom came back to again and again, was that this "Ana" was some sort of tabloid spy. He had come across them before—the people who dug through his trash looking for prescriptions or damning receipts or befriended his assistants and plied them with drinks, mining all possible avenues for any speck of dirt they could find so they could cobble it all together into some salacious story they could sell to the highest bidder. And he knew the gossip rags would pay top dollar for dirt on his family, because they had done it before.

Then there were the people who didn't outright work for the tabloids but who were happy to sell his family out for a few bucks or their own fifteen minutes of fame. There was the too-eager classmate of Theo's at Brown, who had leaked to the gossip rags the parties his brother attended, how many drinks the underage freshman had had, how many girls he had slept with. The maid who had been under his mother's employment for years, who had sold a story to the *National Enquirer* that his father was a closeted polygamist and kept a secret second wife in the basement. People would do anything to feel important, to feel seen or heard. They lusted after the spotlight that constantly trailed his family, wanting to be welcomed into its warm glow.

He tried to catalog in his mind the conversations he had had with Ana, the details he had divulged about himself, his family. What she might have seen or heard while living at the house, anything that could incriminate them or cause public shame. He recalled, with a twist in his gut, the intimate conversation they had had that night in the hotel room in LA. He had told her that he played a part, that he was not who he pretended to be, that he—God, how had Ana put it?—"focus grouped his personality." He'd asked Ana to tell him when she'd last masturbated—not because he'd wanted to know but to prove a point that there were certain things that everyone kept to themselves. Still, he doubted that Ana would provide that context when retelling that particular piece of their conversation. He imagined how his words might sound when played through the distorted mouthpiece of the media, devoid of compassion or empathy, how his actions would look when filtered through the cold lens of public scrutiny. He was an actor, a two-faced, duplicitous liar; he had said as much himself. He was a pervert who harassed a young girl under his employment—that is how they would spin it.

Ransom thought he might be sick when he thought of this image of himself broadcast to the world—stripped down to his basest insecurities, to his most vulnerable, and then offered up to everyone for ridicule, for entertainment. His face plastered across the glossy surfaces of the gossip rags; his name reduced to a punch line on the lips of late-night talk show hosts.

He knew he had to confront Ana. He'd hoped before doing so that he'd have some real knowledge of her true identity, of the motivation behind her deception, so he'd know how best to disarm his adversary, but he was reluctantly coming to the realization that he'd have to go in blind, with only his speculations to guide him. His only choice would be to make her understand how ardently and swiftly he would retaliate if she breathed a word about him or his family to the press. The most powerful weapon he had at his disposal was fear, intimidation.

He would threaten a hellfire of litigation, that he would make of her scorched earth.

And so Ransom found himself at Cliffhaven the next week, unannounced. The Senate was in recess; he was supposed to be attending an agricultural rally in Bakersfield, but at the last minute, he had diverted his plane south, toward his home's private airfield.

When he arrived, Mrs. Talbot greeted him in the hall, as if she were not surprised at all to see him.

"Do you know where I might find Miss Rojas?" Ransom asked.

"She's in the library," she said.

He thanked her and headed off swiftly in that direction.

The library doors were closed, which was unusual. Usually, the double doors stood open so that you could see into the mahogany fireplace and the gleaming floor-to-ceiling bookcases on either side. Normally, Ransom would have walked right in, but something about the strangeness of it made him stop with his hand around the knob, lean in, and press his ear to the door. Through the thick oak came a low, muted moan, a girlish laugh, a sharp intake of breath.

Ransom let go of the doorknob and instinctively took a step back, registering the sounds and their meaning before they could form into coherent thoughts and pictures in his mind.

Ana was in the library, but she wasn't alone.

It was Salvador who was with her, Ransom was sure. An image flashed in Ransom's mind of Ana and Salvador standing side by side on the balcony the night of the Fourth of July, whispering and laughing, leaning into one another conspiratorially as they waited for the fireworks to start. Then there was the way Ana had blushed when Jacqueline had asked her about Salvador during their dinner at the Duchess, how she had admitted she thought he was good looking. And then the last time Ransom had visited, the day he'd kissed Ana in the pool, he had seen them himself, just the way that Saoirse had described—sitting next to one another at the breakfast table, conspiring.

It made a sickening sort of sense. Salvador was a ladies' man, after all: attractive, charming, suave. He'd always had a different girl on his arm at school, lounging on a picnic blanket on the quad on a warm day, giggling and kissing, their fingers intertwined, or huddled together on the sofa in a dimly lit corner of the room at fraternity parties.

Of course Salvador had gone after Ana, and of course she had fallen for him. They lived under the same roof, ate nearly every meal together. The hours, the days, the *nights* they had spent together—it was all but inevitable.

Ransom felt a swift surge of jealousy, hot and stinging, in his gut. Then, he stopped himself. He had fallen into the trap of his feelings again, and again, they had blinded him. Ana wasn't even Ana. He had to remember that. Ana had lied to him from the very beginning. He didn't know this woman, not a thing about her, except that she was there for her own malicious reasons.

Well, he was done playing games. He was done being lied to. This was his house, after all, his family, and he was going to put a stop to this, here and now.

Ransom swung the door open with so much force that it flew back and hit the doorjamb with a thud. He wanted to be loud; he wanted to be obvious. This was not a time for subtlety. Let it be quick, and let it be over.

The effect was immediate. The two figures on the couch went still and turned to look at him. He saw Salvador, naked, hovering over a woman, his mouth slack, his eyes unguarded. And there was a woman underneath him, tilting her head back to look at the source of their disruption, her long dark hair falling over the back of the couch. Only, it wasn't Ana.

Saoirse let out a loud, piercing shriek.

Before he even knew what he was doing, Ransom was across the room. He grabbed Salvador and yanked him off the couch.

"What the hell do you think you're doing with my sister?" Ransom said. He gripped Salvador by the throat, pushing him backward toward the wall.

Salvador cupped his hands over his exposed genitals, straining to breathe. "It's not what it looks like," he choked out.

Ransom clutched his throat harder. "The hell it's not," he said.

Behind them, Saoirse crawled off the couch and hastily threw on Salvador's shirt. It dwarfed her, running past her thighs. She was rushing to button it and settled for clutching it closed over her chest with one hand.

"Did he force himself on you?" Ransom asked, turning to look at his sister now that she was half clothed. Her hair was mussed, her cheeks red and splotchy. The sight of her made him grip Salvador's throat harder, and this time, Salvador abandoned any attempt to cover himself and instead tried to pry his neck out of Ransom's grasp. The veins in his forehead were bulging.

"Stop it," she pleaded. "Just stop it; you're hurting him. You're going to kill him."

She was looking at Ransom like he was the villain in all this, like he was the aggressor. Like *he* was scaring her.

Ransom seemed to recover himself then, and he let Salvador go. Salvador slumped forward onto his knees on the floor, coughing and gasping for breath. Saoirse tried to go to him, but Ransom held up his hand in warning, and she stopped, stood still where she was.

"Put your clothes on," Ransom said to Salvador. "And then get the hell out of my house."

Behind them, Saoirse let out a yelp like a wounded animal. "You can't do that," she said.

Ransom ignored her. He couldn't even look at her.

"Please, just let me explain," Salvador said, his voice hoarse. "It's not what it looks like. I care about her. We're not just—we're in love."

"She's a child!" Ransom said.

Saoirse tried to go to Salvador again, but Ransom stepped into her path. "Take one more step in his direction," Ransom said, "and I swear to God I will call the police right now and have him arrested."

Saoirse froze again. She started to cry.

Salvador picked up his trousers, which lay crumpled on the floor, and hurriedly put them on. He retrieved his belt off the couch and threaded it hastily into his belt loops, looking around frantically for his shirt. His eyes fell on Saoirse, and an awkward silence settled as he realized she was wearing it.

"Go," Ransom hissed. "Leave."

Salvador opened his mouth to protest, but Ransom took a step toward him, and that was all the threat he needed to turn and make a beeline toward the door.

What the hell just happened? Ransom thought. His heart was hammering in his chest, as if he'd just sprinted a mile. He felt dizzy, lightheaded.

The whole thing felt to him like a sickly, out-of-body experience, a nightmare: watching this full-grown, half-naked man flee and his disheveled sister weep, gasping for breath. One thought kept echoing in his mind: Salvador was a predator, and Ransom had *invited* him into his home. If Ransom had his way, he would have Salvador arrested on the spot, but he knew if he did, he couldn't keep it out of the papers.

It all came down to this: even in his own house, he could not protect his sister.

"Stop crying," he said to Saoirse. "He's a predator. He doesn't deserve your tears."

Saoirse's face was screwed up into a tight knot of fury. "Where do you get off, treating him like he's done something wrong, like he's some sort of criminal and I'm some sort of—some sort of hapless victim in all of this?" Saoirse said. "I came on to him, Ransom," she went on, pressing her hand to her chest. "Me. I was an equal player in the whole thing. At least acknowledge that."

Ransom shook his head. "No," he said.

Saoirse was only seventeen—too young to give her consent. Salvador had abused his power. Ransom couldn't see it any other way.

"I put him in a position of authority, and he used it to prey on you," Ransom said.

"You're twisting it in your mind into something that it's not!" Saoirse cried, exasperated. "Salvador didn't . . . prey . . . on me. He loves me."

"He doesn't love you," Ransom said. "He loves what you can do for him."

"That's not true," Saoirse said.

"It is," Ransom said. "He did this all the time at school. He'd pick out girls. They were never the prettiest or the most popular. But they always had money. He would give them attention, and they would buy him things."

"You're lying," Saoirse said. "You're just saying that to hurt me."

"I'm not," Ransom said. "I just never thought he'd have the gall to do that here, under my roof, or I never would have brought him here."

He reached out to touch her shoulder. He only wanted to comfort her, but she roughly shrugged him off.

"Stop it," she said. "Why do you always do this? Why can't I have anything that's mine? My wants? My desires? Even my mistakes, you take ownership of."

"Saoirse, I'm not—"

"No," Saoirse said.

A sudden calm seemed to grip her, a quiet gravity. She reminded him of their mother that time Theo had briefly flirted with the idea of majoring in theater, and Birdie had pursed her lips and said sternly, *We're not theater people, darling. Why be the jester when you can be the king?* And Theo, quite unlike himself, had dropped it.

"I'm not some porcelain doll you need to keep on a shelf for fear of breaking," Saoirse said. "I'm not a puppet whose strings you can pull, or a parrot who will say exactly what you want me to. I'm a person, just like you. And just like you, I'm going to love who I want to love, and do the things I want to do, and say the things I want to say."

Ransom just looked at her; for once, words eluded him.

"And I know you can't accept that right now," Saoirse said, "but one day, very soon, you won't have any choice in the matter."

CHAPTER THIRTY

PRESENT

The Major Crimes Unit at the San Luis Obispo County Sheriff's Office was quiet today. It was just the three of them—Detective Church, Deputy McPherson, and Detective Leland, all sitting at their separate workstations. McPherson had the radio on low, listening to a show on NPR. He leaned back in his chair and stretched.

"I'm gonna grab some coffee from the break room," McPherson said, looking over at Church. "You want anything?"

"I'm good," Church said. "Thanks."

"What about you, Leland?" McPherson called.

Church glanced across the room at Leland, who was bent forward, focused intently on his monitor. He hadn't spoken to Leland since that uncomfortable sit-down with Sergeant Wallis and Sheriff Braverson two weeks ago, when they had handed Leland his ass. It'd been easy enough for Church to avoid Leland since then. Their workstations were on opposite ends of the room. Besides, Church was used to keeping to himself.

Leland shook his head. "Thanks, though," he said.

As McPherson headed toward the door, Church decided it was time he broke the ice. He saved his work on his monitor and got up and crossed the room.

"Hey," Church said.

"Hi," Leland said.

"I saw Nisha the other day," Church said. "She told me about the 3D facial reconstruction you guys are doing on our John Doe. That was a good idea you had."

"Well, what's that thing they say? Necessity is the mother of invention?"

"Ah," Church said. "You didn't get any hits on the DNA?"

Leland shook his head. "And the tox report came back negative."

"Shit," Church said.

"Makes you wonder—how does a perfectly healthy person drop dead in the middle of a party?" Leland said.

"Heart attack?" Church asked, but Leland shook his head.

"Unlikely. Our John Doe was late twenties or early thirties, average weight."

"What about local missing persons?" Church asked.

"No matches," Leland said. "And I checked the entire staff list. Everyone is accounted for. Whoever our John Doe was, he was an interloper. He wasn't supposed to be there that night."

They were both quiet for a moment.

"Listen, all that stuff the sheriff and sarge said the other week," Church said. "Don't take it too personally. They went a little hard."

"I deserved it," Leland said, "a boneheaded move like that."

"Don't beat yourself up over it, is all I'm trying to say," Church said. "It's not like you're the only one who's ever fucked up a case before."

"Yeah?" Leland said. "Somehow, I can't see you making a mistake like that."

"Yeah, well," Church said. He scratched the back of his head. "You'd be wrong."

Leland looked up.

Church hesitated a moment. He glanced over at the door and wondered how long he had until McPherson returned from his break. He didn't want an extended audience for this particular story.

He perched on the edge of Leland's desk and kept his voice low. "There was this case, several years ago," Church began. "The Riley case." It had been one of the first cases he was assigned to when he took over the Cold Case Unit. "I got a call from this woman, Lindsay Banks," Church went on. "Apparently, her mother, Ruth Blackwell, had just passed away after a long, drawn-out battle with colon cancer, and on her deathbed, well, she'd made a confession."

Church still recalled Ruth Blackwell's last words, the three sentences that had sent his life into a tailspin: *"Those two little girls,"* she'd said. *"He did it. Ben did it."*

Lindsay didn't need to ask her mother what she meant; she knew. The Blackwells had lived two streets over from the Rileys when Peyton Riley had gone missing in December of 1973.

Peyton Riley had been only seven at the time. The school bus had dropped her off in her neighborhood in Bishop Falls. Between the bus stop and Peyton's house, which was only five houses away, Peyton had disappeared.

There was another little girl who shared the same bus stop as Peyton—Ashley Lewis, age eight—and she had been the only witness. She'd told the police that she and Peyton had seen a young man walking his dog. It was a white terrier mix with big brown spots, and Peyton stopped to pet him. They struck up a conversation with the man, who told them the dog could do the most marvelous tricks if only they had some treats to feed him. Ashley ran across the street to her house to get some peanut butter, and when she came back, Peyton, the man, and the dog were gone.

The police had been called immediately. They'd canvassed the neighborhood, set up search parties, but found nothing. It was a local hunter who found Peyton—or, rather, her remains—in the woods in the town over the next spring. There'd been a frenzied investigation after—the police had interviewed over one hundred suspects. But slowly, the list had dwindled as alibis checked out and leads went nowhere. The case grew cold.

"Ruth Blackwell had been Ben's alibi the day of Peyton's disappearance," Church went on. "She'd told the police that Ben had been home that afternoon, helping her organize donations for the church rummage sale that would take place the following Saturday. Besides, the Blackwells didn't own a dog. So the police had dismissed Ben as a suspect. But Lindsay told me that not only had her mother recanted Ben's alibi, but that Ben had volunteered regularly with the local humane society, where he cleaned kennels, washed dogs, took them for walks. That was where he'd really been that day that Peyton Riley went missing."

"Holy shit," Leland said.

Church nodded. "So I visited the SLO Humane Society," Church said. "I spent hours in that back room, going through boxes and boxes of administrative paperwork. And then I found it: the old volunteer records from 1973. There was a handwritten sign-in sheet, and on December seventh, 1973, Ben Blackwell had scribbled his name. Time in: one forty-five p.m. Time out: five thirty-eight p.m. It was exactly the window in which Peyton had gone missing."

"Wow," Leland whistled. "That must have felt like striking gold."

Church nodded. "It did. There wasn't any DNA evidence to go off of in the case," he said. "The original investigators had found a hair that didn't belong to Peyton on her remains, but there was no root, so it couldn't be tested. So I conducted a photo-identification lineup instead."

Church recalled arranging an old photo of Ben from around the time the disappearance had taken place with a slew of other headshots. He'd held his breath as Ashley Lewis—the only witness, who was now in her early fifties—leaned over the table, examining each photo, crinkling her forehead as she strained to remember. Then she sat back, tapped her finger on Ben's photograph.

"Him," Ashley said. "That's him."

The jury had deliberated for only an hour after the prosecution and defense had finished presenting their cases. The verdict came back: guilty.

"The paper did a write-up on me," Church said. *"Local Detective Solves Decades-Old Cold Case.* I was the town hero, the department golden boy."

"This isn't really making me feel any better," Leland said.

"Just wait," Church said and trudged on.

Ben Blackwell had protested his innocence and appealed his conviction, not once but twice. By the time of the second appeal, ground had been broken in DNA hair analysis—they now no longer needed the root. The hair that had been found on Peyton Riley was tested, and the results came back: Ben Blackwell was not a match. Instead, it matched a seventy-six-year-old inmate of Kern Valley State Prison: a man by the name of Larry Ferguson, who was serving life in prison for the murder of his ex-girlfriend.

"Holy shit," Leland said.

"Yeah," Church said. "Holy fucking shit, indeed."

"So what happened?" Leland asked.

"The judge overturned Blackwell's conviction," Church said. "And the paper ran another piece: *Man Wrongfully Convicted in Cold Case Goes Free.* There were accusations about shoddy police work and evidence manipulation. The photo lineup that I'd conducted included headshots from the local 1973 high school yearbook," Church said. He recalled the headshots vividly, each young man dressed neatly in a suit and tie with a uniform background. "Only, Ben Blackwell had dropped out before his senior year, so his photo had been a candid one pulled from an old family photo album," Church said. Ben had worn a T-shirt and stared unsmiling at the camera, the sky a bleak, pale canvas behind him.

"Shit," Leland said.

"Yeah," Church concurred, scratching the back of his head. "The judge ruled the photo lineup had been prejudicial. There was talk that maybe I had staged it that way to manipulate the witness into choosing Ben Blackwell's picture."

Of course, he hadn't meant to manipulate anything—he had just been working with the photos that were available to him.

"I was placed on administrative leave while the department conducted an official investigation into my conduct," Church said. He still felt shame when telling this story, even all these years later. "They eventually cleared me, but, by then, the damage to my reputation was done."

Doubt—it followed him everywhere after that. Like a potent, toxic scent that clung to his skin. It preceded him into any room and lingered long after he'd left. People couldn't see him clearly, couldn't see his work clearly, sometimes even now, all these years later, because of the stench of it.

"So, yeah, you're not the only person who's ever fucked up a case," Church said, standing. "And I'm sure everything sucks right now, and it probably will for a while. But you'll get through it. I mean, look at me. I'm still here."

"Any advice?" Leland said. "You know, for surviving the shitstorm?"

Church shook his head. "Sometimes, the only way out is through," Church said.

CHAPTER
THIRTY-ONE

I t was no easy matter to keep RJ fooled. In fact, keeping up the farce was wearing Florence almost to exhaustion. They would always leave the house together, Florence and Astrid, on their way to do preapproved activities. But down the street and out of view of the house, they would part ways—Astrid to the studio in Notting Hill, and Florence to any number of places: the Red Cross to help organize donations, an art class at the local university, tennis lessons at the club. Then they'd meet up again, Astrid slipping into the appropriate attire for whatever activity she was supposed to have come from. They'd get their stories straight so that Astrid could keep up the conversation at the dinner table—how Margaret Thompson had mislabeled the kitchenware at the Red Cross and Astrid had had to spend all afternoon redoing it, how Professor Wallace was having them paint still lifes this week, how she was working on her backhand serve.

Tonight was Astrid's first recital. She was going to wear the steel-boned tutu that RJ had bought her when she'd first started dancing—the one with delicate layers of tulle and organza. Florence and Astrid left the house together at 5:00 p.m., and while Astrid headed to the studio, Florence went to the will call box at the West End theatre to pick up their tickets to *My Fair Lady*, their cover for the evening. She'd leave the torn stubs on the front hall table for RJ to see. Then, she took a cab to Notting Hill.

The studio was set up as a makeshift stage, rows of chairs facing the mirror. It was crowded by the time Florence got there; every chair was taken, so she stood in the back and craned her neck to see. Madame Petrov introduced each act, and Mary accompanied them on the piano. There were young girls, age twelve, doing pirouettes and older girls doing a dance from *Swan Lake*. Florence looked expectantly for Astrid in her grand tutu—surely, she would be impossible to miss—but every act came and went, and she did not see her. Then Madame Petrov was standing in the middle of the stage, thanking them for coming and wishing them all a good night.

Florence waited by the back door as the guests and dancers filtered out. Madame Petrov was one of the last to leave. Florence reached out and touched her arm to stop her.

"Madame Petrov," Florence said, "where is Astrid? I thought she was supposed to perform tonight."

"Perhaps she got cold feet," Madame Petrov said, clucking her tongue. "I gave her the solo she begged for, but she never showed up."

Florence couldn't get home fast enough. She didn't even take her coat off or remove her gloves at the door, she was in such a rush. Her hand was on the railing, her foot on the first step, when she heard his voice.

"Florence," RJ said. "I've been expecting you."

A cold dread filled Florence's body, and she inadvertently shivered. She turned to see RJ standing there, just outside the parlor.

"RJ," she said, "I didn't realize you were home."

There was a party in Mayfair; she'd expected him to be out all evening.

"Yes, there's been a lot of that going around tonight," RJ said. "Misunderstandings. Realizations."

Florence swallowed hard. "I don't know what you mean."

"If you're looking for my wife, she's upstairs," RJ said.

Florence's hand tightened on the railing.

"I'd ask you not to disturb her at the moment, though," RJ said. "She's resting. It's been a difficult night for all of us. You see, she's had an accident."

Florence's heart quickened. "An accident?"

"Please, come sit with me in the parlor," RJ said. "There's much I'd like to say to you."

Florence's knees trembled. For a moment, she contemplated bolting up the stairs to Astrid's room. But what good would that do? RJ could easily catch her, tackle her, do Lord knew what with her if she provoked him. It was his home. Florence knew none of the staff would come to her rescue. They'd done nothing to restrain him or check him, even though everyone knew about the bruises that Astrid hid under her clothes. If Florence remained calm and civil, maybe he would too. So she turned and followed RJ into the parlor. A fire was going in the hearth. RJ poured them both a glass of brandy.

"Is Astrid all right?" Florence asked, trying to keep her voice level.

RJ motioned toward the sofa, ignoring her question. "Please, sit," he said.

Florence sat, and RJ handed her a glass and took the armchair next to her.

"I've underestimated you, Florence," RJ said, crossing one leg over the other. "When I first met you, I thought you to be meek and pious—a timid little church mouse. I thought you'd be a calming presence for my wife, a familiar balm in an unfamiliar place. But you're not a mouse, are you, Florence? You're a snake."

Heat flamed in Florence's cheeks, and she looked down at the floor.

"Don't you think I know what goes on in my own house?" RJ said.

Florence looked up at him. "Please," she said. "We meant no harm."

"I think it's time for you to go back home," RJ said, taking a sip of his drink. "Back to Cliffhaven. I've spoken with Scarlet. It's all been arranged; your ticket's booked. You leave at the end of the week."

Florence's heart stuttered in her chest. "Does Astrid know?" she asked, her voice hoarse.

"I've had a conversation this evening with my wife," RJ said. "We are—as we are in all things—in complete agreement on this matter."

It was the next morning before Florence was allowed into Astrid's room to see her. Astrid was still in bed, the curtains drawn, her body curled into itself, facing the windows.

"Are you awake?" Florence asked.

Astrid sniffled in response. "Yes," she said, her voice hoarse. "But I wish I wasn't. I wish I were dead."

Florence sat down on the bed next to her. "What happened last night?" Florence asked. "Are you okay?"

Astrid pulled the covers back, and that's when Florence saw it—her right foot was in a cast. Her toes peeked out, a gruesome blue-black color, blood crusted under the nails. Florence gasped.

"The doctor says I've fractured the sesamoid bone," Astrid said despondently. "It'll never heal properly, he said. I'll never dance en pointe again."

"How did it happen?" Florence asked, her voice quiet, lest anyone stood at the door, intent on eavesdropping on their conversation.

"I've always envied you," Astrid said.

"Envied me?"

"Yes," Astrid said. "You can go anywhere, be anything."

"So can you," Florence said.

"No," Astrid said, and Florence didn't think she'd ever heard anyone sound sadder. "I've exchanged one cage for another."

"Why do you stay?" Florence asked.

"You act as if it's some choice I'm making," Astrid said. She let out an exasperated laugh. "Where would I go? What would I do? I've nothing that truly belongs to me. Everything I have belongs to my husband or my family. I've no right to any of it without them. And they keep me yoked to them like a . . . like a prized calf."

"We could go to Paris," Florence said before she knew what she was saying.

"Paris?"

"We could get an apartment there, on the Seine," Florence said. "Our own apartment, and no one could tell us what to do."

"That's a pretty thought," Astrid said.

"I'm serious," Florence said.

"How would we get there?" Astrid asked.

"We'd take the train," Florence said matter-of-factly.

"Yes, the train," Astrid said teasingly. "But with what money, my pet? I have but pocket change, and you have even less than I do."

Florence's hand went to the necklace that she wore under her dress, the one Doris had left her. She fingered the canary yellow diamond under the fabric, the halo of pearls.

"Leave that to me," Florence said.

CHAPTER THIRTY-TWO

PRESENT

Detective Church got to the office early, which was not unusual for him lately. He'd been pulling a lot of long days, coming in before the sun rose and leaving long after it had set. He hadn't seen daylight or felt the sun on his face in ages.

He had spent all week trying to track down Saoirse's caretaker from that summer—Ana Rojas. It was a maddeningly common name. There were nearly a hundred Ana Rojases in Southern California alone. He couldn't find any social media accounts linked to *his* Ana Rojas, though, the one he was searching for—she didn't exist on Facebook, Twitter, or Instagram. He figured she had probably married and changed her surname, so he'd consulted the Towerses' tax returns from 1982 that Leland had so disastrously gotten a court order to obtain. From that, Church pulled her social security number and ran it through the criminal databases but got no hits. It wasn't until he searched the Social Security Death Index that he finally found her. His heart sank when he saw it: Ana Rojas had passed away in December of 1982, only a few months after Saoirse had gone missing. He eventually found a newspaper article with her obituary: she'd been killed in a car accident.

A hit-and-run. Church left the office feeling defeated. He'd spent the entire week chasing down a literal dead end.

This morning, he poured himself a hot mug of coffee from the break room and meandered down the hall to the evidence room, which, this early, was dark and empty except for him. He pulled the box he was looking for from its place on the shelf and sat back down at a table to examine it.

It was the box that Florence had given him the last time he was at Cliffhaven. He'd looked through it once before when he'd first brought it in and entered it into evidence but had seen nothing of significance. It contained mostly a medley of party-planning debris, which the evidence and property technicians had catalogued and itemized, sorting everything into plastic baggies and envelopes with the requisite labels. There were filled-out RSVP cards noting the guests' meal preferences, seating charts, a list of special dietary restrictions. Mostly, Church marveled at the fact that Florence had kept these things for forty years. What was the point? He started to absently comb through it all again, starting with an envelope of photographs.

The photos were professionally taken, some candid, others posed. There were shots of guests dancing in the ballroom, close-ups of the band playing, stills of the fireworks. Church gave them all only a cursory glance, moving each photo to the back of the stack until he was at the beginning of the night again, when the photographer had evidently gone around and gotten pictures of each of the tables before dinner. He was just about to put the photos down when one made him pause. He held it up, leaned back in his chair as he examined it. Four people were seated at a white-clothed dinner table, their arms around one another, leaning in, posed for the shot. Four faces gleamed up at him, all smiles, but there was one face in particular that caught his attention.

"Holy fuck," he whispered.

He sat up straight, his blood running cold. He scrambled through the box on the table with both hands now, turning over receipts for the centerpieces and the menu from the caterer, the set list for the band. Finally, he found it near the bottom: Florence's seating chart. He checked it again.

Fuck, fuck, fuck, fuck, fuck.

"It can't be," he said. But he knew it was.

He knew what he needed to do. He grabbed his car keys.

There was one person he still had to talk to.

PART FOUR

CHAPTER
THIRTY-THREE

*AUGUST 28, 1982—THE DAY OF SAOIRSE'S BIRTHDAY
PARTY*

In the early predawn light, Saoirse lay awake in her bed, staring up at the ceiling. In just a few short hours, the guests would start arriving. There would be music and dancing and champagne. They would be celebrating a birthday, but Saoirse was celebrating something else. When the clock struck midnight this morning, she had passed an invisible threshold. She didn't feel any different, but she had suddenly become, in the eyes of the law and the terms of her trust, an adult. Finally, after so many months of being a prisoner in her own house, she was suddenly free.

She wiped a tear that had snaked its way down her cheek, leaving a warm, wet streak in its wake.

For the past year and a half, she hadn't felt like a person. Her thoughts and feelings hadn't mattered; her voice had been silenced. She couldn't go where she wanted or do what she wanted or say what she needed. To be constantly watched, forbidden from leaving the house without a chaperone. Today, she got to start being a person again.

Saoirse had her own plans for tonight that she hadn't told anyone about. For how could she tell anyone? How could she trust anyone? She had seen the way her brother had reacted to the choices she made—always angry, quick to judge, never hearing her out. Salvador, for instance. If Ransom had just listened, if he had taken a moment to try and understand, maybe he would have seen her side of things.

Saoirse was sixteen when she'd met Salvador. She was sullen and surly, and several months pregnant. She had refused to open her textbook or look at him when he spoke to her, but instead of growing angry or irritated, Salvador had closed his book and sat quietly across from her until their lesson time was up. On their third morning together, Salvador wheeled a television set into the library.

"Do you mind if I watch my show?" Salvador asked. "I've been taping it, but if we're going to sit quietly during our lessons, I figured I might as well watch it live."

Saoirse shrugged but didn't look at him.

The show was in Spanish, so Saoirse didn't understand what was being said. Occasionally, her eyes would wander to the screen. There was a girl about her age in many of the scenes. She was on a ranch somewhere out in the country, learning how to ride a horse, how to muck a stall, even though you could tell she didn't want to be there and didn't belong. Her jeans were designer, the kind you wore out to lunch, not the kind that was meant to get dirty. In one scene, she fell into a cow patty in the field, and Saoirse gasped.

Salvador looked over at her.

"They were beautiful pants," Saoirse said wistfully.

He laughed, his eyes drifting back to the screen.

Saoirse couldn't bring herself to ask Salvador what was going on because that would mean admitting interest, so she made up the story in her head. The girl's name was Lucia. Her parents had died in a car crash. She had lived this beautiful life before, in the city. They had a lot of money, a nice house. She had a lot of friends and a boyfriend whom she loved. But when her parents died, everything changed. She found out that her father was in debt; she was left with nothing. Her estranged aunt took her in, but her aunt lived on a hacienda far out in the country, and it was a very different way of life. Lucia had to learn to muck horse stalls and milk cows. She went to public school, where people thought she was difficult and stuck up. They didn't understand her. She had a hard time.

There was a boy who appeared in some of the scenes, about the same age as the girl, maybe a little older. He was handsome, but the way he looked at the girl sometimes made the hairs on the back of Saoirse's neck stand up. One day, the girl was off by herself on the property, going for a swim in a secluded lake. The boy found her there.

No one would hear her if she screamed, Saoirse thought.

She couldn't help herself. She had to know.

"Is he the bad guy?" Saoirse asked.

Salvador looked over at her, startled that she had spoken. He thought for a moment. "In Spanish telenovelas, there is no clear-cut line between good and evil characters, like you have in America," he said. "There are protagonists and antagonists, sure, but the protagonists have weaknesses and flaws, and the antagonists often have noble motivations. It is not uncommon for an antagonist to gain the sympathy of their audience or to enjoy a happy ending. In this way, our telenovelas are a bit more realistic than, say, *The Young and the Restless.*"

"You don't think there's such a thing in real life as a bad guy?" Saoirse asked.

"No," Salvador said. "People are more complicated than simply *good* or *evil.*"

"You should meet my ex-boyfriend," Saoirse said. "He would change your mind."

Salvador chuckled. "I used to watch telenovelas with my grandmother," he said. "We'd sit at the kitchen table, eating tortillas she'd make each morning by hand, and watch. Watching them now reminds me of her. Makes me feel like I'm home."

"I used to watch soap operas with my dad sometimes, when I was home sick from school," Saoirse said.

She would lay her head on his lap, and he would rub her back. He'd bring her Sprite and saltines, and he wouldn't say anything about the crumbs on the coffee table or the seat of the couch, the way her mother would have.

That was the kind of parent she wanted to be, she decided, her hand moving to rest protectively over her stomach: the kind who wouldn't say anything about the crumbs.

On the screen, the boy was talking to the girl.

"What's he saying to her?" Saoirse asked.

"It's a quote by Concepción Arenal," Salvador said. "It basically means those who face adversity and fail but get back up are greater than those who never experienced hardship or failure at all," he went on. "It's about the power of resilience, how hardships make us stronger. You see, Concepción Arenal was a founder of the feminist movement in Spain. She went to law school when such a thing was unheard of for a woman. She was the first woman in Spain to attend university. She spent her life defending women's right to an education, that their purpose was not just to be wives and mothers but to be people in their own right."

"Imagine that," Saoirse said. "People in our own right."

The next day, Salvador wheeled in a chalkboard and started conjugating verbs into the past perfect. This time, Saoirse didn't protest. She took out her notebook and started copying them down. At the end of the class, Salvador wheeled in the TV again, and they watched the episode with the subtitles on.

For her homework, Salvador had Saoirse translate pieces of Concepción Arenal's *La Mujer del Porvenir*. They'd sit out front on the grass on a nice spring day, a breeze teasing its way through the branches of the oak trees overhead. Saoirse would take off her shoes and stick out her bare feet, the green blades tickling the skin between her toes.

"I hope he's a boy," Saoirse said, her hand on her belly. "Sometimes I wish I'd been born a boy. How different things would have been. It's crazy how much of your life is determined by what's between your legs."

"A lot of your life is determined by things that you have no control over," Salvador said. "Not just your gender, but where you're born. Who you're born to. What you look like. The color of your skin. The language you speak. Things you didn't choose. Things you cannot change."

Saoirse looked over at him. She knew parts of his story, but she had never before really considered what things must have been like for Salvador. To be born poor, to grow up without his parents. To go away to school in another country where he knew no one, where the language they spoke was not his own.

She had always viewed Salvador as one of her brother's friends. But he wasn't, really, was he? At school, Salvador had been their tutor, the guy who helped them cheat on exams. And now here he was again, the hired help.

She saw in him a twin hurt, a mirrored rage, a deep wanting.

A few weeks later, when the baby came too soon at six months and Saoirse labored for a day and a half to deliver a child, blue hued, silent, and still, she held the infant to her chest for hours, skin to skin. A little girl. Saoirse was exhausted and spent, her hair stuck to her forehead, the sheets to her thighs. The nurse and the doctor begged to take the child away, but Saoirse wouldn't let them. She cradled the baby in her arms, trying to memorize every inch of her: her eyes closed, her mouth slack. The impossibly small fingernails and little lashes. She wouldn't let them take her away until she had given her a name—Cetta Josephine Towers—and said a prayer to a god that Saoirse had never before believed in to watch over her in the next life.

Ransom was away when it happened. Tabby dabbed at her sweaty forehead with a sponge, changed her sheets, brought her her favorite meals to eat. But it was Salvador who sat with her in the afternoons while they watched the soap opera with the misplaced girl and the boy who was neither bad nor good in her dimly lit room.

Her love of Salvador was slow and grew out of grief and rage and wanting, out of loss and a shared understanding of the cruelty of the world. It was a deep-rooted, stalwart love, but it had not been her first. It was as different from her first love as it could possibly be. A counter. A study in opposites.

She'd never felt about any boy the way she felt about Teddy. It wasn't just that he was beautiful, even though he was. It was that he had a way of drawing everybody in, like he was the sun and everyone else just planets stuck in his gravitational pull, orbiting around him. When Teddy spoke, people listened. He was fun and shrewd. And when Teddy paid attention to you? Well, it felt like the summer sun warming your cheeks. And when his attention drifted, it was like a cold coastal fog had drifted in and you'd been caught without a sweater.

The summer that Saoirse was fifteen, Teddy came to Newport a single man, and all his attention was focused on Saoirse, as if she were his singular purpose for existing. He took her out to lobster dinners at the club, strolled with her—fingers interlaced—barefoot on the beach in the moonlight. He opened her car door and brought her flowers and called when he said he would. Once, when it was just the two of them smoking pot in his father's boathouse, he told her about how his older brother had committed suicide with a hunting rifle right before Christmas three years before, and she held his head in her lap, stroking his hair as he cried. It was the only time she had ever seen him look vulnerable, like a little boy. She was sure that she was the only one who got these pieces of him, the only one who knew what he was really like.

He took her out one day, on his boat, and kissed her urgently, but when his fingers trailed to the hem of her shirt, Saoirse pulled away.

"What's the matter?" Teddy asked.

"I wouldn't want to do that with, well, someone who wasn't serious about me," Saoirse said.

"You think I'm not serious about you?" Teddy asked, sounding hurt, with a hint of accusation. "I thought it was obvious, the way I feel about you."

"It is," Saoirse said. "I mean, to me, it is. But I'm not sure it is to everybody else."

"I didn't know you cared so much about what everyone else thought."

"I don't," Saoirse said. "I guess I just need, like, a sign of commitment, that's all."

"What, like, a promise ring?" Teddy asked.

"No, not like a promise ring," Saoirse said. Her face burned. She wished he would just get it, just understand her, not make everything so hard. Not make her practically beg.

"God, Teddy," she said, "I just want us to call this what it is, to finally put a name to it, that's all. *I* don't want to see anyone else, and I don't want *you* to see anyone else. And frankly, I don't know if you feel that way, because if you do, you've never actually said so."

She felt embarrassed for needing it, for saying it all out loud. She felt childish. Small.

When she had brought it up to Teddy before, always in roundabout ways, he always shrugged it off, saying that titles and labels were stupid, arbitrary, which puzzled Saoirse, because she knew that he had consented to them before, with someone else. Besides, titles and labels, they mattered to Saoirse. They existed for a reason. She wanted everyone to know that she belonged to Teddy and Teddy belonged to her. She wanted to draw a line in the sand, not to box them in but to keep them from losing each other. She steeled herself for his pushback, his teasing, his admonishments for her conformity to what he saw as tawdry societal norms.

"Is that all?" Teddy asked.

She nodded, but she couldn't look at him.

He climbed down onto his knee in front of her, pulled her hand to his chest.

"What are you doing?" she asked.

"Meerkat," Teddy said. "My little mongoose. Light of my life."

Saoirse tried to pull her hand away. "Don't," she said.

But Teddy held her hand anchored to his chest. "I'm serious," Teddy said. "Meerkat, I'm crazy about you. Lover, sweetheart, *boyfriend*. Call me whatever you want. I'm yours."

She wasn't entirely sure if he was making fun of her or if he was being completely genuine. That was the maddening thing about

Teddy—sometimes, you couldn't tell. But she decided to believe him, to take him at his word. To, as she had time and time again, give him the benefit of the doubt. She laughed and let him kiss her. She didn't protest when he swept her up into his arms, or when he carried her belowdecks, or when he unbuttoned her blouse.

Afterward, he rolled over onto his back and fumbled for a cigarette and lighter from his discarded pants' pocket.

"You're such a tease," Teddy said.

"What?" Saoirse asked. She felt cold suddenly, and she pulled the bedsheet over her bare chest.

"You didn't bleed," he said. He handed her the cigarette. "You're not a virgin."

She took a drag from the cigarette and stayed quiet.

It didn't count, before, she wanted to say. *It was just for practice.*

By the time they both went back to school in the fall, things had shifted between them, the distance loosening the threads that held them together. When he didn't call when he said he would, and she'd get angry because she had stayed in, waiting to hear from him, he'd say she was being unreasonable. It was dizzying the way he always turned everything on its head, inverted it, turned her hurt against her like a weapon wielded back against herself. Somehow, anytime she voiced a need, she was the one being insensitive; she was the one who misunderstood. If she started out needing reassurance, by the end of the conversation, she was the one reassuring him. With Teddy, she was always on the wrong side of everything. He made her feel like she deserved it, the push and pull of their relationship.

Once, after they'd broken up for the last time and Ransom had pulled her out of school and brought her back to Cliffhaven, Saoirse had called Teddy late at night, when everyone else in the house was asleep. She had the number to the fraternity house at Columbia where he stayed. When someone answered, she asked for Teddy, and they set the phone down to go look for him. She heard noises in the background—lots of people talking all at once, and music. A party. After several minutes, she was sure that whoever had answered the phone had forgotten about her, or maybe they had found Teddy but he didn't want to talk to her. She was about to hang up, but then she heard Teddy's voice on the other end.

"Meerkat," Teddy said, and her heart soared at the sound of his voice curling itself around her nickname. "Where have you gone off to, my little mongoose? I called around to Choate a couple weeks ago, and some girl told me you were no longer enrolled. Said you were sick or something."

"I'm not sick," Saoirse said. She took a deep breath. "I'm pregnant."

There was a pause on the other end of the line.

"That so?" Teddy said. "And who does the little wretch belong to?"

Saoirse pressed her lips together tightly. For a moment, she thought about telling Teddy the truth.

"Don't worry," she said after a moment. "It's not yours."

She couldn't tell if he really believed her or if he just wanted to believe her. Either way, he didn't press the issue.

"Anyway, Ransom's super pissed," Saoirse went on hurriedly. "He pulled me out of school because he doesn't want anyone to know, and he made up this whole story. And now he's keeping me here, in my own house, like a hostage or something. I'm not allowed to see or talk to anyone."

"Seems like a bit of an overreaction," Teddy said.

"Yeah, you think?" Saoirse said, irritated. She expected him to be more concerned about what was happening to her, the grave injustices she was being subjected to. He should be outraged. Instead, he sounded only vaguely interested, almost bored. "I was thinking, um, that maybe you could come get me?" Saoirse said. For some reason, it came out sounding like a question.

Teddy laughed. "What, you're serious?" Teddy asked when he noted her silence on the other end. "Meerkat, listen. I know this seems like the end of the world right now, but it won't be forever. You've got, what, like nine months? And then you give the thing away, and you go about your life again, pick up right where you left off, like nothing ever happened."

Saoirse felt like she might throw up, and this time, it wasn't the hormones. This was the boy who had told her that he loved her when they were pressed together in the back seat of his car. The boy who had cried in her lap that night at the boathouse, as she had stroked his hair. All this time, she thought she'd been privy to some secret, that she knew the one true Teddy Mountbatten, while everyone else got the glossy surface stuff. The charming, arrogant man versus the vulnerable boy she thought she knew. *So which is it?* she wanted to yell into the phone. *Who are you?*

"Teddy," Saoirse said instead, "you're being such an asshole."

"Hey now, don't be like that," Teddy said, growing irritated. "You know I care about you. I do. We're friends, right?"

"Sure," Saoirse said. "Friends."

She felt something warm and wet on her cheek and realized she was crying.

On the other end of the line, she heard someone call Teddy's name. It was a girl's voice. She sounded pretty.

The sound grew muffled, as though Teddy had cupped his hand over the phone. Saoirse heard him say, "Just a minute, sweetheart," his voice muted. Then, a moment later, louder, his voice clear, Teddy said, "Meerkat, I've got to go. It's Sunday night, and I've got a lot of studying to do. I have a big exam tomorrow."

"Yeah," Saoirse said. "Sure. Okay."

"And a bit of friendly advice, Meerkat," Teddy said, "next time some Joe Schmo comes on to you, keep your legs closed."

Saoirse hung up the phone, hard.

Saoirse had loved Teddy; maybe a part of her still loved Teddy, even if she wasn't supposed to, even if another part of her loathed him. In the pit of her stomach and the marrow of her bones, she knew he wasn't good for her. It was toxic, this thing between them.

But Salvador had seen her at her worst, and he loved her anyway. And it was love, despite what Ransom had told her or might believe. With Salvador, it wasn't up and down like it had been with Teddy. It was steady, even keeled.

Saoirse sighed and sat up. Today was the first day of the rest of her life, and she couldn't wait to start it.

CHAPTER THIRTY-FOUR

AUGUST 28, 1982—THE DAY OF SAOIRSE'S BIRTHDAY PARTY

The first guests arrived early, hours before the party was scheduled to start.

Ana had been in the drawing room with Saoirse and Mrs. Talbot, helping to write out the place cards, when a maid informed them a car full of guests had just turned down the drive. They hurried out to meet them. Ransom and Jacqueline were there, too, already at the bottom of the steps. Ana knew they had arrived sometime the night before, but she had been so busy this morning she hadn't yet seen them. She gave Jacqueline an enthusiastic wave.

"Why, darling, hello!" Jacqueline waved back. "We missed you at breakfast."

"Yes, I was helping with the place cards," Ana said.

"A hostess's job is never done," Jacqueline said.

Ana's eyes met Ransom's next. She smiled and started to say hello, but his eyes slid past her, to the car that had come to a stop at the front step.

The first girl who got out of the car was tall and lanky, with a pixie cut. Ana recognized her from somewhere, but she couldn't place exactly where.

"Evie, darling, it's been too long!" Saoirse said, flinging her arms around the girl. They rocked back and forth enthusiastically, almost losing their balance, then laughing.

"Handsome Ransom!" the girl called out.

"Miss Vanderbilt," Ransom said, giving a small nod of his head.

And then it clicked. Eve Vanderbilt. The heiress, the model. She walked on some of the world's biggest runways: Yves Saint Laurent, Armani, Gucci. She had just been featured in *Vogue*. Ana surveyed her more closely. She was pretty in the way that most models were pretty: she was tall and painfully thin, with wide-set eyes and high cheekbones. On the runway, she looked exotic—long necked, long legged, like a giraffe. Up close, there was something striking and androgynous about her features.

Eve kissed Ransom on the cheek and hung on to his arm, and Ana tried hard not to hate her. Her one respite was that Ransom didn't appear interested in Eve Vanderbilt at all. He looked almost bored with whatever she was saying to him, his gaze sliding away from her, back to the car and its passengers.

Another woman slid out of the back seat next. She was blond, with wavy hair and blue, sullen eyes. Ana recognized her from some of the pictures in Saoirse's room—Tessa Montgomery, her best friend and former roommate at Choate. She tucked her hair behind one ear and nervously readjusted the strap of her purse on her shoulder but made no move to embrace Saoirse.

"Happy birthday, Serse," the girl said tepidly.

Saoirse nodded. Her smile didn't quite reach her eyes. "Good to see you, Tessa."

Ana wondered at the lukewarm greeting but barely had time to ponder it, because a young man was getting out of the front passenger seat—he was tall and broad in the shoulders and undeniably handsome. His eyes were a salient blue.

"Teddy, you're here," Saoirse said flatly, crossing her arms across her chest, as if she'd just been assaulted by an icy breeze.

Ah, Ana thought. She'd overheard Saoirse and Hugh talking in covert whispers about Teddy Mountbatten, the dreaded ex. Though they rarely referred to him as Teddy—their nicknames were much more creative and impolite.

"You're looking well, Saoirse," Teddy said.

"You've gained weight," Saoirse said. "I've heard of the freshman fifteen, but what do they call this unfortunate phenomenon? The sophomore thirty?"

Teddy merely laughed. "Have I put on a few pounds?" he asked good naturedly, putting his hands on his toned stomach. "Well, I daresay you've lost some." He reached out and poked Saoirse's bare midriff, and she jumped back, as if he had shocked her.

"There are refreshments on the patio," Jacqueline announced. She gestured toward the two attendants who flanked her. "Tom and Jonathan will take your bags up to your rooms. There's croquet set up on the back lawn, if anyone has an interest."

"Yes, let's," Eve said. "Lead the way."

They shuffled up the stairs and down the hall, toward the back patio, and Ana found herself following behind Ransom and Jacqueline at the front.

"One of us should probably go see about the tent rental for tonight in case the weather takes a turn," Ana heard Jacqueline say. "The other one of us should stay and hold down the fort. Shall we flip a coin for it?"

"No," Ransom said, sighing. "They're my guests. I'll stay."

Ana was relieved to hear it and realized she'd been holding her breath, waiting for his answer. She wasn't sure, with the chaos of the party, whether they'd actually get to spend any time together, and they hadn't spoken in weeks—not since that kiss they had shared in the pool.

"There's a good sport," Jacqueline said, clapping him on the shoulder. "Try not to have too much fun." Then, she darted off in the direction of the kitchen.

The croquet court was set up on the back lawn. They decided to play singles—every person for themselves—and each person took a ball. Saoirse got blue because she was the birthday girl and got to go first. She gave Teddy the black ball. ("Black, like your heart," she told him.) One by one, they took their first shot, following their ball across the court, until it was just Ana and Ransom left.

He still had not really looked at her, and Ana tried hard not to get in her head about it. He was probably just distracted. There was a lot to think about with the party. He was just preoccupied, she told herself.

"After you," Ransom said, motioning for her to take her turn first.

Ana strode forward and made a steady stroke that sent her ball cleanly through the first wicket. Ransom followed, with his own close behind her. They paused and waited for the others to take their turns.

"You must be relieved," Ana said.

"Relieved?" he asked. "About what?"

"That all of your hard work is almost at an end," she said. "What are you looking forward to the most tonight? The dinner? The fireworks? The dancing?"

This last one was a joke, but Ransom didn't even crack a smile.

"Oh, I remember," Ana said. "That it will all be over soon?"

"Yes," he said dryly. "That does have a nice ring to it."

They watched the others taking their turns. Saoirse and Teddy were out in front. Teddy was talking to Saoirse, but they were already too far away for Ana to really hear what he was saying. She saw Saoirse roll her eyes and then lean forward, focusing on her shot.

Ana glanced back over at Ransom, who was watching the others, too, not looking at her. He was being weird. Standoffish. Cool. She wanted to break whatever this strangeness was that had settled between them.

"I got you something," Ana said.

Ransom looked over at her.

"It's, uh, back in my room," Ana went on. "I went into town the other day and found a copy of Judy Blume's *Are You There, God? It's Me, Margaret*. I thought you might like to read it."

Ransom kept his face blank, a vacant stare. Then, he looked away.

"I don't know why I'd want to read a silly children's book," he said.

Ana blinked at him. She wasn't sure if he was making a joke, or whether or not she should laugh. "I'm sorry?" she said.

"Miss Rojas, if I'm being perfectly blunt, you're behaving a bit more familiar than I find appropriate," Ransom said. "I am your employer, and you are my employee, and the only matter on which we are to converse is my sister. Other than that, as far as I'm concerned, we have nothing to say to one another."

Ana stood, shell shocked at his words. She felt as if she had just been slapped. "I don't understand," Ana said when she finally found her voice.

"Well, I don't know how I can state it any more clearly," Ransom said.

"The other day, at the pool—" Ana started, but Ransom cut her off.

"If I gave you the wrong impression the other day, then I apologize," Ransom said quickly, clearly impatient for the conversation to be over.

The wrong impression? It had been more than that. He had pulled her into his arms and kissed her. He had said the words out loud, how he didn't want to just be her friend. And now he wanted to act like none of that had ever happened?

"You kissed me," Ana said.

"A momentary lapse in judgment," Ransom said. "I assure you, Miss Rojas, it won't happen again."

Ana's cheeks flamed. Of course, it wasn't just about the kiss. She had shared things with him, and he had opened up to her. He had seen her, really seen her, and she thought she had done the same for him. But now she could feel the stark difference in how he looked at her, the way he held himself, tall and bracing, like an impenetrable wall. What the hell had happened? Ana didn't understand it.

"It's your turn, Miss Rojas," Ransom said, nodding toward the ball. "We're all waiting."

Ana glared at him but didn't answer. She dropped her mallet in the grass and turned back toward the house. She had to get away from here; she couldn't let him see. There were tears pricking the backs of her eyes—tears of anger, yes, but also something else.

She didn't offer any explanation, just strode purposefully toward the house, toward her room. But what was most disheartening was that he didn't ask. He didn't call after her or ask her to stop; he just let her go.

CHAPTER
THIRTY-FIVE

*AUGUST 28, 1982—THE DAY OF SAOIRSE'S BIRTHDAY
PARTY*

The ballroom was nearly full by the time Ransom showered, dressed, and came down for dinner. When he reached his assigned table, his cousin, Hugh, got up to greet him.

"There he is, Mr. Congressman, our family's shining star, our saving grace," Hugh said, giving him a hug.

"Hugh, it's good to see you," Ransom said. "I understand I have you to thank for the synchronized swimmers in the pool?" he asked as he took his seat.

"If there's one thing I know how to do, it's throw a party," Hugh said. Hugh's gaze slid over Ransom's shoulder, and his eyes lit up. "My God," Hugh said. "Who is this beautiful creature?"

Ransom turned in his chair. Ana stood behind him, dressed in the blue-green Yves Saint Laurent gown he had picked out for her that day on Rodeo Drive. It skimmed the curves of her body, the slit climbing all the way up her thigh. It was strapless, the neckline straight, showing off her bare shoulders and the olive tone of her skin. Her hair was sleek and straight, parted on the side and slicked back into a low ponytail that fell down her back. She wore a simple silver chain and pendant at the base of her neck. Ransom had never found collarbones so attractive before. He recalled that day in the pool when he had run his hands over them and down her shoulders and felt a deep fervent thrumming of desire pulse through him. He swallowed hard.

"Table two?" Ana asked, holding up her place card.

"You're in the right place," Hugh assured her, pulling out the empty chair between him and Ransom. "That dress, my dear, was made for you," Hugh went on. "You're a dark-haired Marilyn."

Ransom normally found Hugh's flirtations amusing, but now he found his grip tightening on his dinner napkin beneath the table.

"Come now," Hugh said. "You've earned yourself a drink for surviving the summer. Or should I say, for surviving Saoirse. Lord knows I love the girl, but she can be hell on wheels. And the two of us together—" He whistled. "Forget it." He motioned to a waiter passing by with a tray of champagne and lifted off two glasses. "Ransom, will you partake?" Hugh asked.

Ransom shook his head. He couldn't afford to be off his game tonight, to be operating at anything less than 100 percent. Tonight, it was too important that everything went according to plan. "No, thank you," Ransom said.

Hugh took a third glass anyway. "Ah, come now, we're celebrating," Hugh said. He set the glass down in front of him. "Now, I rather pride myself on giving toasts," Hugh went on. "It's a little hobby of mine. I'd make it a profession if I could, but I've vowed never to take a profession." He lifted his glass. "To you, my dear, for surviving the summer," Hugh said to Ana. "Saoirse's not just a little firecracker; she's the whole damn show."

Ransom raised his glass but didn't drink; he was saved from any protest from Hugh by the arrival of Jacqueline, who took the empty seat on Hugh's other side without waiting for anyone to pull out her chair.

"I can't believe you're drinking without me," Jacqueline said, admonishing the entire table. "Where's my glass?"

"Have mine, love. I'll get another," Hugh said, passing her his drink. He half stood to motion to the nearest waiter holding a tray and grabbed another glass.

"How was the croquet game earlier on the lawn?" Jacqueline asked, taking a sip of her drink. "I was sorry to miss it. I'm a very good player, you know. I could have gone pro if I didn't have such weak wrists."

"Are there professional croquet players?" Hugh asked.

"Oh, yes," Jacqueline said. "Anything where you hit a ball with a stick can be a profession."

Ransom glanced over at Ana. He watched the rise and fall of her collarbone as she drew breath, and he hated what it did to him, how he wanted to kiss the hollow of her neck. He looked away from her, stared down at his porcelain dinner plate. What was wrong with him? She was a liar, a manipulator, a con artist. He knew nothing about her aside from that.

"Picture?"

There was a man standing next to the table, a photographer. He held up his camera.

"Oh, yes, please," Jacqueline said. "I haven't eaten for a week. I need photographic evidence of how great I look."

She leaned in toward Hugh, already cheesing.

The photographer crouched slightly and looked through his lens.

"Congressman Towers," he said. "If you would, sir, lean in closer to the young lady."

Ransom reluctantly scooted his chair closer to Ana and leaned toward her until the lapel of his jacket was practically touching her shoulder. He stared straight ahead at the camera, but he felt Ana stiffen next to him. He could smell the store-bought shampoo she used, the faint whiff of strawberries. He held his breath.

The photographer snapped the picture. A second. A third.

Then he stood. "Thank you," he said and moved on to the next table.

Ransom scooted away from Ana, back to his place setting.

The salads came. Then dinner. Ransom had barely finished eating when the band started up and Saoirse was opening the dance floor with—to Ransom's immense surprise and disappointment—Teddy Mountbatten. He thought they were at odds with one another? But here they were, smiling, holding each other close. Everyone applauded when they finished, and then the band broke out into a banger, and Saoirse's friends flocked onto the dance floor.

"Come on, you ninnies, we can't be the last ones out there," Jacqueline said, throwing her dinner napkin onto the table and standing up.

Ransom shook his head, but Jacqueline pulled on his arm anyway.

"You have to dance at your own party," Jacqueline said. "Ana, you too. Don't make me throw you over my shoulder and carry you out there myself, because I *will* do it."

Ana stood reluctantly.

Hugh was already on his feet. They all followed Jacqueline, winding their way around the tables to the dance floor by the stage.

Ransom didn't mind dancing when there were rules prescribed to it—the waltz, the foxtrot, even a simple box step. But this solo dancing next to your partner, the ungoverned swaying and swinging of one's arms, one's hips, felt silly to him. Jacqueline bumped her hip into his and clapped her hands, and then Hugh took her hand and twirled her around. Then the music changed to a slow song, and Jacqueline and Hugh paired off, leaving Ransom and Ana standing there, just looking at each other.

Ana's eyes were cold and hard as she looked at him. She crossed her arms over her chest, as if she were cold, and something about the bareness of her shoulders and the way she was standing there, all alone, looking at him, made him feel weak in the knees. She opened her mouth to say something, but Ransom cut her off.

"I need a drink," he said brusquely.

He turned away from her quickly and made a beeline for the bar. When he caught sight of the line there, he thought better of it; he grabbed a glass of champagne from a proffered tray instead and headed for the open doors to the patio. Outside, the night air was cool and crisp against his face. He hadn't realized until that moment that he'd been sweating, the collar of his shirt sticking to the back of his neck. He took a swig of champagne and felt the bubbles, hard and abrasive against the inside of his throat.

What was wrong with him? What was he doing?

He stared out into the dark night. He couldn't see the water anymore with the lateness of the hour, but he could hear the waves in the distance beating against the shore.

"What the hell was that about?"

Ransom turned to see Jacqueline standing behind him, looking winded and irritated.

"What?" he asked.

"You left that poor girl stranded on the dance floor."

Ransom shrugged. "I didn't feel like dancing."

Hugh came up behind Jacqueline, jovial and oblivious, two fresh drinks in hand. "An old-fashioned for you, my dear," he said, handing Jacqueline hers. "What'd I miss?"

"Nothing," Ransom said. "I'm going to bed."

"Bed?" Jacqueline said, sounding insulted. "It's barely nine thirty."

"You two enjoy yourselves," Ransom said curtly. He had to get out of there.

"Huzzah!" Hugh said, lifting his glass in mock salute while Jacqueline huffed in blatant disapproval.

"You're not really going to turn in early at your own party? Ransom?" she called after him as he walked away, his back to her.

The night was already a disaster, and it had barely started. He couldn't wait for it to all be over, for all this to finally be behind him once and for all.

CHAPTER THIRTY-SIX

PARIS, 1961

On Tuesday evenings, they played cards with their neighbors, crowded around the tiny table next to the hot plate and sink and freezer box that comprised their makeshift kitchen.

"I don't think I would have ever left my husband if he spoke French," Astrid said, taking a drag on her cigarette in one hand and surveying her cards in the other. "French is such a romantic language. Every time they speak, it sounds like they're making love to you. But English, it's so vulgar, all the harsh consonants, the *r*'s. We sound like barking seals. And it's easy to be cross and fight when you sound like that. But I don't think French men ever say anything ugly."

"Never mind how they speak," Gisele said. "It's how they make love that sets them apart. I've never been so pleasured by an American man, an English man, even an Italian, as I have by the French."

Astrid laughed and laid down a card. "Well, I can't speak to that—yet."

Astrid and Florence had been in Paris for over a year now. They'd settled in Montmartre, a hilltop neighborhood on the northern fringes of Paris, where the rent was cheap. Rent went down as the hill went up, so they'd taken an apartment near the top, a few blocks from where a young, struggling Picasso had once lived in his artist abode, Le Bateau-Lavoir.

Their apartment was small—a single room, with a shared bath down the hall. Just a few steps from the table where they now sat was the bed where Astrid and Florence both slept at night. Their laundry hung from a drying rack near the solitary window that they'd left open in hopes of tempting in any passing breeze.

"What about you, Florence?" Gisele asked. "Have you experienced all that French men have to offer?"

"No," Florence said, blushing. "I'm a tabula rasa when it comes to love."

"How very Lockean of you," Hugo said, exhaling a plume of smoke from his cigarette.

"A virgin? At nineteen?" Gisele said, sounding horrified. "Mon Dieu! Mon pauvre. Is this by choice or circumstance?"

"My Florence is an ingenue," Astrid said, wrapping an arm protectively around Florence's shoulders. "I happen to think it's quite romantic that she's saved herself for so long. I, for one, would love to go back and experience it all again for the first time—that heart-pounding first kiss, the first time you fall in love. But we all only get one first."

"Paris is the perfect place for that," Gisele admitted.

Gisele and Hugo only left when all the wine was gone, so it was after midnight when Astrid and Florence got ready for bed. They undressed at separate ends, unbuttoning their blouses, unzipping their skirts, rolling down their pantyhose. Florence always turned away to dress or undress, facing the wall, but Astrid would strip down to the nude facing any which direction, without a stitch of self-consciousness. But then, what did she have to be self-conscious about? She was thin and beautiful.

"You never told me," Astrid said as she slid her nightgown over her head, "was there a boy in school you were sweet on?"

"No," Florence said, still facing the wall. She buttoned the top of her own nightgown and turned around to help Astrid turn back the coverlet.

"Have you never been kissed, Florence?" Astrid asked, very serious now.

Florence shook her head.

In truth, Florence had never felt an ounce of attraction when she looked at a boy. Even Adam Cunningham, arguably the handsomest, most sought-after boy at the high school she had attended—the quarterback of the football team and senior prom king. She could admit that he was objectively good looking, but she never felt that drop in her stomach when she looked at him. Her palms didn't sweat, her voice didn't quiver, her face didn't flush when he looked at her. Florence always felt that women were more attractive and pleasing to look at than men. The soft curves of their hips, the thin circles of their waists, the fullness of their breasts—there was a poetry, a real beauty, in their shape.

"Every girl should be kissed properly at least once in their life by someone who really knows what they're doing," Astrid said as she climbed into bed.

"Mm, is that so?" Florence asked, sitting down. She turned to fluff her pillow.

"Yes," Astrid said. "I'm no Elizabeth Taylor, but I fancy myself fairly experienced."

"You?" Florence asked, finally catching on. "You don't mean that you want to . . . you're not suggesting that we—?"

"Don't be such a goose," Astrid said. "I've kissed plenty of girls. We did it all the time at Choate. How else were we supposed to get any practice? We didn't want to be complete ninnies the first time a cute boy kissed us. We wanted to know what we were doing."

"I suppose that makes a certain sort of sense," Florence said.

"Shall we give it a go?" Astrid asked.

They sat facing one another on the bed, Florence with her legs crossed in front of her, Astrid perched on her knees. Astrid leaned forward and tucked Florence's hair behind her ear, and Florence's skin burned in the wake of Astrid's touch.

"Relax," Astrid whispered, and her warm breath against Florence's face sent goose bumps down her neck.

Florence tilted her chin up and closed her eyes. She felt Astrid cup the side of her face with her hand, and then Astrid's lips were against her own, warm and soft—gentle, like a question.

Florence had never known anything like it before, the wanting that erupted low in her belly, the way her heart galloped in her chest. She leaned forward into Astrid, and the kiss shifted with a wild urgency. She reached up and touched Astrid's neck and heard Astrid's sharp intake of breath. After that, the kiss became something else entirely. They broke apart a few moments later.

"So that's a kiss," Florence said, slightly out of breath.

"I suppose we got carried away," Astrid said, laughing.

Florence only nodded.

"Good night, dear," Astrid said. She reached over and turned out the light and climbed under the covers.

Florence rolled onto her side, facing the wall, and pulled the covers close, even though it was a warm evening. She touched the tips of her fingers to her lips in the dark, still feeling the reverberations of Astrid's lips on hers.

Florence worked at a café down the street from their apartment. She got there early, before it opened, folded pats of cold butter into the creases of dough that the baker made fresh every morning, piped chocolate into the hot centers of croissants. She always had flour dust in her hair and grains of sugar under her nails, and she stood all day at the counter, taking orders, handing the patrons their warm rolls in wax paper bags, frothing their milk at the espresso machine.

Astrid had worked for a while at a gallery when they'd first moved to Paris. She'd taken art history at school and was proficient in French, so she could talk at length about impressionism and postimpressionism, cubism and surrealism, and the burgeoning new realism that was all the rage. But while she was knowledgeable and charming, she often arrived late and left early. She was prone to taking long breaks, where she'd wander off from the gallery and leave it unattended, and once, the owner had found her napping in the storage room in the middle of the day. It wasn't her fault. The pills the doctor had given her for her foot made her groggy, and then they started to wear off before they should have, leaving her in pain, so she'd take more than she ought to, until they were gone. Florence and Astrid both agreed when the gallery let her go that it was useless for her to work until she was fully recovered, and so she spent her days sleeping late. She took up sketching and painting and even cooking to some degree, making rabbit stew on the hot plate in their apartment.

In the evenings, they would go to the ivy-covered cabaret Au Lapin Agile and sit at a table in the back by the bar, sipping their beers as they listened to poets read their work from worn notebooks and activists ardently recite their anarchist manifestos to the dimly lit room. Some nights, they'd get dressed up and wander down to the Moulin Rouge to watch the girls dance the cancan. For the first time in their lives, their time was their own. Florence had never felt more alive. She couldn't remember a time when she had been this happy.

Once a week at first, and then more often, they'd go down to the foot of Montmartre to Pigalle, the red-light district, where there was a brothel that doubled as an opium den. It was the only thing after the pills ran out that gave Astrid some relief. Florence never partook in the ritual, but she'd sit at the back and observe as they passed around the oil lamp; the ceramic pot of the tarry, amber-brown drug; a needle; and a bamboo pipe. The room was filled with an acrid smell. Afterward, Florence would put her arm around Astrid and help her home, tuck her into bed.

When Florence came home from the café late one afternoon, she found Astrid at the kitchenette, busying herself with the electric kettle, her back to the door. A well-dressed man was sitting at the table. It took Florence a moment before she recognized him.

"Charles," Florence said. The shock stole the breath from her body.

"Florence," he said. "It's good to see you."

"He's tracked us down," Astrid said brightly. "A regular Sherlock Holmes, this one."

She set a steaming cup of tea down in front of Charles at the table and sat next to him with one of her own. She was wearing a silk kimono, her hair loose around her shoulders, and she had dark circles under her eyes from the previous night's opium-induced haze.

"What're you doing here?" Florence asked.

Charles gave Florence a reassuring smile. "Scarlet was worried sick when your letters stopped," Charles said. "She phoned RJ, but he was evasive. First, you were always out. Then, you had gone on a trip. It was weeks before he admitted that the two of you had left and he didn't know where you had gone off to or if you were ever coming back."

"We're not," Astrid said, taking a sip of her tea. "Sit, darling," Astrid said to Florence. "You're making me nervous, just hovering by the door like that."

Florence sank into a chair at the table, her knees weak. "But how did you find us?" Florence asked.

"I came to London myself after RJ admitted that you'd taken off," Charles said. "I hired a private detective. You rented this place under your real names. It wouldn't take RJ half a week to find you if he put his mind to it."

He sounded slightly admonishing when he said this part. Florence couldn't decide if the censure in his voice was directed at them for running off and hiding or the fact that they hadn't done it well enough. Or perhaps it was directed at RJ for not putting an ounce of effort into finding them.

"Scarlet was fit to be tied when she heard you'd run off," Charles said. "The doctor prescribed her bed rest. She refuses to eat."

"Mother has always loved her theatrics," Astrid said, sounding exasperated.

"Astrid, this is serious," Charles said. "Scarlet was devastated not knowing where you were, if you were all right."

"We're fine," Astrid said dismissively. "In fact, we're better than fine. We're more fine than we've ever been in our entire lives."

"I can see that," Charles said, looking around the room.

"Tell her we're living in a quaint little apartment in Paris," Astrid said. "I've taken up painting. We'll come home for Christmas if that'll make her happy. Tell her to eat something."

Florence looked over at Astrid—how flippantly and casually she had offered for them to fly home and back again for the holiday. Did she not know the cost of two round-trip transcontinental tickets? Did she not grasp the stark reality of their financial situation? They were barely getting by, week to week. They were barely making rent.

"Now, I'm starving," Astrid said, as if she were bored with the conversation. "I'm going to go rinse off, and then let's go out. There's a Peruvian restaurant down the street that you'll just die for, Charles." Astrid gathered her towel and her bath caddy and disappeared out the door.

For a moment after she'd gone, Florence and Charles just looked at each other across the table.

"She's not well," Charles said.

"I know how it looks, but—it's because of her foot," Florence said hurriedly, wanting to reassure him. "It bothers her. It's the only thing that helps."

"How did it happen?" Charles asked. "Her injury?"

Florence paused, bit her lip. "When she told RJ that she wouldn't give up dancing, he told her he'd make it so she couldn't anymore," Florence said. "He took a hammer to her foot while the butler held her down."

A vein flared in Charles's neck. Florence knew him to be an even-tempered man. She'd never seen him angry before.

"Animal," Charles said under his breath.

"Please," Florence said, leaning forward. She set her hand on top of his on the table, imploringly. "Don't send her back to him, Charles. He'll kill her."

Charles thought for a moment. "And I suppose she won't come home?" Charles asked. "I mean, more than just for the holidays. To stay."

"That would kill her, too, but in a different way," Florence said. "I'm not sure which would be worse, in her eyes. She's happy here, you know."

Charles looked around the room again. His eyes landed on the single bed. "There's a sanatorium about a day's drive from here," Charles said. "I don't suppose she'd go?"

Florence shook her head. "I know her too well to ask."

After their newly found freedom, to go to a place where she didn't have any—Florence knew that would break Astrid.

"She's happy here?" Charles asked. "Truly? You both are?"

Florence nodded. "Yes."

They ate at the Peruvian restaurant, and Charles paid for their dinner. He stayed a week. He found a nice apartment for them on a quiet cobblestone street in the sixteenth arrondissement and rented it under a false name. Before he left, he took Florence aside and said he'd send her a weekly allowance to get them by.

"Take care of her, will you?" Charles said.

Florence nodded and promised him that she would.

Eight weeks later, Astrid was dead.

CHAPTER THIRTY-SEVEN

AUGUST 28, 1982—THE NIGHT OF SAOIRSE'S BIRTHDAY PARTY

Ana glanced down at the velvet purse she carried in her left hand. A clutch, it was called, because you had to clutch it to carry it; there was no handle. She'd been fearful the bag would be too small to fit the snub-nosed revolver, that it would bulge and give her away. But the bag was roomier than it looked at first glance, and the gun was so compact and slender that it fit easily into her purse with her compact mirror, powder, and lipstick.

Ana had stolen away from the party early. She could still hear the loud bass of the band playing and the hum of conversation as she crept up the stairs. She had one object in mind—Ransom's notebook. Ana hadn't been able to get it out of her mind since she'd first laid eyes on it that night in their hotel room—the daily journal of Ransom's private thoughts. It was the very thing she'd thought she'd had when she'd taken the black notebook from his locked desk drawer several weeks prior, only to find out it was a sketchbook instead. But this time, she was sure. The only tricky part about obtaining it was that Ransom always had it with him. Which meant it was only at Cliffhaven when Ransom was there. Which meant that Ana's opportunities to steal it were few and far between. But tonight, with the distraction of Saoirse's party, she finally had the perfect chance. As host, Ransom would be occupied all night, and the staff was busy catering to the guests, leaving the hallway of the family wing empty, free of prying eyes.

When Ana reached the second floor, she took off her shoes—the straps of her heels had rubbed the backs of her ankles raw, and they stung. She padded silently down the hallway and stopped outside Ransom's room. She glanced left and then right, and when she was sure that she was alone, she reached for the doorknob. But before she could turn it, the door opened on its own.

Ransom stood there in his shirtsleeves, his tie loosened, the buttons under his collar undone. He had a drink in his hand, and he looked harried.

"Ana?" he said. "I thought I heard someone out here."

Ana's heart leaped into her throat, and she took a step back. "Ransom," she said. Her mind was a fog. "I—I, um, saw you leave the party early. I just wanted to see if you were all right."

It was the first lie she could think of, and she wondered if it landed, because she could give fuck all if he was all right. She hadn't really seen him leave the party. In truth, she'd seen him leave the dance floor for the bar. She figured he was still carousing with his guests—and if not carousing, then at least, well, present. It seemed rude for him to leave his own party so early.

"Am I all right?" he echoed her, as if it were a question he was wondering himself. "Come in. Have a drink with me."

Ransom took a step back to make room for her. She hesitated, but what choice did she have? She'd just told him she'd come up to check on him. Ana clutched her purse to her stomach, and she could feel the hard metal barrel of the gun pressing into her, just north of her belly button, and its presence gave her some reassurance. She took a deep breath and stepped over the threshold; Ransom closed the door behind her.

He busied himself at his liquor cabinet, and Ana surveyed the room, her head still spinning from the sudden turn of events. There was a fire going in the hearth behind him. The doors to his balcony were open, ushering in a cool breeze and the sounds from the party below.

"Please, sit," Ransom said as he handed her a glass of brandy, neat.

She took a seat on the sofa, next to the fireplace, and kept her purse close on her lap. Ransom sat in the armchair across from her, between her and the door.

"So tell me, Ana," he said, sitting back. "Who are you, really?"

He looked at her so coldly, without feeling, that it sent a shiver down her spine.

"What?" she asked, trying to keep her voice steady. The question threw her off guard. What did he mean, who was she? She would have thought it was a joke if it weren't for the cold look in his eyes and his unforgiving tone.

"I know you're not who you've pretended to be," Ransom said. "You are not Ana Rojas, twenty-three, nursing student from California State University, San Bernardino."

He recited the most basic facts about her—her name, her age, her occupation. All those things laid out on the résumé she'd given him. All of them damningly false.

Ana shifted in her seat. She brought her glass to her lips and took a sip just to buy herself some time as she grappled for a response. Here it was, then, the moment she had been dreading, the thing that kept her up at night: that she would be exposed, caught, found out, before she was ready. Before she had accomplished what she had come here to do.

"You should know that the NDA you signed upon your employment is still binding," Ransom said, his voice so hard and cold it sounded foreign to her. "Signing a false name is fraud, and I plan to prosecute you to the full extent of the law. And if you should ever be so foolish as to put pen to paper, know this: I have vast resources at my disposal and a lethal team of lawyers."

Ana's mind was grappling with his words, trying to make sense of them. *Put pen to paper?* What was he talking about?

Ransom leaned forward, his elbows on his knees, looking at her intently.

"Everything you have, I will take from you," he said, his voice like ice, subhuman. "Every person you love, I will hunt them down. I will bury them in lawsuits so labyrinthine and costly that I will drain from them every penny they have ever made. I will bring down upon you and everyone you know a hellfire of litigation so intense that you will rue the day you stepped foot inside this house. I will make scorched earth of you."

The breath left Ana's body, as if she had been slammed against a wall. Once, she'd been in the front passenger seat while teaching her younger brother Jorge how to drive. They'd been going down a back road at night when a coyote had darted in front of their car. Jorge veered right, slamming on the brakes, and they skidded off the road, over the embankment, and landed upside down on the roof of their car in the dirt, twenty yards from where they'd left the road. Ana would forever remember the strange feeling of being so forcefully and unexpectedly knocked off center. The feeling of going so steadily, so assuredly in one direction, only to be slammed in another one altogether. To lose all sense of which way was up or down. As the car rolled, Ana's seat belt had hugged her body so tightly that it cut into the skin of her collarbone, and afterward, she'd had a bruise across her chest for weeks, so tender that it hurt to breathe.

This felt uncannily like that. Except then, she had felt fear. Now, she felt only anger.

"You'll make scorched earth of me?" she said.

The anger was a tight ball in her throat, so big she almost couldn't get the words out. What a self-important, entitled motherfucker. Of course he would go and hide behind his lawyers like he'd always done, have them fight his battles for him. He would sit in his ivory tower while his mercenaries eviscerated a grieved, working-class man and his wife. A family that had only ever asked for answers.

"You know, for a moment, I thought maybe there was more to you than some cold, calculated, callous man," Ana said. "But I had it right the first time. You're a monster."

Ransom's mouth settled into a grim, hard line. "I'm the monster?" Ransom said. "You're all the same. Coming at us like we're some zoo animals in a cage, only there for your amusement and entertainment, rather than flesh-and-blood human beings. The ones with the cameras and the microphones that they thrust into your face are bad enough, but you lot are worse. Pretending to be something you're not so that you can pick at our insides like scavengers."

"Ransom," Ana said, "what the hell are you talking about?"

"Don't play coy," Ransom said. "You're a tabloid journalist." He said these last two words as if they tasted foul in his mouth. "A vulture trying to get a scoop you can sell to the press."

Ana let out a shocked, bitter laugh.

A tabloid journalist? How could he think such a thing of her? That she was here for mercenary reasons? That she had interpolated herself into his household, his family, out of cruelty? How could he get her so wrong? Did he think so little of her character?

No, she decided. It had nothing to do with her character. The impenetrable walls he had built around himself were made of glass, but he didn't see through them like he thought he did. Instead, they reflected back at him all his own worst fears and insecurities.

"I'm not a—" She paused and shook her head. "I'm not a tabloid journalist, Ransom. My name is Elena Castillo. Rosie Castillo was my cousin."

For a moment, Ransom looked utterly confused. "Rosie Castillo," he repeated, as if trying to place the name.

Recognition slowly dawned on Ransom's face, then horror. He turned away from her, toward the window, his hand on his forehead, as if he were trying to stave off a coming migraine.

"My God," he whispered under his breath. He looked back at her in disbelief. "This whole time, I thought you seemed familiar," he said. "You look like her. I don't know how I didn't see it."

Elena didn't say anything. Every time he had asked her if they'd met before, a thrill of terror would rush through her. She swore, twice now, that she had given herself away, that he would know, with just one glance, who she was.

"You're here to expose me in some way?" Ransom asked.

Elena shook her head. "No," she said. "All I want is the truth."

"The truth," Ransom said sarcastically. "Coming from someone who posed under a fake name, who came into my home under false pretenses. Has anything you've told me since I met you had any semblance of truth?"

"If I've been dishonest, it's because you've given me no other choice," Elena said heatedly. "Any time my family has tried to get answers, we have been met with silence or legal sleights of hand. We do not have—how did you put it? 'Vast resources at our disposal.' Or 'lethal lawyers.' I saw a way to finally get answers, and I took it. If that makes me a liar, so be it."

Ransom rubbed his forehead, trying to puzzle it out. "I don't understand," he said. "How did you come about the job posting?"

"Sophia, my sister, is a nurse at UCLA," Elena said. "She saw the job posting that Jacqueline put out. She knew who Jacqueline was, who she worked for, and she told me about it. I thought—if I could just get through the doors, I don't know—maybe I could find something that would finally tell me the truth about what happened that day. But I knew you'd never hire me if you knew my real name, if you knew my connection to Rosie."

"And Ana Rojas—who is she?" Ransom asked.

Elena shrugged. "I don't know her. My cousin, he sort of runs a side business making fake IDs. This time, of course, the ID had to be a real person. He knew a girl who fit the profile we were looking for—someone our age who was going to nursing school—and he paid her to use her information."

"So everything you've told me about yourself is a lie?" Ransom asked.

"No," Elena said. "Mostly, I've been myself. I've told the truth. My relation to Rosie and the real reason I'm here are the only things I've been dishonest about."

"Well, I'm sorry you've wasted your time," Ransom said. "Everything I have to say about what happened that day, I've told to the police."

"I've read their report," Elena said. "Your version of events doesn't make any sense to me."

"Well, those are the facts," Ransom said. "Whether or not you can make sense of them is beyond my purview."

Elena bristled at his condescension. "The facts contradict themselves," Elena spat.

"You weren't there!" Ransom said, raising his voice now. He breathed deeply, tried to rein in his temper. "Any view you have on the matter is pure speculation," he said.

"It's not," Elena said. "Rosie and I, we talked on the phone most days. She told me about the people she met while working the front desk at the Duchess—celebrities, politicians, once, the Prince of Wales. She told me when you and Theo came in."

Ransom grew very still.

"You probably didn't notice her at first, didn't think anything of her—but she took note of you," Elena said. "You were quiet and aloof, she said, standing back from the desk, barely acknowledging her with a glance. There was a girl with you who didn't speak, and you held on to her arm. Your brother, Theo—she thought he was handsome and charming. He smiled at her, asked her for her name. You can imagine what a rarity that is for a front desk girl. The next day, he came by himself to ask for directions, and he leaned against the front desk like he had nowhere else to be. They talked for half an hour. He seemed kind. Later, he called down for more towels, and she brought them up.

It was the Lotus Suite you were staying in—do you remember? One of the nicest suites in the hotel."

Ransom had a look of quiet panic in his eyes.

"Theo answered the door when Rosie knocked; he invited her in," Elena went on. "You were playing cards around the coffee table in the sitting room—Go Fish, she said. It was you and Theo and that girl. Theo asked Rosie if she wanted anything to drink. She asked for a Coca-Cola, and the two of them stood out on the balcony, talking. She stayed for over an hour. When she had to leave, he walked her to the door. The three of you were going sailing the next day, on your yacht, to Catalina, he told her. It was Rosie's day off, and he asked her to join you. She was so excited that night when we spoke on the phone. It was all she could talk about," Elena said. "The next day, she was dead."

Silence settled between them.

"I am very sorry about your cousin," Ransom said. "Truly sorry."

"I don't need your condolences," Elena said. "I need answers. You claimed it was just you and Theo and Rosie on the boat that day. Just the three of you—no mention of the other girl who was there, the one from the hotel room. Why? Who was she?"

Ransom didn't answer.

"Your story—it's not the whole truth, is it?" Elena said. "You're leaving something out."

Ransom took a deep breath. "If you don't believe my account of things, then read the coroner's report. He ruled it an accidental drowning."

"He also said there was evidence of blunt force trauma," Elena countered.

Ransom didn't speak.

"Rosie never would have gotten into that dinghy without a life jacket," Elena said. "She was terrified of the water. She didn't know how to swim." Elena leaned forward, pleading. "Ransom, please. You have to understand—this was the dearest person to me in the whole world. Rosie was like my sister. And the not knowing—I can't do it anymore.

Please. I'm not here to gather dirt on your family. I'm not here to take you down. I just need to know what happened that day. What *really* happened."

Ransom fixed her with a steely gaze.

Over the past several months that she had known him, he had been cold and prickly and aloof. But there had also been moments when she had seen something else in him—flashes of kindness and generosity, real moments of vulnerability. Moments that made her think—hope—that he was the type of person capable of telling her the truth that she was so desperately seeking, someone who could set her free from her torment of not knowing.

"I don't think it was you who hurt Rosie," Elena said. "It was Theo in the dinghy with her. And Theo, he had a history of—"

"Those were all unsubstantiated rumors," Ransom said. "The girl from Vassar, she never pressed charges."

Elena pursed her lips. "You said yourself Theo was many things."

Ransom fell silent.

"I understand why you'd want to protect Theo when it happened," Elena said. "He's your brother, and you loved him, however flawed he may have been. But he's gone now. What's the use in protecting him anymore?"

"I'm sorry," Ransom said, "but I can't give you what you want."

There was a finality in his voice, and Elena felt his words to her core—the cold, swift kick of denial.

"Coward," she said, the ball of anger slipping into her belly. It was a fire that heated her whole body. She stood up.

She had come so far; she had gotten so close. She had never felt so angry and so helpless at the same time. She clenched and unclenched her hands. *This can't be it.* This couldn't be all there was. She hadn't spent the past three months at Cliffhaven for things to end like this, to return home with nothing.

She grabbed her purse and stood up, walked toward the door. The whole time, her mind was spinning, grappling for an idea, a plan, to turn everything around before it was too late. There had to be something she could still do.

She paused at the door and glanced down at the purse clenched at her side. She thought of the hard, cold metal gun it hid. She had only ever brought it with her as a means of protection. She was going to live in the house with the very man who might have had something to do with Rosie's death. She couldn't walk into the lion's den without a chair. She had never before imagined using the gun for harm or intimidation. But.

But. But. But.

She was desperate, wasn't she? And she was out of other options. If he wouldn't give her the truth, there was still something she could do to pry the truth from him, whether he was willing or not.

CHAPTER THIRTY-EIGHT

AUGUST 28, 1982—THE NIGHT OF SAOIRSE'S BIRTHDAY PARTY

Sometime around 10:30 p.m., the rain started. It was no more than a light sprinkle, but the strong, late-summer gale that accompanied it sent all the guests inside. The girls patted at their damp hair and flocked to the bathrooms to apply fresh powder to their noses; the men shirked out of their wet jackets and left them hanging on the backs of their dinner chairs to dry.

Saoirse grabbed another glass of champagne from a passing tray. She wasn't of legal drinking age yet, but hell, it was her party, and no one was going to tell her that she couldn't enjoy herself.

She waved across the room at one of her old school friends from Choate. In her alcohol-induced haze, she couldn't remember the girl's name, but they had been on the equestrian team together, and once, the girl had shared her cherry lip balm with her when it was cold and Saoirse's lips were chapped. The intimacy of the gesture had struck Saoirse at the time, as she had pressed the slick balm to her lips and then handed it back, and the girl had, without hesitating or thinking twice about it, applied it to her own lips and then slipped it back into her coat pocket.

"Don't worry," Jacqueline said, appearing by her side, her red dress noticeably speckled with raindrops, "we have the tents in the garage. We can have them up in no time."

"No, no, I already told you we don't need the tents," Saoirse said.

Jacqueline had tried to set up the tents before the party started as a preventative measure, but Saoirse had argued to have them taken down. The tents were ugly. You couldn't see the stars through them. Besides, Saoirse couldn't help but feel that putting up the tents was unlucky, as if the gesture would manifest the rain.

"Okay, but the storm—" Jacqueline said, clearly confused.

"Don't be dramatic," Saoirse said. "It's only misting."

Saoirse took a swig of her champagne. She felt gloriously warm and elated, buoyed up. It was her birthday, and everything was—*would be*—perfect. The mist would stop soon, and they would all go out and enjoy the fireworks.

"So that's a no to the tents, then—you're sure?" Jacqueline asked, sounding concerned.

"Yes," Saoirse said happily. "No tents!"

"All right, dear, it's your birthday," Jacqueline said resignedly before wandering off.

No sooner had Jacqueline left her than Bass was at her side, leaning forward to give her a kiss on the cheek. She could smell the brandy on his breath, sweet and nutty.

"Happy birthday, my dear," Bass said cheerfully.

"Yes," Saoirse said, raising her glass to toast herself. "Happy fucking birthday to me!"

She took a swig.

"I didn't care for how we left things the other day," Bass said.

For a moment, Saoirse didn't know what he was talking about, and then she remembered—the financial plan that Bass and Ransom had drawn up, the one that she had unceremoniously deposited in the trash can.

"Oh, that," Saoirse said. She didn't want to think about that now. It was her birthday. She wanted to think only about happy things.

"I believe it was a misunderstanding, on both of our parts," Bass said. "I think, if we could just sit down, the two of us, and talk—"

"Yes, but not now," Saoirse said, trying hard not to slur her words. Her mind was warm and fuzzy; she couldn't think straight. "This is a party." She gestured to the room around them. "Let's drink. Let's enjoy ourselves."

She raised her glass a little too heartily, and champagne sloshed over the edges and onto the floor.

Bass didn't seem to notice. "Yes, yes, of course," Bass said. "You're right. Actually, I just came over here to give you your gift."

He fumbled in his suit jacket, and the anticipation rose in Saoirse's chest. Bass was great at giving gifts. Masterful, even. For her thirteenth birthday, he had taken her to Studio 54, and she had seen Bianca Jagger ride a white horse across the dance floor in an off-the-shoulder red evening gown. For another birthday, he had gotten her a navy blue Hermès bag in crocodile skin, just like the one Grace Kelly owned. Of course, Saoirse couldn't bring herself to use the bag anymore, but she also couldn't bring herself to get rid of it. It sat on the shelf in her closet like a prized art exhibit, its beauty bringing her joy anytime she saw it.

Bass pulled out a thin, long box and opened the lid. Inside was a bracelet with a delicate gold chain, and from it hung several charms: a sun, a moon, and a dozen stars.

"I wanted to give you something to go with your necklace," he said.

Saoirse's hand went subconsciously to the pendant at the base of her neck, the one she always wore. Its inscription was emblazoned in her mind—the celestial bodies named there, echoed now in the charms of the bracelet Bass presented her with: the sun, the moon, the stars.

"Mother gave me this," Saoirse said. "For my fourteenth birthday."

A lump rose in her throat at the memory.

"It's from an E. E. Cummings poem," Bass said.

"Yes, I know," Saoirse said. "Mother's favorite poet. She kept a book of his poems on her bedside table."

"Yes," Bass said, nodding. He looked like he was somewhere far away in the past in that moment, in a time when her mother was flesh and blood, rather than just a memory.

"You know it?" Saoirse asked.

"Of course I know it," Bass said. "I was the one who gave her that book, for her fortieth birthday."

Something cut through Saoirse's champagne-induced haze—a needling feeling underneath her rib cage. She shook her head to clear it. Bass's words didn't make any sense. She recalled the hand-scrawled inscription on the inside title page of the poetry book that her mother kept on her nightstand: *Love defies reason.* It was unsigned, but it had always been obvious to Saoirse who had gifted her mother the book, who had written that inscription. It was a book of love poems, after all.

"Daddy gave her that," Saoirse said.

"Charles?" Bass said, breaking from his reverie. He laughed. "No, Charles was always more of a Keats man. Or Tennyson. He always said Cummings was too esoteric, too idiosyncratic, to be to his liking."

Saoirse instinctively took a step back.

It didn't make any sense, what he was telling her.

Or perhaps the problem was that it did make sense, a great deal of sense—it was more that Saoirse didn't want it to. The pieces were falling into place against her will. Every memory like a puzzle piece fastening itself together, forming a picture she didn't want to see. Bass at every birthday party, every Christmas, every family vacation. The way he rested his arm on the back of her mother's chair when they were at dinner. One time, while stepping off the boat onto the pier, Saoirse's mother had lost her footing and fallen back into the boat, and Bass had cried out, as if he had been the one to fall. He'd jumped down into the boat after her to make sure she was all right.

"You're lying," Saoirse said. "You're a liar."

Only then did Bass seem to realize that something was wrong. He reached out and grabbed Saoirse's forearm to steady her.

"My dear, are you all right?" he asked.

Saoirse's throat was constricting. She couldn't breathe.

The next realization was cold and sharp, like a knife cutting through her: of course her mother hadn't given her that necklace, the one she always wore, the one that proclaimed how her mother really felt about her. It had been Bass all along. Bass, the master of gifts. Which meant that Saoirse had never misunderstood her mother's resentment. Her dislike, her lack of regard—which had always shown so plainly in her mother's actions toward her—was probably exactly how she had really felt.

Saoirse groped for the chain around her neck. It wasn't tight, but still, it felt like it was choking her; she had to get it off. She grasped at it and pulled hard—one sharp yank, then two. She felt the clasp give; there was a sharp pain at the back of her neck. She pulled the chain off her, and she felt the pendant slide off and fall into the neckline of her dress, but she barely noticed. She clasped the chain so hard that the sharp stars that jutted out cut into the flesh of her palm, and the pain was a welcome, if insufficient, distraction from her thoughts.

"Saoirse—what?" Bass started, alarmed, but she cut him off.

"Did Daddy know?" she asked. She could barely get the words out.

Out of everyone in her family, her relationship with her father had been the only one that hadn't been riddled with complications. He had loved her without strings. That had been the one pure thing in her life.

And it wasn't even real.

Bass looked confused at first and then panicked. He removed his hand from her arm and looked away from her.

"I don't . . . I'm not sure what you think—"

"Tell me the truth, for once," Saoirse said, her voice loud.

The people closest to them stopped talking, turned to look.

Bass stuttered, red in the face, but he wouldn't give her an answer.

Saoirse felt a lump rise into her throat.

Maybe her father had died thinking she was still his little girl. But if there was a heaven, if there was an afterlife, maybe now he knew the truth: that she didn't belong to him. That the one thing that had been good about her life was actually a lie.

Saoirse ardently wished there weren't a heaven or a hell, or any sentience or omniscience granted to us after death. She wished for oblivion. Blinding and numbing oblivion. That way, at least, things would never change between them. They'd go on, just as they had been, until she died.

Saoirse dropped the chain of her necklace at Bass's feet.

"I don't know how you live with yourself," she said.

Desperate, Bass grabbed Saoirse, hard, by the elbow. "Saoirse, please—" he said, but Saoirse ripped her arm out of his grasp.

"Don't touch me," she shouted, and several more people turned to look.

Saoirse felt someone next to her then, a man, but she was too disoriented to notice who it was. She was dizzy. She thought she might pass out. She reached out to steady herself, and the man took her arm, wrapped it in his.

"There you are, Meerkat," the man said, as if he'd been looking for her.

She didn't hear what the man said after that, but she let him steer her across the ballroom. The next thing she knew, they were standing at the bar, and he was handing her a drink.

"Teddy," she said, as if she had just noticed him.

"Yes, of course it's me," Teddy said.

She took the drink he handed her and downed it in two swigs. It burned the back of her throat, warmed her stomach. She wiped the back of her mouth with her hand, and Teddy laughed.

"Attagirl," Teddy said. "Fancy another turn around the dance floor?" he asked.

He didn't wait for her answer; he already had his arms around her waist, as if they belonged there. As if they belonged together. Saoirse tried to push him away, feeling repulsed.

"Don't touch me," she said.

"What's this?" Teddy asked, confused.

"I said, get your fucking hands off me."

She broke away from him and walked in the other direction as fast as she could, out of the ballroom, toward the bathroom, where he couldn't follow her. There was a line in the hallway, but Saoirse didn't care. She cut to the front of it, and as soon as the door opened, she rushed inside, then slammed the door shut behind her and locked it.

Saoirse sank to the floor. She pressed her lips together to try and muffle her sobs, but she knew they all could hear her anyway in the hall—her gasps, her pitiful sobs.

How did she end up here, she wondered, at her own party, hiding in the bathroom, a weeping mess?

The tiles under her were muddied with heel prints and mud from the rain earlier. Her beautiful, perfect dress was probably streaked with mud now, ruined, but she didn't care. Everything was ruined anyway.

There was a knock at the door.

"Go away," Saoirse said harshly.

"It's me," a woman said, and Saoirse recognized Tessa's voice. "I just wanted to make sure you were all right."

Tessa. There would have been a time in her life, not too long ago, when Saoirse wouldn't have hesitated to let her in. Tessa was the closest thing Saoirse had ever had to a sister. They'd sat next to one another in their algebra class at Choate, passing notes surreptitiously back and forth; borrowed one another's eyeliner; squeezed themselves onto a sofa, lying side by side like sardines, one summer night at a house party in Martha's Vineyard when they were too stoned to stumble home. There was a time when Saoirse couldn't imagine keeping anything from Tessa.

But then Teddy had happened, and Saoirse suddenly couldn't find herself divulging the biggest secret she'd ever had: that she was pregnant. She knew that Tessa would tell Teddy, and she didn't want Teddy to know the baby was his. She wanted him to care, but not because he had to. She had shut Tessa out, and Tessa had bristled at her sudden distance, her silence, her coldness.

Now, Saoirse wiped her snotty nose on the back of her hand and stood on shaky legs to unlock the door.

Tessa looked at Saoirse a moment—her mascara-streaked face, her rumpled dress—and then turned toward the women still standing in line, the ones staring at the two of them curiously, craning their necks to get a peek.

"There's another bathroom down the hall, on the other end," Tessa said.

The women just looked at her, not moving.

"Get out of here," Tessa said, louder, more firmly. "Go."

She started waving them away, yelling at them to hurry up, asking them what they thought they were looking at. When the line had dispersed, Tessa entered the bathroom and closed the door behind her. She grabbed a fresh hand towel from the basket, and Saoirse joined her at the pedestal sink.

"Was it Teddy?" Tessa asked as she wetted the towel and dabbed at the charcoal streaks down Saoirse's cheeks.

Saoirse shook her head. "For once, no."

Saoirse's breathing slowly steadied, and she hiccupped her way back to a semblance of calm. It was such a relief not to be poked or prodded with questions, to just be cared for. She felt raw, her head too big for her body, like it couldn't possibly be connected to the rest of her at all.

"That's better," Tessa said when she was done.

Saoirse glanced at her reflection in the mirror. Her eyes were red rimmed and watery, but other than that, she looked normal.

"What a fucking disaster of a night," Saoirse said.

Tessa shrugged. "I don't know," she said. "I mean, if some girl isn't absolutely losing it in the bathroom, is it even a party?"

Saoirse caught Tessa's gaze in the mirror and laughed so hard she snorted.

"Ow," Saoirse said, touching her nose.

"What do you say we grab some cake and go watch the fireworks?" Tessa asked.

"Fireworks?" Saoirse said, a panicked thought suddenly percolating in her mind. "It's midnight?"

"Thereabouts," Tessa said, checking her watch.

"I have to go," Saoirse said, darting toward the door. "There's somewhere I need to be."

"What, is your carriage going to turn into a pumpkin or something?" Tessa called after her, but Saoirse didn't answer.

Saoirse speed-walked down the hallway, past the entrance to the ballroom, telling herself not to run, not to attract attention. A woman she didn't know, who was very much inebriated, exuberantly wished her a happy birthday as she passed, raising her glass high into the air and sending champagne sloshing over the sides and onto the wood floorboards. Saoirse only nodded at her.

She was flat-out running after she turned the corner, down another hallway, this one much quieter than the one outside the ballroom. She started up the staircase, taking the stairs two at a time, and then took a sharp left down the next hall to the library. She was going so fast she almost ran right into him.

"You came!" she said excitedly, throwing her arms around him.

"Of course I came," Salvador said. "Did you ever doubt I would?"

He was wearing a suit and tie. She had never seen him so dressed up before. He looked handsome.

"I don't know," she said into his chest, smelling the familiar spicy scent of him, like cloves and bergamot. It was a comforting smell. "Everything tonight has been such a disaster."

"What happened?" he asked, stroking her hair.

"Nothing," she said. "I don't want to talk about it. I don't want to think about it. I just want to forget it ever happened. Can we do that?"

"It's your birthday," he said. "We can do whatever you want."

"Good," Saoirse said. "Well, I want to go watch the fireworks."

She led him by the hand out the back into the dark. People were gathering on the balcony, but there was almost no one in the yard or in the garden. Saoirse and Salvador took the rickety old staircase on the cliffside down to the beach. They made their way down slowly, carefully, as the steps were slick with the recent rain.

"Do you think it will storm later?" Salvador asked, looking up at the sky dubiously.

"It wouldn't dare rain on my birthday," Saoirse said. "Again."

When they reached the bottom, Saoirse took her shoes off so she could feel the sand between her toes. They were the only ones on the beach. Probably the daunting look of the staircase and the earlier rain had put everyone off it, but she didn't care. It was better this way, just the two of them. She lifted up the hem of her dress and stepped into the water lapping at the shoreline. The cold salt water felt good against her skin. Salvador followed suit, kicking off his dress shoes and rolling up the hem of one pant leg and then the other to follow her.

When the fireworks started, they stood on the beach, looking up at the sky. Saoirse leaned into Salvador, and he wrapped his arms around her.

This is perfect, Saoirse thought. *Everything is perfect now.*

In between the breaking of the waves along the shore and the loud crack of the fireworks erupting overhead, Saoirse heard the creaking of the stairs behind them. She turned her head. There was a figure there, stepping down onto the beach. At first, Saoirse thought it might be one of her party guests coming down to enjoy the fireworks, but who would venture down here by themselves in the dark? Besides, they weren't looking up at the sky, admiring the show. They were staring right at her and Salvador.

"Hello?" Saoirse called out, trying to keep the quiver out of her voice. "Who's there?"

The person didn't answer. They took another step forward. Saoirse couldn't see from this distance who it was, if she knew them.

She tugged on Salvador's arm, and he turned to look too.

"Who is that?" she whispered to him, and she felt his arms tighten around her.

Just then, the sky lit up again, not with a colorful explosion but with lightning. Saoirse saw who the person was and what they were holding.

"Oh my God," Saoirse said.

And then the sky went dark, plummeting them into pitch blackness.

CHAPTER THIRTY-NINE

AUGUST 28, 1982—THE NIGHT OF SAOIRSE'S BIRTHDAY PARTY

I t was Ransom.

It took Elena a moment to realize he had his hand on the door, keeping it shut. That she couldn't leave. She turned her head—he was right behind her, standing so close the heat of his breath hit the side of her face.

"Wait," he said.

His voice was soft, barely a whisper. She hated the way her body responded to him, softening, turning toward him, when she was so angry, when she wanted to hate him. For a moment, they just looked at each other, merely inches apart.

Ransom cleared his throat, took a step back. He motioned toward the sofa facing the fireplace. "Let's sit," he said. When she didn't move, he added pleadingly, "Please."

"Okay," Elena said. Her grip lightened a little on her purse. She returned to the couch, and Ransom sat next to her this time, but carefully, a good distance apart, as if he were afraid of getting too close.

"I'll tell you as much as I'm able to," he said. "I'll be as honest as I can be. And in return, I ask that you give me your word that whatever

I relay to you tonight is never talked about outside this room. People's lives depend upon it."

"People's lives?" Elena asked.

"That's all I can say until you agree," Ransom said. "You said you want the truth about what happened that night. That knowing will grant you some sort of peace. Fair enough. I will tell you what you want to know, what really happened to Rosie, but it's for you to know and no one else."

Elena sat back. "What? No nondisclosure agreement for me to sign this time?" she asked. "Just my word?"

"Anyone can wiggle their way out of legal entanglements if they really want to," Ransom said. "A person's word is more binding if they have a certain level of integrity, which I believe you to possess."

Elena thought about this for a moment. Then, she extended her hand. "Okay," she said. "You have my word. Whatever you tell me will never leave this room."

They shook on it.

"Who was the girl that was with you on the boat that day?" Elena asked. "The other one—the one Rosie saw with you at the hotel?"

"Her name is Vivienne Smith," Ransom said. "She's my sister."

Elena blinked at him. "Your sister?" she said. "I don't understand. You have another sister besides Saoirse?"

Ransom nodded. "I didn't know about Vivi until after my parents passed away," he said. "They kept her hidden away at a nunnery in Santa Maria—a secret to the world."

"Why would they do that?" Elena asked.

"Vivi was born severely developmentally handicapped," Ransom said. "My parents wanted to protect her. Or, maybe, they wanted to protect themselves. I don't know. I won't excuse it, what they did, but there it is."

Elena waited for him to go on.

"It was Vivi's birthday that weekend," Ransom said. "Our parents had just passed away, and Theo and I wanted to do something nice for her. We never got to be a family together, growing up. Vivi wasn't a part of our holidays or any of our family trips. So we took her away for the week, to Los Angeles, to the Duchess Hotel, just like our parents used to take us when we were kids. We were trying to make it up to her—everything she had missed out on, everything *we* had missed out on by not having her there."

He fell silent, and Elena waited for him to continue.

"Vivi had never been sailing before, and Theo thought it would be a fun way to spend the day," Ransom said. "So we rented a boat—a sailing yacht, about fifty feet, just small enough that Theo and I could handle it on our own and we wouldn't need a crew. It was supposed to just be the three of us, but, well, Theo was being Theo. He thought Rosie was cute, and he invited her along. I was pissed at him, to be honest," Ransom said. "That weekend was supposed to be about Vivi. But Theo always had a way of making things about himself."

He paused and stared down at the floor. He didn't like to think about that day. He had never talked about it, about what really happened, with anyone.

Ransom took a deep breath and went on.

"We anchored off the coast of Catalina. Theo wanted to take the dory out and take some pictures with Rosie. Vivi wanted to go, too, and she was upset when we told her she couldn't, that she should stay back with me. She didn't understand why she was being left out. But the truth was she couldn't swim, and we were worried about her going along in the dory with the wind and the water being as rough as they were. There was an argument, and she stormed off. I thought she had gone off belowdecks and that I would just let her cool off, and then I'd go after her, maybe try to rouse her interest in casting a line off the back. So I helped Theo and Rosie into the dory, and it was at least half an hour before I went to look for Vivi belowdecks and realized she wasn't there. It took about as long for Theo and Rosie to figure out Vivi was on the dory with them. She'd hidden beneath a pile of blankets. By then, they were so far out it didn't make sense for them to turn back. Rosie took off her life jacket and gave it to Vivi when she saw she wasn't wearing one. It was selfless, what Rosie did. It probably saved Vivi's life and ended up costing her her own."

Ransom paused. This next part was the hardest to talk about. His heart squeezed in his chest like a fist was gripping it.

"A wave hit the dory, and it capsized," he said. "Theo's oar struck Rosie in the head as he went over, knocking her unconscious. It all happened so fast. He got the boat upright and went to Vivi first. Once she was secure, he went after Rosie. He didn't realize until it was too late what had happened, how badly off Rosie was. By the time he rowed them back to the yacht, she wasn't breathing; her lips were blue. We tried CPR, pumping her chest with our bare hands until we left bruises, but it didn't do any good. When we got back to the harbor, Theo wanted to call for an ambulance right away, but I wouldn't let him. Rosie was already gone; we couldn't help her. I told him we had to get Vivi back to the hotel first, that Vivi couldn't be there when the ambulance came. There would be police once they found out Rosie was dead; they would have questions. And we couldn't explain Vivi without upending her whole world. And I never, ever wanted Vivi to feel like she was somehow responsible for what had happened to Rosie. I don't think she could handle that. I told her that Rosie was sick, that we were getting her help, when I took her back to the hotel. And she believed me."

Ransom fell silent.

"I think about your cousin often," he said after a while. "How senseless her death was. I will carry the guilt of what happened that day with me for the rest of my life. But it *was* an accident. There was no foul play."

Elena sat back in her seat. This heavy thing that she had carried with her for the last four years—this hollow ache in her chest, this anger, these questions—she could finally set it down, release it, let it go. She felt at once relieved and, strangely, very, very tired.

Rosie had acted selflessly in her last moments, Elena thought. Even though she must have been very afraid, she had given up her life jacket to keep Vivi safe. And she had. Elena took comfort in that. Rosie had saved Vivi's life. Elena wouldn't dishonor Rosie's final act of bravery by ever breathing a word about Vivi and what had really happened that day. She would do her part to keep Vivi safe too.

"Can I ask you something?" Elena said after a while.

Ransom looked at her grimly, as if he were afraid of what she might ask. Still, he nodded. "Sure," he said.

"Why don't you have any pictures on the walls?"

He blinked at her. "What?"

"Your bedroom," Elena said, looking around. "It's so . . . impersonal. You've lived here your whole life, and yet there are no photos of you or your family or your friends. Your bookcase looks like it was curated by a college professor. I don't think there's a single book in there a normal person would actually want to read unless it was required. You don't even have any lube or condoms in your bedside table."

"How do you know what's in my bedside table?" Ransom asked.

"Not important," Elena said. "Just answer the question."

Ransom sighed, ran a hand through his hair. "Truthfully, I couldn't tell you what's in that bookcase," he said. "My mother renovated my room one summer when I was gone, and she stocked it with whatever looked nice. I think it was more about aesthetics than anything."

"And the no-personal-photos thing?" Elena asked.

Ransom shrugged. "I suppose it just never occurred to me to put anything up. This place has never been home to me, not really. I went off to boarding school when I was twelve. And then it was on to college and grad school and then DC. I never actually spent much time here. I still don't."

Elena nodded. "I guess that makes sense. When I first saw it, I sort of thought, I don't know . . ."

"That I was devoid of a soul or personality?" Ransom asked.

Elena smiled. "*Sociopathic* is the word I would use."

"You seem to use that word a lot, don't you?"

"Just with you," Elena said.

Ransom laughed. "I assure you, Miss Castillo," he said, "at my town house in DC, where I *actually* live, there are plenty of pictures on the wall and books you would want to read."

"And in your bedside drawer?" Elena asked, raising her eyebrow.

Ransom smiled wryly. "As we've previously established, Miss Castillo, everyone has things they'd like to keep private."

Elena nodded, bit her lip. "Please," she said. "You can call me Elena."

CHAPTER FORTY

PRESENT

There was a woman coming up from the gardens. She had on running shorts and a T-shirt, her short salt-and-pepper hair tied back at the nape of her neck. Detective Church watched her from the top of the terrace as she ascended the steps. She had AirPods in, so she didn't notice him until she was almost to the top and just a few feet away.

"Detective Church," she said pleasantly enough, though she looked slightly puzzled to see him. Her forehead was sweaty, and she was out of breath.

"Mrs. Towers," he said.

"Please," she said, "you can call me Elena."

"Elena," he said.

"Are you looking for my husband?" she asked. "I believe he's up at the house."

"Actually, I was looking for you."

"Me?" Elena asked, sounding surprised.

"I've been looking for you for quite a long time, actually," Church said. "Or, should I say, I've been looking for Ana Rojas."

He heard her breathing alter, but her face remained unchanged. He pulled a picture from inside the breast pocket of his jacket.

"This is you, is it not, sitting there next to Ransom, at table two?" Church said, holding the picture out to her.

Elena looked but didn't move to take the photo from him.

"Would you like to sit down?" she asked. She raised a hand to shield her eyes from the bright sun and squinted at him. It was a hot and sunny day. "I'm parched, and if I don't get out of this heat, I think I might pass out."

"Lead the way," Church said.

They settled at a table under a shaded part of the terrace. A maid brought them a giant pitcher of lemonade and two tall glasses full of ice.

"Did you grow up around here, Detective?" Elena asked as she poured him a glass.

"Not far," Church said. "Just south, in Morro Bay."

"Ah, so you're familiar with the house, then?" Elena asked. "Of that feeling of looking up at it from a distance?"

Church nodded. "When I was a boy, I used to think that King Arthur and his knights lived here, in this castle on the hill."

Elena chuckled. She poured a glass of lemonade for herself and took a sip, settled back into her chair. "I can tell you it's a completely different experience from the inside," Elena said. "There are leaky faucets and creaky stairs; sometimes, the toilets run. This house is just a house, however big it may be. And the people in it are just people. Skin and bone. Flawed, just like anybody else."

"Did you know Ana Rojas?" Church asked. "The real Ana Rojas, I mean?"

"No, not really," Elena said, setting down her glass. "She was a friend of a friend."

"So she was aware you were impersonating her that summer, that you had taken her identity?"

"She was more than aware, Detective," Elena said. "It was her idea."

Church leaned forward in his seat. "What do you mean?" he asked.

"Well, it's a funny story, really," Elena said. "Ana applied for this caretaker job as a summer gig, but when she got the request for the interview, she didn't want to go. She'd met a boy; he was in a band. Young love, you know?" Elena said, waving her hand, as if all this were obvious. "She wanted to spend the summer traveling with him, but her mother didn't approve. Ana still lived at home, you see. They were a very Catholic family. So she came up with this idea to cover her absence, that someone else would go in her place. My friend told me about her predicament, and I volunteered. I needed a job that paid well. We struck up a deal. And the rest, as they say, is history."

Elena took a sip of her drink.

"And when did Mr. Towers come to learn the truth?" Church asked.

"A few weeks before Saoirse's party, I came clean to him," Elena said. "We'd started to spend a lot of time together by then. We'd become quite close, and I felt guilty lying to him."

"And how did he react when you told him that you weren't who he thought you were?"

"He was upset at first. Shocked. But he eventually got past it."

Church thought for a moment, considered this. "The night of the party," Church went on, "did you go to Mr. Towers's room then?"

"Yes," Elena said without hesitating.

"At about what time?"

She bit her lip, looked around. "I don't know," she said. "After dinner, after the dancing had started."

"Around ten o'clock?"

"Yes, that sounds right."

"And what was the nature of your interaction that night?" Church asked. "In Mr. Towers's room?"

Elena raised her eyebrows. "Really, Detective?" Elena said. She shifted in her chair. "We talked. We enjoyed each other's company."

"And when did you leave?"

Elena thought for a moment. "Late," she said. "Maybe one or two in the morning."

"So you weren't with your husband the entire night?"

"No," Elena said.

Church pondered this. "Did he seem off at all to you the next morning, when you saw him?" Church asked. "Was there anything unusual about his behavior?"

"Just what are you suggesting, Detective?" Elena asked.

"I'm not suggesting anything," Church said. "I'm simply asking a question."

"No," Elena said. "Nothing seemed unusual about his behavior. He seemed tired, agitated. He didn't care for large social events, and he'd taken great care to make sure the evening had been perfect. He had more duties to carry out that morning before everyone left. It drained him. Everything seemed perfectly within the realm of normal."

"And what of his appearance?" Church asked. "Were there any scrapes, cuts, or bruises on his arms or face? Any odd abrasions?"

Elena laughed. "Detective Church, do you think I would marry someone I thought was a murderer?" She leaned forward. "You don't know my husband's character as I do," she said. "Despite what people may say or what the public perception of him may be, he is a good man. An ethical man. He feels things very deeply. He is steadfast and loyal. He would never harm his sister. *Ever.* And that's the end of it. Whatever happened to Saoirse, my husband had nothing to do with it."

Church's phone rang in his pocket.

"I apologize," Church said. "I thought I'd shut this off." He pulled out his phone and went to silence it, but when he saw the name on his screen, he paused. "Excuse me, just one moment," he said to Elena. "I have to take this."

Elena watched Detective Church get up from the table and move a little way off, the phone pressed to his ear, his voice too low for her to make out. His forehead creased, and at one point she heard him mutter, "Jesus Christ." A few minutes later, he returned to the table, looking rattled.

"Everything all right, Detective?" Elena asked.

Church put his phone back in his pocket and rubbed his chin. "That was Detective Leland," he told her. "He's just identified the second body."

Elena's eyebrows shot up. "Really? That's wonderful," she said. "Who is it?"

"I'm afraid I can't say—not just yet, anyway," Church said. "Thank you for your time, Elena," he went on. "I appreciate your candor, but there's one more person I need to speak with before I go."

"My husband?" Elena asked, already scooting back her chair. "Shall I go get him?"

"No," Church said. "I'd like to speak with Florence Talbot."

CHAPTER
FORTY-ONE

1961

It felt surreal to Florence to be back in her old rooms again at Cliffhaven. The last time she was here, three years before, she'd been mourning the passing of Doris. At the time, she thought she'd never again know a grief so raw and harrowing, but she'd been wrong. Astrid's passing had gutted her. This time, a part of her was missing. A part of her was gone, and she knew she'd never get it back. She'd never be whole again.

Charles had flown to Paris as soon as he'd heard the news of Astrid's overdose. Florence had come home from work to find Astrid still and unmoving in their bed, her lips tinged blue, her eyes vacant and staring. Charles took care of closing out the apartment, arranged for the body to be flown back with them. And he brought Florence home with him to Cliffhaven.

Scarlet was despondent at the funeral. She shrieked and fell to her knees when they lowered the coffin into the ground, and it took the strength of two men to pull her up again. She wept hysterically, and Florence's heart couldn't help but pinch at the glimmer of Astrid she saw in the display.

After the funeral, Florence wandered the halls vacantly, like a ghost. No one asked anything of her. She slept late and went to bed early and pushed the food around on her plate, barely eating.

After a while, Florence started to wonder if she really had become a ghost. People no longer tried to engage her in conversation when they saw her. She wondered sometimes if they even saw her at all as she glided through the rooms of Cliffhaven silently. It was almost like she wasn't there, the way that people's gazes slipped past her (or was it through her?).

One afternoon, she went into the library to get a book, and she saw them standing there, silent and still as statues. Birdie, Charles's wife, her hair swept back into a low chignon, and William Bass, standing over her. Florence stopped instantly and breathed in sharply as the cold realization of what was happening washed over her. Bass's hand was on the top button of Birdie's silk blouse, and he leaned toward her, possessively, and she toward him, as if they belonged to each other. Birdie's eyes drew toward Florence, reflexively, across the room. But Birdie didn't say anything, and her expression didn't change when she saw her watching them. Bass leaned forward and kissed Birdie's neck, and, after a moment, Birdie closed her eyes. Florence retreated from the room, as quietly as she had come.

A few months later, Scarlet Towers died silently in her sleep. She was only forty-seven. The medical examiner said there was nothing wrong with her, aside from the fact that she was dead. But nobody was surprised by her passing or questioned its cause. It was obvious that Scarlet had died of a broken heart.

Three years passed at a pace that felt, to Florence, impossibly slow and, at the same time, much too fast. Suddenly (or so it seemed to Florence), her old companion Verity—her first playmate, the girl with whom she had shared the nursery and been tutored side by side—had graduated from college, married, and had a son. Florence could barely recognize her old playmate anymore—Verity had grown tall and lean, leggy and lithe. Gone was the round face Florence had known so well, the pudgy hand that had held hers in the dark of the night when the strange noises of the old house settling around them had seemed the hungry grumbles of a monster's belly. Verity had grown chic, with her hair cropped short and oversize sunglasses, her brightly colored shift dresses and her chunky knit sweaters worn over button-down shirts and stirrup pants. She had landed a coveted position as a guest editor at *Mademoiselle* magazine in New York City, and she had married a stockbroker named Francis Gordon, who, while he himself was rather plain looking, owned an attractive brownstone on the Upper West Side. At the christening party for their son, Hugh, which Birdie hosted at Cliffhaven, Florence looked across the room full of guests she only half recognized and wondered where the time had gone. How had she not changed at all, while the rest of the world went on around her? It was like she was wading through a vat of molasses, her movements sloth-like, her progress slow, even though it felt to her as if she were exerting far too much effort to have traveled so little distance in such a length of time. It was amazing to her that simply existing with no real purpose other than to make it from one day to the next could be so exhausting. The raw pain and emotion she had felt for the first few months after Astrid's passing had settled into a low, throbbing ache below her ribs. A constant presence, but one that was not as all-consuming as it once had been.

Florence could feel Charles's eyes on her from across the room, even though her back was to him. She'd felt him looking at her all day. It was as if, somehow, this milestone of Verity's had called attention to her in the most unexpected and unwelcome way. Verity's achievements threw into stark relief Florence's lack thereof. Verity had an education, a profession, a marriage, a child. A place in the world. While Florence was like a spinning top—constantly moving but always staying in the same place. It raised the uncomfortable question: What to do about

Florence? It was a suffocating question. It made Florence's head dizzy to think about.

Florence left her drink on the side table and meandered down the hall to the library, away from the hum of the party. She ran her hand across the spines of the books in their cases and settled into the leather sofa by the fireplace.

She heard his voice before she saw him.

"Not enjoying the party?" Charles asked.

"Just getting some air," Florence said.

"Can I join you?"

"Please," Florence said, motioning to the empty seat next to her.

Charles sat. For a moment, they just looked at each other.

"I know these past couple years must have been quite hard for you," Charles said. "Seeing Verity get married, become a mother."

Florence picked at the hem of her dress. "Not really," she lied. "I don't think I'll ever do those things." This part, at least, was the truth. She said it practically, matter-of-factly, without an ounce of emotion. "They're just not what I imagined for myself."

"Birdie thought you might want to go east for school," Charles said.

Here it was, then. The time had come. She'd worn out her welcome.

"We could help you, if that's what you wanted," Charles went on. "I'm close with the dean at Wellesley, and, of course, Birdie has ties at Vassar. We could help with your lodging and tuition and then get you settled after, wherever you wanted to go."

Florence's heart ached. It was ironic, what he was offering her. It was the kind of offer Astrid would have leaped at and exactly the thing that Florence dreaded. Maybe everyone was cursed to want the thing they could not have. Or maybe they only wanted it because they couldn't have it, and that was the curse? Her whole life, Astrid had longed for an open door, the opportunity to go and be whatever she wanted, to separate herself from her family. But all Florence had ever wanted was to stay at Cliffhaven, to be accepted into the Towers family fold. Astrid had been hedged in her whole life, desperate to get out. And all her life, Florence had been desperate to be let in.

"That is a very generous offer," Florence said. "But then, you've always been generous, and very kind, to me, Charles. I hope you won't find it impertinent of me to say, but I'm not like Verity, with her grand ambitions to go out into the world and make something of herself. I'm not like Astrid either—I don't have a passion for art or dance; I don't need to create something. I've always been a creature who is firmly rooted in people and place. I want to be *here*. I want to make myself useful *here*."

She'd never been able to be so honest with Scarlet, but the past few years had changed her. Besides, she'd always looked up to Charles as a big brother.

Charles looked relieved. "I'm glad to hear you say that," he said. "I thought it would be selfish of me to ask you to stay. I thought it might be hard for you to be here, after all that's happened."

Florence nodded. "It is," she said. "But it would be harder for me *not* to be here, if that makes any sense."

"It does," Charles said. For a moment, he looked deep in thought. "I will have to run this by Birdie, of course," he said. "But—" He leaned forward, his elbows on his knees. "Birdie is expecting," he said, very seriously.

For a moment Florence sat there, waiting for him to finish. Expecting what? And then, it dawned on her: a baby.

"Oh," Florence said, unable to hide the shock from her voice.

"Yes," Charles said. "It surprised me as well. She's due at the end of the summer."

"I'm—I'm very happy for you," Florence said, but in her mind, she saw Bass's face—Bass, leaning into Birdie in the library, kissing her neck.

"Thank you," Charles said. "We will need someone to look after the baby—a nanny. Birdie doesn't want to take much time away from her charities or the foundation. It would be such a comfort to me—and

I'm sure Birdie will agree—to have someone close to us, someone we really trust, in that role."

He looked at Florence, and Florence understood.

"I don't know anything about babies," Florence said.

"I saw how you looked after Granny Doris when she was sick," Charles said. "And the way you cared for Astrid. You have a nurturer's heart, Florence. You'd be a natural."

Florence wavered—it was never a role she had envisioned for herself, but then again, here was a way forward, a way to make herself useful and needed at Cliffhaven. A way to stay.

"Okay," Florence said. "Yes. Of course."

Birdie gave birth to Saoirse early one late-summer day at Cliffhaven. Florence was the first to hold her after the doctor pulled her from between Birdie's legs, red faced and squalling. Florence clasped her gently to her chest and marveled at the existence of her. Impossibly small. Impossibly soft. Still covered in the thin film of vernix from the womb.

Florence moved into the nanny's quarters off the nursery, her days fading into a delirious haze of bottle feedings, changing cloth diapers, baths, and rocking Saoirse back and forth in the chair next to her crib, her downy head lilting against Florence's chest as she fought off impending sleep. Saoirse curled her hand around Florence's index finger, and Florence could almost burst with how full she felt—how content, how happy, even.

Florence read to Saoirse from picture books as Saoirse cooed and pawed at the pages with her pudgy fingers. When Saoirse could crawl, Florence went down onto her knees with her on the nursery floor, played at blocks and Barbies, made *choo choo* noises while dragging a toy train across the carpet. Florence stitched up the baby blanket that Saoirse wore to threads, the one she couldn't sleep without, and checked under her bed for monsters before turning out the light. When Saoirse had a nightmare, it was Florence she called out for in the middle of the night—"Tabby, Tabby, my Tabby"—Saoirse's first word she ever spoke after "No."

Charles was a frequent visitor to the nursery, leaning over Saoirse's crib to tuck her in, putting her onto his shoulders, and bouncing her around the room during playtime. Florence would watch them from her chair, but she could never bring herself to tell him what she knew, the truth that simmered beneath the surface. She wondered if time would lay bare the sins of Saoirse's mother—if, as she grew, Saoirse's light hair would settle into a vibrant blond, if her chin, the arch of her nose, might betray her.

Time could bear witness, Florence decided, but she would not, could not, bring herself to do it. She loved the child too much to ever harm her, even with the truth.

CHAPTER FORTY-TWO

AUGUST 28, 1982—THE NIGHT OF SAOIRSE'S BIRTHDAY PARTY

O h my God," Saoirse said, her hand on her chest. The lightning illuminated the sky again, turning the pitch-black night momentarily bright as day, like a temporary, fleeting sun. It illuminated the woman standing there at the bottom of the staircase, angled toward Saoirse and Santos on the beach.

"Tabby," Saoirse said, breathless, "you scared me half to death."

Florence proffered the umbrella she held in her hand. "I'm sorry, child. I didn't mean to frighten you," Florence said. "It's going to be raining cats and dogs any moment, and I saw you headed down here earlier without an umbrella."

It was just like Saoirse to do something like this, to wander down that rickety old staircase in the dark. A staircase that was hazardous enough when traversing it in broad daylight when it was sunny and dry out, let alone in the wet dark. And on top of that, she came down here with *him*, of all people. It was as if she was deliberately putting herself in harm's way.

"Mr. Santos," Florence said coldly. "I don't recall seeing your name on the guest list."

She had seen Saoirse hanging on to a boy as she made her way down the stairs, but in the dark and with the distance, she hadn't been able to make out who it was.

"Please, Tabby, don't be cross," Saoirse said. "I invited him."

"I see," Florence said, the displeasure plain in her voice. "You should come back up to the house, both of you. The weather's turning."

"It's not going to rain," Saoirse said defiantly.

Then, as if to spite her, the sky opened up, and it started to pour. Saoirse swore under her breath.

"Come up to the house," Florence said again. "You'll catch your death out here."

This time, Saoirse didn't need persuading. Florence opened the umbrella, and Santos held it as best he could over Saoirse and Florence as they climbed the stairs, slowly and arduously in the dark. Though, in truth, with the winds as bad as they were, the umbrella did them little good.

When they got to the top, the yard and terrace were empty. Everyone had gone inside.

"Does Ransom know that Mr. Santos is here?" Florence asked.

"No," Saoirse said. "Of course he doesn't know."

Florence nodded. "Well then, it may be best if the two of you come around the back way with me. You can dry off in my room. The last thing we need is for your brother to see this and cause a scene."

They took the back entrance to the servants' quarters, which were quiet and empty. Everyone was busy working the party tonight. When they got to Florence's rooms, she shut the door behind them and started a fire in the hearth. Santos shrugged out of his jacket and hung it up to dry. Saoirse shivered and hugged her bare arms. She was drenched to the bone.

"Child, go to your room, and put on a change of clothes," Florence said. "You look like a drowned rat."

Saoirse laughed and rolled her eyes. "Thanks, Tabby," she said through clattering teeth. "I'll be right back," Saoirse told Santos. She stood on her tiptoes to give him a kiss.

When Saoirse had gone, Florence inquired if Santos had had anything to eat.

"No," Santos said. "I came after dinner."

"I'll make you something, then," Florence said.

Her rooms, the biggest in the servants' quarters, had a small kitchenette. She pulled open the refrigerator door and bent down to look inside.

"How about navy bean soup?" she asked. "I have some left over from the other night. I can heat it up for you."

"That sounds great, thank you," Santos said.

She pulled out a small pot from her cabinet and clicked on the burner on her stove. Then she fiddled around in her drawers.

"I can never find my big wooden spoons," she said.

Santos turned his back to her and went to warm himself by the fireplace. He sat down on the ottoman and held his hands out toward the heat.

"It's good of you, to be so nice," Santos said. "I know you don't approve of me and Saoirse together."

"No," Florence said. "I don't approve. But I know Saoirse, and she's going to make her own decisions. There's no standing in the way of that. Ah, here it is."

She retrieved a wooden spoon from her drawer and poured some of the soup out of the Tupperware and into the pot. When it was warm enough, she ladled it into a bowl and brought the bowl and a spoon to Santos.

"Careful, it's hot," she warned.

She sat down across from him in her armchair.

He sipped at it. "Mm," he said. "It's very good."

"Chef made a batch the other night, and I took some with me," Florence said.

"It tastes different from how I remember it," Santos said, taking another sip.

"You know Chef," Florence said. "Always experimenting." After a moment she asked, "So what will you and Saoirse do now that she's of age?"

"We plan to be married," Santos said. "We leave for Vegas in the morning."

"Married?" Florence said, surprised. "Don't you think that's a little fast? You should take some time to really get to know one another first."

"We know each other," Santos said. "We don't want to wait any longer to start our lives together."

"I see," Florence said. "And what does that look like? Your lives together?"

"Traveling," Santos said. "There's a lot we want to see. I want to take her to South America, first. Then Europe. We've talked about doing an African safari."

"And after that?"

"We'll settle down somewhere," Santos said. "Perhaps abroad. Saoirse's talked about trying to start her own fashion line. I've always been interested in the markets, in investing."

"Those sound like risky ventures," Florence said.

"Well, luckily, we'll have the means to take some risks," Santos said. He coughed, cleared his throat.

"And what if your temperaments are not suited for one another?" Florence asked. "Saoirse can be headstrong, stubborn, and capricious. What if you fight often? Or you find her too combative? Or you grow tired of her constantly changing fancies? What then?"

"I think we'll manage," Santos said. He cleared his throat again. "Besides, we'll have more means than most to be happy."

"Take it from me," Florence said. "Money is not a balm for unhappiness. I've lived around the rich for my entire life, and they have been some of the most unhappy, wretched souls I've ever met." Florence clucked her tongue in disapproval. "I fear," she said, "that you're on a path to ruin both your lives, forever."

Santos didn't answer. His bowl clattered to the ground. He gasped for breath, clutched at his throat.

Florence picked up the fallen bowl and spoon and went to deposit them in the sink. She grabbed a dishcloth to clean up the spill.

Santos was on his knees now, his eyes large and bulging as he looked at her for help. He reached out an arm for her, tried to speak, but his throat was swollen shut.

"That'll be the peanut oil I added to your soup, dear," Florence said. "Don't worry; this will all be over soon."

Santos tried to crawl toward the door, but he didn't get far. He collapsed by the hearth, and, after a moment, his body grew still and stopped moving.

CHAPTER FORTY-THREE

PRESENT

Elena and Detective Church found Florence Talbot in the upstairs drawing room, sitting in one of the upholstered chairs next to the fireplace. Ransom Towers sat across from her on the tufted sofa. Both had their afternoon tea in front of them; they were going through the household accounts.

"Darling, I thought you went for a run," Ransom said when they entered the room.

"I did, but I had to cut it short. It's so hot out I can hardly breathe," Elena said. She crossed over to her husband and gave him a small peck on the cheek before sitting next to him. "Anyway, look who I ran into on the terrace on my way back."

"Detective Church," Ransom said, sounding less than pleased to see him.

Church nodded his head. "Senator." He looked over at Florence. "How are you today, Florence?" he asked.

"Tired," she said, giving him a weary smile. "I've had two maids quit this week, and hiring has been a nightmare. I just interviewed a girl who had two visible body piercings and a face tattoo. At this rate, I shall have to scrub the toilets myself."

Church smiled, but it didn't quite reach his eyes.

"I wasn't expecting to see you today, Detective," Ransom said. "Has something happened? Is there news?"

"They've identified the second body," Elena said.

"They have?" Ransom said. He looked over at Detective Church expectantly. "Who is it?"

"I'm afraid I can't disclose that information," Church said.

"Well, why the hell not?" Ransom said.

Elena placed a calming hand on Ransom's forearm. "Temper," she said softly.

Ransom exhaled sharply. "I apologize, Detective. I'm normally a very patient man. But I've been patient for forty years now, and I fear if I practice any more patience, I'll be dead and buried before the answers come."

"I understand," Church said. "And I promise you you'll have your answers soon enough. But for now, I'm not authorized to divulge that."

"Well, why come here at all, then?" Ransom said. "Just to bait us?"

"He came to speak with me, dear," Elena said.

Ransom glanced over at her, a crease between his brows. "What?"

"He found out about the whole Ana Rojas bit," Elena explained. "It's fine. I explained everything."

Ransom glared back at Detective Church. "What does Ana Rojas have to do with my sister?" he asked.

"Nothing, it turns out," Church said.

"Forgive me, Detective," Ransom said. "But my patience has run out. If you've finished interrogating my wife and you cannot tell us any pertinent information about the second body or the case, then what are you still doing here?"

"I need to speak with Florence," Church said.

"Absolutely not," Ransom said.

Elena put her hand on her husband's arm, but this time he was too angry to heed her.

"This is unconscionable," Ransom said to Church. "You come into my house, you harass my wife, you refuse to give us any information, and now you want to do the same with Mrs. Talbot? I won't allow it."

"With all due respect, Senator," Church said, "that's not up to you."

"I'll speak with him," Florence said. "I don't mind."

Ransom seethed. "Fine," he said through gritted teeth. "But you'll talk to her here. You have five minutes, Detective, and then my patience will have officially run out." Ransom glanced at his watch, marking the time.

Detective Church took the armchair next to Florence. He leaned forward and set his tape recorder on the side table between them. "Do you mind if I record this?" he asked.

"Why would I mind?" Florence said.

"Very good," Church said, hitting Record. "I was speaking with Mrs. Towers just now, and it got me thinking that you and I have never had a proper interview. Recorded, and all that."

"No, we haven't," Florence said, as if she were well aware of the fact and, on top of that, disapproved. "I must admit I was starting to feel a little left out."

Detective Church smiled. "I've come at this case from every angle, Florence, just like those who worked it before me," he said. "I've cycled through all the regular motives. I've considered jealousy and greed. I've looked at what one might do for self-preservation, the lengths someone might go to protect their own self-interests. But there was one motive that I hadn't considered, one that all of us overlooked. And perhaps it is the most powerful motivator of all."

"And what, pray tell, is that, Detective?" Florence asked.

"Love," Church said.

"Love," Florence repeated. "I don't think I follow."

"Yes, get to the point," Ransom said. He checked his watch. "Four minutes, Detective."

Church shifted in his seat. "Let me try to come at this another way," he said. "This whole time, we've been looking at Saoirse as the primary victim. Who would want to hurt her? What would someone gain from her death? But what if we've been looking at this all wrong? What if Saoirse was never supposed to be a victim at all?"

Florence didn't flinch; she held his gaze. She opened her mouth to speak, but Ransom interrupted.

"What are you saying?" Ransom asked. "That Saoirse was just collateral damage?"

"Yes," Church said. "The second body that was discovered—what if that was actually the *first* body, the first victim?" His mind shot back to the phone call he'd just received identifying the remains. He wasn't yet authorized to divulge that information, and he had just blatantly refused to do so, but now, he had to make a gamble. He took a deep breath. "Salvador Santos," he said.

Again, Florence opened her mouth to say something, but Ransom cut in.

"Saoirse's tutor?" Ransom said. "He's the second body?"

Church kept his attention on Florence. "He was very suddenly and unceremoniously let go, from what I understand."

Florence's eyes flitted from Detective Church to Ransom.

"No official reason was ever given for the sudden end of Mr. Santos's employment," Church said, "but one thing is clear: Salvador Santos was promptly removed from the premises, the payroll, and the party guest list. It begs the question—what sort of misconduct would require such drastic actions? And why would they be kept so hush-hush?" Church asked. "Florence, were Mr. Santos and Saoirse having an illicit romantic relationship? Were they sleeping together?"

Across the room, Ransom Towers stood up. "There is a line, Detective, and you have crossed it," he said, fuming. "My family has endured enough abuse from your department over the course of your investigation. I will not sit idly by and let you slander my sister's name with your wild, unfounded allegations."

Detective Church looked back over at Florence, a whisper of hope in his chest that she would answer his question, but she only stared indignantly back at him.

"I've had just about enough," Florence said.

"Don't worry, Mrs. Talbot," Ransom went on. "I will remove Detective Church from the premises myself."

"I've had just about enough *of the interruptions*," Florence went on, heatedly. She looked pointedly at Ransom. "Detective Church and I are trying to have a conversation, and I would very much like to finish it."

"But, Mrs. Talbot," Ransom said, confused.

"Ransom, please," Florence said curtly. "Sit down and be quiet. You need to hear this too."

Ransom looked dumbfounded. Florence gave him a stern look, and he sat back down on the sofa like a chastened child. She turned her stern gaze on Elena next, who looked equally confused but made no move to protest.

"Now, Detective Church," Florence said, looking at him expectantly. "You were saying?"

Church cleared his throat. He didn't understand this turn of events, but he wasn't about to question it. "Mr. Santos was the perfect victim in many ways," Church went on. "He had no family to miss him. He lived an itinerant lifestyle. He was no longer under Senator Towers's employment or on his guest list. He wasn't supposed to be here that night, so no one gave any thought as to his absence. And," Church said, "he had a peanut allergy, which you would have certainly known about."

"I am very meticulous about the household's dietary restrictions, yes," Florence said.

"You loved Saoirse," Church said. "More than anything. More than you loved even yourself. You caught Mr. Santos and Saoirse trying to run away together that night, didn't you? And you couldn't bear to see it happen, to see Saoirse taken away by that man. So you took care of him, made it so he couldn't take her away. You gave no thought to yourself, of what it would do to you, or the potential consequences. You did it to save her."

Florence was silent for a moment.

All these years, she had carried this secret of what she had done silently, by herself. How strange it must be, Church thought, to have someone finally speak it aloud to her. For someone to finally know and for her to be able to talk about it. It must be freeing, in a way.

"I knew what would happen if they ran away together," Florence said. "I've seen firsthand what happens when a man marries a woman under false pretenses, for his own selfish reasons. What happens when he takes her away from her family. What a man is allowed to do to a woman. I've lived it. I wouldn't let it happen again. Especially not to her."

Across the room, Ransom Towers let out a breath. "Mrs. Talbot, what are you saying?" he asked.

Detective Church ignored him and remained intently focused on Florence. "You had the best of intentions," he said. "You wanted to protect her, to save her. But something went wrong."

"I sent her off to change her clothes," Florence said. "She was soaked to the bone. I didn't want her to catch a cold. And I dealt with . . . that man . . . while she was gone."

"And what happened next?" Church asked. "Did Saoirse come back before you were expecting her? Did she see what you had done?"

Florence shook her head. "No," she said. "I dragged Mr. Santos's body into the next room, hid him under my bed so she wouldn't see. She never knew."

Church was puzzled by this. "So the two of you didn't get into an altercation regarding Mr. Santos?" he asked. "You didn't—maybe, in a fit of desperation, the heat of the moment—inadvertently harm Miss Towers?"

He had been so sure that this was the direction her confession was headed—that Saoirse had discovered what Florence had done and Florence had had no choice but to kill her, too, to keep anyone from finding out.

"No," Florence said, shaking her head adamantly. "No, never. I would never harm a hair on that child's head. Never, never."

Church leaned forward, on the edge of his chair now. "Then, what exactly did happen to Saoirse, Florence?"

Florence had tears in her eyes. She took a deep breath.

"The very worst thing," Florence said, her voice full of despair. "The very worst thing that could happen, did."

CHAPTER FORTY-FOUR

When Saoirse returned to Florence's rooms, Florence was standing over the stove, stirring a pot. The fire in the hearth was still going, and the room was warm and cozy, much more comfortable than the drafty hall that Saoirse had just come from.

"Ah, good, child, you're back," Florence said when she saw her. "Can you do me a favor and fetch me the salt? It's in the pantry, just over there."

Saoirse retrieved it for her. She leaned against the counter next to her and surveyed the room. She thought at first that Salvador must be in the bathroom, but she saw now that the door to the little bathroom that abutted the living area was open and the bathroom was unoccupied.

"Where's Salvador?" Saoirse asked.

Florence didn't seem to hear her. She spooned some soup from the pot on the stove and held the ladle out to Saoirse.

"Taste this, will you?" Florence said. "Chef never puts enough salt in for my liking."

Saoirse acquiesced. The soup was warm and thick. She could taste the savory bacon and soft shells of the navy beans. In her opinion,

Tabby had been a little too heavy handed with the salt, but she wasn't about to say so.

"Mm," Saoirse said. "It's good."

"Wonderful," Florence said. She turned off the stove and spooned the soup into two bowls, one of which she handed to Saoirse.

"Tabby, where's Salvador?" Saoirse asked again.

"Let's sit, child," Florence said.

"Why?" Saoirse asked, the panic starting to rise in her throat. "Just tell me where he is."

"Now, none of that," Florence chastised. "There's no reason for nerves. Let's just sit and eat, and I'll tell you. There's no use talking on an empty stomach."

They sat around the little table in Florence's kitchenette that was barely big enough for both of them. Saoirse felt almost sad thinking of Tabby sitting there by herself most nights, eating her meals alone.

Now, Florence ate several enthusiastic spoonfuls of soup, while Saoirse couldn't even bring herself to lift her spoon to her mouth. She felt so jittery, as though if her skin were not there to contain her, she would fly everywhere at once.

"Tabby, please," Saoirse begged. "Please, just tell me."

"All right, child, if you must know," Florence said. She set down her spoon. "Mr. Santos has gone."

"Gone where?"

"He didn't say," Florence went on. "He just said that he was going, that he had a change of mind and that, well, he didn't have the heart to tell you himself. Rather cowardly if you ask me, but there you have it."

Saoirse went limp. Her shoulders slumped, and she braced herself against the table so she wouldn't fall out of her chair.

"He's gone?" she echoed.

Florence reached a hand across the table and patted Saoirse's arm. "Yes, child, but I'd say you're better off," she said. "This is a blessing in disguise, really. That Mr. Santos was not a good man. Anyone who would just run off like that, well, you're better to let them run. There'll be others. Better men. Or, maybe, you're better off without a man at all."

Saoirse nodded vaguely, though she wasn't really listening.

Everybody leaves, she thought.

It made a certain sort of sense. Everyone else she'd ever loved had left her. Her father. Teddy. Why wouldn't Salvador be the same?

She'd been too eager. She'd missed the signs. He had probably been pulling away for a while now, and she just hadn't noticed. Maybe he had come here tonight to break it to her gently, because he was a good person, because on some level, he did care about her, just not enough. And then, of course, he'd gotten cold feet and couldn't do it after all.

There was something wrong with her. Saoirse was sure of it now. There was a cold void inside her that people sensed when they got too close, something that they couldn't bear to be around. Something that made her unlovable.

Before Saoirse registered what she was doing, she had stood up from the table. Then, she was halfway across the room.

"Child, where are you going?" Florence asked, but Saoirse didn't answer her. Instead, she started running.

She was going to the one place she always went to when the world was crumbling around her, when the people she loved and trusted the most, the people who were supposed to care for and protect her, decided to abandon and betray her instead. She was going to that little stretch of beach that no one besides her ever visited, that lonely and abandoned patch of sand that matched her lonely and abandoned heart.

Florence knew this instinctively because she knew Saoirse better than anyone, and she followed her out into the storm.

A heavy gale was pushing up against the cliffside, so strong that it almost thrust Florence backward into the house when she tried to follow Saoirse out the back door. But Florence trudged onward, out into the cold, wet night, calling Saoirse's name, her voice swallowed up in the wind and the rain. She tried with all her might to run after her, to stop her, but she wasn't fast enough. For the rest of her life, she would always wonder if Saoirse had meant to do it or if it was truly an accident, the way her feet slipped when she reached that wet and rickety staircase, the way she fell.

Later, Florence would drag Saoirse's limp, soaked body back to her room. She would dry her hair and change her into fresh clothes and, many nights later, lay her to rest in the ground outside the east wing, where the holes had been dug for the new footings. And she would carry that secret for over four decades, all alone, never telling a soul. For it was some small, strange comfort to her, always knowing where Saoirse was, that she would never leave Cliffhaven and, above all else, that no one could ever hurt her again.

CHAPTER FORTY-FIVE

Detective Church reached forward and turned off the tape recorder.

"My God," Ransom Towers muttered from his chair across the room. There were tears in his eyes. "Mrs. Talbot."

Detective Church stood and unclipped the handcuffs from his belt. "Florence Talbot," he said, "you are under arrest for the murder of Salvador Santos. You have the right to remain silent. Anything you say or do can and will be used against you in a court of law."

"Surely that's not necessary," Ransom said, rising from his seat. "She was acting in defense of my sister. Saoirse was just a child. That man—he was a predator. That's not murder, that's . . ." He trailed off, searching for the word.

"I'm sorry, Senator Towers," Church said, and part of him really was. "But that'll be for a judge to decide."

"At least put away your handcuffs," Ransom said. "Let us have some dignity. I can bring her down to the station in my car."

"I'm afraid I have to follow protocol here," Church said. He couldn't be sure that Florence wasn't a flight risk. With Ransom being sympathetic to her case, and the vast resources at his disposal, Church couldn't be sure whether she would indeed make it down to the station or disappear into the ether. He couldn't take that chance.

"You cannot be serious," Ransom said. He had made his way across the room at this point and was hovering protectively over where Florence sat on the sofa. He looked pointedly over his shoulder at Elena. "Get Mr. Ferguson, our attorney, on the phone."

Elena looked frozen and startled, like a deer caught in headlights.

"Senator Towers, please," Church said, but Florence cut in, her voice soft and placating.

"My dear boy," Florence said, standing, "it's all right." She put her hand on Ransom's cheek, and he stilled. "I've carried this with me for a long time, and the weight of it was getting too heavy for me to bear," she went on. "I'm grateful to finally put it down, to be able to tell you what really happened to Saoirse, to put an end to the not knowing. But that peace comes with a price, I fear, and I must pay it. I knew that from the moment they pulled her from the ground. I've spent the last several weeks coming to terms with it, and I finally have. And if I can, then you must too."

Church saw Ransom Towers's face soften and fall. In that moment, he didn't look like a powerful politician or the stalwart patriarch of the great Towers dynasty, but like a child. Helpless. Small.

Elena made her way over to Ransom, slipped her hand into his. As she planted a kiss on his shoulder, Church noticed that she was crying.

"We can bring her home after you book her?" Ransom asked, looking at Detective Church again. "Whatever the bail amount, I'll pay it. It doesn't matter."

Church cleared his throat. "That'll be up to the judge too," he said.

"Penny can fill my spot until you find a replacement," Florence told Ransom. "She's a smart girl, and she knows how I run things. And I already put the request in to the cook for dinner—pot roast, your favorite," she said.

She gave Ransom one more comforting pat and then offered up her wrists to Church. He cuffed her, and she walked with him, stalwartly, toward his car, the staff gathering in the halls and on the stairwell, open mouthed, heads bent in whispers as they passed.

As they pulled out of the drive, Church glanced in the rearview mirror at Florence in the back seat.

"Are you comfortable?" he asked. "I can turn up the AC if you're hot."

Florence chuckled. "Detective Church," she said, patting her arthritic knees. "I haven't been comfortable since 1996." She turned and looked thoughtfully out the window at the house as it slowly receded from view. "I always thought I'd die here," she said.

Her words made Church's heart pinch painfully in his chest.

"Can I ask you something, Florence?" Church said.

He saw her nod in the rearview mirror.

"You seem very composed," he went on. "Very calm, despite everything. Why is that?"

Florence chuckled again and shook her head. "You young people are very preoccupied with the present, with what's happening right this instant," she said. "You think of everything as so final, so permanent. When you get to be my age, you start to realize that it's never the end, not really. Things always go on, in some way. Things always change. If today, things look terrible, well, tomorrow, they might look differently. Even death," Florence said after a moment, "is not final. I've carried Doris with me, Astrid, Saoirse, for over half a century now. I don't think we really die until the people who knew us, who loved us, are gone too."

Florence looked out the passenger-side window again. Now, all that was in her view was the ocean and, above it, a gray, bleak sky. But Church could still see Cliffhaven as he looked at her in the rearview mirror, framed in the car's back window. It was much smaller now, the stone a pale yellow as it reflected back the overcast sky.

"I suppose, in a way, then, I *will* die here," Florence said, "one day."

EPILOGUE

Detective Church wasn't entirely sure what made him do it, but the Wednesday after his grandmother's funeral, he got in his car and drove the two hours inland to Wasco State Prison.

Usually when Church solved a case, he felt a sense of fulfillment. There was a certain self-satisfaction that came from untangling the web, a comforting peace that resulted from finally having answers where before there had been only questions. But the Towers case had been different. It stuck with him, kept him up at night. Did it matter, he asked himself, if Florence's actions had been motivated by something good and pure, if they had ultimately resulted in something so ugly and destructive—cutting short not just one young life but two? Sometimes Church answered this question one way in his mind and then the other. Even so, he didn't like to think of Florence at Wasco, dressed in a stale jumpsuit, lying on an old mattress in a concrete cell.

Now he sat at a table in the sterile visitors' room, his knee bouncing up and down beneath the table as he waited. The lawyers whom Ransom had hired to represent Florence Talbot had worked out a plea deal on her behalf. She'd been charged with first-degree murder, the obstruction of justice, and the concealment of two bodies, but in the deal she brokered with the prosecution, she pleaded guilty to the lesser charge of voluntary manslaughter, and the other charges were dropped. In exchange, she was sentenced to three years in prison, but she'd be out in two with good behavior. They'd sent her to Wasco State Prison, outside of Bakersfield, to serve out her term. Church had not seen her since the plea hearing six months ago.

"I'm glad you came."

Detective Church looked up at the voice and saw Florence standing there, a guard behind her. She looked smaller in her orange jumpsuit; it dwarfed her.

He stood up as she pulled back a chair on the opposite side of the table. He wondered what the proper greeting was in a circumstance such as theirs, the captor and the captive. He sat back down when she sat.

"I got your last letter," Florence said. "I was very sorry to hear about your grandmother."

He nodded. "Thank you."

It had been sudden. His grandmother's heart had stopped in the middle of the night while she slept.

"It was the way she wanted to go," Church said. "No fuss or commotion. Quick. Peaceful."

"Yes," Florence said. "But still, you must miss her terribly. Regardless of the circumstances, it can be hard to say goodbye."

Church swallowed.

He shifted in his seat and pulled out the silver rosary ring from his pocket. Because it was a religious item, he'd been permitted to bring it through security. He turned it slowly in his fingers.

"I want to return this to you," he said. "I can leave it at the security desk when I go. They'll add it to your things."

"I wish you wouldn't," Florence said. "That's for you. To remind you of the good."

"I'm not sure it does that anymore," Church said.

Florence held his gaze. "You said in your letter there was something you wanted to ask me in person?"

Church stared back down at the ring in his hands. He had written that. Ever since he'd made the arrest, there was such a sense of unease, uncertainty, that he'd carried with him in the hollow of his chest and the pit of his gut. He wanted to put those feelings into questions, exorcise them from his body. He had thought by the time he saw her, face to face, he'd be able to metabolize those feelings into words, into concrete questions, but he'd been wrong. He opened his mouth and closed it again.

He didn't know how to come to terms with the fact that sometimes justice didn't feel like justice at all. Having the answers, knowing the truth, resolving a case wasn't always completely satisfying. He wanted things to fit neatly into boxes—good and bad, right and wrong. But the ambivalence of this case thwarted his efforts.

Florence lifted her hand from the table, as if she meant to place it on top of his but then remembered they were not allowed to touch, so she set it back down again.

When Church passed the security desk as he left, he slipped the rosary ring back into his pocket. The drive home was quiet; he kept the radio off, his mind untangling the rope of emotions in his head that he still couldn't find the words for. He took Highway 46 west and, just north of Harmony, turned left onto the Pacific Coast Highway.

When Church was almost home, he could see it there in the distance, jutting out from the coast: Cliffhaven. Somehow, the house didn't look the same to him anymore. It wasn't the mythical, impenetrable castle he'd viewed it as when he was a child; nor was it the cold, austere stone estate he'd considered it to be as a grown man. It was something else now, something he couldn't yet name.

ACKNOWLEDGMENTS

While my first book flowed out of me without too much resistance, this book was another matter. It took a lot of excavating, a lot of time and patience, to unearth. And I couldn't have done that without the fresh eye and skill of so many talented people. Thank you to Suzanne Gluck for helping me hone the tone, to J. J. Spitz for telling me the staircase should play a bigger role, to Haley Heidemann for helping me shape it and fearlessly taking it out into the world, to Chantelle Aimée Osman for seeing its potential and pushing it to be even better, to Faith Black Ross for helping me fine-tune the final draft, and to Emily Freidenrich for shepherding it across the finish line. Without all of you ladies, this book would not be what it is today.

To my multihyphenate little-sister-best-friend-ride-or-die Annie Klehfoth, for always being my first and most enthusiastic reader.

To Mom and Dad, for being quite possibly the best parents who ever existed. Thank you for all your love, support, and encouragement. This book would not exist without you telling me I could be anything I wanted to be when I was little, and then a hundred times after.

To Mark Klehfoth, for being you.

To Brendan Kenney and Amy Amendola, just because.

Trevor, thank you for creating the time and space for me to write. Time becomes such a sparse resource when one becomes a parent, and you went out of your way to make sure I had the time to do the thing I loved. I love you for that. And for a million other reasons. Thank you for all the amazing meals you cook, for always making me laugh, and for staying up late to watch bad reality TV with me. My home is wherever I'm with you.

Milo, thank you for sitting next to me while I wrote each draft and trying not to snore too loudly or hog too much of the blanket.

And, lastly, to Olivia. I wrote the first words of this book sitting on my bed in my old apartment on Barrington, before you were a glimmer of a thought in my mind. I put that first mess of a draft away for a while and took it back out again years later in our new home, where you were a dream, and then a soon-to-be reality. I worked on drafts as you slept soundly next to me in your Boppy on the couch in my office or on the back patio during your cozy newborn days. I worked on it during early mornings while you were still asleep in your crib and on Saturday afternoons while I could hear you, through my office wall, laughing and playing with Daddy in the next room. You have taught me so much about love and patience and true joy. May you always know, without a shadow of a doubt, how loved you are.

ABOUT THE AUTHOR

Photo © 2018 Trevor Wineman

Elizabeth Klehfoth grew up in Elkhart, Indiana. She studied creative writing, earning her BFA from Chapman University and her MFA from Indiana University, where she also taught fiction writing and composition. The author published her first novel, *All These Beautiful Strangers*, in 2018. She currently lives in Los Angeles.